9/16

Make Me Love You

Center Point
Large Print

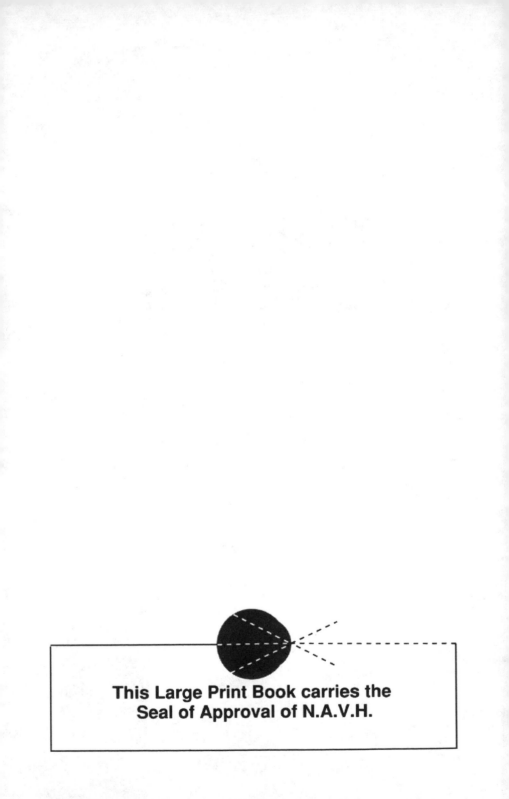

This Large Print Book carries the Seal of Approval of N.A.V.H.

Make Me Love You

Johanna Lindsey

CENTER POINT LARGE PRINT
THORNDIKE, MAINE

This Center Point Large Print edition is published
in the year 2016 by arrangement with Gallery Books,
a division of Simon & Schuster, Inc.

The text of this Large Print edition is unabridged.
In other aspects, this book may vary
from the original edition.
Printed in the United States of America
on permanent paper.
Set in 16-point Times New Roman type.

ISBN: 978-1-68324-087-7

Library of Congress Cataloging-in-Publication Data

Names: Lindsey, Johanna, author.
Title: Make me love you / Johanna Lindsey.
Description: Center Point Large Print edition. | Thorndike, Maine :
Center Point Large Print, 2016.
Identifiers: LCCN 2016022772 | ISBN 9781683240877
    (hardcover : alk. paper)
Subjects: LCSH: Nobility—Fiction. | Large type books. | GSAFD:
Romantic suspense fiction.
Classification: LCC PS3562.I5123 M27 2016b | DDC 813/.54—dc23
LC record available at https://lccn.loc.gov/2016022772

Make Me Love You

❧ Chapter One ❧

"This is intolerable. How *dare* that dissolute joke of a royal heir give the Whitworths an ultimatum!"

Aging badly, twenty-five years his wife's senior, Thomas Whitworth still had a face that defied the passage of time. Though his hair had turned pure white, he had no wrinkles to speak of. He was still a handsome, if old, man, riddled with pain in most of his joints. But he had the constitution and stubbornness to appear otherwise, could stand hale and hearty in the presence of others even if it took every ounce of his will to do so. Pride demanded it and he was a very prideful man.

"He is Regent now, officially sworn. England *and* her subjects are in his hands," Harriet Whitworth said, wringing her own hands. "And not so loud, Thomas, please. His emissary isn't out the front door yet."

But with the emissary gone from the room, Thomas collapsed on the sofa. "D'you think I care if he hears me?" Thomas snarled at his wife. "He's lucky I'm not adding my boot to his arse to help him out the damned door."

Harriet hurried over to the parlor door and closed it, just in case, before she turned back to her husband and whispered, "Even so, we don't want our opinions of the Prince Regent carried straight to his ear."

She had been young when she married Thomas, Earl of Tamdon, a prime catch in her day and a beauty still at the age of forty-three with her blond hair and crystal blue eyes. She had thought she could love this husband her parents had picked for her, but he did nothing to encourage that emotion from her and so it never came to pass. Thomas was a hard-tempered man. But she had learned how to live with him without becoming subject to his rants and rages, and never, ever to cause them.

She'd had to become as hard and callous as he was and didn't think she would ever forgive him for turning her into a copy of himself. But at least he didn't scoff at her opinions, even heeded her suggestions occasionally. That said a lot for a man such as Thomas, so maybe he did care for her a little even if he never showed it otherwise. Not that she wanted affection from him anymore. Frankly, she wished he would just die already so she could be herself again—if there was even anything of herself left. But Thomas Whitworth was too stubborn to even do that in a timely manner.

She brought him a lap robe and tried to tuck it around his legs, but he pushed her hands aside to do it himself. Summer was upon them and yet he easily took chill while others sweated. He hated his infirmities and aching joints. Most of his rages these days were directed inwardly because he was no longer the robust man of old. But his current rage was solely directed at the Prince Regent.

"What outrageous audacity!" Thomas said. "D'you think he isn't aware of what the entire nation thinks of him? He's a hedonist with no interest in politics, only the pleasures his royal blood affords him. This is just a ploy to confiscate our wealth because, as usual, he's utterly in debt from his extravagances and Parliament won't grant him relief."

"I'm not so sure of that," Harriet disagreed. "One duel could be ignored, despite that old ban on them that the emissary was keen to mention. Two duels would raise eyebrows but could still be ignored since no one has died yet. But the last duel Robert had with that northern wolf was too public and has become a scandal because of it. This is our son's fault. He could have declined."

"And be branded a coward? Of course he couldn't decline. At least he nearly killed Dominic Wolfe this time. The bastard may still die of his wound and we can be done with this vicious vendetta of his and the Regent's bold ploy to take advantage of it."

"You think Prince George is bluffing? That he will do nothing if we don't form this alliance with Lord Wolfe that he's demanding? I fear he isn't. One duel is for honor, but three is simply attempted murder, and there have been far too many public outcries against dueling from sectors that will fully support the Regent in this case. I say we end it this way, or d'you want to see our son forced to risk his life yet again? Need I remind you that he's already been wounded himself in those duels?"

"I don't need reminding of *that*, Wife. But the Prince Regent is as insane as his father is if he thinks a marriage between our families will end Dominic's vendetta. The wolf is as likely to murder your daughter as he is to take her to his bed, if we give her to him."

Harriet pursed her lips. It infuriated her that her husband never referred to *his* daughter as his, only as hers. But it had been that way since the day Brooke was born. Thomas had taken one look at the beautiful daughter she'd given him and turned away with a snarl. Sons he'd wanted and lots of them, not mewling females. But Harriet had only given him two children, not by choice. Five other pregnancies hadn't come to term.

But now she said what she knew he would want to hear and just as callously as he would state it. "Better her than Robert. Robert is your heir. Brooke is just another mouth to feed in this house."

The Whitworth heir chose that moment to open the parlor doors and join them. He had obviously heard the last remarks. In a bored tone, Robert said, "Send her immediately. The wolf won't

10

accept her. He'll be the one to lose his lands and title while we comply with the Regent's underhanded 'suggestion' of an alliance."

Harriet expected no less from her son, who bore no love for his sister. No taller than his father at five feet ten inches and every bit as handsome and strapping as Thomas had once been, Robert had his faults, but she loved him in spite of them.

Both of her children took after Thomas with his once black hair and pale green eyes. Brooke was even taller than Harriet by several inches. But Robert was just as much a hedonist as the Prince Regent was and at twenty-three had already racked up quite a few mistresses at home in Leicestershire and in London. But then he *could* be charming—when he wanted something. Otherwise he was much like his father, disdainful of peers and servants alike.

Thomas was too furious over the entire matter to let Robert shrug it off with his usual disregard. "If you've gotten yourself into another situation like the one we had to deal with last year . . . If you've broken your word—"

"I haven't," Robert was quick to cut in.

"You called these duels trifling, but this man's determination to gain satisfaction smacks of a dispute that is anything but trifling! What the devil did you do to him?"

"Nothing. I've run into him only a few times in London. Whatever his real reason is for wanting me dead, he's not fessing up to it. I imagine it's jealousy or some slight I dealt him that is so ridiculous he's ashamed to admit it."

"Then you had good reason to decline those duels."

"D'you think I didn't try? He called me a liar! I couldn't very well ignore that, now could I?"

Harriet knew her son. He was inclined to be less than candid when the truth did not serve him well. But Thomas believed him. Of course he did. He would not want to punish his precious son.

Less volatile now and more to the matter at hand, Thomas demanded, "You knew this outrageous demand was coming?"

"I had warning George might try this, yes, which is why I've returned from London. He heeds foolish advice from his sycophant cronies who bemoan that his purse strings have been tied yet again. He is hoping we will ignore his ridiculous assertion that this silly alliance will result in a peaceful end to the violence, so he can carry through with his threat. I assume you will not please him in that regard?"

"Then you don't think he's bluffing either?"

"No, unfortunately. Napoléon is killing enough Englishmen on the Continent. The Regent's counselors do not believe it is good for the nation's morale for the nobility to be killing each other at home, and the Prince is making the rounds to ensure that exact sentiment is shared by one and all. He'll have all the support he needs to wield the royal hammer against us if we defy him."

Thomas sighed and glanced at his wife. "Where is the chit? I suppose she will have to be told she is to marry."

❖ Chapter Two ❖

Now that they would be looking for her, Brooke quickly abandoned her crouching position below the open parlor window and ran straight for the stable. She'd heard it all, even what the emissary had said to her parents. She had been on the way to the stable when the man arrived in his fancy coach, and she'd been too curious not to stay and find out why he was there. Her parents rarely had visitors. They didn't socialize at home, only when they went to London, so they had few friends in the shire. And they never told her anything, which was why eavesdropping had become a habit.

They would look for in her room first, then the conservatory, then the stable, her three haunts. She didn't want to be found yet so she didn't stop to check on the stallion's sprained right foreleg or greet the new foal. She simply urged the stable-boy to hurry with her mount, Rebel. She'd named her horse that because it was what she was, at heart anyway. She despised most everything about her life and wanted to change it. Of course she was powerless to change anything and had finally accepted that.

She didn't wait for the groom, who was off having his lunch. It wasn't mandatory that he accompany her since she was only allowed to ride on Whitworth land. That land was extensive, though. Only a quarter of it was devoted to the large sheep farm that had made the Whitworths rich in the wool trade for decades. Not that anyone in her family had ever sheared sheep! But the rest of the land was open or wooded, allowing for a good gallop, which is what she needed today. She wanted ample time to digest everything she'd just overheard before her parents shared the "news" with her.

Her immediate reaction was extreme disappointment that Robert's dueling was going to cost her the Season in London that she'd been promised. The planning of that trip had brought her and her mother together. Brooke hadn't seen that much of her mother in years. If Brooke didn't know better, she might even have thought Harriet had been excited about it.

Brooke would have been packed and ready to leave for London soon. She already had the trunks and the new wardrobe to go in them. Harriet had been giving her a Season in London not because Harriet wanted to or thought it would please Brooke, but because it was what society expected of her parents, and Harriet always did what was expected of her. Brooke had never looked forward to anything as much as she had that promised trip. So much for promises.

Then the fear hit her. She would have to marry a complete stranger. But as she and Rebel raced across the meadow, she realized this change of plans might be a blessing in disguise because it was a quick, sure way of getting away from her family. She *had* been worried that she'd go to London and not fit in because she had so few social skills, that she might not find a man who would marry her. *That* worry was gone now.

In the end, the disappointment and the fear were still with her, yet she was hard-pressed to get a smile off her lips. She'd never before experienced such contradictory emotions, but she supposed her fear of this unknown man who would be "as likely to murder her as to bed her" and lived far away couldn't cancel out her delight at leaving home. Being thrown to a wolf was not the escape she would have preferred, but anything was better than living with a family that didn't love her.

She slowed her horse when she came to the woods and took the path she usually used when accompanying her maid, Alfreda, on an herb-gathering expedition. They'd created the path themselves on their many trips to the deepest part of the forest. Alone there in a small clearing flooded by sunlight, she dismounted and looked up at the sky and screamed her rage, then cried out her fear, and finally laughed with relief that she would be out from beneath the thumbs of the heartless people whose blood she shared.

God, she would *not* miss this place or these people . . . well, except for the servants. Alice, the upstairs maid, had given her a box of hand-embroidered ribbons for her Season. Brooke had cried when she realized how much time and love had gone into making them. Or Mary, the cook, who always had a hug and a pastry for her. Or William, her groom, who went out of his way to make her laugh when she was in a dismal mood.

But she would be inconsolable if her maid couldn't go with her to Yorkshire. She would miss Alfreda Wichway too much. The maid had been with her since the week Brooke was born when Harriet's milk had dried up and Alfreda, having just lost her own baby, had been hired as a nursemaid. Then Alfreda had become her nanny, then finally her maid. Thirty-three now and with black hair and eyes so dark they could be considered black as well, Alfreda was more a mother to her than Harriet had ever been. She was also Brooke's dearest friend. Earthy, bossy, outrageously blunt at times, Alfreda wasn't the least bit servile and considered herself the equal of anyone. Brooke spent much time tending plants in the conservatory so that Alfreda would have the herbs she needed year-round.

The villagers of Tamdon relied on Alfreda to cure their ills. They came to the kitchen and passed their requests through the kitchen staff to Alfreda, who then passed her herbal remedies back the same way in exchange for coin. Alfreda had been helping people for so long that Brooke imagined she was rich by now. Even though people called her a witch instead of a healer, they still came begging for her potions. Alfreda wasn't a witch; she just had ancient knowledge of the medicinal properties of plants and herbs that had been passed down through generations of her family. Alfreda kept her healing skills a secret from Brooke's family out of concern that they would accuse her of witchcraft and cast her out of their household.

"You usually have reason to rage and cry, but why are you laughing? What has pleased you, poppet? The London trip?"

Brooke ran toward Alfreda as the maid stepped out from behind a tree. "Not London, but a trip nonetheless. Come, I have somewhat good news to share."

Alfreda laughed. "Somewhat? Have I not taught you the peril of contradictions?"

"This one can't be helped. I am being given in marriage to an enemy of my brother's, not by choice, of course, but by the Prince Regent's request."

Alfreda raised a brow. "Royals don't make requests, they make demands."

"Exactly, and threaten dire consequences if their demands are not met."

"You would refuse to comply?"

"Not me, my parents. But they have decided not to see if the Regent is bluffing and will send me to this man instead. Robert thinks the man will refuse me, so I may not be forced to marry him after all."

"You still haven't said what pleases *you* about this arrangement."

"I will marry him willingly if it means I will be done with my family for good. And he has one thing in his favor: he's tried to kill my brother three times. For that I am already inclined to like him."

"The recent duels your parents spoke of?"

"Yes."

"Honor is usually satisfied with one duel. Did you ever find out why there were three?"

Brooke smiled because Alfreda knew of her proclivity for eavesdropping. "My mother asked Robert the last time he was home, but he fobbed her off, saying it was just a trifle, not worth mentioning. It was obviously more'n that, but when my father asked him today what had incurred this northern lord's wrath, Robert

18

claimed he didn't know. But you and I are well aware that he is a liar."

Alfreda nodded. "At least you have common ground with this man they will give you to. That is a good start."

"Well, yes, we have in common a dislike of my brother, but I didn't try to kill Robert as he accused me of doing when I was a child," Brooke said adamantly. "I really did trip that day when I was trying to beat him to the bottom of the stairs and stumbled into his back instead. I was lucky and caught the railing, whereas he tumbled to the bottom. Yet he claimed I pushed him deliberately and my parents believed him, of course, as they always do. So I was confined to my room until he was hale and hearty again, but I swear he pretended to need an extra few weeks for his sprained ankle to mend because he knew I disliked being cooped up! But I don't care what he thinks. He hated me long before then, as you well know."

Alfreda put an arm around Brooke's shoulder and hugged her close. "It will be good for you to not see that hateful boy anymore."

Brooke would have included all of her family in that statement, but didn't say so. "I may leave within the week. You will come with me? Please say you will!"

"Of course, I will."

"Then let us spend the day stocking up on your

supplies and gathering rooted herbs you can replant. We don't know if we will be able to find in the north all the herbs you need."

"Where in the north?"

"I don't know. They haven't actually told me any of this yet. I just—"

Alfreda's laugh cut her off. "Yes, we know how you gather information."

❦ Chapter Three ❦

Having spent all afternoon helping Alfreda gather her favorite herbs, Brooke returned to the manor house at dusk. She intended to sneak up to her room, change out of her riding habit, and eat dinner before she made herself available to her family. If they had sent riders out to look for her, none had gone near the woods. But her parents didn't need to speak to her immediately. It was more likely that she would hear of the arranged marriage the very day she was to depart and not sooner. That's how little consideration her parents afforded her.

She hurried down the hall and passed the dining room where her parents and her brother were likely seated at that hour. She never ate in that room.

He doesn't like to be reminded that you weren't another son, so we shan't remind him with your presence.

She had a vague memory of her mother telling her that when she was old enough to leave the nursery. It was one of the few kindnesses she could recall her mother ever doing for her, because she would not have had an appetite if she'd had to eat with them. She liked taking her meals in the kitchen with the servants where there was laughter and teasing and camaraderie. Some people in the house cared about her and would cry when she was gone. Just not her family.

As she started up the stairs, the third step creaked. With no one in the dining room talking at that moment, it was heard.

"Girl!" her father yelled.

She winced at the tone of his voice but immediately went to the dining room and stood in the doorway, her head bowed. She was an obedient daughter. At least they *thought* she was. She never broke rules—unless she knew with absolute certainty that she wouldn't be caught. She never argued, raised her voice, or defied an order, even though she wanted to. Her brother called her a timid mouse. Her father had made it clear she was to be seen, not heard, and preferably not seen at all. The few sparks of rebellion she'd had as a child had been met with slaps or harsh punishments. She'd learned quickly to appear docile even when rage boiled within her.

"Has it been so long since I've clapped eyes on you, Sister, or have you just grown up overnight? You certainly no longer look the mouse."

She met Robert's gaze. *Him* she could look at squarely. He didn't deserve any deference from her and would never get any. But it was so galling that this entire situation, and the part she was going to be forced to play in it now, was Robert's fault. He had done something horrid, she didn't doubt, to get the northern lord enraged enough to demand a duel not once but thrice.

"I don't recall seeing you for years either, so quite possibly you are correct that it has been that long," she replied tonelessly.

She kept her facial expression devoid of all emotion. It was easy to do when she had mastered the art of deception. Her unloving family never guessed how much pain they had caused her over the years.

Although her father had called her into the room, he hadn't spoken yet. Perhaps he, too, was surprised that she was no longer the little girl he'd occasionally spotted in passing. She took pains to stay out of his sight. It was a big house and easy to do when she knew his routines. Like Robert, Thomas used to spend a lot of time in London until the last few years, when his joints had started aching him. Her mother hadn't always gone to London with him. When she and her mother were alone in the house, Harriet had taken an interest in her and would talk to her as if they had a normal relationship. She had found her mother's behavior confusing and assumed Harriet was just lonely when Thomas and Robert weren't around, or maybe she was a bit loony, because as soon as Thomas or Robert returned, Harriet acted as if Brooke had ceased to exist again.

Robert stood up and tossed his napkin down on his plate, saying to Brooke, "I will speak with you later. There is a strategy you might employ to come out ahead in this endeavor."

Him help her? She would sooner hug a poisonous adder than trust any offer of assistance from her brother. But since no one had actually told her yet why she'd been called into the dining room, she said nothing and just waited for her future to be unfolded for her.

Her mother began, explaining everything that Brooke already knew. A daughter would normally ask dozens of questions, might even protest. Not her.

"Why did you not say she had reached the age to marry?" Thomas interrupted his wife at one point. "We could have arranged a betrothal to someone of our choosing, then we wouldn't be in this preposterous dilemma now."

Brooke smiled inwardly. Her mother had taken steps to prepare her for marriage because she didn't want Brooke to shame the family by being a complete imbecile. Although she wasn't included in her family's social activities in

London, she'd had all sorts of teachers—for riding, music, dance, language, and art, as well as for rudimentary reading, writing, and arithmetic. No one ever praised her for doing well since she wasn't expected to excel at anything, but she did well nonetheless.

"Since she will be eighteen next month, she was going to have a Season this summer in London," Harriet explained. "The offers would have poured in for her. I did tell you, Thomas. You have merely forgotten."

He grunted in response. Brooke figured he probably forgot a lot of things at his age. He was old enough to be her grandfather. He winced whenever he moved. Alfreda could have eased his pain with an herbal remedy but would probably have gotten dismissed for even offering. Brooke could have eased it, too. With Alfreda as her constant companion, she'd learned about herbs and their wonderful uses. A kind, decent man could have been helped, even if done secretly by adding beneficial herbs to his food or drink. Cold, heartless men deserved what nature dealt them.

Harriet was staring pointedly at Brooke, waiting. She realized that Harriet might expect a response from her to the mention of the London trip. Although she already knew the disappointing answer to the question she was about to ask, she asked it anyway. "Then there won't be a Season in London?"

"No, this marriage is more important. The servants have already begun packing for you. You will depart in the morning at first light with an escort and chaperone."

"You?"

"No, your father is doing poorly so I need to stay with him, and Robert is likely to get challenged to another duel if he accompanies you, so that is out of the question. Dominic Wolfe comes from an eminent family of means that has been based in Yorkshire for centuries. I know his mother socially, but not very well. I've never met her son. He bears the title Viscount Rothdale, but that's all I know about this belligerent man who seems to prefer the wilds of Yorkshire over London society. If he refuses you, all the better. The ax will then fall on his head, as it were, and you may then return home and we will go on as before. But in no way can you refuse *him*. All Whitworths will comply with the Prince Regent's request so he can find no fault with us."

"A viscount is beneath us," Thomas grumbled. "But pay heed, gel. It would be madness for you to refuse to marry the wolf. If you did so, I would have to have you locked away as a lunatic for the rest of your life."

Brooke found it incredible that, apparently, she held her family's future in her hands, but her father's threat made her shudder inwardly. She didn't doubt he'd do exactly that if his title and lands were lost because of her. But this was her escape from *them*. She wasn't about to refuse Lord Wolfe.

She bowed and left the room, and only then could she breathe freely again. Tomorrow. She hadn't anticipated leaving this soon, but the sooner the better suited her just fine.

Chapter Four

"Make him love you, precious. Make him fall deeply in love and you will have a good life with him," Brooke's mother whispered to her before Brooke stepped into the coach.

It took hours for Brooke's shock to wear off. Her mother had called her "precious" and given her advice? She had already been surprised that Harriet had come outside to see her off, when last night Harriet had sent the butler up to Brooke's room to give her money for the trip instead of coming herself. Those words, however, had almost sounded as if Harriet cared about her but Brooke's entire life vouched otherwise. Why couldn't her mother be consistent? Why did Brooke only ever get these confusing glimpses of the mother she wished Harriet could be, but so rarely was?

If the wolf of the north became besotted with her, then he'd leave Harriet's darling Robert alone and stop trying to kill him. Brooke was no fool. Only one child had ever been loved in her family, and her parents would do or say anything to protect him, including lie to their daughter about her chances of charming a man who hated her family as much as she did!

The family-crested coach had pulled up to the front door for her. Her parents' pride demanded that she arrive at the enemy's door in style, she supposed. Besides the driver, two footmen escorted her. Earlier that morning, she'd gone to the stables for one last visit with the horses. She'd informed the head groom that she'd be taking Rebel with her. If she was not coming back here, and she truly hoped she wasn't, then she didn't want to leave behind anything that she cared about.

Most of the staff came out to bid her good-bye.

She didn't think she would shed tears for this place, but she did for the people she'd grown up with, servants who actually cared about her. Her groom, William, even handed her a wood carving he'd made of a horse, telling her he hoped it reminded her of Rebel. It didn't—he wasn't good at carving—but she would cherish it anyway.

The servants accompanying her had their instructions. They were to bring her straight back home if the wolf didn't allow entrance into his lair. Otherwise, the servants, except for Alfreda, were to return to Leicestershire with the coach.

Brooke hoped she gained entrance. She hoped she would find something to like about Dominic Wolfe other than their mutual dislike of her brother. But it was possible she wouldn't, and possible, too, that she wouldn't get through the door.

The emissary had come to the Whitworths first. From Leicestershire it was half a week's ride by coach to Lord Wolfe's home near York. The Regent's man was only a day ahead of them on the road, which meant Lord Wolfe was still blissfully unaware of any of this. If he was going to be enraged when he was told—and rightfully so, Brooke thought—she wished he could have more than just one day to calm down before she arrived.

It would have been logical for her family to wait until they'd learned his reaction to the Regent's demand before sending her north. To dispatch Brooke so soon smacked of fear. They might have raged and railed about this, but they would never have called the Regent's bluff. The consequences meant too much to them to do so.

And her brother, what a blackguard! When he'd come to her room last night, he'd had a calculating look in his eyes that warned her she wouldn't like the "strategy" he had mentioned in the dining room.

"Marry him first, then poison him," Robert had simply stated. "We can claim half his lands or all of them, if he has no other relatives. I know he had a sister who died, but no one knows much else about Dominic Wolfe."

"And what if I like him instead?" Brooke had replied. It could happen. She wasn't hopeful that it would, but it could.

"You will not. You will be loyal to your family and despise him."

She might end up despising Dominic Wolfe, but it certainly wouldn't be out of loyalty to her family. She hadn't said that, though. She had kept her incredulity over Robert's suggestion to herself. She knew he was mean and spiteful, even cruel, but murderous, too? Yet he was so handsome! He had so many blessings, was even an earl's heir. There was no excuse for him to have turned out as he did, except that he was his father's son. "Like father like son" had never been so true as it was in the Whitworth family.

She refused to even acknowledge his preposterous suggestion and instead asked, "What did you do to Dominic Wolfe to make him challenge you three times?"

He snorted. "Nothing to warrant such persistence. But don't cross us on this, Sister. We don't want him as a relative through marriage. His death will remove any further demands the Prince Regent can make of us."

She gestured to the door. He gave her such a vicious look for dismissing him that she thought he might use his fists on her to make his point. It wouldn't be the first time he'd done that.

But he was still scheming and in parting said, "As a widow, you will have your freedom, more freedom than family or a husband will ever give you. Keep *that* in mind, Sister."

Her fondest wish! But not at the cost *he* was suggesting. Yet she'd lost her chance to learn something about the man they were sending her to. Robert knew him, could have told her something about him, but didn't. She'd almost asked before the door closed behind him, but she'd never asked anything of him in her life and wasn't going to start now.

It was ludicrous that the only thing she knew about Lord Wolfe was that he wanted her brother dead. She didn't know if he was young or old, infirm, ugly, or even as cold and callous as her own family was. He could already be engaged to marry someone else, too, could be in love . . . How horrible to think that his life was going to be turned upside down just because he'd wanted justice from her brother that he obviously couldn't get from the courts. She already felt sorry for him!

When the coach stopped for lunch that day, they'd already traveled farther from Whitworth manor than Brooke had ever before been. By evening they would be out of Leicestershire! The trip to London was to have been her first long journey and her first time out of the shire. She'd been to Leicester and a few other towns around it, but those had been short visits that hadn't required spending the night away from home. So she was determined to enjoy this journey despite what would happen at the end of it, and she spent much of that first day staring out the window at countryside she'd never before seen.

But she still couldn't stop her thoughts and anxieties from churning. By late afternoon she got around to telling Alfreda about Robert's nefarious suggestion.

The maid merely raised a brow, not showing the least surprise. "Poison, eh? As cowardly as he's always been, that boy. He'd ask this of you but he wouldn't do it himself."

"But he fought those duels," Brooke reminded her. "That took some bravery."

Alfreda scoffed. "I'll warrant he fired his pistol before he should have. Ask your wolf when you meet him. I'm sure he'll confirm my guess."

"He's not my wolf and we probably shouldn't call him that just because my parents did," Brooke said, even though she'd been doing just that.

"Well, you might want to."

"Call him a wolf?"

"No, poison him."

Brooke gasped. "Bite your tongue, I would never."

"No, I don't suppose you would. I will if necessary. I won't have you suffer at his hand, if he has a heavy one."

Despite the subject, Brooke was comforted to know how far Alfreda would go to protect her from the stranger who was to become her husband.

❦ Chapter Five ❦

Having joined the ancient Great North Road that led all the way to Scotland, the Whitworth coach was making much better time the second day. Although the road was bumpy, Alfreda's pet cat, Raston, didn't seem to mind and purred on the seat between them. Raston had never been allowed in the house. He'd lived in the rafters of the Whitworth stable. Oddly, the horses had never been bothered by his presence. Alfreda had brought him food. The stableboys had given him more. Now Raston was fat and heavy to hold due to all those meals.

"Your father told the damned driver to make haste," Alfreda grumbled when she was jostled on the seat for the third time that morning. "But this is too much. I don't think Lord Whitworth wanted you to arrive in York *before* the Prince Regent's emissary did. I will warn our driver to slow down when we stop for lunch today. They can go as fast as they like on the return trip."

Brooke grinned. "But this is fun. I really don't mind a bouncy ride."

"You will tonight when you feel the aches from it. But I'm glad to see you smiling. You know you can be yourself now, laugh when you want, cry when you please, even lose your temper from time to time if you feel like it. Away from that house that choked the life out of you, you no longer need to keep your inner self contained, poppet."

Brooke raised a black brow. "You're suggesting I let this Prince-picked groom see who I really am?"

"You could. Why pretend with him?"

Brooke laughed. "I'm not really sure who I am anymore."

"Of course you are. You are yourself with me and always have been."

"But only with you, and only because you were the only one in that house who actually loved me."

"Your mother—"

"Don't defend her to me. She spoke to me only when she had to, or when my father and Robert were away and she was in one of her chattering moods. And even then she only wanted me to sit there and listen, not participate in a real conversation."

Many times Alfreda had tried to convince Brooke that Harriet loved her. At times Brooke had thought it might be true. Occasionally, her mother would smile at her when no one else was around or stand in the doorway of the study watching her during a lesson with her tutor. Once, when Brooke cut her arm, Harriet brushed Alfreda aside to tend it herself. She'd even given Brooke Rebel, her most prized possession, for her thirteenth birthday. Yes, a few times Harriet had acted like a mother toward her, but Brooke knew what love felt like and what it looked like. She saw it every time Alfreda looked at her. She never saw it in her real mother's eyes. Yet she knew Harriet was capable of love because she displayed it in abundance for Robert.

"She could be like two different people, Freda. Most of the time, cold and indifferent, and on rare occasions, caring and interested. Sometimes I thought . . . but if I'd been myself with her, I would have been caught in the crosshairs when she reverted to being as cold as my father. The hurt she caused me would have been so much worse if I'd allowed myself to hope it could be otherwise. But you—I wished so many times that you, not Harriet, were my mother."

"Not as many times as I wished you were my daughter. But you are the daughter of my heart, never doubt that." Then Alfreda cleared the emotion out of her throat and added more formally, "We know why you hid yourself from that unnatural family of yours. It was the only way to save yourself pain and abuse. Let us both hope those days are gone for good."

"What d'you think will happen if Dominic Wolfe doesn't like me and sends me back home?" Brooke wondered aloud.

"Nothing other than you will likely get that Season in London that you were promised, and soon after, some other husband. But there would have to be something very wrong with Lord Wolfe for him not to like you, poppet."

"But he hates Robert and will hate me because of it."

"Then he would be a fool."

"He could be that anyway." Brooke sighed a little forlornly. "I knew I would marry eventually, but I expected a courtship."

"As well you should have."

"To at least know my husband well before we reached the altar."

"We have passed beyond 'usual' circumstances here. You could ask for a brief courtship, though. If your wolf is a good man, he might agree."

"Or he could be as afraid of the royals as my family and drag me straight to the altar instead."

Alfreda chuckled. "Which is it you want, to be turned away at the door or married straightaway?"

Brooke sighed again. "I won't know until I meet him. I wish none of this had happened."

"Take heart, poppet. This northern lord could be wonderful. The Prince Regent could be doing you a very big favor."

"Or Robert could have done me the biggest

unplanned ill yet. Getting me stuck with a husband who could well repulse me."

Alfreda tsked. "Then perhaps we shouldn't speculate?"

"Perhaps not."

On the third day of their journey, when they stopped for lunch, no one at the inn knew who Dominic Wolfe was. But they found out that the Regent's emissary was traveling so swiftly that he was probably on his way back to London by now. Apparently, he was traveling day *and* night, merely changing horses when he could, and sleeping in his coach.

That night, they were only a few hours away from Lord Wolfe's estate, but Alfreda refused to continue on in the dark. She wanted Brooke to be refreshed and looking her best when she faced the wolf for the first time. They took a room at an inn and Alfreda went down to order a bath for Brooke and to have food delivered to their room. When she returned, she had information about the Wolfe family.

"You aren't going to like this," Alfreda said with a dour look. "As if you already don't have enough worries on your plate, this family you've been ordered to join apparently has a curse hanging over their heads, so I think now we need to hope you get turned away at their door."

"What sort of curse?"

"The nasty sort, centuries old, a curse that has

killed all the firstborns in each generation in their twenty-fifth year—unless illness or accident takes them sooner."

Round-eyed with amazement, Brooke said, "You're joking, right?"

"No, just repeating what the barmaid, then the cook, and then one of his own villagers who is visiting a relative near here had to say about Lord Wolfe's family."

"But we—I mean, I don't believe in curses. D'you?"

"Not really. The thing is, poppet, many people do, including those who are supposedly cursed. If you are told you are going to die by a certain age, you might be more reckless with your life so the harm invoked by the curse ends up happening anyway. But I doubt the Wolfe heirs just dropped dead for no reason. Ask yours to explain when you feel comfortable with him."

"I will. There's obviously some simple explanation that the family just doesn't bother to share, thus the rumor never got quashed as it should have."

"Undoubtedly."

"And maybe they like having such a rumor floating around—for some reason."

"You don't need to convince me, poppet. But it's the 'centuries-old' part that worries me. That means this rumor has been around for a *long* time and has been kept alive because firstborns *have* died, and at least a few of them in their twenty-fifth year. That's a lot of bad luck for one family to have if it is only bad luck."

Brooke was scowling but she wanted to know what else Alfreda had heard about the Wolfes. "Was anything said about Dominic in particular?"

"He's young. No one gave an age, but obviously he's not twenty-five yet."

Brooke rolled her eyes and accused, "You *do* believe in curses!"

"No, just a little levity on my part that obviously failed abysmally."

"Robert mentioned that Lord Wolfe had a sister who died. The wolf might not even be the first-born of his generation."

"Which might be good news if we believed in curses, but a death is never good news. He could have other siblings your brother doesn't know about."

"Or be the last of his line and determined to get himself killed in a duel. I *wish* we knew more about him."

"Well, there is another rumor, one even more absurd. They say he prowls the moors as a real wolf and his howls are the proof of it."

Brooke's mouth dropped open before she demanded, "Tell me that's more levity?"

Alfreda grinned. "No, but you know how rumors get embellished every time they are passed along. They end up being so far from the truth that they are no more than wives' tales."

"Well, *that* rumor is obviously superstitious nonsense. A wolf man? Maybe they have an ogre living in a tower, too."

Alfreda chuckled. "I don't think anything would surprise me at this point. But there must be something unusual about the Wolfe family for these rumors to have started in the first place."

"And aren't wolves extinct in England now?"

"Indeed."

"But they weren't centuries ago when superstitious people started these ridiculous rumors," Brooke said with a nod, making her point.

"I'm not arguing with you, poppet. However, because wolves are extinct, no one would believe they hear a *real* wolf, only an unnatural one. But if people really have heard howling, it's no doubt just the cries of a long-snouted dog."

Brooke huffed. "Well, you found out more about the Wolfes than I wanted to know. I think I will be most disagreeable when I arrive so I *do* get turned away at his door."

❧ Chapter Six ❧

Dominic stood at the window in his bedroom watching the coach moving along the winding road in the distance. Sweat beaded his brow and dampened his hair. His whole body ached so it was hard to distinguish if his wound did. He'd been informed last night that a Whitworth had stopped at an inn only hours away. The message had passed through four people before it reached him, so which Whitworth it was didn't survive the repeating. He hoped it was Robert Whitworth, come to finish this, but he doubted it. The man Prince George had sent had assured him that the Whitworths would comply with the Regent's suggestion. Suggestion!

His blood still boiled at the manner in which that suggestion had been relayed and the blatant threats that had followed it. Yet the Regent's emissary had been so disinterested. He didn't seem to care how his words were received or what disastrous outcome would follow them; he was only doing his duty.

Gabriel Biscane stood beside him, not watching the coach approach, but frowning at Dominic instead. Not quite as tall as Dominic's six feet, Gabriel, blond and blue eyed, was more than a servant and often took advantage of his status.

The viscount and the butler's son had grown up together in this house. They were the same age and enjoyed the same things. No one was surprised that they became friends before their disparate social stations prevented it from happening. Dominic's father might have broken up that friendship if he had lived beyond Dominic's fifth year. His mother didn't care. And Gabriel's father didn't dare. So Dominic and

Gabriel now had a unique relationship that defied class distinctions.

"You need to get back in bed," Gabriel was bold enough to mention.

"You need to stop giving me orders because you think I am presently weak. Did you send that letter off to my mother? I'd prefer that she hear about the Regent's abominable demand from me and not the gossips, should word of it leak out."

"Of course. This very morning." Gabriel was supposed to be the valet, yet he had audaciously hired another valet for Dominic, leaving himself underfoot with no specific duties. Dominic had offered his friend other jobs that he might prefer, but Gabriel had done none of those, either. Gabriel finally said he would be a jack-of-all-trades, a servant of none. He didn't actually give his current job a name, but he promised to be available for anything Dominic needed and expected a wage for that. And got one. Though Dominic had fired Gabe a number of times, Dominic knew he would have missed him if his friend had actually taken him seriously and left.

Gabriel shook his head. "I give good advice, not orders, so it wouldn't hurt you to pay heed from time to time. Just don't expect me to get your naked body back to bed if you collapse. I'll fetch footmen to do it—"

"I'm not so weak I can't cuff you."

Gabriel sidestepped before he replied, "You

are, but I won't say another word, so don't feel you need to prove otherwise—though truly, when you can't get your own pants on . . ."

Sometimes it was just easier to ignore his friend, Dominic decided. Gabriel usually kept him in top form, with verbal and physical sparring, and Dominic usually welcomed both, just not since he'd come home with this particular wound. The last one had been a scratch. This one was going from bad to worse.

He didn't need a doctor to tell him that. He knew very well he wasn't healing as he should be. He'd just regained some strength after losing a lot of blood when the fever started and was steadily sapping it again.

He had been a fool to come home to Yorkshire this time. He should have stayed at his London town house to recover after the last duel with Robert Whitworth. But he hadn't wanted his mother to know how seriously wounded he was or for word to spread of how close Robert had come to killing him. He didn't want *Whitworth* to know. He'd rather die than give him that satisfaction. Which could still happen. He still *felt* half-dead, but only because of the damned fever that he couldn't shake off.

The anger wasn't helping. Having to deal with the Regent's threat and the enemy's showing up at his door when he wasn't at his best just infuriated him more.

Dominic told his friend, "Put her in one of the towers when she gets here, until I decide what to do with her."

"I believe the decree given you was—marry her," Gabriel said drily.

"Like hell I will."

Gabriel lifted a golden brow. "So you're going to refuse her?"

"I won't have to. She will go running back to her family posthaste. The Whitworths can deal with the consequences of her doing that."

"And how are you going to make that happen?"

"There are ways to scare off virgins," Dominic assured him with a dark look.

Gabriel raised a brow. "Very well, but do I need to remind you that you only have one tower left that is even remotely habitable?"

"Then you won't have trouble finding it, will you," Dominic managed just as drily.

Gabriel started to walk away, but swung back around to say in earnest this time, "I must point out that your war is not with this girl, but with her brother. Treating her ill will serve no purpose."

"Actually, it serves a very important purpose. It will cause Robert Whitworth and his family to lose their lands and title."

Gabriel's eyes flared. "I'm reassured that there is method to your madness. Pardon me, I meant—logic."

"This is *not* a good time to test my patience,

43

Gabe," Dominic warned, then yelled for his valet. "Andrew, bring my riding clothes. I'm not going to be in this house when the enemy knocks."

Gabriel sighed in exasperation. "Dr. Bates ordered bed rest."

"I'll rest when I get back from riding off this rage."

"You will need Bates again if you persist in doing that! Damnit, Dom, be reasonable. You'll rip out your stitches if you ride. Royal won't like the smell of blood."

"My horse doesn't like a lot of things, you included. How he will react to blood remains to be seen. Now enough dire predictions. For once, just do as you are told."

Gabriel made a sound of pure frustration before he grumbled, "I'll fetch Bates back here, *then* deal with your bride."

Dominic started walking slowly toward his dressing room to meet Andrew halfway. "She's not going to be my bride."

Already heading to the door, Gabriel didn't look back as he promised, "I will put her in the most inhospitable room you have."

"The tower," Dominic stressed.

"Certainly, even though it doesn't have a bed."

"She can sleep on the bloody floor!"

The door closed on that order.

✥ Chapter Seven ✥

"There's another one," Brooke said, pointing out the coach window at the ruins of a small castle.

"Many of the smaller ones in Yorkshire were built to protect against incursions from Scotland. Yorkshire was meant to be a stalwart wall that would keep the Scottish armies from reaching the south."

Brooke glanced at the maid and giggled. "You were listening to my history lessons, weren't you?"

Alfreda nodded. "I had to. That tutor wasn't supposed to be teaching you history. Your parents would have fired him if they'd found out. So I guarded the door. You don't remember tempting him to lose his job with all your questions?"

"Vaguely."

Looking out the window again, Brooke wondered if this small ruin was on Wolfe land. They should be on it by now unless the Wolfes didn't actually own much land in Yorkshire.

"I wonder if we'll be here long enough to see all this heather bloom." They'd been told it would flower in late summer. "It must be beautiful when it does, there's so much of it."

"The Yorkshire moors are quite striking, even without the heather in bloom. But I prefer more heavily forested terrain," Alfreda replied.

The sky was cloudy this morning, and without the sun the landscape looked a bit bleak and gloomy to Brooke. She wondered if her thoughts were just coloring it so.

"Where the deuce *is* it?" she said impatiently, still looking out the window on her side of the coach.

Alfreda didn't need to ask what Brooke was referring to. "On my side."

Brooke gasped and quickly changed places with the maid, but she sighed dismally when she saw the house she'd been looking for. "I hope that's not it."

"I'll wager it is."

The façade of the three-story manor house was made of dark gray stone that looked almost black, though that might be because moss or ivy was covering it. It was hard to tell at this distance. Two corner towers rose above the massive rectangular edifice, giving it the appearance of a castle. A large tree stood in front of each tower. Both were in full bloom, obscuring her view of the rest of the manor.

"It looks forlorn, gloomy, forbidding."

Alfreda laughed at that and stressed, "No, it does not. It would not appear that way to you if the sun would stop hiding from us. It's going to rain soon. Let's hope we get inside first."

"If they let us in."

"Stop it." The maid loudly tsked. "If you are

46

turned away at the door, I will spit on it. See how they like *my* curses added to theirs."

Brooke couldn't help laughing. Alfreda wasn't a witch, but sometimes she liked to pretend she was. Alfreda swore that centuries ago the *t* had been removed from her surname Wichway. It was part of her mystique, which she cultivated with the villagers to keep them in awe of her, warning that she'd prove the *t* really belonged there if they told anyone where they got their potions.

Brooke spotted something else and exclaimed, "I see hedges behind the house, on this side of it at least, tall enough that I can't see over them. D'you think he's got a maze in there? Now that might be fun!"

"I know you were denied many things growing up, but mazes are something you should be glad to have missed out on. You can get lost in them."

"You know that from experience, do you?"

Alfreda snorted. "Me? Go in a bloody maze? Ha, not in this lifetime I won't. But Cora from Tamdon village used to work at an estate in the south that had one. She and her beau thought it a lark to have their trysts in that maze. It was so big that no one could hear them yelling for help. They were lucky it was only days, and not weeks, before they were found."

"They should have dropped bread crumbs to leave a trail they could follow on the way out."

"They did, but Cora's cat followed them in and ate them all."

Brooke shook her head. "Was any of that actually true?"

Alfreda didn't deny or confirm it. "I'm just saying, if you enter a maze, leave a trail, just not an edible one."

"I'll remember that, if there's even one there."

Brooke leaned back in the seat, beginning to feel anxious again now that their destination was in sight. She could be meeting her future husband within the hour. If he was even there. The emissary had obviously assumed he was. But what if Dominic Wolfe wasn't at his home in Yorkshire and knew nothing about this marriage yet? A reprieve for her! That would suit her just fine. Maybe Lord Wolfe had been warned of what was going to be demanded of him and intended to keep himself unavailable indefinitely to avoid receiving the news. She might just like living here if he stayed away so she could have the house to herself.

Alfreda nudged her shoulder and nodded toward the other window. Their coach had gone beyond the manor house and had rounded the last curve in the road, which turned them back toward the house. Now they could see a large stable at the side of the house and beyond it a fenced-in pasture that stretched as far as the eye could see. Brooke's pale green eyes flared wide seeing the small herd of horses grazing in it, some small enough to be foals.

"He might be a horse breeder!" she exclaimed excitedly. "How ironic that he's already doing the very thing I want to do."

Alfreda chuckled. "You still have that silly notion of breeding horses someday?"

"Not just any horses, but champion racers, and I most certainly do."

"But women don't," Alfreda said bluntly. "It would be scandalous and you know it."

"The devil it would. Oh, you mean—no, no, I wouldn't actually be on hand for the breeding. I'd have a manager for that, of course. But I'll own them and make the selections and be involved in the training. Yes, I most certainly can do all the rest of that. And I'll make a very nice income at it once I'm done with family and husbands."

"Or you could devote yourself to your children instead."

"If I ever have any, but who says I can't do both? I can raise horses *and* horse breeders!"

Brooke laughed. Lord Wolfe's liking horses as much as she did was a plus on his side. Two pluses boded well, didn't it? She was suddenly feeling much better about him and this place where he lived.

"Well, the idea has at least put some color back in your cheeks, and in good time," Alfreda said. "We are turning into the last stretch of road to the house."

Chapter Eight

Trees lined the drive but not evenly, so perhaps they hadn't been planted there by design. Ivy did indeed cover the manor house's dark gray stone exterior walls, but it had been trimmed back from the front windows. Brooke saw a large circular stained-glass window centered above the front entrance, but couldn't tell from the outside if the colored glass formed a picture. Manicured shrubs hugged the walls on either side of the double doors. Eavesdropping below the windows here wouldn't be easy.

One of the Whitworth footmen assisted Brooke out of the coach. She straightened her lilac pelisse coat, which fell to her knees, and looked down to make sure the hem of her pink dress reached her shoes. She decided not to put on her feathered bonnet, which she had removed during the drive, and just carried it in her hand. The sun broke through the clouds just then. A good omen? she wondered. Probably not. Just no rain, after all.

Alfreda followed her out of the coach with Raston in her arms and remarked in a disagreeable tone, "You would think they would have seen or heard us arriving and be out here to greet us. They must have a lax staff if we have to knock on the door."

"Perhaps no one lives here. We could be at the wrong house."

"Don't sound so hopeful, poppet. We had good directions from that last coaching inn."

It could also be a not-so-subtle way of saying she wasn't welcome, but Brooke didn't mention that again. Her stomach was tied in knots and had been for days, but now it was much worse. If she vomited, she would be mortified. Whichever servant had to clean it up would hate her. *Not* a good start if they did get in.

The footmen were waiting for her order to unload the trunks. She didn't give it yet, didn't move, either. Alfreda didn't notice that Brooke was rooted to the spot, merely said, "Come on, then," and started toward the doors. But Raston hissed loudly as the maid got closer to the house and fought to get out of her arms. They watched as he ran along the side of the house and disappeared.

"What the devil's got into him?" the maid said in surprise.

"Maybe they keep dogs in the house that he can sense."

"Or maybe it's because there really is a wolf in there," Alfreda countered, hinting that she believed in folklore after all. "Raston usually scares dogs away. I've yet to see one that frightens him."

"It's a new place. He doesn't feel at home yet."

"And neither do I with this lack of welcome."

51

"Let's go after him."

"No, let's get you settled first. Raston won't go far. He'll likely head straight for the stable. It's what he's used to."

"Let's wait," Brooke said. "If that door doesn't open, we'll have good reason to leave."

"I know you're nervous, but—"

"Really, let's wait. The sun is out now. I'd like to enjoy . . ."

Brooke fell silent before she started babbling. She *was* nervous. So much hinged on what happened today. Alfreda, peering closely at her expression, quickly nodded. Did she look that afraid? She took a few deep breaths, which didn't help.

Ten minutes passed, possibly more. It really did seem as if no one was in residence today. Or maybe the Wolfes didn't have servants? No, her mother had said they were an eminent family of means. This *was* a rebuff. The wolf was going to tell her to be gone if she came face-to-face with him. This was his way of avoiding that. She almost breathed easier, until she realized she had too much hanging over her own head to just make assumptions like that.

Brooke finally straightened her shoulders and nodded at Alfreda, who took the last few steps and raised her fist to the door—and almost lost her balance when one of the two doors finally opened and she hit air instead. Alfreda glared at the man standing there. Brooke said nothing. She had taken one glance at him and lowered her eyes as she was accustomed to doing with strangers. But in that glance she'd seen a tall man with short blond hair, cut in the current fashion that her brother favored, and light blue eyes. A handsome man, dressed nattily in buff breeches, a neatly tailored coat, and a thick cravat. It was not how a servant would dress. If this was Lord Wolfe, she'd be pleased, indeed she would. Her stomach stopped feeling quite so knotted.

But then she heard him say, "I was in a quandary of sorts, so I was not going to open the door until you knocked."

"Do you realize how long we've been waiting out here?" Alfreda demanded.

"No longer than I've been standing in here waiting for your knock."

Brooke was incredulous. Logic like that boggled the mind. Alfreda swore, then, sounding exasperated, asked, "What was your quandary that you chose to ignore us?"

"I would never do that! You are immeasurably unignorable, 'deed you are. I just wanted to make sure the halls were cleared before I invited you in."

"Cleared of what?"

"Furious encounters," Brooke thought she heard the man say, but he'd spoken so softly she wasn't sure. Then he added, "Do please come inside."

Alfreda complained, "If you're the butler, I'll see that you're fired."

"I'm not, and you won't," the man said cheekily. "You'll warm toward me before long. You'll love me."

"In your dreams, puppy. Show us to your lord."

"No, but I'll show you to your rooms."

So he wasn't Lord Wolfe. How disappointing! But Brooke glanced up at him again only to find him staring at her now as if he'd only just looked her way. And continued to stare for a long time. Alfreda cleared her throat loudly at his rudeness.

He heard it but didn't blush. He did grin and say to Brooke, "If he doesn't love you, I will. You already have my heart, 'deed you do. At *your* service, M'lady Whitworth. I am Gabriel Biscane and so very pleased to meet you."

The lighthearted, silly remarks brought a brief, courteous smile to her lips. She wasn't used to meeting young men of any sort and had certainly never experienced this reaction from any of them.

"So you were expecting us?" Brooke said.

"Not this soon, but you and your mother should come inside."

Alfreda growled, "I'm not old enough to be her mother—well, I am, but I'm not, and if I catch you staring at her again like you just did, you'll think I'm *your* mother, I'll box your ears so hard."

Alfreda was definitely annoyed by the welcome they were receiving from Gabriel Biscane. But he wasn't the least bit cowed by her. With a wink he said to Alfreda, "See? You already love me."

He stepped back from the doorway so they could enter the house. "Come along, then. I will show you to your room, though in my opinion it's not a room. Very well, you might not think it a room either. Oh, bloody hell, it's a tower."

Brooke didn't like the sound of that and reiterated Alfreda's previous request. "Perhaps you should take me to Lord Wolfe?"

"I can't do that. When he's ready to see you, he will request your presence."

"Today?"

"Possibly not."

Another reprieve, and this one brought a sigh of relief, another smile to Brooke's lips, and the last of the knots in her belly dissipated. He had to have been joking about the tower, she decided. But if he wasn't, tower be damned, she wouldn't mind it at all if it meant she wouldn't have to deal with the lord of the manor anytime soon— well, as long as the tower had a bed. Surely it would have a bed. Alfreda was about to protest, though, but Brooke shook her head at the maid, who had done too much complaining already. And Mr. Biscane had already turned about and was heading down the hall.

As they walked past two Grecian columns that bordered the foyer, they entered a gray-marble-floored hallway that was two stories high. Oil paintings lined the white walls above the dark wood wainscoting. Brooke saw that they were portraits of men and women, a few of whom were wearing clothes that dated to the sixteenth and seventeenth centuries. She assumed they were the viscount's ancestors.

A large crystal chandelier was in the center of the hall, but so high up a servant would have to climb a tall ladder to light it, so she doubted it was used often. They passed several sets of double doors, which no doubt led to parlors and the dining room, before they came to the grand staircase.

Splashes of color on the white walls made her glance back at the foyer. The round stained-glass window above the front door threw beams of blue, red, and yellow light on the white walls. The window did indeed have a design—the head of a wolf baring its teeth. Brooke assumed the emblem was part of the family crest—the wolf's head because of their name. But why had they chosen the image of a ferocious wolf? Perhaps the current Lord Wolfe had a sense of humor and had had the window made as a way of poking fun at the fanciful rumors. But, on second thought, she figured he probably didn't like the rumor that he howled on the moors any more than he liked the one about his being cursed and doomed to die young.

At the top of the stairs, Gabriel Biscane led them

to the right, down a wide carpeted hallway that had doors on only one side. These rooms would face the back of the property, Brooke realized. Soon they turned a corner and headed down another corridor that led back to the front of the house. Here a few of the doors on both sides of the corridor had been left open to let in light. The house certainly had many bedrooms and was bigger than it appeared from outside. At the end of the corridor, Gabriel stopped at a circular stairway. Brooke guessed it led to the tower room he'd mentioned. She hadn't thought he was serious about putting her there until that moment.

She tensed, waiting, but he didn't move, just stared at the dark winding stairs in front of them for a long moment. Then without a word he turned about and marched them back down the corridor and returned to the other. As he passed the door at the end, he glanced back at Brooke and Alfreda and put a finger to his lips, suggesting they needed to be quiet, and moved to the next door, just to the right of the stairs. Brooke was reminded of what had happened to her as a child when she'd disturbed her father's solitude upstairs. She'd only done it once. Lessons had been learned quickly in that house.

Gabriel entered the room, walked across it, and opened the two windows to let in some fresh air. Brooke followed him, wanting to see the view. She'd been right. The tall hedges she'd seen from a distance surrounded a large parklike area behind the house with bright green lawns and pathways bordered by beds of roses and other pretty flowers. There were a few shade trees with benches beneath their leafy, green canopies and a tiny pond. Lampposts were placed here and there to light the way at night or just look pretty from the house. Right in the center was indeed a maze, not huge, but with hedges so tall she couldn't see the pathways inside it from her window. Too bad. She would have liked to memorize them before venturing into it, and she would be doing that—if they were staying.

Before Gabriel left, he said in a whisper, "I will bear the brunt of his wrath for not putting you where he ordered, but I'd rather not wake him just yet, so do try to be as quiet as you can so he doesn't hear you in here."

Appalled that he hadn't been joking about the tower, Brooke replied, "Please, I'd prefer another room not so close to his, even one in that tower."

He smiled, apparently not as worried about the lord's wrath as he'd sounded. "Nonsense. Most of the rooms up here aren't cleaned regularly unless guests are staying in them. This is the only unoccupied room that is clean and doesn't have a permanent 'don't use' sign on the door."

She hadn't noticed any signs. "Why is Lord Wolfe sleeping in the middle of the day?"

"I'd be amazed if he is." Gabriel was already

heading briskly toward the door, adding without pause, "I will have your trunks sent up."

Brooke might have thanked him if the door hadn't closed so quickly and she weren't wondering now if the wolf was as ill-tempered as her father, if he needed to be tiptoed around. And then she was staring at another door, one that could very well connect to Lord Wolfe's room, and all sorts of alarming thoughts entered her head, the worst of which was that the wolf would have easy access to pounce on her while she slept!

❧ Chapter Nine ❧

Gabriel arrived just as Dr. Bates was leaving. Bates paused to give him the same instructions he'd given everyone else in the room. Dominic caught Gabe's expression and might have laughed if it wouldn't hurt, but it would. They'd all been right. He had ripped open his stitches and had been forced to cut short his ride. But the doctor's embarrassing lecture had done what the ride was supposed to do—temporarily distract him from his anger.

Carl, the servant assigned to stay with him to fetch whatever he needed today, sat in a chair by the door. Carl had winced in sympathy when the doctor had given his instructions. Dominic's valet,

Andrew, was also in the suite, but he was busy in the dressing room.

Gabriel closed the door after the doctor left and approached the bed. "Leeches? Really?"

"Whatever you wrote in the message that summoned Bates here again apparently led him to bring bloodsuckers," Dominic replied. "He warned he won't be available for the next few days because he's committed to visit patients up north, but he's confident the leeches will soon bring down this fever. That is his opinion, not mine."

With his wounded leg left bare on top of the bedsheet, the leeches by the restitched wound were quite visible. Gabriel refused to look at them and stared instead at Dominic's dog sleeping on the foot of the bed.

After a moment Gabriel shook his head and picked up a tan hair off the sheet. "You shouldn't allow that mutt in here, at least not while you are being leeched. He's shedding. You don't want dog hair in the wound, d'you?"

"Wolf is fine. He's worried about me. He refused to leave when Carl tried to get him out. You can take a horse brush to him later if you're worried about him shedding." Then, turning to the matter uppermost on his mind, Dominic asked, "Was it the Whitworth's daughter in that coach?"

"Indeed."

"How did she like the tower?"

Gabriel glanced back to nod at Carl to leave the room before he met Dominic's eyes. "We didn't find out."

"She's already left?"

"No, actually, Lady Whitworth is probably quite happy with her room."

Dominic immediately frowned. "Where did you put her, Gabriel?"

The reply was mumbled so low Dominic didn't hear it. He was too drained to repeat himself, so he waited, staring pointedly at his friend.

Gabriel finally sighed and said in a louder tone, "Next door."

"Gabe," Dominic said warningly.

"Well, Ella's room is locked and will always be locked. And your old room can't be used because you left most of your childhood mementos in it."

"There are numerous bedrooms on this floor! How dare you presume to put my enemy's sister—"

"Wait! Don't bite my head off until you're stronger, and—I really didn't have a choice. None of the guest rooms are kept readied because anyone who wants to visit you and stay for a time gives you prior warning so that rooms can be prepared for them. Those were your mother's instructions, which you never bothered to change. So only these family rooms at the back of the house are kept spotless at all times. As for that particular room next to yours, your grandmother had that door installed and moved into that room when she could no longer sleep because of your grandfather's snoring. If she hadn't done that, it wouldn't even be part of your suite of rooms."

"You know very well I consider that room my mother's and always will. She moved into it after father died and lived in it until . . ."

"Until she left after Eloise's funeral. And swore she would never return. You've never found a use for it other than to keep it available for her just in *case* she changes her mind and comes back."

"She won't," Dominic said tonelessly. "She was raised in London and prefers London. Here she grieves too much, there she is distracted from it."

"But if Lady Anna did return, she wouldn't want that particular room again anyway and would insist on another. She would want you to have the entire lord's suite. Besides, this arrangement is nothing more'n temporary, but if you *must* know, I thought it rather appropriate, putting Lady Whitworth there, since now she won't have to be moved after the marriage."

Dominic could not care less how logical all of that sounded—except the marriage part. There wasn't going to be a wedding if he could help it. But there was no point in being angry at Gabriel when it wouldn't last. It never did, and at the moment he simply didn't have the strength to maintain it for even a little while.

But he still growled, "Lock that bloody door."

"Of course!"

Gabriel rushed to the now-offensive door and turned the latch, even tested the knob to make sure it wouldn't open. He came back saying jauntily, "Besides, it's not as if you'll be roaming the halls for a while, where you might run into her more often than not. Are the leeches working?" he added, trying to change the subject.

It didn't work. Dominic said succinctly, "You disobeyed my wishes. Aside from your convoluted logic, why did you really do that?"

Gabriel winced, but stood his ground. "You can move her to the tower when you're well. I simply didn't have the heart to do it."

Dominic sighed and closed his eyes.

Gabriel guessed, "I've worn you out. I'll leave—"

"No, you won't. Which member of her family came with her?"

Gabriel sat down in the chair that had been moved next to the bed. "None, which seemed rather odd. However, she was well escorted by servants, though only her maid is staying with her. Charming woman, that one. Full of fire and dire threats. You'd think *she* was the lady, but obviously, she's very protective of hers."

"And the lady?"

"She didn't treat me like a gnat under her boot, like you-know-who did. That last mistress of yours, well, I won't repeat myself. But *some* ladies are just—just—"

"Yes, I know your sentiments in regard to snobby bitches. You still haven't answered my question."

"The lady seemed a bit cowed if you ask me, like she's not used to strangers—or she wasn't expecting to be invited in. Or she's just very demure. Yes, that's probably all it was, considering her young age."

"She's not too young is she?" Dominic demanded sharply, his eyes open again and narrowed. "If they sent me a child—"

Gabriel interrupted with a laugh. "D'you really think the Prince Regent would have made his demands without first finding out if there was a Whitworth daughter of marriageable age? No, she's at least old enough for that. Would you like me to read more of—"

"No." Dominic waited. But Gabriel merely put the book he'd just picked up back on the nightstand and got comfortable in the stuffed chair to take a nap as soon as Dominic nodded off for one. As if there weren't more to tell of his meeting with the Whitworth chit. As if Dominic weren't the least bit curious about the girl who was being forced on him. He wasn't. She wouldn't be staying. He'd even supply a coach for her return trip when she refused to marry him.

But when Gabriel still said nothing else, Dominic finally snapped, "Bloody hell, what's she look like?"

"I was hoping you wouldn't ask, but since you did . . ." Gabriel paused for a long sigh. "She's got a wart on the left side of her jaw and another one by her nose. I didn't stare at them too long, I promise. Red, florid cheeks more suited to a farm wench, big owlish eyes. But if you can overlook all that and her weight—"

"She's fat, too?"

"A little—" Gabriel shook his head. "Very well, a lot. But a good diet and exercise could surely fix that. I can start a regimen for her if you—"

"No. And do not befriend her. I want her to hate this place and leave on her own."

"So her chubbiness is a problem?"

"Don't be obtuse, Gabe. I could not care less what she looks like."

"Then why did you ask?"

"Because I would prefer not to be surprised one way or the other, and truth be told, I feared she might be a beauty sent here to tempt me, since her brother is a handsome fellow despite his black soul. I'm glad at least that she's not comely, because my course was determined the moment that royal toady threatened me with the consequences of not following his master's wishes. Justice will be served if Robert Whitworth loses everything that he cares about because of *his* sister. So she has to refuse to marry me, and we are going to assure that she does. Are we clear on that?"

"Crystal."

"Then fetch her to me."

"You don't care if she's repulsed by what the doctor left on you?"

"I don't care if she faints. Bring her—and some smelling salts with you."

⚜ Chapter Ten ⚜

"We need to find out if there is a conservatory or a greenhouse where we can plant your herb cuttings," Brooke said to Alfreda.

They were on their way to the stable to look for Raston, and Brooke also wanted to make sure Rebel was going to be well cared for. She'd left her bonnet and pelisse in the bedroom since the day was comfortably warm. Her Empire-style pink dress had short capped sleeves and, for modesty during daytime, a matching chemisette that was tucked into the deeply scooped neck-line. Brooke had never had occasion to leave off the tucker, though she knew she would have been expected to when she attended evening gatherings in London.

"Those cuttings need to be planted soonest before they wither and die," she added. "I know you've been worried about that."

"You are my only worry, poppet. You are and always have been my one true focus, since the day they put you in my arms to nurse. The cuttings I can plant in the ground for now, perhaps behind the hedges where no one but the gardeners will notice them. There's good, fertile soil here. That park behind the house attests to that."

"Yes, but we can also build our own greenhouse if there isn't one here. Harriet gave me money for this trip, more'n I needed. Not because she wanted to, but because it would reflect badly on her if she sent me here with empty pockets. You know how she is, always doing what's 'expected of her' whether she wants to or not."

"She loved you in her own way, poppet."

"Don't defend her. I know my mother and I don't want to think about her now." To keep that old hurt from joining all of the other unpleasant emotions she was dealing with right now, Brooke quickly changed the subject. "Do you think that's a greenhouse?"

Alfreda followed Brooke's gaze to a small building by the tall hedges bordering the park. "Hard to tell what's in it from here. It could just be the gardeners' shed."

"I can't tell from here if that's glass on the roof and sides or just light-colored boards."

Alfreda squinted her eyes at the little rectangular shed. "If it's glass, it's very dirty glass. But we'll have a look after I find Raston."

As soon as they stepped inside the stable, they

heard a loud meow that seemed to come from above them and made both of them laugh. Raston didn't get up from the long support beam where he was lying; he had just wanted them to know he'd seen them.

An elderly white-haired man approached with a teenage boy beside him and said, "The cat will be fine here, ma'am, actually a welcome addition. I spotted a few mice in the hay pile this morning and I was just thinking of fetching my sister's cat from the village since our resident mouse-catcher seems to have abandoned us. Can't have vermin underfoot here spooking the horses. Your cat will likely take care of that problem—if he's yours?"

"Indeed," Alfreda replied.

The man's weathered face creased further when he grinned at Alfreda slightly because he'd guessed correctly, but when he glanced at Brooke, he appeared undecided whether to say anything else. For a moment, she could have sworn his expression turned pitying. But then he seemed to shake off whatever emotion that had been and introduced himself. "I'm Arnold Biscane, head groom here at Rothdale Manor. And this is my youngest son, Peter."

"You're related to Gabriel Biscane?" Brooke asked curiously.

"Gabe is my nephew. And Peter has already put your mare out to pasture with the other mares and will fetch her when you need her. She will be well cared for here."

"Thank you." Brooke smiled. "Indeed, Rebel is precious to me."

She didn't just love her horse. Rebel represented hope for her future. She wanted to breed the mare while Rebel was still young. She hadn't been allowed to at home because their head groom had orders not to increase the stock. When she was younger, she had devised all sorts of plans to accomplish her goal anyway, even trying at midnight when the grooms were asleep. But she was afraid to get near her father's stallion that Rebel favored. But Brooke might be allowed to breed Rebel here, if the wolf did indeed breed horses.

She would ask the viscount that when, or rather if, she ever met him. At the moment she was more concerned about Alfreda's herb cuttings and asked Arnold, "Is that a greenhouse we saw over by the hedges?"

Arnold nodded. "Lady Anna, Viscount Rothdale's mother, had it built. She loved to garden and didn't want to mar the design of the house by adding a conservatory. She grew special flowers that were later replanted in the park. Some even survived after she left, though everything inside the greenhouse has long since withered and died."

"D'you think I could do some gardening in the greenhouse?"

He didn't answer, probably didn't know if she would be allowed to, but he did ask instead, "You think you'll be staying then, m'lady, and marrying his lordship despite the curse?"

She wondered why he suddenly looked so sad and then realized he must believe in that silly curse. She almost giggled at his question though. What a deplorable subject to raise, and she didn't even know the answer!

So she said, "That's a very good question, but the answer remains to be seen, since I haven't even met him yet. Thank you for seeing to my horse. I'd like to meet all of the Rothdale horses when I have more time, but just now I'm going to go check on Rebel out back while my maid has a closer look at the greenhouse. I'll meet you there in a few minutes, Freda."

Brooke walked through the large stable and out the open back door. The pasture fence began back there and stretched far to the west. She spotted Rebel grazing in the far field. The male horses were kept in the near pasture. She watched them for a while, noting that no slugs were in the bunch. Prime horseflesh, all of them. One trotted toward her. He was solid black, even his mane and tail, and beautifully sleek even as big as he was. He stuck his head over the fence trying to reach her.

She moved closer to rub his nose gently. "Well, aren't you pretty. Yes, I know you're not a mare, so don't take offense. You're still pretty."

"You're a brave one, aren't you? Dominic's stallion isn't usually friendly to anyone. He's tried to bite me a time or two."

The horse galloped off as Brooke swung around to see Gabriel standing behind her. "I love horses. Perhaps they sense that."

He shook his head. "I love horses, too. Who doesn't, as handy as they are? But that brute still tries to bite anyone who approaches him, carrot in hand or not. Just be cautious if he comes near you again, or just don't go too close to his fence. He's king of the roost." Gabriel laughed and waved his hand behind him. "Like his owner is of all the rest."

That didn't sound like an order, merely friendly advice that she could take or ignore as she pleased, but she nodded. "Have you come to give me a tour of the property?"

"No, he's ready to see you." Gabriel extended an arm toward the house.

Her feet might as well have just grown roots. She wasn't moving. "Why?"

He laughed. "Why? And here I thought you wanted to meet him today."

The devil she did. That sick feeling was back, churning in her belly. Dread. She ought to be used to it when she had lived most of her life with it for one reason or another.

She still couldn't seem to move and distracted

him from noticing by asking, "What exactly is your post here?"

"I'm a jack-of-all-trades." He grinned. "I do whatever Dom wants done."

She was surprised to hear him speak so familiarly of his lord and to refer to him by a nickname. "You care about him?"

"Friends usually do."

If she hadn't just met other Biscanes who had claimed Gabriel as a relative, she might have thought he was minor gentry who had latched on to a benefactor. Robert had had one such friend, as hard as it was to believe he had any, who often came home with him and stayed as a guest. Servants, however, didn't usually consider their employers friends. She'd thought she was unique among the nobility in befriending servants. Her family certainly didn't. Good grief, did she and Viscount Rothdale have this in common, too?

"So he's a likable fellow? I'm so—" Her mouth snapped shut when she saw all humor leave his expression. The knot in her belly tightened. And he didn't answer her!

"I don't mean to rush you, Lady Whitworth, but he doesn't like to be kept waiting."

"I'm not moving a step without hearing your answer first."

Gabriel sighed. "You must know the reason why you are at Rothdale Manor. The hatred for your brother runs deep here."

"You share it?"

"Yes, I do."

"Why?"

"You don't know?"

"Robert and I don't speak. I don't think even my parents know what he did to cause your lord to challenge him to so many duels. Actually, I think Robert fobbed them off by calling it a 'trifle.' "

Gabriel looked angry when he muttered, "Despicable blackguard."

She wholeheartedly agreed, but she wasn't going to share that with a servant. Maybe he would tell her what had made the viscount challenge her brother. "What did he do?"

"That isn't for me to say. I'm sure Dominic will tell you if you ask—actually, you might not want to broach that subject with him, at least not today."

"So I'm to be tarred with the same feather as my brother?" she demanded. "Is that what I can expect from this meeting with Lord Wolfe?"

"I honestly don't know what you can expect. But if he sends someone else to find you, neither of us will like the results. *Do* start walking toward the house, please."

She did get her feet moving, though slowly, and tried *not* to dwell on what was about to happen in that house. She turned to Gabriel for distraction. "You have a lot of family that work here."

"Not a lot. A few cousins, an uncle, my mother. The Cotterills and the Jakemans have more. Our ancestors lived in and around Rothdale village. You can see it from the west tower, or could, before the tower almost burned down. No one goes in there now. My father was the butler here before he died. He wanted me to take over his position, tried to groom me for it when I was a child, but I was too busy having fun with Dominic to want to spend time doing that! So a new butler was hired after my father died."

"What caused the fire?"

He followed her gaze up to the tower and said solemnly, "Dominic did."

"Quite the nasty accident. What was he doing up there?"

"Setting the fire."

She gasped. "Deliberately?"

"Yes. It was his sister's favorite playroom when she was a child. The year she died, she took to going up there again, but not to play. She would just stand in front of the window for hours at a time. She died that fall."

"I'm sorry."

"We all are. Everyone here loved her."

"Does Lord Wolfe have any other family?"

"His mother and a few distant female cousins, but he's the last Wolfe to carry the name—and wants to keep it that way."

⚹ Chapter Eleven ⚹

Brooke was still dragging her feet by the time they got upstairs, desperate now for a delay that would keep her from entering that room at the end of the hall. She stopped for the umpteenth time, asking Gabriel, "Why did you put me in a room that connects with the viscount's?"

He glanced back to say, "As I told Dominic, it will save us the trouble of moving your belongings after the marriage. But I assure you the door is locked—now."

That would have been a relief if she weren't so anxious. "Do you know for a fact there's to be a marriage?"

He didn't answer. All he said was "One of these family rooms was his sister's. It is locked and will always be so. One is his old room—"

She interrupted hopefully, "Instead of telling me, why don't you show me?"

"Perhaps another time. He is waiting."

He marched ahead of her and opened the dreaded door. She glanced at the one to her room and wondered if she could barricade herself in there. But did she really want to appear cowardly? She was cowardly! No, she wasn't, she reminded herself.

It took courage to live with *her* family, and

75

cunning, and masterful avoidance and deception skills. But at home she knew all the variables and exactly what she had to deal with. This was different. This was the unknown. Her behavior now might affect the rest of her life. First impressions were important. She didn't want to be labeled a coward here—if she would be staying. It was time to find *that* out.

She stepped into the room, her head bowed respectfully. A movement to her left drew her eyes to a fellow in a chair, wiping sleep from his eyes. He quickly stood up and bowed to her, muttering, "M'lady."

In a movement to her right, yet another man, this one middle-aged and dressed more formally like a butler, came around a corner on the east side of the suite.

He bowed, too, and offered a respectful "m'lady" before a third voice said commandingly, "Leave us."

She got out of the way of the exodus, stepping farther into the room, closer to the alcove, and winced when she heard the door close behind her. She knew vaguely where Lord Wolfe had spoken from, somewhere in front of her, but without looking up, she saw only the foot of a bed in that direction.

Then a dog ran over to her and sniffed at her shoes. Her instinct was to crouch down to get acquainted, but that would reveal that she liked animals, and she didn't want to reveal that much about herself yet. The dog stood almost three feet high and had a long snout and a short coat of brown-and-gray hair with light cream on the neck and underbelly. She couldn't tell what breed it was, but she imagined that with a snout that long, it would sound like a wolf when it howled.

When the animal sat down beside her, she was bold enough to ask, "What is his name?"

"Wolf."

"He's not actually . . . ?"

"No, I found him on the moors a few years back, still a pup, but half-dead from starvation. He thought he could chew on my leg. I liked his determination not to die so I brought him home and fed him."

"Does he howl on the moors?"

"Not that I've noticed. So you heard that rumor?"

"Yes, but I paid it no heed."

"Come here."

She tensed. Well, there really was no help for this. And they'd just had a somewhat normal conversation. He might not be as cold and vengeful as she'd been expecting him to be. Maybe her brother had lied and *he'd* been the one demanding the duels, while Lord Wolfe was just an innocent in Robert's vendetta for some imagined slight. It was possible. She and the viscount might both be victims of Robert's vicious nature.

She moved forward some more, but she was still hesitant to look at him. When she did, she would instantly know his nature. She was good at reading people, a side effect of not letting them read her. But she wasn't seeing his feet in front of her and she'd be reaching the wall pretty soon!

Then she did see them, at the foot of the bed. One was under a sheet, and the other, a big bare foot, lay on top of the sheet. He was receiving her while he was in bed?! That was so inappropriate it boggled the mind. She was mortified and prayed her cheeks weren't showing it.

She raised her eyes and took in his face and his whole body. Her red cheeks couldn't be helped now. He sat propped up in bed against a dozen pillows, one leg entirely exposed! His whole chest was bare as well. The bedsheet was draped over his hips. She didn't miss the leeches on his left thigh, which explained why his leg was uncovered.

She saw too much with that first glance so she kept her eyes on his face. She definitely wasn't expecting this. He was more handsome than her brother, and she'd thought no one could overshadow Robert in looks. But this man did in a wild way. The bare shoulders, the upper chest matted with black hair, the thick neck and arms, were a study in stark masculinity. She'd never before seen this much bare male skin.

Did he *have* to be such a big, strapping specimen? Wasn't she intimidated enough without having to worry about his size, too? She wouldn't be able to outrun legs as long as his, and she definitely wouldn't be able to get out of arms that strong. And why was a confrontation with him the only thing that came to mind at the sight of so much brawn and muscle? Because he really did look wild.

It was the hair, long, black, very, very unkempt. And the feral eyes. They were light brown with many golden flecks. Amber eyes—like those a wolf might have. She had to bite back a hysterical giggle. But who could blame her for being fanciful? Fraught by shredded nerves, fears, rumors of wolf men and curses, of course her imagination was going to run rampant.

"Brooke Whitworth?"

She banished the wolf from the bed and focused on the man. "Why aren't you sure?"

"You don't have warts."

"No, none that I've ever noticed."

"Gabe alluded . . ."

"Did he? Shame on him. Does he often tease you like that?"

"Unfortunately, yes."

She smiled, but only to herself. "You must not mind if he still has his job."

"Unfortunately, we've been friends since childhood, so he takes advantage of that."

"That is an odd way to describe a longtime friend . . . as 'unfortunate.' "

"He is likely the only one who will cry when I'm gone. I regret that."

What a sad thing to say, as if he might want her sympathy. Or was he just testing her to see if she had any? When his expression hardened, she decided it was neither. He probably hadn't intended to reveal something like that to her, so she quickly said, "You have a wound?"

"A gift from your *brother* that refuses to heal."

He said "brother" as if speaking of the most reviled thing imaginable. They really did have something in common, but she didn't want to talk about her feelings for Robert.

Instead she glanced at the leeches on his thigh and said, "He wasn't aiming for your heart, was he?"

"I think it's obvious what he aimed for."

A crude gentleman? No, he was no gentleman at all, or he was attempting to shock her. The latter was more likely, but it didn't work. The long bare leg shocked her. The bare chest shocked her. That her brother had tried to make sure there would be no more Wolfes didn't. But that wouldn't be Robert's goal. Robert would have aimed to kill.

So she said, "I disagree. What's obvious is that he has no more skill in shooting pistols than you do."

She realized too late that she'd just insulted

him, so she was surprised when he admitted, "I'm not in the habit of dueling."

"That's too bad. With more experience you could have saved us both this . . ." She didn't finish. Telling him she didn't want this marriage was revealing too much.

But he guessed anyway, saying drily, "Unwanted marriage?"

She could have lied, but she chose not to answer. She'd meant she wished his aim, not Robert's, had been true, but there was no point in clarifying that. He was going to think the worst of her simply by association. She was a Whitworth, the sister of the man he'd thrice tried to kill.

But she couldn't hold back her curiosity. "Why didn't you practice? Wouldn't that be the logical course of action, practice first then issue your challenge?"

"Rage doesn't acknowledge logic."

Well, for some people such as *him* it might not, but—oh, very well, he had a point.

"Are you even old enough to marry?"

The question, out of context, drew her eyes back to his. The anger appeared to be under control for the moment, but she couldn't be sure. She wasn't getting a sense of the man yet, other than that he was quick to anger, quick to blunder, and was not giving her a welcoming smile. Perhaps he never smiled. But if he was going to be civil again, she could be as well.

"I don't think anyone cares if I am or I am not—certainly not the Prince Regent, who is demanding that our families be joined in marriage—but as it happens, I will be eighteen in a few weeks."

"And what would a spoiled earl's daughter as young as you know about marriage?"

She stiffened only a little. "I understand what's expected of me."

"Do you? I highly doubt it. Your mind is more likely filled with misconceptions, but how could it not be, when half the *ton* beget their children without ever taking off their nightclothes?"

Her mouth dropped open. She quickly closed it.

"Come closer."

She didn't. With two feet between her and the bed, she was close enough to a naked wolf. They weren't married yet. He was *not* getting any samples . . .

"Already you show that you don't know the first thing about marriage, or did your mother fail to mention that above all else, you will *obey* your husband?"

She knew that rule, but she also knew that without some sort of mutual respect and devotion a marriage could end up being quite odious—for her. But what the deuce was he doing? Just making sure that she would be a dutiful wife? Or making sure that she knew that being *his* dutiful wife wasn't going to be pleasant?

She took a step forward before he made the

demand again. But when he just stared at her, waiting, she knew he wanted more. Decide! Call his bluff? Be compliant? Remind him . . . no, he *had* to marry him or else her family would lose their lands and title. He *had* to marry her for the same reasons. They might as well already be joined.

She took the step that brought her upper thighs to the edge of his mattress. His arm closest to her slipped around her waist and up her back as he drew her closer. It was so sudden she almost sprawled across his chest, but caught herself in time, placing one hand on the bed's headboard above his shoulder. But he was still pressing her closer, and his arm had too much strength for her to resist. Her mouth got captured by his, and the heavy arm around her back kept her there.

He kissed her. His anger made it seem passionate. It *was* passionate. It was illuminating, a promise of what could be had in his bed if he accepted her. A promise that there would be no clothes between them if he did, that he was a lusty man who would take what he wanted when he wanted it. Her heart pounded erratically, loudly. Her senses were assailed with the rasp of a persistent tongue, the scrape of stubble on his upper lip against her skin, fingers at the back of her neck that caused her to shiver, the smell of whiskey on his breath. She was in no way repulsed, rather she was lured to the forbidden.

But she quickly stepped back when his arm left her back, his tongue left her mouth. She imagined he'd just gotten bored with the lesson, and she didn't doubt that was all it was.

He verified that when he said, "That's what you can expect."

She wanted to bolt from the room, but she stood her ground. She knew what her father would do to her if she refused to marry Lord Wolfe. Tucking an errant wisp of hair back into her coiffure as she took a deep breath to calm herself, she noticed the glass and the bottle of Scotch whiskey on his bedside table. The wolf drank during the day? That didn't bode well. Or was he taking the whiskey as medicine for his wound?

"Are you in pain?"

"Why are you still here?" he grumbled. His golden brown-eyes narrowed on her. "Does it matter?"

"If you are a drunkard, then, yes, it would."

"Then, yes, I am a drunkard."

She tsked. Was no part of this meeting going to go well? They'd almost had a normal conversation when he'd asked her age. She tried to get back to that.

"I told you when my birthday is. When is yours?"

"It was last week."

"So you just turned twenty-five and expect to die at some point during the next twelve months?"

"Or, thanks to your brother, in the next few

days from this wound. But how do you know of the curse?"

"Last night at the inn near here we heard more'n one rumor."

"And that didn't scare you off?"

"I don't believe in such things, so it wouldn't."

"Too bad."

She stiffened. "I beg your pardon?"

"You are sister to the man responsible for my sister's death. You will never find welcome here."

Good God, what had Robert done? It took a moment for her to absorb how much this man hated her. Of course he did, if Robert had harmed his sister.

"What did he do?"

"Don't pretend you don't know!"

Brooke wasn't sure what to do in the face of such rage. If she wasn't going to be welcome here, did that mean he had no intention of marrying her? So why had he agreed to see her? And why had he tried to shock her with that kiss?

"Should I leave Rothdale?"

"Yes."

She gasped and turned, about to head straight for the door. If she'd done so more quickly, she would have missed his adding, "If that is your choice."

She paused to say bitterly, "You know very well that choice isn't mine."

"Nor mine!" he growled behind her.

❧ Chapter Twelve ❧

In the upstairs hallway, Alfreda was drawn to the far end of it where Gabriel stood with his ear pressed to Lord Wolfe's door. She approached to do the same, but he stepped back, saying in an urgent whisper, "Wait! I think she's about to burst out the door."

"It's not gone well?" Alfreda said with a frown.

"Indeed not."

After a few moments when the door hadn't opened, they both pressed their ears to it. Facing each other, Alfreda saw Gabriel grinning, as if he did this sort of thing often. Alfreda was only concerned for Brooke and would enter the room without permission if she thought Brooke needed help. Gabriel's amusement annoyed her. She didn't like sharing an intrigue of any sort, even one so minor as eavesdropping, with such an impertinent fellow.

Halfway between the bed and the door, Brooke was having trouble dealing with her own anger. She understood Lord Wolfe's rage. Her father had been just as furious after the Regent's emissary had left. Men who commanded everything around them naturally balked when they had to accept commands from someone more powerful than they were. But she shouldn't be on the receiving end of that rage when she'd played no part in causing it. Robert had caused it.

You are sister to the man responsible for killing mine.

Brooke didn't doubt that her brother was capable of any perfidy, but murder? *Responsible* could mean all sorts of things. But she couldn't ask the wolf again for an explanation no matter how rampant her curiosity now was, not after the way he'd reacted to the subject. He might get out of that bed to demand an eye for an eye by killing her. She didn't know him and what he was capable of, and he obviously wasn't going to let her find out.

She didn't leave the room. She was still angry enough at him for refusing even to pretend to be civil anymore to march right back to the side of his bed. He'd no doubt thought he'd just chased her out of his house. Too bad for him.

But he didn't look disappointed, though his single raised brow spoke volumes. Was he waiting for a fight? Hoping for one? Or just curious about why she hadn't fled?

As she gazed at the half-naked viscount who lay before her, she thought it was a good thing that she'd been raised by down-to-earth Alfreda rather than a proper lady. Otherwise she would be more embarrassed by Lord Wolfe's undress. She noticed the sweat on his brow. It was early summer, but the room wasn't warm enough to cause it. He must be running a fever. She stepped closer to the bed and looked at the wound on his left thigh to see if it was inflamed.

Watching her, he asked, "The sight of leeches doesn't bother you?"

"I'm not repulsed by something that helps to heal."

Brooke knew some herbs that could draw out the poisons in his wound more effectively than leeches, but she didn't say so.

Instead she said, "May I?" Without waiting for his answer, she gently pressed a finger to his flesh near his stitches to see if yellow liquid would drain from the wound. It didn't occur to her, at least not immediately, that she shouldn't be touching him at all, that she was breaking a clear rule of etiquette. She felt her cheeks warming but she willed away the blush, reminding herself that he'd broken a couple of more important rules by insisting she enter a room where he lay less than half-covered by a sheet and by kissing her!

"These stitches look fresh."

"How would you know?"

Now he sounded a bit testy. He obviously didn't want her help for any reason. Yet she did have a reason, but she wasn't going to explain to him that hating her brother as much as she did, it would give her perverse pleasure to heal his mortal enemy. The wolf's dying wasn't going to help her—unless he did it after they were married. Damn Robert for putting *that* thought in her head.

Keeping her eyes on his wound, she answered, "There is fresh bleeding around your stitches and not because of the leeches. I think you haven't been following your doctor's orders."

"*You* are the reason the wound needed to be re-stitched today."

Truly? He was going to blame her for that, too? Because he was too stubborn not to stay in bed and give his leg time to heal?

She still wouldn't meet his eyes, afraid she'd get mesmerized by them again—or frightened into backing off—but she said, "Good. Reopening the wound drained it, which will heal the wound faster than those leeches will."

"How d'you know?"

How to answer that without revealing too much of herself? Evasively! "It's common knowledge in Leicestershire. And there are other ways to draw out the poisons more quickly."

"A woman doctor? I'm impressed that you found a school to teach you."

She heard the sarcasm. But he was right, no school would teach her. But Alfreda had. It wasn't in her to let his condition worsen if she could prevent it, no matter if she might suffer for it afterward.

"D'you realize you are in danger of losing your leg if the poisons spread? Your leeches aren't even close enough to the wound to do any good, and they will draw more good blood than bad."

He snorted at her. "Your prognosis is not a trained one, so don't expect me to believe you know what you are talking about. Dr. Bates would have warned me if my condition were as dire as you are suggesting. In a few days the doctor will return and prove you wrong."

She supposed Dominic's reasoning was sound from *his* perspective . . . well, from any male's perspective. Like most men, he was absolutely certain that a woman could not possibly know more about any subject than a man did.

So she moved back away from him with a shrug. "You will do as you please, of course. But should you change your mind, my maid, Alfreda, who has great knowledge of herbal remedies, might know how to fix you, if I can convince her to help."

"Convince?" he scoffed. "She's a maid. You give her the order—"

"No, I do not. She raised me. From the week of my birth she's been more a mother to me than mine ever was. I don't treat her like a servant and never will. And she's only ever helped people who can't afford a real doctor, which means she's never helped a lady or a lord before. So as I said, I could try to convince her to have a look at your wound, but she may balk at breaking that rule of hers."

"So she's a healer, just not a traditional one?" he speculated.

Brooke didn't answer. She wasn't about to give away Alfreda's secrets. She shouldn't even have made the offer. He would probably survive for a few more days.

But her silence prompted him to say, "I'm aware there are self-trained healers with knowledge that has been passed down from one generation to the next who still treat the sick in areas where doctors are not available. This far north, we are lucky to have even one doctor who lives nearby. But why would your maid have a rule against helping the nobility?"

She'd revealed too much! This closeness to him must be rattling her thoughts. She blanched when he added, "Is she a witch?"

"Don't be absurd! There are no such things."

"Of course there are. It was a witch who cursed my family."

He *believed* he was cursed? She was incredulous. He was an educated man, wasn't he? He should know better than to succumb to superstition. But then it dawned on her that he was going to use that supposed curse as another means to get her to flee. He must think that if he professed to believe in it, then she would, too. Ha! She wasn't falling for that ploy.

He didn't say anything more about his family curse. He closed his eyes instead. Apparently, he'd taxed what little strength he had. They shouldn't have met yet. He should have waited until his fever was gone and he was not in pain.

"You should rest if you hope to survive until your doctor returns," she suggested matter-of-factly, and turned toward the door.

"You can ask your maid," he said, opening his eyes. "But why do you even want to help me?"

Not expecting the concession, she glanced back at him. "Because you are going to be my husband."

He growled at that answer. She raised a brow, silently questioning if he was going to be the one to fail to comply with the Regent's demand.

"So you think you can make me love you by healing me?"

"Not a'tall. I'm confident that you will find many other reasons to love me."

He didn't seem to like that answer and scowled darkly. "You are mistaken, Brooke Whitworth. I am not pleased to allow you into my home, nor should you feel welcome here, because you are not."

Her back stiffened. She had been nothing but cordial, even helpful to him. "Then tell me to go."

He didn't. No, of course he wouldn't. He'd already made it clear he wanted *her* to do the fleeing on her own.

"Just as I thought," she added bitterly. "You are as stuck with me as I am with you, no matter how much we both hate it."

❦ Chapter Thirteen ❧

Brooke was too upset to notice that Alfreda was in the group of people waiting outside the viscount's door. She turned away from them and ran down the narrower corridor to that tower Gabriel had led her to earlier. She peeked into the dark stair-well and saw only a faint light emanating from above, but she mounted the stairs anyway. She wanted to see for herself exactly where the wolf had wanted to put her. When she reached the top of the stairs, she blanched. Nothing was in that circular tower room except cobwebs.

The windows were small and narrow, letting in only a few narrow sunbeams. This wasn't a bedroom, it was a dismal cell.

"Well," Alfreda huffed, coming to look over Brooke's shoulder at the empty room. "Now we know."

"And have Gabriel to thank for not making me sleep on the floor in here tonight."

"Don't *you* thank him. I will find some way to—if he ever stops annoying me."

Brooke turned about and hugged Alfreda because she needed a hug just then. She didn't want to stay in this house. She didn't want to argue with Dominic Wolfe again. Even as sick and wounded as he was, he'd quickly lost his temper.

God help her when he regained his full strength. If that happened. Maybe she shouldn't ask Alfreda to intervene, should just let nature and one incompetent doctor take their course.

Rubbing Brooke's back soothingly, Alfreda said, "If he's not really a wolf, it will be all right."

Since neither of them believed he was a real wolf, Brooke knew the remark was meant to lighten her mood. She appreciated Alfreda's effort, but it didn't work. She'd clung to a slim hope on the way to Viscount Rothdale's estate that he and she might get along eventually—if he didn't simply refuse to marry her. That hope was gone now that she knew how deep his antipathy ran for her whole family.

Such a dismal thought and such a shame. Had she met Dominic Wolfe under different circumstances, she could have been quite attracted to him. He was young and handsome, after all. A very different outcome might have been possible, even a courtship if her family had approved—no, that was only what should have happened, not what could have happened, not when he was only a viscount. Her father would have aimed higher, not for her, but for himself. Not that it mattered when Dominic despised her and was determined to make her despise him as well. He had made that abundantly clear.

Brooke turned toward the stairs, wanting to

leave this horrid room, confessing, "The wolf hates me. He wants me to flee."

"We anticipated this outcome."

"I know. It was illogical to hope that he might like me and *not* immediately hate me because I'm Robert's sister."

"No, just optimistic. But it won't be pleasant for you at home if you do flee."

"My parents won't *have* a home if I do."

"Well then, we need to consider that there are ways to have a marriage that is not really a marriage."

"To pretend?"

Alfreda paused at the bottom of the stairwell to clarify. "It's probably too soon to consider this, but what I refer to is a mutual agreement not to live together intimately. You would be surprised how often such arrangements have been made over the centuries, when families, especially noble ones, joined for reasons that had nothing to do with love and esteem and everything to do with land, power, or wealth. An heir is usually needed first, but once that has been accomplished, the husband and the wife go about their own interests, even living in different households—if they can agree to such an arrangement."

Brooke thought that sounded incredibly promising. "Is any of that actually true, or are you just trying to make me feel better?"

"Did it work?"

"So it's not true?"

"It is. You have so very little knowledge of the *ton* because your parents socialized in London without you. But my mother worked in London before I came along and she moved back to the country. She was privy to a good deal of gossip in that big town and used to amuse me with tales of the inner workings of the nobility's house-holds."

"So if such couples do hate each other, why wouldn't they agree to such an arrangement?"

"Because the husband will do as he pleases anyway and might not care about his wife's feelings—unless he is afraid of her family."

Well, that was a brief hope, wasn't it? It didn't even last one minute.

Brooke sighed. "The wolf doesn't fear my family, just the opposite. I wouldn't be surprised if he wants to kill us all because of what my brother did."

"Do we know yet what he did?"

"All I learned is that he blames Robert for the death of his sister. He got too angry for me to want to press for more information about it."

"That's a good reason for a duel, but it's an even better reason to get your brother imprisoned or hung. I wonder why Lord Wolfe didn't pursue that course of action."

"Because he wants to be the one to kill Robert. Three duels definitely suggest that."

"Possibly," Alfreda conceded. "We can find out what really happened from the servants here."

"I asked Gabriel, but he just said I should ask Dominic about it. I have the feeling no one here wants to talk about it."

"To you, maybe. But servants will talk to other servants. Let me give it a try . . . So, did you decide to be yourself with him?"

"I wasn't going to, but he got me so angry, I'm afraid I couldn't hide my true feelings."

"He must have provoked you."

"Deliberately."

"Yes, but that wouldn't tell him much about you, poppet, now would it? It wouldn't reveal that you're as quick to laugh, that you aren't vindictive and wouldn't seek revenge even if warranted, that you have a good, pure heart, despite the family you come from."

Brooke sighed. "Suggesting a pretend marriage would probably just make him laugh because he would be the husband who would do as he pleases with no care a'tall for my feelings. Besides, he doesn't want *any* marriage to me, he made that perfectly clear. All he wants is for me to leave, which I can't do."

"Would you like a love potion instead?"

Brooke blinked in surprise and choked back a laugh. "There's no such thing."

"Yet there are herbs—and I do have a tiny supply left—that will stimulate . . . Well, the villagers called the tonic I made from these herbs a love potion because it stimulates desire, and some people equate that with love. But if the wolf suddenly wants to bed you, then he will look more favorably on the marriage, and everything can go uphill from there."

"He already kissed me."

"Did he?"

"But it was just a ploy to frighten me off. He got quite angry when it didn't work."

Alfreda raised a brow. "Did you like the way he kissed?"

"I didn't mind it. It was quite—surprising."

Alfreda looked pleased. "That's an excellent start, poppet."

"For me, not for him. He's certainly not repulsive. I wouldn't mind a'tall having him for my husband—if he didn't hate me."

"You've only just met him. We've only been here a few hours. In time he won't hate you."

"That's not a certainty, Freda. And, no, don't give him one of those potions you mentioned. He's got far too much rage in him right now for me to want him to want me. It could turn out much too unpleasantly."

"We'll just keep it in mind as a last resort then." Alfreda winked.

Brooke rolled her eyes before she broached Dominic's condition. "Speaking of your herbs, would you be willing to have a look at the wound

Robert gave him? It's not healing and his fever appears high."

Alfreda snorted. "Just because you take pity on every sick dog you come across doesn't mean you need to feel sorry for a wolf."

"Pity is the last thing I feel for him right now."

"Then why do we want to help him?"

"Because then he might be inclined to deal with me more reasonably and not see Robert whenever he looks at me."

"Well, we're going to have lunch first to give him a bit of time to take in his first glimpse of you and realize the remarkable favor the Prince Regent has done him." Alfreda put her arm around Brooke's waist to lead them back up the corridor. "Besides, we are not in a hurry to fix him after the insult he's dealt you."

"You were listening at the door!" Brooke accused, hearing Alfreda use the word *fix* and the same phrase she used with the wolf.

Alfreda didn't admit whether she had, she just nodded toward the tower. "I'm talking about that room we just left. That was an insult, poppet, of the worst sort."

Brooke agreed, but she still grinned. "Lunch sounds like a good idea. He's not going to get worse in the next few hours—I don't think."

✦ Chapter Fourteen ✦

Brooke and Alfreda found a big kitchen at the back west corner of the house. Two men and four women were in it, and two older children doing menial chores. Two Biscanes, three Cotterills one Jakeman, and two others who weren't members of those three families that had worked at the "big house," as they called it, for hundreds of years. But the two newcomers didn't learn all that until Alfreda got angry when their lunch was set before them in the dining room.

Brooke felt discouraged as she looked at her plate. It was obviously another ploy the wolf had arranged to get them to leave his house. But Alfreda was livid when each of them was served a plate with only two thin slices of toasted bread, burned actually, on it and nothing else, not even a crock of butter.

"Come with me," Alfreda said, going straight to the kitchen.

Brooke agreed that something needed to be done about the shabby way they were being treated, but she wasn't expecting the approach Alfreda took. First, Alfreda demanded that the servants intro-duce themselves. As the staff warily gave their names and positions, they stared nervously at Brooke. They probably weren't used to a lady invading their domain, but she might have confused them, too, when she sat down at the kitchen table. They didn't know that she was used to eating in a kitchen.

Marsha Biscane, the cook, was much older than the other women in the room. Short and blond, she had laugh lines around her blue eyes, which hinted at a jolly disposition. Unfortunately, she wasn't displaying it now as she stood quite stiffly, looking offended by Brooke and Alfreda's presence.

Alfreda pointed a finger at the cook, saying, "You'll serve us a proper meal if you don't want to grow warts."

Marsha turned quite red in the face. "I follow his lordship's orders."

"To starve us? How many warts would you like? I can be very accommodating."

Brooke almost laughed, the other servants looked so horrified. But frightening the servants probably wasn't a good idea, especially if she ended up marrying Dominic. So she told Marsha, "She's joking."

"She don't look like she is."

"She has an odd sense of humor," Brooke assured Marsha before she got assertive herself. "I'm sure you know I am to marry your lord\ and eventually bear his children, so I do need to be in good health for that. You can either agree that he wasn't serious when he told you to feed us scraps, or you can vacate the kitchen and we will make our own meal."

Alfreda added as she sat down at the table, "And you might also want to keep in mind that once Lady Whitworth becomes Lady Wolfe, she'll be wielding the household ax, as it were. If you like your jobs, you might want to agree that Lord Wolfe, being in a feverish state, wasn't thinking clearly about any orders he's given you concerning my lady."

Absolute silence followed that. It probably wasn't the best time for Raston to wander in and hop onto Alfreda's lap. Or maybe it was. "Witch" was whispered from more than one direction, but the cook filled two new plates in a hurry and set them on the table. Were all the servants here superstitious? Possibly. But Brooke didn't want herself and Alfreda to be treated as pariahs *if* they were going to be living in this house, so she needed to put the staff at ease.

She tried a simple common courtesy first. "I was very sorry to hear about Lord Wolfe's sister. When did she die?"

"It was nigh two years ago when it happened and, and—" The girl, named Janie, wiped a tear from her eye before insisting almost angrily, "We don't speak of Lady Eloise's death. You'll need to ask his lordship about that sad matter."

Brooke wondered why no one would talk about

Eloise's death, but she didn't press. Maybe the servants didn't even know the circumstances. But she did wonder why the wolf had waited so long to challenge her brother if his sister died almost two years ago.

Alfreda was quite pleased with the new meal and seemed more relaxed. Perhaps to convince the kitchen staff that she wasn't a witch she complimented them on the meal and got them talking in a more natural manner after she told a few amusing stories about Leicestershire.

Marsha took to Brooke first, or at least she stopped being so stiff and formal. More comfortable with members of the nobility than the other servants due to her elevated position in the household, she seemed pleased by Brooke's praise for the cottage pie she'd served them and even laughed when Brooke told a story of her own about her midnight foray to try to get her mare bred when she was only fourteen and how she'd chickened out.

Marsha was Gabriel's mother and aunt to the young woman Janie. Once Marsha let down her guard, Brooke understood where Gabriel had gotten his chipper, good-humored nature.

Before Brooke and Alfreda left the kitchen, Marsha told her niece, "Go and inform his lordship that I'm feeding his children."

Confused, Janie pointed out, "But he doesn't have any."

"He will one day and he'll understand. Just tell him."

Brooke hid a grin. The woman could have just kept it a secret that she'd be feeding them proper meals, but Marsha obviously didn't fear the wolf. She didn't appear to fear Alfreda now, either, so Brooke had accomplished at least one goal today.

When they returned upstairs after lunch, they found Gabriel still waiting outside Lord Wolfe's room. He grumbled to them, "He's annoyed with me. He won't let me back in. But now that you're here, you can help by distracting him so he won't kick me out again."

"So he's sleeping?" Alfreda guessed.

"I doubt it. He's too stubborn to actually rest. It's been hell keeping him in that bed, er, beg pardon, ladies, but it *has* been difficult."

Since neither Gabriel nor Alfreda appeared to want to open the door to find out if Dominic was awake, Brooke did and entered the room. "Brave, ain't she?" she heard Gabriel whisper behind her.

It was unnerving to know that even Dominic's friend could be wary of him. When she peeked into the room's alcove, she saw that the wolf wasn't sleeping. His eyes had latched on to her immediately. And narrowed. She still led her little group forward to the bed.

"My *companion*," Brooke stressed in the introduction, "Alfreda Wichway."

"It took you *this* long to convince her?" Dominic said to Brooke.

She hadn't realized that having given her permission to bring Alfreda here, he'd expected them to come back immediately. She took the blame, saying, "No, I wanted to have lunch."

"So you kept me waiting over a trifle?" Dominic demanded surly.

Alfreda tsked, her own tone not the least bit conciliatory when she said, "She did nothing of the sort. It *did* take this long for her to convince me. And I am still not convinced. I will look at your wound, though, with your permission."

He'd just been hit with two salvos, both pointing out that they didn't like him much. He didn't say another word, just nodded his head slightly. Brooke suspected he found it galling to be at the mercy of his enemies. He must feel as bad as he looked to agree to this. He probably did think he might be in danger of losing his leg, and thus their help was better than none.

Alfreda only had to glance at the wound to say, "That's quite a serious inflammation, Lord Wolfe. Your body fights it vigorously, which is why you are feverish and likely feel like hell warmed over."

He didn't confirm how he felt and instead asked, "So you *are* a healer?"

"I've never called myself that. I am merely familiar with remedies that have been commonly known since olden days, as are most women who

105

grow up in rural villages. You can continue with the course of treatment your doctor recommended, or I can find an herb that will do the same thing, only quicker."

Brooke knew that Alfreda didn't want the people at Rothdale to know they were both prepared for medical emergencies such as this one. That was why Alfreda hadn't brought her satchel of potions, salves, tools, herbs, and plant cuttings. The less others knew of her healing abilities, the better.

"There's actually such an herb that grows here?" Dominic asked.

When Alfreda didn't answer him, Brooke quickly interjected, "I brought some common herbs with me from Leicestershire. One of those may be what she refers to."

"These will need to be removed," Alfreda added matter-of-factly, placing a finger near the leeches. "Or we can wait until they fall off. If you've been treated with leeches before, you know they will leave tiny wounds that will bleed. They will itch before your bullet wound does. But do not scratch them. Scratching could worsen the inflammation."

"Stop treating me like a child." He swiped a hand over his thigh to remove the leeches himself.

Brooke's eyes flared at that display of impatience. Alfreda's hand was knocked away from him as well as the leeches, which were now squirming on the bed beside him.

"That, m'lord, was very—detrimental. There was time—"

"If you insult me again . . ."

The wolf didn't finish his threat, but threat it certainly was. Brooke was amazed that Alfreda wasn't already on her way out the door. How had Alfreda insulted him? By not rushing immediately to help him? By giving him sound advice that he apparently already knew? Perhaps he'd guessed, as Brooke had, that Alfreda had been about to say "foolish" instead of "detrimental"? Or maybe he was feverishly imagining some other slight?

That was possible. In fact, all of his churlishness thus far could have been induced by his fever and his discomfort. But that might just be wishful thinking on her part.

If anyone had been insulted, it was Alfreda. Brooke thought about leading her maid out of there and leaving the wolf to his fate. If only she could. If only she could defy everyone, even the Prince Regent. But she was still by law in the hands of her parents, and they had thrown her to this wolf. High dudgeon would only lead to embarrassment afterward because she couldn't leave this place. She would still have to deal with Dominic Wolfe, and getting him beholden to her could definitely make those dealings go easier.

But she was still angry enough to tell Alfreda, "I think the less time we spend in here the better."

She said it deliberately to direct his anger away

from Alfreda and back to her. She hoped it would prompt him to kick her out of his house. If he was going to make that costly mistake, he would do it when he was in a rage. But she didn't hear the words that would free her, and he didn't even glance her way. He was still glaring at Alfreda.

But amazingly, Alfreda wasn't done with offering her help. "It's too bad your doctor doesn't wield a needle better. Your wound is going to leave a jagged scar. We could make it much neater."

"You or her?"

"Me, m'lord."

"Then say 'me,' damnit."

Alfreda stiffened and stood back. "I am not your maid, I am hers. Do not presume—"

"You truly wish to butt heads with me?" Dominic cut in darkly.

"I am not butting heads, merely stating a fact," Alfreda insisted.

"Careful, wench. If this marriage occurs, I will be the one paying your wage."

"You are welcome to, but it isn't necessary. Lady Whitworth is dear to me. I will serve her with or without a wage."

Alfreda was annoying him more and more with every word she said. Brooke could tell from his increasingly feral expression. Finally he growled, "I think you should stay out of my sight."

Alfreda was quick to make that happen. Brooke was speechless as she watched her dearest friend leave the room. When Brooke looked back at the ungrateful wretch in the bed, her light green eyes blazed with anger. "That was very ungracious of you, Lord Wolfe, considering she was only here to help you at my request."

"Do I look miraculously healed by either of you?" he shot back.

"You look like a beast determined to be a nasty churl. She *can* fix you. You would mend quicker —more's the pity!"

Brooke marched out of the room, slamming the door behind her. The satisfying sound did nothing to quiet her rage.

❧ Chapter Fifteen ❧

Out of sight, out of mind. How Brooke wished that were true! But Dominic Wolfe had used a single word that had eased some of her rage before she got to her room. *If.* He'd said, *If this marriage occurs* . . . Was there still a possibility that he might do something to keep it from happening?

She found Alfreda collapsed in one of the reading chairs. The maid looked tired. She wasn't any more used to nasty confrontations such as that than Brooke was.

Collapsing on the bed herself, leaving her lower legs to dangle over the side, she said, "He's intolerable. We need to consider other options."

"I wasn't expecting him to be so handsome," Alfreda remarked.

"What's that got to do with anything?"

"Well, it does sort of make him tolerable, I would think, at least in your eyes."

Brooke snorted.

"Or not. But we don't know what he is really like yet. A man in pain is never at his best."

Brooke was good at reading people, but the only thing she got out of the wolf was that he was despicable. "He's not going to have a 'best.' "

"Then you should wait to make sure of that. And what other options have we?"

Brooke was precariously close to tears. "I don't know! There must be something—other than poisoning him as my brother wants me to do."

"If we leave here, we won't be able to go home."

"I know."

"They will just drag you back here."

"I know!" And probably beat her, too. She wasn't old enough for her "no" to matter at the altar if her parents were saying "yes."

A long moment passed before Alfreda said determinedly, "Then we go somewhere else."

Brooke latched on to that kernel of hope. "I speak fluent French."

"We are at war with those people. We can't go there. They'll think we are spies and hang us."

"Scotland isn't far from here."

"Exactly—it's too close. We'd be found easily there."

"We can catch a ship then. The coast can't be too far from here."

"A day or two, but did your mother give you enough money for a long voyage? And to survive wherever we end up long enough to figure out how to earn more money to live on?"

Brooke figured she had enough for passage, maybe, but not enough to survive on for long. The tears got closer.

But then Alfreda added, "Or we can sneak back to Leicestershire and fetch my money from the forest."

Brooke let out a near-hysterical laugh. "You buried it?"

"Of course I did. I suspected we might not stay here. And even if we did, I suspected you might want to escape every so often and could use the excuse of visiting your parents to do so. In any case, I assumed we would return to Leicestershire at some point. But you realize, no matter where we go, we still might be found. Your parents have too much to lose. They will send an army of lackeys after you."

"But it will be too late. The Regent will have taken what he will take."

Alfreda raised a brow. "Do you really want to do that to them? To your mother?"

"She doesn't care about me," Brooke insisted. "Why should I care about her?"

"Because you do. And because she does. I know you don't like to hear it, poppet, but she does. I don't know why she's chosen to hide it, but she must have good reason. Did you never consider it might be because of your father? When a man decides something has no value, everyone around him must agree with him or risk punishment."

Brooke shook her head, unconvinced. The times Harriet had acted like a real mother were too few. Although she'd gotten quite involved in preparing for Brooke's Season in London, almost as if she were looking forward to it more than Brooke, none of that made up for the years of neglect, never giving her a hug, never telling her "I love you." Brooke couldn't even eat dinner with her parents! But Robert certainly did. Still, Alfreda was right. She couldn't do that to her mother. It would break her own heart.

Out of options, she sighed dismally. "I'll move up to that tower room so I will be reminded every moment I'm in it that it's where my future husband wanted me to be."

Alfreda tsked. "We don't pout."

"You don't. I might find it refreshing."

"Pouting hurts you more'n it hurts anyone else. We don't pout. But you can make him love you."

Brooke sat up. Her mother had said the same thing. *Make him love you, precious. Make him fall deeply in love and you will have a good life with him.*

"You suggested a pretend marriage earlier," Brooke reminded Alfreda. "Love wouldn't be a part of that."

Alfreda shrugged. "You need to reach common ground with him so he stops pushing you away. He might find an arrangement or a bargain acceptable, and that might get you a truce. Then you can move in for the kill."

Brooke burst out laughing. "I wouldn't exactly call enticing him to love me moving in for the kill."

"It's his animosity you'll be killing. Anything is possible after that."

This interesting thought was a much more palatable option. She might indeed get the wolf to bargain with her if she convinced him she wasn't going to leave no matter what. She just needed to figure out a bargain that would benefit him. It would be a way to become friends with him. Like before love. Friends before lovers. It would give her time to endear herself to him, time to get into his thoughts and then his heart. It would certainly be a challenge, probably the biggest of her life, but if she set her mind to it . . .

But one obstacle she might not be able to surmount. What if she couldn't get past her dislike

of him? Yet she was adept at hiding her feelings
. . . well, she was before she came here! But she
could get that under control. So as long as he
didn't guess that she didn't like him . . .

❧ Chapter Sixteen ☙

After Alfreda helped Brooke out of her traveling
garb and into a simple day dress, the maid
immediately went off to her room in the servants'
wing to get the herbs they needed for Dominic.

Brooke hadn't expected her first day at Rothdale
to be so trying and fraught with unpleasantness,
surprises, and anger. She supposed there were a
few bright spots, though. The greenhouse was not
being used, so she and Alfreda could cultivate
their herb garden there. She had a pretty bedroom
and no one had yet come to tell her to get out
of it. She walked over to a window. She found
the views of the lovely park and the two horse
pastures soothing. Oh, and she'd gotten in the
wolf's door. All in all, she'd made her escape from
her unloving family. She really ought to keep that
in mind and do everything possible to get along
with Dominic Wolfe, at least until he and she
could come to some sort of special marriage
arrangement.

She turned away from the window when Alfreda
returned and handed Brooke two colored pouches

and a small potion bottle. "The herbs in the red pouch will draw out the poisons that are causing the inflammation. Mix them with water and make a paste, and apply it to the wound three times a day until the redness is gone. Then use the herbs in the blue pouch. They will make the wound close more quickly and form a scab. The potion will help him to sleep more soundly, which will also aid the healing, but you might want to explain that to him before you offer it." Then Alfreda added stubbornly, "I'm never going back in that room. I don't care if he's taking his last few breaths."

Brooke nodded. She didn't blame Alfreda for feeling that way. She also knew Alfreda didn't mean what she'd said. The maid wouldn't ignore someone close to dying, no matter how she felt about the person. But the wolf probably wouldn't die now, so Alfreda was no longer obliged to deal with him.

Brooke concurred, "I'm not going back in there either. We've done more'n enough for him when we shouldn't have helped him a'tall."

Alfreda tsked, giving Brooke a look of disapproval before reminding her, "We settled on a plan. The more you help him, the more his heart will open to you. When he's better, he will remember what you did for him and start to love you."

Brooke sighed. "Very well."

"Be pleasant."

"I doubt that's possible."

"Be soothing,"

"I know that's not possible."

"Then just be yourself."

Brooke laughed. "I think I've been doing just that!"

She knew Alfreda had given her sound advice so she decided to at least try a combination of all three. If she didn't lose her temper again. If she could ignore his surliness.

Gabriel answered Brooke's knock and let her into Dominic's room, even though he whispered, "He's sleeping."

"No, I'm not" came from the bed.

He had keen hearing like a wolf—that was an unnerving thought. But approaching that bed again was even more unnerving because his long, muscular bare leg was still on top of the sheet, not beneath it.

She tsked when she saw that the leeches were back on his leg.

He admitted in a somewhat normal tone, "I assumed you were done helping me."

"Did you? You were half-correct." She set the medicine on his nightstand. "These leeches will have to come off. The sooner I apply the salve, the sooner you will start to heal."

"A servant can do that."

"A servant will not know how."

"Your maid does—"

"You've offended her. She won't be back."

"She's offended—"

"I was present. I know exactly who got offended. But as your soon-to-be-wife, it's my duty to assist you, and it is your duty to be grateful for it."

He stared at her incredulously. "You overstep. And you aren't even correct. I have no duty to you."

"Well, I will still honor my duty to you."

She removed the leeches carefully, picked up the red pouch, and went to find water. She walked through the sitting room, which contained a few reading chairs that matched the one next to the wolf's bed, and a small dining table, to the two other rooms in the suite, which she'd caught a glimpse of when she'd stormed out of here earlier. She saw the valet in one of them folding clothes. She guessed the other was the bathing room.

She was surprised to find a second fireplace inside the bathing room. It wasn't as grand and ornamental as the one that heated the main room of the viscount's suite, but it certainly was useful for warming up the room in cold weather and for heating water for baths. A metal bucket of water currently hung over a low fire. And what a tub! A long porcelain tub that had to have been specially made for his size dominated the room. The wolf certainly liked his luxuries.

She went over to a large cabinet with glass doors that contained stacks of towels and an assortment of items, including a supply of clean shaving cups.

She grabbed one and poured water from a pitcher in it, just a tiny bit, then sprinkled some of the powdered herbs in to make the paste. She stirred it with a clean spoon she found in the cabinet and washed her hands.

When she returned to the main room, the wolf was eyeing her and the cup in her hand suspiciously.

"This will only sting for a moment, then you won't notice it." She'd dipped her finger in the paste so she could dab it on his wound.

He grabbed her wrist when she leaned toward him, demanding, "Only sting? If it does worse, you may not like the consequences."

"How much more unpleasant can you be?" she countered, then reprimanded herself. She had to stop reacting to his surliness. "You were shot. Nothing I do will equal the pain of that."

He let go of her wrist without further comment. Without the leeches on his thigh distracting her, she was suddenly too aware of his body, all of it, and how close she was to such a big, strapping *handsome* man—fully naked under that sheet. And his wound was so close to his . . .

Her cheeks suddenly too hot, she tried not to think about where she was touching him and quickly applied the salve, saying, "Perhaps I'll have dinner here with you tonight?" Without waiting for his permission, she glanced up and gave him a brilliant smile. "Yes, that's a splendid idea, since I will need to apply the salve again come evening. We may even see some improvement by then." And less churlishness, she added hopefully to herself.

"That soon?"

"It may only be minimal, but, yes, I do expect there will be a little less inflammation and perhaps your fever will go down. We shall hope."

He merely grunted, so she went to wash her hands. When she returned, his eyes were closed. Had he fallen asleep that quickly? Or was this his way of dismissing her? Likely the latter, she decided, but she left the room quietly anyway.

✖ Chapter Seventeen ✖

"You're still here?" Janie asked when Brooke entered the kitchen.

Brooke was taken aback. Janie wasn't exceptionally pretty, though she did have lovely red hair and bright green eyes to keep her from looking plain. The girl was glaring at Brooke accusingly. And here she'd thought she'd charmed the kitchen staff over lunch.

"Why wouldn't I be?"

"Because he was so angry when I gave him my aunt's message about her feeding his children."

"Ah, that." Brooke managed not to grin. No, indeed, he wouldn't have liked hearing that.

But the cook swung around from the counter where she was chopping meat. Knife still in hand, Marsha said angrily, "That's all you have to say? We're lucky he didn't send us all back to the village. We serve *him,* m'lady, not you— yet."

"I understand where your loyalty lies. But you need to understand that no matter how hard he tries to push me out the door, I'm not leaving. You also might want to take into account that he's feverish and in pain, so he probably won't even remember that you took my side in this matter after I finish healing him."

"*You're* healing him?"

"Yes. With my maid's help, we'll have him back on his feet much sooner than his doctor can manage. So please have two dinner trays delivered to the viscount's room at precisely seven o'clock this evening. I will be dining with him."

Both women appeared startled by the news that Brooke would be spending time with their lord. She could even hear them whispering about it behind her back as she left the house through the kitchen door. She hoped they would now stop taking sides, at least in the battle for decent food.

With the rest of the day free, she would have liked a tour of the house, but since Gabriel wasn't around, she decided to treat herself to a pleasant ride with Rebel instead.

While her mount was brought in from the pasture, Arnold Biscane gave her the lay of the land. The village of Rothdale was to the west, within walking distance, with hills and dales beyond it. The seacoast was more than a day's normal ride to the east, as she'd guessed, but the distance could be traversed quicker with a heavy hand.

Of the northern route, Arnold said, "If you come to woods, you'll know you've gone too far."

"The woods aren't on Wolfe land?"

"Only partially, m'lady."

He also cautioned her to always keep a landmark or a road within sight, so she wouldn't get lost. She kept her grin to herself. Some men just had to treat women like children. She didn't mind Gabriel's uncle's advice. She was sure he meant well. And she was too excited that woods were somewhat nearby and went in that direction. Alfreda, who loved forest and woodlands, would be pleased.

On the way back she spotted a church halfway between the manor house and the village and wondered if Dominic and she would be married there. A graveyard was behind it. She decided to

121

stop to see if Eloise was buried there. The inscription on her marker might even indicate how she died. Brooke was curious about that since no one would say. But only the villagers were buried in the churchyard. The Wolfes had a crypt at the back of the graveyard, but the door to it was locked. So much for that.

Brooke was late getting back, so she stopped by the kitchen again and told the servants to delay the dinner she'd requested by three-quarters of an hour so she could take a bath and requested that water be heated and sent up to her room. At least there were no objections this time.

Alfreda arrived with the servants carrying the water buckets. She stayed to help Brooke undress, then laid out a frock that didn't smell of horses while she bathed. Brooke wanted something a little more fancy and said so.

"We're going to tempt tonight?"

"No, just hopefully look pretty."

"You look that no matter what you wear, poppet. The yellow, then? It enhances the brightness of your green eyes."

The gown did more than that, but Brooke didn't blush. She'd done enough of that when her first evening gowns had been made for her earlier this year in preparation for her Season. They weren't her first Empire fashions, but they were her first fancy gowns that didn't include a chemisette tucked between the low neckline and her throat.

The yellow gown was sleeveless and had a short ruffle that edged the entire neckline, front and back. A sprinkling of gold sequins that sparkled in the light was stitched to the ruffle.

Apart from the embarrassment she felt at her unaccustomed exposing of so much skin, Brooke found the current fashions quite comfortable. The thin, soft muslin was pulled tight beneath her breasts and flowed loosely down to her ankles. Beneath the gown she wore flesh-colored pantaloons! Brooke had laughed at the notion, but Harriet's seamstress had explained that all fashionable women were wearing this under-garment because the Empire-style gowns should appear as if nothing were worn underneath them.

To fill in the bare expanse of skin above the gown's low neckline, Brooke put on the necklace Alfreda had given her, an ivory cameo on a silver chain. A jewelry box had been delivered with her new wardrobe, but nothing in it was as precious to her as the cameo. It was mostly filled with inexpensive baubles of every color that matched the new gowns that Harriet had picked out for her. The only expensive items were an emerald set Brooke was to have worn to her first ball.

With her hair yet to be styled more elegantly for the evening with a lot of short ringlets around her brow and temples, Brooke said anxiously, "Hurry with my hair, please. I'm really running late for dinner with the wolf."

"Nonsense," Alfreda replied. "You're going to look so beautiful he will find you worth waiting for. So stay calm and remember your plan to make him love you."

Easier said than done, Brooke thought. But he probably wasn't going to wait for her, had most likely sent someone to fetch his food. She hoped he'd done that. A hungry wolf wouldn't make for a pleasant wolf—and whom was she kidding? He was never going to be pleasant with her. Not growling was the best she could hope for.

On her way out the door, she told Alfreda to hurry to the kitchen to have the food for her dinner with Dominic sent up immediately, if he didn't already have his. She then knocked softly on his door, but didn't wait for permission to enter since he was expecting her. It was beyond the dinner hour but not dark yet, with the sun setting so late in June, so no lamps were yet lit. Dominic appeared to be alone in the room this time.

He was still in bed, still propped up on his many pillows. But at least he was wearing a white nightshirt, though it was mostly open down his chest. And he'd combed his hair! He hadn't been shaved, though. The stubble on the lower half of his face was darker now. But perhaps he was feeling somewhat better . . .

"Why the devil are you dressed like that?" he growled as she approached the bed.

Brooke was embarrassed by the way his eyes focused above the décolletage, but she didn't pause. She might love how comfortable the current fashions were, but she would never get used to these low necklines that were so popular in London.

"I always dress like this for dinner," she lied.

"Not with me you won't."

She was so pleased to hear that, she smiled. "As you wish. I can be very accommodating." He snorted. Since he already sounded like a beast, she added, "I suppose I don't need to ask how you are this evening? No better a'tall?"

"Hungry, that's how I am. Twice I have been given excuses for why my dinner doesn't sit before me. How have you managed to charm my cook?"

"I haven't," she replied pleasantly. "In fact it's very obvious your staff doesn't like me a'tall."

"Then why are they listening to you instead of me?!" he yelled.

"Because I'm a lady, of course," she said pointedly. "And servants don't dare pit themselves against a noblewoman without serious consequences. It must be your fever that has made you overlook that. Besides, your trying to starve me while I'm here isn't going to work. At least wait until you're well enough to guard your kitchen yourself, because in the meantime, I'll chase your cook out with a broom and prepare my own meals if I have to. So you might want to reconsider that nasty plan. Burned bread and nothing else? Really?"

His face just got redder. She ought to be angry, too, but having gotten a proper meal for lunch, she could now see a little humor in his attempt to starve her. So she tried to mollify him a little by saying, "I expect our dinner will arrive at any moment. But in the meantime . . ."

He was done yelling, perhaps done talking at all, so she glanced down at his wound and was relieved to be able to say, "It does look a little better, not quite so red."

She hurried to the bathing room to mix the salve. When she returned to his bedside, he was still glaring at her. But she was surprised when he grabbed her wrist as she reached for his wound and said, "You are closest kin to the man I hate most in this world. That should terrify you. Why doesn't it?"

That gave her pause. If he thought she should be afraid of him, then she probably should be. But then he didn't know how she felt about her brother. She decided to tell him.

"Because, believe it or not, I hate Robert, too. And believe it or not, I would rather be here with you than with my own family, no matter that you're a churlish beast."

"You might want to stop calling me names."

"You might want to give me a reason to."

She had kept her tone pleasant thus far. She'd

126

even smiled at him, which was obviously confounding him. Good. It was a start. Make him curious. Catch him off guard.

"Why would you hate your brother?"

She'd never told anyone but Alfreda. She shouldn't share the reason with him, but suddenly she did.

"He's hated me from the day I was born, I don't know why. But he used to come into my room in the middle of the night, put a hand over my mouth and hit me, leaving bruises where they wouldn't be seen, and promising to kill me if I told on him. I was too young to realize I could lock my door against him. I think I was only four or five. Most people don't remember much from that age, but Robert's beatings are something that I can't forget and still can't forgive. He became sick for several weeks after the last time he did it, justly deserved."

That had been after Alfreda had found out what Robert had been doing and began sleeping on a cot in Brooke's room *and* locking the door to prevent any more middle-of-the-night visits. Alfreda did that for nearly two years, although Robert stopped trying to get in the room when he started finding the door always locked to him.

"You wished him ill?"

She laughed. "D'you think I can make wishes come true?"

"Can you?"

"I didn't take you for superstitious . . . well, actually, you must be if you can believe you are cursed. But if I had such a talent, I wouldn't be here, would I? I'd be having my Season in London as I was promised."

"That's all? You wouldn't wish for something more grand than that?"

She realized suddenly that they were having a normal conversation, with neither of them growling or snapping. "It's something I've looked forward to for the last two years."

It had made those two years tolerable, at least, better than all those before it. She'd had something to be excited about. The trip promised something better in the end, possibly even happiness. It promised escape. But this man could give her those things, too, couldn't he? At least the escape.

So it was quite annoying to hear him say, "You know I have no reason to believe you about your brother and every reason not to."

"How true! But I don't feel a need to convince you of anything, so it's all right if you don't. You asked, I answered. And as long as we are making confessions—"

"*We* aren't."

She ignored that. "I should warn you that I don't usually reveal my feelings. I have become quite accustomed to keeping them under wraps, as it were."

"Why?"

"Because the alternative would be—unpleasant," she admitted.

For me, she wanted to add, but she was not going to try to win him to her side with pity, if he was even capable of it, by telling him what her life with her family had been like.

"So instead of this light, chipper nonsense I'm hearing, you're really seething with anger inside? Is that what you're implying?"

She blinked at that guess, then laughed. "Exactly! Oftentimes that is the case, but not right now. And earlier I felt angry and, as you might have noticed, I couldn't hide it from you because—"

"But how will I know whether you are concealing or revealing your true feelings?"

"I admit it might be difficult for you to tell. So shall we both simply agree to be forthright with each other?"

"I hope you will not be here long enough for it to matter."

That was not exactly what she'd hoped to hear after being honest with him and revealing so much personal information. "Well, I will continue to share my feelings with you. *You* are already doing exactly that. So I suppose we don't need to agree to anything."

If he couldn't tell that he'd finally annoyed her, then he was blind. But he didn't reply because the food arrived and he finally let go of her wrist. She almost laughed it was so obvious that he'd only done so because he was hungry and the sooner she was done treating his wound, the sooner he could eat.

She made quick work of dabbing the paste over and around the stitches, though she stood back as far as she could from him to do it. "Let that dry while we eat. I will bandage it before I go so the paste does not rub off while you sleep."

"You know I don't want your help?"

"Yes, you have made that quite clear."

"Then why do you persist?"

"As I mentioned earlier, you're going to be my husband, so it's my duty to assist you."

"Your life will never be pleasant here. You need to think about that very carefully and figure out that you only have one option."

She raised a brow at him. "To leave? That is actually the only option I don't have. So maybe *you* need to do some thinking instead and give in graciously—if you know how to do that."

"Get out!"

She almost said, *Make me!* But she bit the words back. She had to stop succumbing so quickly to anger! Where had this willingness to fight with him come from? If he weren't bedridden, she wouldn't dare. And Alfreda's herbs were likely to get him out of that bed sooner. More fool her for helping to that end!

✤ Chapter Eighteen ✤

Brooke didn't leave the wolf's den, although she stared at the door for a few moments, tempted to walk out. She finally chose to ignore Dominic's order and picked up one of the two food trays that had been set on the little dining table and took it to Dominic. A small vase of flowers had been added to one tray. Marsha must have tried to make amends to the viscount for delaying his dinner until Brooke was ready. He probably wouldn't even notice how pretty the flowers were. She knew she ought to offer a smile as she set the tray on his bedside table, but she couldn't quite manage it. He was lucky that she didn't dump it in his lap.

"Would you like me to feed you?"

She had to stop goading him! It got her the glare she expected. He didn't thank her for putting the tray within his reach or for handing him the dinner plate. Did the man have no manners at all, or was his abundant rudeness reserved just for her?

After removing the ceramic dome that had been put over his plate to keep it warm, she took it back to the dining table, where she intended to eat, far from him. She was doing it again—reacting to his churlishness and forgetting her resolve to make him like her. So she removed the dome from her plate and took her tray with her as she went to sit in the chair at his bedside. She would be pleasant despite him and show him it would be nice to have her around.

He didn't reiterate his order for her to leave. He was probably too busy eating to care just then. The baked fish was served with a tangy cream sauce topping it. Brooke found it quite tasty. Crisp vegetables filled the other half of the plate. The dinner trays also had biscuits, little bowls of butter, and cinnamon scones for dessert.

Dominic didn't appear to have any trouble reaching for whatever he wanted to add to his plate. But then, aside from the wound on his thigh, nothing was wrong with his body and his arms were long. She imagined she was going to be impressed by his height when she saw him standing. Would she find him even more intimidating then? She wished they could come to some sort of peace before then.

With fork in hand, Brooke tried to introduce a topic of conversation that didn't touch on their impending marriage. Since she was curious about his family, she asked, "Your mother isn't in residence?"

He didn't answer. Actually, he must have debated whether to respond, so she was pleased when he finally got around to saying, "She lives permanently at our house in London now. There are too many bad memories here for her to want to return to the moors."

"You're estranged?" she guessed. "You could say the same thing about me and my mother, but I didn't have the luxury of leaving home. Until now, that is. Odd that we would have that in common."

He gave her an incredulous look, which ended in a dark frown. "We don't have *any*thing in common. That's a nasty habit you have, of jumping ahead with your assumptions, particularly when it couldn't be further from the truth. I am quite close to my mother. She merely refuses to come back to Yorkshire because all the memories of my sister are here, which is understandable. And she was raised in London. The social whirl and her old friends there at least distract her from her grief."

Since he mentioned his sister without getting enraged this time, she added carefully, "Yet keeps her from you. Does she even know you were wounded?"

"She knows I dueled and why, but, no, I didn't want to cause her worry over this wound. But I'm in the habit now of spending half of each year in London with her. We keep a town house there and another in Scarborough on the coast. Here is where we come to hide."

To hide from what? she wondered, but pointed out, "It's not possible to hide when you are in the open with next to nothing blocking your house from view."

"You haven't grasped the size of Yorkshire, have you? We are the proverbial needle in a haystack."

"Then you probably shouldn't have built a road that leads straight to your door."

"We didn't. It winds."

She laughed. She couldn't help it. She knew very well he didn't mean to be funny, which was why he was scowling at her now for laughing. She didn't care. At that moment she decided to be herself while she was here . . . well, mostly—at least when he wasn't frightening her with his scowls and bared teeth. Though maybe she should ask if he would mind.

So, trying to keep her tone light, she confessed, "I've never been able to be myself with anyone except Freda. I was trying to explain that earlier— before you annoyed me. But it seems fitting that I be myself with you since you will soon be my husband. Don't you agree?"

He raised a curious brow. "Am I supposed to understand what you're implying? How could I stop you from being who you are? Actually, explain that remark. Is something wrong with you?"

She choked back another laugh. "Not a'tall. I've just been stifled, raised in a house that never felt like a home. I was an unwanted daughter, you see. And when no more sons arrived after me, I got blamed for that. So your calling me a spoiled earl's daughter could not have been farther from the mark."

"As if I would believe that any more than I

134

believe that you and your brother aren't thick as thieves. Don't try to garner pity for nonsense of that sort."

She bristled. "I bet you don't even know the meaning of the word *pity*—and you probably even kicked puppies as a child. I assure you it's been quite obvious that you are a man without grace or kindness. Really, you don't need to work so hard at convincing me of that," she added drily.

That got her such an icy look she shivered. So much for conversation and getting to know each other before they reached the altar. And when would that be? Was there a time limit involved?

She didn't ask and said no more to him. When she was finished eating but still had two biscuits left, she put them on his tray. She did it out of habit. She was used to sharing her food with Alfreda. After taking her tray back to the dining table, she wanted to leave, but she had one more task to perform.

She approached him again. "Did your doctor leave a supply of bandages?"

He waved a hand at his night table. She hadn't noticed the shelf underneath it until then, but a tall stack of white cloths was already cut into long strips.

She shook one out, then stared at his left thigh, wondering how she was going to get the cloth wrapped around it without getting too close to him. She didn't think she could, was already blushing, and keenly felt his eyes watching as she hesitated.

"You should not stare like that," she said curtly.

"You shouldn't deign to tell me what I can and cannot do."

"I didn't. I wouldn't presume. 'Should not' implies that what you are doing is making me uncomfortable."

"Is that supposed to make me ashamed for doing so?"

"No, I—" She snapped her mouth shut. He wanted a fight, she realized, anything to get her out of there soon. He was simply still trying to get her to refuse to marry him. Was it going to be like this every time she came in here to help him?

Maybe it was. Maybe he hated *needing* her help, too, and that's why he was so nasty about it. No. She had a feeling that his animosity was never going to end, even when he was hale and—

She'd hesitated so long he yanked the bandage from her hand. She sighed in relief as he started to wrap the cloth around his muscular thigh. "Be careful you don't rub off the salve. Freda advises airing wounds, not covering them up. They heal quicker that way, and I have an herb to help with that, too. But until the wound has fully drained, you need the bandage."

"Whatever will get me back on my feet sooner."

That had been said tonelessly. She glanced at

him. Though his brow was dry, he was still pale and likely tired.

As he tucked in the end of the cloth strip to hold the bandage tight, she tapped the potion bottle on his bedside table. "You can take a sip of this when you are ready to sleep. It will keep you from waking due to the discomfort of your wound. An undisturbed sleep is wonderful medicine. Or you can drink more whiskey, which will basically do the same thing. Just don't mix the two."

"Why not?"

"It will make you grow warts." She grinned to show she was joking. He scowled, not amused, so she added, "It might make you queasy in the morning is all."

"Take it with you. I don't trust potions that haven't been given by a doctor."

He clearly didn't trust *her* was what he meant. She didn't take offense. There was no point.

She picked up the bottle. "I will come in the morning to apply the salve again. Have hot water on hand. A hot compress should be soothing for you."

With that she headed straight for the door. She didn't expect any thanks and didn't get any. Lines had been drawn. They were basically at war. Well, in *his* mind. She just needed to persevere, to be patient, and to fire only soft bullets in return.

So she forced herself to say "Sweet dreams" before she closed the door on whatever nasty rejoinder he would have for that.

❧ Chapter Nineteen ❦

When Brooke opened her eyes in the large, darkened room, she didn't know where she was. She sat up, startled, and looked around, then lay back down on the soft pillows, remembering she was in Yorkshire at the home of the angry, churlish, handsome man who was going to be her husband. She reached for her pocket watch on the night table to see that it was eight thirty. She'd overslept.

When she'd got back to her room last night, she'd taken a sip of that sleeping draft the wolf had refused, and when it didn't work quickly enough, she'd taken another sip. She was afraid she was going to have trouble sleeping in this room every night. Because of the door that connected her room to his. Because while she couldn't open it, he could from the other side.

She saw that Alfreda had already been here. On the washstand was fresh water, still slightly warm, though the drapes were still closed. Brooke opened those now and smiled down on the park below. It was quite lovely with the morning sun shining on it. She might read a book today, if she could find one, on one of the many benches.

The tall bookshelf in her room was empty, as had been all of the other furniture before she'd unpacked. The room's decor made it obvious that a woman was the previous occupant. The large four-poster bed was covered with a thick white spread that was dotted with pink flowers and edged with a set of ruffles.

The carpet was a darker shade of pink, mixed with yellow and maroon, while the wallpaper on the walls was lavender and pink in yet another floral design. The sitting area by the two windows had a love seat and a comfortable-looking chair next to it, both thickly upholstered in silver-threaded lavender brocade. A low, intricately carved table was centered between them.

Brooke had put her toiletries and jewelry box on the vanity. A small desk was still empty and would remain so, since she didn't own any stationery, though perhaps she should try to buy some in Rothdale village. She had a mind to let her mother know she was having *so* much fun here.

She made quick work of dressing, which was quite easy to do with the current Empire fashion. She merely tied back her hair with a white ribbon to match her frock. She was more used to wearing her hair this way than the way it had been styled last night and for the trip to Yorkshire.

While the wolf might be expecting her, she was so not looking forward to entering that room again that she went downstairs first. Passing through the kitchen on her way to the stable, she grabbed two sausages, one for herself and one for

Raston, and two carrots, just in case Dominic's stallion got curious again.

Raston came down from the rafters when she waved the sausage at him and followed her out the back door. After he devoured his treat, she picked him up for some petting while she waited for Rebel to notice her standing at the fence that separated the two pastures.

Dominic's stallion trotted toward her again and didn't hesitate to take a carrot from her hand. She found it hard to believe that he was as vicious as Gabriel claimed. But when Rebel arrived, the mare didn't even glance at the carrot Brooke offered her; she was too busy lifting her tail and swatting it toward the stallion barely a foot away.

Oh, dear, Brook thought. Rebel was definitely making her preference in stallions known. While Brooke would love to have her bred while they were at Rothdale, she had a feeling Dominic would object to his horse being the stud, just as he was objecting to everything else she suggested. Besides, it was much too delicate a subject to broach with him before they were married. But afterward, if there was going to be an afterward . . .

There might not be. He might still give in to his rage and kick her out of his house. But it would have to happen in a moment of blind rage. He wouldn't give up everything that mattered to him just to be rid of her when he was rational. *That*

140

was why he was so angry and was doing his best to force her to leave.

How much time did he have to win their battle? *Was* there a time limit on when they had to marry or forfeit? Her family had certainly wasted no time in sending her here. She ought to ask him, and maybe she shouldn't keep him waiting when he was expecting her.

With that thought she hurried back to the house and straight upstairs. Dominic's dog was sitting outside his door waiting to get back in. She was surprised no scratch marks were on the door if he wasn't always allowed immediate access. The animal apparently had more patience than she did! She knocked smartly on the door. The dog growled at her.

She glanced down and saw him sniffing near her hand and grinned. "Smell Raston, do you? You might want to get used to his scent if you and I are going to keep running into each other."

The door opened, Gabriel holding it wide and giving her a quick grin. "Might I say you look divine today, Lady Whitworth?"

She didn't answer. The effusive compliment embarrassed her because she wasn't used to receiving compliments of any sort. The room was crowded again with Dominic's servants. Even the valet poked his head around the corner to bid her a cheery morning.

She offered her own smile as she neared the bed.

Dominic was still wearing a nightshirt, and at least both his legs were under the sheet this time.

"Do you always have such an entourage in here?"

His golden eyes had been on her from the second she appeared, and he was already frowning. Yet he deigned to answer, "One is here to assist and fetch, one won't leave my clothes alone, and one has arrived to be a bloody annoyance."

Her cheerful smile disappeared, though her resolve remained. "If you mean me—"

"I mean Gabriel, but you can definitely be added as an annoyance."

"Some things don't require repeating. I'm quite aware of your feelings, as you are of mine. A truce might be in order."

"Promise me you'll leave before the wedding and you'll have a quick truce."

She wondered if she should pretend to agree to that just to see what he was like when he wasn't growling and scowling. No, she didn't dare give him hope, then snatch it away.

She reached the side of the bed and pulled the small scissors from her pocket. "Shall we see if the inflammation has receded?"

"I feel better," he mumbled.

"Do you? But the salve still needs to be applied —unless you've been miraculously healed?"

Throwing back at him those words he'd used yesterday to chase her away wasn't the wisest thing she could have done. She curbed the bit of anger that had snuck up on her because of his annoyance remark and dredged up another smile, though she was sure he could see how fake it was.

But he wasn't looking at her. He raised the sheet covering his left leg high enough to unwrap the bandage himself before she could get her scissors near him. So he did sense her anger? So be it. Hiding it every time she was around him was a recipe for an explosion.

"Your wound drained well," she said as the last of the bandage fell away. "Three more applications today and—"

"Three?" he balked. "You can tell me how to make the salve and I will apply it m'self."

"I could, but too much of the herb could draw out the poisons too quickly and enlarge your wound, while too little will do nothing."

That was an absurd lie. She ought to tell him it was. No, she wouldn't. He might want to see her as little as possible, but nothing would get resolved if they just counted the days down in separate rooms until they were standing at the altar. Besides, for her tactic to work instead of his, she had to keep helping him. And she had to stop being so sensitive to his insults.

"Is there hot water for a brief compress?" she asked.

"The water has been kept hot for two hours. When you request something, be on hand to receive it."

She ignored the surliness as she headed to the bathing room to find the water, tossing back, "The room *is* a little warm from that fire, isn't it?"

It wasn't really. She guessed the window in the bathing room had been left open to draw out the heat from the fireplace and she found that she was right. She dipped a small towel in the bucket of simmering water, then dropped it in a clean bowl to take back to his bed. She wrung out the towel and placed it over his wound. It was no longer hot enough to burn, but he must have thought it was. He roared. She raised a brow at him and got a nasty look for it.

To distract him she mentioned what was on her mind. "How soon do we need to marry?"

"Too soon."

"Would an engagement do instead?"

"No. The Prince is fickle. He has a tendency to change his mind so he sets specific time limits on important matters he wants to see done. He wants money out of this absurd arrangement to pay off his debts, wants one of us to refuse to go along with it so he can dip his hands into fresh coffers. He wants that immediately, so if we don't marry in the time he has prescribed, he will get what he really wants out of this absurdity. The first of the three banns was read yesterday at Sunday mass. The emissary saw to that before he left."

She felt a little queasy hearing that news. "So in only two more weeks? I'm surprised he didn't bring a special license with him to shorten the time."

"He did. I got the delay only because of the severity of my wound, which he could clearly see since I had to receive him in bed. It was his stipulation that you remain here for the duration. If you leave . . ."

"Yes, yes, we already know your sentiments. Mine are the same as yours. Believe me, I wish none of this had happened. As I told you, I was looking forward to having a Season in London, but instead I was thrown to the wolves, or wolf as it were. Oh, I beg pardon I suppose you don't like that nickname."

"You shouldn't try to provoke me," he warned darkly.

Her heart skipped a beat. When he got all feral like that, he really was frightening. She had to remind herself that she didn't know what he was capable of. Then again, maybe she should try to find out.

So she steeled herself to say drily, "Only you are allowed to be provocative? Oh, wait, that assumes I'll still be here to see what happens if I don't heed your advice? Which means you won't say the words to end this, will you? Which suggests a truce is still the best path forward for both of us."

She grabbed the herb pouch and headed back to the bathing room to mix another batch of salve. She was surprised he didn't retaliate with another resounding no.

When she was back at his bedside, she risked raising his ire once more by asking, "Will we marry here or in London?"

"I refuse to plan for an event I don't believe will happen," he said darkly.

His ire didn't rise because it hadn't subsided! So she quickly spread the salve around his stitches, then handed him a fresh bandage, saying, "I will return again after lunch. Take heart that I won't suggest we share all three meals each day. But I will be back to have dinner with you again."

"Be precisely on time, vixen, or I will fire my cook."

Her eyes flared. Her mouth opened to revile him for that threat, but she snapped it shut. She didn't doubt he would do exactly that, even though his cook was his friend's mother. How despicable!

In answer she wriggled her nose. "You stink. The fever has made you sweat quite heavily. You can't take a bath yet, but that doesn't mean your manservant can't bathe you."

"You dare—"

"An unclean body can affect—"

"If you're not out of my sight in two seconds, I will share this *unclean body* with you!"

She hurried out of the room, trying to suppress a grin. She hadn't really insulted him. He did stink and probably knew it. He just didn't like being told about it.

❧ Chapter Twenty ❧

Returning upstairs after lunch, Brooke caught Gabriel coming down the corridor from Dominic's room and stopped to ask him, "Am I ever going to get a tour of the house?"

"This is going to be your home, so you're welcome to explore all you like."

"Tell me about Eloise then?"

All of a sudden he looked wary. "Why? It's not good to talk about the—"

"Nonsense. What was she like?"

Gabriel was silent for a moment. "She was beautiful, wonderful . . ." He blushed a little. "I was a little in love with her myself, but she didn't know and of course I could never tell her. She was so full of spirit and fun, but she was a bit headstrong, too, and could be as wild and reckless as her brother. She loved to ride just as fast as Dom, and those two were always racing across the moors together, *actually* racing each other. She also had her own sailboat, identical to his, which he bought her after he taught her to sail, and they would even race those down the coast. And she used to tag along with Dom and me, even when Archer and Benton, his best friends from school, visited. She refused to be left out of whatever fun we were up to."

His description made Brooke wish she could have known the girl. Eloise Wolfe sounded quite fun to be around. Brooke had a feeling they could have been close friends.

"Anything else about her that was special?"

"She liked making her own choices, about clothes, friends, even charities. Lady Anna didn't always agree with her daughter, and she couldn't curb Ella's buying whatever caught her fancy because Ella had her own money, an inheritance from one of her grandmothers. Lady Anna is a patron of the arts and she encouraged Ella to pick a worthy cause to support as well. Ella surprised us all when she didn't pick one, but three!" Gabriel chuckled. "A hospital in York, a church-run foundling house just outside of London, and a home for elderly mariners in Scarborough. Not exactly what Lady Anna had in mind, though she couldn't deny they were worthy causes. And to honor her daughter, Lady Anna continues to support them now."

Generous, this family, at least the women in it. Ella had been so lucky to be able to make her own choices. Brooke couldn't imagine what having that sort of freedom would have been like.

"I do admit I was a bit jealous when Ella and her mother returned from London at the end of that summer, and Lady Anna declared her daughter's first Season a success."

"Why?"

"Because it obviously was. A couple of besotted young lords followed Ella home to continue the courtship they started in London. I suspected marriage proposals would soon follow if Ella hadn't already been asked. But then Ella accompanied her mother to Scarborough before the weather turned too nippy. I'll never forget how touched I was when she told me before she left that day with her mother that she loved me because I was such a good and true friend to her brother. Dom was closer to Archer Hamilton and Benton Seamons, the lords he went to school with, yet she seemed to think I was the better friend. It was the last thing she ever said to me. She never returned from Scarborough."

When his expression turned sad, she asked gently, "How did she die, Gabriel?"

She didn't need to hear the words. She could tell what he was going to say from the wary expression that returned to his face. "You'll need to ask Dominic if you want to know about that."

She sighed. As if that subject were ever going to be safe with the wolf. But she glanced behind her at the locked room he'd mentioned yesterday, trying a new tack. "What about that room?"

"Ella's? I told you it's kept locked."

"You also said I could see her room another time. Now's a good time."

"Why do you even want to?"

"So I can understand a little better the people

149

responsible for my being here, Dominic, Robert—and Ella."

Gabriel hesitated before he nodded and moved past her to unlock the door. "Please don't tell Dom I allowed this," he whispered.

She held out her hand for the key. "I promise he'll never know. I'll lock the door when I leave."

Gabriel nodded, then continued on his way downstairs.

Brooke entered the room and quickly closed the door. Would she find anything of interest in the dead girl's room? It wasn't going to tell her how Ella died. It was dark and musty in here with the thick drapes closed. She opened one panel before slowly walking about the room.

She might be seeing it exactly as Ella had last seen it, except for the portrait of a beautiful young woman leaning against one wall. Eloise Wolfe? She had a strong feeling that it was, and it must have been painted right before her eighteenth year —black hair, amber eyes, joyful. Excited about her upcoming Season? It had probably had a prominent place downstairs until her death made it too painful for her family to look at, and it had been stored behind a locked door instead.

Nothing appeared to be out of place or missing from the room. The vanity was still filled with perfumes and baubles, the small dressing room was still cluttered with clothes, bonnets, and shoes. There was a painting of a beautiful white horse, and another of two sailboats on the sea. Ella definitely liked the outdoors. A miniature of Dominic sat on a night table next to the bed, a younger Dominic, though old enough for the image to closely resemble the man he'd become. Ella loved him, had been close to him from what Gabriel had said. A jewelry box had a wolf's head carved on the top of it. A family heirloom? She opened the box and was surprised to find it nearly empty except for a tarnished pair of small silver earrings. If Ella had her own money, why wasn't that box filled with expensive jewelry?

The girl had also liked frilly things. Ruffles were on the bedcover, the drapes, the vanity—or perhaps she'd never got around to redecorating after she grew up. A large bowl of small seashells was at the center of her bureau, with large shells placed around it. She must have had fun on that Scarborough beach as a child. With Dominic? Did they build sand castles together? Swim together? Brooke wondered if he would ever talk about the sister he'd lost.

She started opening the bureau drawers and felt guilt creeping up on her. This was snooping of the worst sort. But how else was she supposed to find out what happened to Dominic's sister when he wouldn't tell her anything beyond Robert's being responsible for her death?

The first drawer of the bureau she opened was filled with fans. Brooke was amazed to find so many. She started opening them and saw that they were all quite fancy, each made with a different-colored lace and with different gems dotting the painted frames, no doubt to match Ella's large collection of evening gowns. Then she opened an unusual one. The frame was plain, unpainted wood, no gems attached, and the panels were made of white paper with a faint cursive handwriting design on it. Well, that made it more unusual, and since no gems were on it, she didn't think anyone would mind if she borrowed it for a while.

She didn't own any fans herself. Harriet had completely overlooked that accessory or they hadn't been delivered to Leicestershire before Brooke had been sent here. But a fan would certainly come in handy to hide a grin if she felt like grinning at an inappropriate moment, or to keep Dominic from seeing her gritting her teeth. She stuck the fan in her pocket before opening more drawers.

She found nothing else of interest, and the only other thing to open and look inside was the chest at the foot of Ella's bed. As she'd suspected, it only contained bedding. But just to be thorough, she reached inside and ran her palm across the bottom of the chest and touched a piece of hard leather. She pulled out a large book, but it had no title on the cover. Opening it, she read, *Stay out*, which was written in a childish scrawl. She was incredulous when she realized she was holding

Eloise Wolfe's childhood diary. She quickly flipped through the pages and saw that the handwriting changed, becoming more formal and mature. Her eye caught phrases about fittings and gowns and house parties. It wasn't just a childhood diary but one that Ella had kept later in her life. Maybe she had written about Robert. Maybe the diary contained clues about Ella's death. Brooke wanted to read the entire thing. So she left the room with the diary, locked the door, and hurried to her own room.

She spent the rest of the day as well as the next two days combing over seven years of Ella's life, from the day the eleven-year-old girl started the diary to her eighteenth year. Brooke found the diary quite entertaining and actually laughed out loud when she read about Ella and Dominic's getting lost in a snowstorm and being led home by a big white wolf—Ella's description of the dog that had helped them. The girl had had a childish crush on one of her brother's friends and worried that he'd marry someone else before she was old enough to propose to him, though she never mentioned it again, so she must have outgrown the notion.

The diary contained so many amusing anecdotes. Ella's peeking in on Dominic in a corner of the gardens when he tried to kiss one of the local girls, who ran away screaming. Dominic's pretending it was an accident when he fell on their sand castle—they did build them together!—just so they'd have to start over. Ella had even beat him at some of their races and mentioned every win, though she did suspect he had allowed her to. Brooke hated to put the diary down when she had to exercise Rebel, help Alfreda set up her new herb garden, or perform her least favorite task—visiting the wolf's room to tend his wounds.

She was terribly disappointed when she reached the end of the diary because there were only a few entries from the summer of Ella's Season and none from the autumn when she died. Those pages had apparently been ripped out, everything after the day she met "him." That's the only way Ella referred to the man who had fascinated her at her first ball. The six pages after that were missing. Brooke's breath caught in her throat when she saw that whoever had ripped them out had missed the last page of the dairy that contained Ella's handwriting. Had Ella removed the evidence before she died? No, Brooke realized Dominic must have ripped them out in the rage that overcame him when he found the damning words that had sent him to kill Robert. But no wonder he'd overlooked that last page when only two lines were on it:

laughed when I told him about the baby, but the baby leaves me no choice. Damn Robert Whitworth for ruining my life!

Brooke didn't know what to think when she read that last page. So her brother didn't just take Ella's virginity, he'd left her pregnant? Lied to his own parents about it, refused to take responsibility for it, even laughed when Ella told him? Brooke was horrified that her brother could be that cruel to Ella, and he didn't even care about his own unborn child! Brooke cried when she realized she'd lost a niece or nephew when Ella died. Yet, Dominic didn't just blame Robert for seducing his sister, he blamed him for her death. Did Dominic think she took her own life—because of Robert? Was it in those missing pages? Just those two last lines might have made Dominic think that. If that was so, he didn't just hate Brooke because her brother caused the death of his sister, but also the death of his niece or nephew.

Why couldn't someone here at Rothdale have just told her that? Or did everyone else think Ella's death was a tragic accident? But Brooke was no closer to feeling comfortable about asking Dominic about it.

She'd lied the other night when they'd had their second dinner together, telling him she had an earache so she couldn't hear well. That had helped to keep her from reacting to his barbs. For the next two days he stopped trying to get her angry enough to leave; he simply stopped talking at all, waiting for her "deafness" to go away. While the quiet had been nice for a couple days, it wasn't getting her anywhere. His fever and the inflammation were gone, and so was her excuse to enter his room.

Now that she'd finished reading the diary and had even more questions about what had happened to Ella, she decided her ears would make a full recovery by tomorrow morning.

✢ Chapter Twenty-One ✢

"This is why you sent me off on that errand!" Gabriel accused when he returned to Dominic's room and found him standing at one of the back windows. "So you could sneak out of your bed again?"

"I don't sneak." Dominic didn't glance back, though he lifted the cane in his hand to show how he'd gotten to the window. "I hobbled with this."

"Still—"

"There's nothing wrong with the rest of me, Gabe. The fever broke a few days ago, and I'm damned if I can see any redness around the wound."

"*That's* good news." Gabriel joined Dominic at the window. "I'll let Miss Wichway know her—"

"No, you won't."

"But it will give me an excuse to seek her out."

Dominic glanced to the side. "Why would you want . . . ?" He didn't finish. Gabriel's expression was quite explanatory. Dominic rolled his eyes. "You haven't noticed she's too old for you?"

"She's nothing of the sort."

Dominic snorted. Those two women were wrecking his household, charming his cook, charming his best friend. Even his reticent valet had smiled more in the last five days than Dominic had ever seen him smile before. And Wolf didn't even bark at either of the women when he should have. The dog didn't like strangers. If Dominic didn't know better, he'd think both women were witches.

But the younger of the two sat on a bench beneath a white willow reading, shielded from the sun that flooded the park, her long black hair no longer tied back but flowing loosely around her narrow shoulders. Like a young girl, she didn't appear to care about her appearance when she thought no one was around—or watching her.

Her lips were plump. He imagined she was biting the lower one as she read, as he'd seen her do three times since she'd arrived here, his eyes drawn to her mouth each time. Bloody hell, he was counting? Her eyes were fascinating, so pale a green, like dew-glistened grass. Lightly tanned skin, which indicated how much she enjoyed the outdoors. How unladylike was that?

She should be fashionably pale, but she wasn't. Other ladies rode and walked outdoors, but only with hats, veils, or parasols to shield their delicate skin from the sun. She should be demure but was bold instead. She should have been mortified to enter his bedroom the day she'd arrived, but he hadn't noticed pink cheeks. She had pretended to be cowed, but how quickly she'd dropped that pretense.

She was a wisp of a girl, only slightly taller than most, narrow of frame, and yet the plumpness of those breasts she'd flaunted at him in that yellow gown her first night here . . . Good God, how was he surviving this?

It had been a gut-wrenching blow that she looked as she did. Unexpected, unwanted. And why hadn't she run crying from the room when he'd kissed her . . . ?

He wasn't going to think about that backfiring failure again, but her reaction to it suggested she wasn't a virgin. Was she as immoral as her brother?

She'd been hiding in her room the last few days, according to the staff. He thought her ears might be paining her, yet she'd showed no evidence of discomfort when she'd rushed in and out of his room to apply the salve with barely a word the last couple of days. She seemed more distracted than anything else. He'd had to repeat himself too many times, loudly, to want to continue baiting her. Yesterday they'd barely said two words to each other. He didn't *like* the silence.

"Is she appealing to you yet?" Gabriel asked, following Dominic's gaze if not his thoughts.

Dominic looked toward the pastures before he said, "Like fungus."

Gabriel tsked but didn't comment.

Good. Dominic did *not* need to hear her praises sung again. "My guess is George didn't know what he was sending me or he would have added her to his own tally. Our prince has led a life of dissipation, wild extravagance, escapades, and has had too many mistresses to count, yet he can raise a brow over a few duels? Someone put this scheme in his ear. I would like to know who to thank for it."

"You mean who you can challenge to a duel next?"

Dominic didn't answer. He felt an urge to look down at the park again, so this time he focused his attention on the pasture. "Royal needs exercise."

"Don't look at me! You know my uncle is afraid of him, too."

"Do I need to hire a rider? Find someone willing."

"He gets exercise. Anytime anyone enters that pasture, he gallops around in a threatening manner."

Dominic chuckled. "Does he?"

"And he's been prancing a lot, showing off for the new mare."

"What new mare?"

"Lady Whitworth's."

She actually brought a horse with her? She *did*

159

plan to stay. She'd come here with no idea what she would find, yet she came prepared to stay and marry no matter what—or long enough to kill him.

He'd thought that, at least the first day when she'd offered to help him. It was illogical for her to do that when he'd tried to kill her brother. Illogical for her to accept marriage graciously to her brother's mortal enemy no matter that they had no choice. She should be as furious as he was at the Regent's interference, not offering smiles and ridiculous truces. Yet she'd been playing the angel of mercy when she didn't have to. For some other reason?

On the surface she didn't appear to be as vicious as her brother, but Dominic wouldn't put it past Robert to force his sister to play a more subtle game. The Whitworths' guilt would be too obvious if she killed him right away. Perhaps Robert had counseled his sister to cultivate the appearance of a caring fiancée so that no one would suspect her of poisoning him once they were married.

He didn't doubt that the only honest thing she'd told him so far was that she was more accustomed to hiding her feelings than revealing them. So she might well be a liar, too. In either case, he'd be a fool to trust a single thing she said or did until he could figure out what she was really up to on her brother's behalf.

Robert Whitworth was a decadent scoundrel without conscience or morals, and his sister had been raised with him. That ridiculous tale she'd spun about why she didn't like her own brother, they'd probably concocted it together *and* devised a lethal plan to get her out of this forced marriage and back to *their* plans for her. And those plans would have aspired high. She would have been introduced to society this year. Her family would have had much higher expectations for her than a viscount from Yorkshire.

His eyes drifted back to her in time to see her put the book down and enter the maze not far from the willow tree. He glanced back at the pendulum clock on the wall of his sitting room to time how long it would take her to give up going too far in, or to get hopelessly stuck as had happened to Ella the first time she tried to find her way through the maze. A wooden bench was at the center. Ella had later carved *I win!* on the seat and challenged him to a race to the center of the maze so she could show him.

He and his sister had spent a pleasant hour just talking that day and sharing a few secrets. He'd told her he was worried about his friend Benton, who had gotten too fond of gambling after they left school the year before. She'd confessed she'd decided several years prior that she would marry Benton one day, but now she wouldn't! They'd laughed.

He was surprised he could remember that without getting furious. Had enough time passed for fond memories of Ella not to end with thoughts of the man who'd ruined her life? Thoughts of the man's sister came instead this time, and he glanced back at the clock again. Fifteen minutes had passed. He was about to tell Gabe to go rescue the Whitworth chit when she walked out of the maze, returned to the bench, and began reading again.

He was annoyed and realized it was because she'd gotten in and out of the maze much faster than he had his first time in. He snorted at himself. As he gazed down at her, he doubted she was even reading, was more likely plotting. He couldn't deny he'd thought that potion she'd offered him her first night here had been poison.

Poison was a woman's weapon and so hard to detect if administered correctly, but he had to concede now that his suspicion had been wrong. Nonetheless, as he looked out on her reading in the park, appearing so beautiful and innocent, he would have to remind himself frequently that appearances could be deceiving. And he should have made her drink that potion just to see if she would.

Disgruntled by hindsight, Dominic forgot to favor his wound when he walked back toward his bed. When he realized it barely hurt, even that annoyed him, because she'd obviously succeeded in hurrying the healing along, and he'd be damned if he would thank her for it.

He yelled in the direction of the dressing room, "Are you not done yet, Andrew!"

The valet quickly appeared around the corner of the room with a shirt, a cravat, and stockings draped over his arm as he held up a pair of Dominic's butchered trousers for his inspection. "The hem still needs hemming, sir." Indeed, one leg of the trousers had been cut off.

"Never mind the hem. I'm not going to town in them, just get me dressed."

Gabriel raised a brow. "And why are you suddenly making yourself presentable . . . well, partially presentable? You aren't thinking of hobbling downstairs, are you? Opening your stitches again will only delay—"

"You're going to make a good mother one day, Gabe, but do stop practicing on me. I am expecting a visit from Priscilla Highley today. Show her to me when she gets here."

"What the deuce is *she* coming here for? And how do you know she's coming? I brought no missives up from—"

"I had Carl send for her."

"Why?!"

Dominic waved Andrew away with the rest of the clothes; a shirt and pants were enough. He got back in bed and only draped the sheet over his bandaged leg this time. Presentable and covered enough for Priscilla. He didn't want her thinking she'd been invited for prurient reasons.

But Gabriel was still waiting for an answer, so Dominic said, "Why not? Lady Whitworth needs to know what she can expect from a marriage to me."

"That you won't be faithful? Or that you'll flaunt your mistresses in front of her?"

"Ex-mistress, though Lady Whitworth doesn't need to know that."

Dominic and the widow Highley had ended their affair last year when she'd made it clear she wanted to marry again. He didn't, at least not to her. She'd merely been convenient, living in York, not so far away. However, she'd been unfaithful to him twice during their brief dalliance, not that he'd demanded faithfulness from her when she cost him nothing, being independently wealthy herself, but marriage wouldn't change her roving eye.

"You'll just be spiting yourself if you open this can of worms," Gabriel warned. "Jealous women are not pleasant to be around."

"A jealous woman might walk away from a marriage, too—before it happens."

Gabriel sighed. "Why don't you just admit it's not going to be all that onerous having this lady as your wife?"

"Because I will never be able to trust her," Dominic said simply.

"Because of her brother?"

"Exactly because of him."

The widow had arrived after all and didn't bother to knock as she was quite familiar with Dominic's room. "What am I doing here, Dominic? You and I parted amicably, but you were clear you were done with me."

He ignored the pouting tone. Lady Priscilla looked exceptionally pretty today in a dark violet pelisse and gown, amethysts glittering at her neck and ears. The colors went so well with her blond hair and violet eyes, but then she knew that. Her beauty had never been in question, and she'd been widowed young. She was a few years younger than he was. And rich. It's too bad he'd only been attracted and not quite smitten by her.

He offered Priscilla a smile and patted the side of his bed to beckon her forward. "You're looking splendid as usual, Cilla."

She grinned slightly. "Yes, and just for you, though I don't know why I would bother."

"I could use your company for a week or two, if you have no pressing plans."

"Well, that's a shame. I do have plans, the first grand ball of the Season, which is next week, and I'm not about to miss it. I intended to leave for London tomorrow. But I suppose I could stay one night if you've missed me. And you're already in bed." She grinned. "I can take a hint."

She came over to the bed, sat on the edge of it,

165

and leaned forward to kiss him. He put an arm around her waist to keep her there, but ended the kiss before it encouraged her even more.

"You didn't hear of my last duel with Robert Whitworth?"

"London gossip takes a while to reach York." Priscilla leaned back. "You refer to the second duel?"

"There was a third."

"Goodness, what did he do to warrant so many? He thinks you're unhinged, you know, at least that's what he's telling anyone who asks. He says that you imagine he committed some slight. No one really believes that."

"What do they believe?"

"That it's some woman, of course, that you two are fighting over. Who is she?"

"Let's not discuss that, but rather the results of the duel."

"Fine," she pouted. "That's such a bad habit you have of never giving me anything juicy to pass along. What results?"

"I was wounded. It was serious, but I am already on the mend. However, because of it I've been ordered to marry into that despicable family by the Crown Prince, to end the animosity, as it were. And the only way to make it not happen is if Whitworth's sister refuses me and leaves."

"Leaves? She's *here?*"

"Right here," Brooke said from the open doorway.

❧ Chapter Twenty-Two ❧

Brooke should have had lunch first. She should have refrained from finding out why Dominic's door had been left open. That reason was eyeing her curiously. The young woman sitting on the edge of Dominic's bed with his arm around her was beautiful, elegant, and had a worldly air. Brooke felt as if she were fresh out of the school-room, and in fact she was. And out of her depth.

"You must be Brooke Whitworth?" the young woman said. "I'd heard Robert had a sister who would be enjoying her first Season in London this year, but this is a far cry from London, isn't it?"

"You know my brother?"

"Who doesn't know your brother? Such a handsome young man, quite dashing, though he's considered a bit of a rakehell."

Brooke was surprised to hear that, but not by Dominic's scowl when he corrected the lady, "A blackguard is all he is."

"Yes, yes, your sentiments are well-known"—the woman patted his cheek—"but the mystery is why? Why do you harbor such virulent antipathy toward Robert Whitworth?" She glanced at Brooke again. "Do you know why?"

Brooke didn't know the full story, but even if she did, she wouldn't reveal it to this young woman, and Brooke's expression must have confirmed that because the lady sighed before offering Brooke a bright smile. "But how forgetful of me! I'm Lady Priscilla Highley of York. We would have met in London if you had gotten that far, but you've come here instead. What a marvelous tidbit to share when I reach—"

"Must you, Cilla?" Dominic cut in.

"Oh, indeed, I must, darling."

"I would as soon not be gossiped about," Brooke said coldly as she crossed the room to grab the herb pouch. "And unless you would like to tend to his wound instead . . . ?" She gestured toward the door, not caring how rude she was being. Dominic could wait until *after* he was healed before he romped with his mistress. She almost said so. Almost.

"Goodness, no!" Priscilla laughed, then whispered to Dominic as Brooke marched to the bathing room, "She already treats you like a wife? Lucky you."

Bristling over that whispered remark that she couldn't help hearing, Brooke put a little more of the herbal dust in the bowl this time than she ought to. It was going to sting him. She knew it would, but she didn't start a new batch. It only occurred to her belatedly that she had no right to evict anyone from his room.

Returning to the bedroom, she gazed around the entire area to make sure the woman had left.

Everyone had left, even Carl. Only the dog remained, curled before the fireplace.

She wasn't going to apologize for her rudeness. Dominic shouldn't have received that woman in his bedroom no matter what she was to him, not when his soon-to-be-bride was in the house. If he thought she would tolerate . . . Her emotions spiraled down until only despondency remained. What choice did she have in the matter? None.

"Jealous?"

Her eyes snapped to his, and she couldn't stop the words that came out of her mouth. "Of a gossiping harlot? Hardly."

She lifted the sheet off his leg, relieved to see that his wound was still easy to get at and not covered by the pants he'd donned. If she'd had to stand there and wait for him to remove his trousers . . .

Some pink rose up her cheeks. She might have seen a lot of his skin since she'd arrived at Rothdale, but watching him undress would be her undoing. He was watching her, though, too closely as usual. It was unnerving how his eyes rarely left her when she was in his room. Was he gauging reactions? Searching for something to use against her?

"I notice I didn't have to yell today," he pointed out.

"What?"

"You can hear again?"

"My hearing was only mildly impaired, but, yes, I have recovered," she replied without blushing.

"Priscilla is quite sympathetic to my plight," he remarked casually.

Did he really think she wanted to hear about his mistress? "So am I, though I do pity myself more'n you. You'll just go on as you did before, doing whatever it is you do. What is that, actually?"

He began unwrapping his bandage for her. "Aside from meeting with my managers who handle the many enterprises my ancestors dabbled in, I breed horses for the continental army, for officers to be precise."

"So no thoroughbreds for the common solders?"

"Your tone implies you don't like discrimination?"

"I don't."

"And I don't stipulate who can ride the animals I send to the army. I'm even tasked occasionally with purchasing larger herds for special units. But the common soldiers aren't given mounts of any sort. They walk. That's one of the reasons why it's taking us so bloody long to wrap up the war."

Brooke was pleased to see that a scab had formed over his wound and there were no signs of inflammation. Alfreda's treatment had worked. He had to be feeling much better now. So why hadn't he said so? Because he didn't want her to stop visiting him? More likely he didn't want to have to thank her and Alfreda for helping him.

She probably wouldn't have used this herbal salve today if his damn mistress hadn't shown up. She heard the hiss of his breath as she applied the extra-strong mixture, but he said nothing and she refused to glance up at his face as she gently rubbed the salve over and around his wound. She wished she hadn't been so thin-skinned and pretended to have an earache the last two days, because although she was spending so much time in proximity to him, they were no closer to getting along than they had been the day she'd arrived. Now, more than ever, after reading those few lines in Ella's diary, she wanted to talk to him about Robert and Ella, and the baby, and find out how Ella had died. But knowing how the subject of his sister enraged him, she decided to start out with a less offensive line of conversation.

Before she could do so and not realizing she'd absentmindedly applied more salve than was necessary, he asked, "Will you miss rubbing my thigh once I've healed? You seem to be enjoying it today."

Brooke snatched her hand away. "My mind was wandering for a moment."

"Thinking of other parts of my body you'd like to soothe?"

Brooke gritted her teeth, forcing herself not to take the bait and get angry. "I was wondering about what sorts of family enterprises you were referring to earlier."

"Of course you were," he scoffed, but he deigned to answer her. "Coal mines, but after my grandfather expanded those, competition got rather fierce, so he built a fleet of ships, which enabled him to sell the coal abroad. The shipping business turned out to be quite profitable and now transports other commodities besides coal. And then there are tenant issues that I usually handle personally."

"No sheep farms?" she asked, curious. "I saw so many sheep as we traveled through Yorkshire. I bet sheep love the heather, which grows here so abundantly. And wool is probably just as profitable as coal."

"How would you know about sheep?"

"I don't know much about them. My father owns sheep farms, but he certainly doesn't run them."

"I don't want to hear about your family."

She sighed to herself before she handed him the new bandage and went to wash the salve off her fingers. She had intended to offer to read to him today after discovering a wonderful collection of books in the library. But he would probably rather spend time with his harlot while she was here. Then Brooke blanched when it occurred to her that the woman might have been his fiancée instead of his mistress, in which case Brooke's behavior went beyond the pale.

"Were you otherwise engaged?" she blurted out as she came back to his bedside.

"Engaged in what?"

"To marry someone else? Is that why you're so dead set against us?"

"There is no 'us.' "

If he prevaricated once more, she might growl in frustration. Being absolutely direct this time, she said, "*Were* you engaged to marry Lady Highley?"

"No, Priscilla likes London society too much to be a good wife for me. She's just one of my many mistresses."

"Many? How many do you keep at one time?"

He shrugged offhandedly. "However many it takes to satisfy me—usually two or three."

Her mouth dropped open, but only for a moment. This was obviously just another of his attempts to scare her off—it *better* just be that. She decided to play along instead, pretending to be curious. "One at a time or all at once?"

He looked surprised, and also as if he might laugh, but didn't. "That's an interesting notion. But as to your original question, I wasn't committed, but once I put your brother in the ground, I intended to begin courting my neighbor Elspeth Shaw."

The sound of truth in that statement made Brooke feel horrible. She remembered that it had occurred to her in Leicestershire that he might be in love with someone else. Yet she remembered Gabriel's telling her, too, that Dominic was the last Wolfe to carry the name and wanted to keep it that way. Which didn't mean he wouldn't marry, only that he didn't want to sire children. But if that was so, she had a right to know, didn't she? Especially since she *did* want children eventually.

"So you intended to marry, but never to touch your wife?"

His brows snapped together. "Where the devil do you get such ideas?"

Her cheeks went a little pink. Had Gabriel lied to her? But she shouldn't have asked! It implied that the thought of their never sharing a bed might worry her for reasons other than children.

She quickly explained, "It was a logical question. Gabriel told me that you wanted to be the last of your line."

Dominic snorted. "That was a notion I shared with him one night long ago when I was deep in my cups. I wasn't aware he thought I was serious."

"Then you weren't?"

"I was, but for barely a week. It was a silly notion, wrought from—"

She wondered why he didn't finish, but guessed, "Because of the curse?"

He gave her a calculating look for a moment. "No, because of the ridicule those rumors generated after they reached London. The young bucks in that town found it amusing to howl like wolves whenever they passed me on the street. Didn't know what you were actually marrying into, did you?"

He seemed pleased to be able to add that. She felt like snorting. One day she would laugh at the way he was drawing every card from the deck to push her away. She didn't doubt he'd just told her an absurd whopper and decided to call him on it.

"No one would dare do that to you, as feral as you look when you're angry. They'd be terrified you'd kill them on the spot. So what really made you want to end your line, even if you only felt that way for a mere week?"

He stared at her for a long moment. She *did* just call him a liar, she realized belatedly. Maybe she should be running from the room . . .

But then he admitted, "Because my sister had just died and I was full of despair, with no hope for the future. But now revenge against your brother brightens my future."

Now that she could believe. She waited for him to ask her to leave again, because that would complete his revenge, stripping her family of everything. Or would only Robert's death satisfy him?

But he didn't say that, instead he fessed up. "The howling incidents did happen, but only twice and over the course of a few years, and it was just college pranks. Not that I wasn't angry the first time it happened. But I caught one of the lads that day, and he was so terrified he blurted out that it was a dare that would have gotten him into a brotherhood at school—if I had just ignored them. The second and last time there was a larger group of young bucks, courage in numbers, I suppose, but I had two school friends with me that day, Benton Seamons and Archer Hamilton. Benton chased four of them down the street. The two remaining just stood there laughing at how quickly their friends were trying to get away—until Archer punched one and slapped his glove across the face of the other, getting the response 'Don't be a bloody ass,' before that chap ran away, too. Archer wouldn't really challenge the young buck to a duel over such nonsense, but it did give me a good laugh at the time."

She was incredulous that he'd just shared that with her. There was a different man inside the wolf, one that she hadn't met yet, one that she might be able to laugh with someday—one that she might be able to love. But then it occurred to her again that he'd had plans for his life, specific plans that were now ruined because of her—no, because of her *brother.* She could still only guess at what Robert had done to set these events in motion.

She was about to ask again, but bit the words back. That subject provoked nothing but rage in him. She'd pressed him enough for now. And he had a guest he'd probably rather spend time with.

"Don't let your lady friend tire you today. Rest is your friend just now. I will return in the morning to check your wound."

"You will return for dinner tonight as is your habit."

She wasn't going to argue *or* join him for dinner tonight if Priscilla Highley was still in the house. As if she didn't know what he was up to, rubbing it in her face that he had and would continue to have mistresses, marriage or no.

"Unless you've finally decided to leave? In which case, you can give the salve to Cilla. She will take care of me tonight."

Brooke didn't answer, but she did slam the door shut on the way out.

❧ Chapter Twenty-Three ❧

Lady Highley was spending the afternoon in Dominic's room. Brooke was spending the afternoon in hers, pacing close to the wall that separated her room from his, trying to hear what they were saying. After taking care of Dominic all week, it annoyed her that he could so quickly turn his attentions to another woman. Now she understood why her brother had told her parents in that conversation she'd eavesdropped on that "the wolf won't accept her." It was because Dominic was used to being with beautiful, sophisticated women.

She was neither beautiful nor sophisticated, just a constant, blatant reminder of his sister's death and always would be. It was still possible that he would fail to comply with the Regent's demand and simply tell her to get out. He could probably do so and manage to hold on to a least one of those family enterprises he'd mentioned. The coal mines or the shipping business alone would still make him a rich man. Maybe he'd already sent off a missive to the Prince to suggest it? Or that harlot might put the idea in his head today . . .

Brooke glanced down at her fingernails and pictured what she'd like to do with them right now. Then she pressed her ear to the wall again. Still no sounds in his room. They might as well be whispering—or doing something that didn't require words. That thought sent her out for a good gallop before the dinner hour.

When she got to the stable, she found that Wolf had finally got around to searching for the cat he'd smelled on her. He was standing in front of the door barking, his hair bristled straight up, while Raston sat just inside calmly grooming a paw—or sharpening his nails.

Arnold's approach shooed the cat back up to the rafters. The dog charged in, trying to give chase, but that wasn't going to happen. Brooke said a few commiserating words as she stopped beside the dog and tried to rub him behind his ears, but he wasn't interested.

"He'll give up shortly, so don't be worrying about the cat," Arnold said.

Brooke grinned slightly. "I'm more worried about Wolf. Raston can be nasty in a fight."

"I'll send for Gabe to take the dog back to the house." Then Arnold surprised her with a request. "Royal fancies your Rebel, m'lady. But no one fancies giving that brute the exercise he needs while his lordship recovers. Royal barely tolerates me grooming and saddling him and lets no one on his back except Lord Dominic. Would you mind if Peter rides your mare along the fence between the pastures? We're hoping Royal will give chase or at least keep pace."

"I could try to ride him." The elderly groom looked so appalled, she quickly amended, "Never mind. Go ahead and give it a try when I get back from my ride today."

"Don't be gone too long, m'lady. My wife saw two rings around the moon last night, which foretells the coming of a wicked storm. It was just such a stormy day some hundred years ago that the eldest Wolfe daughter met her death. Whether it was the curse or just an accident that her carriage slid off an embankment in a rainstorm, no one knows."

She stared at Arnold. Was he that superstitious? Were all the villagers? That would explain why rumors of that silly curse had persisted for hundreds of years, and why the wolf-man rumor had started, too.

Brooke smiled politely, though she was skeptical

that it would rain today since the sun was shining and the clouds weren't at all dark. Alfreda also often predicted rain that never came.

But having just spoken of the two horses that obviously wanted to breed with each other, Brooke thought it was a good time to mention one of her goals. "I wouldn't mind if you pastured Rebel and Royal together for a spell."

Arnold's face reddened. "I would, but Royal is a champion racer. His get is worth thousands of pounds. He's actually not been bred since his lordship began breeding stock for the army. But you might discuss that with him after you marry."

Everyone else assumed there was going to be a marriage. Only the bride and groom were still holding out hope that there wouldn't be. Reminded that Dominic was at that moment working on his latest tactic to get her to leave, she didn't set off at a trot when Rebel was saddled for her, she raced away at a full gallop.

She rode northwest this time, away from the roads. She passed several plowed fields where crops were already growing. Farms dotted the area north and south of the village. There was even a cultivated orchard with fruit trees lined up in rows. She passed only one sheep farm, though. Dominic had said he had tenants, so he owned the land but let the people who lived on it do what they wanted with it? She thought about visiting the village, which was so picturesque from a distance, but she wasn't in a friendly mood today, so she rode on.

The Yorkshire countryside was so beautiful, and she enjoyed feeling the warm wind whip through her hair as she galloped across the land. She liked the landscape here better than in Leicestershire for some reason.

Maybe because it was wilder, the terrain alternating between farmland and barren moors. Or maybe she simply liked it because it was so far away from her family.

Even though she was dealing with a churlish, impossible viscount, she felt freer here. But what if Dominic had his way and she would have to leave soon? She decided to take this opportunity to ride farther than she'd intended, to see more of Yorkshire while she still could.

She was surprised to come upon a herd of cattle, one of the long-haired Scottish breeds mixed with some stout Angus stock. The people here were so self-sufficient, growing or breeding everything needed for the pantry.

She crossed a creek, but farther north it widened considerably, becoming a river. She paused to watch the rushing water and wondered if the fish she'd had for dinner the other night came from this river. She continued on, then veered toward a lone sheep she spotted in the distance. When she got closer, she realized it was a dog, a rather big dog. She reined in, but was curious enough to trot forward a little more. No dwelling was nearby from which the dog might have wandered away, nothing habitable this far north in any direction that she could see, just the ruins of another of those small castles to the north, this one with only a few walls left standing, so not worth investigating. She wondered if the dog was lost.

Rebel refused to get any closer to the animal, so Brooke dismounted and hobbled the mare's legs so she wouldn't run off. The dog didn't shy away as she approached; it just sat next to a large grassy mound watching her. It resembled Dominic's dog but was bigger and mostly white with a few streaks of gray on its back, which was why from a distance she'd thought it was a lost sheep. It was beautiful, actually, face all white except for a thick border of black around the eyes, which were so pale they looked white as well.

Four feet away from it, she held out a hand so the dog could sniff it, but it didn't approach her and she didn't go any closer to it either. Trying to make friends with a dog this big might not be her brightest idea. But someone owned this animal. It didn't seem feral. It was too calm, too curious. Then it raised its nose as if sniffing the air. Had it caught the scent of Dominic's dog on her hand?

The dog suddenly let loose a mournful howl. Brooke shivered and nervously stepped back, then stepped back again when the dog stood up. "Well, you probably know—"

She paused when it whined and flicked its ears. She had the incredible thought that it had never heard a human voice before. That was highly unlikely, so she started talking again. "You probably know how to find your way home better'n I do. Or you could follow me. As pretty as you are, someone at Rothdale likely knows who you belong to."

She turned about and rushed back to Rebel. Mounted again, she felt much safer and glanced back at the dog—*if* it was a dog. It was certainly big enough to be a wolf. But she quickly dismissed that notion, not only because wolves were extinct in England, but because this animal wasn't the least bit wild or threatening as a wolf would surely be.

The dog sat down again and was still watching her. She wished she had something on her to feed it, but all she had was the one carrot she'd brought for Royal, who hadn't come to the fence to get the treat. She dug it out of her pocket and tossed it halfway to the dog. She had no idea if it would eat a carrot. Maybe she should try giving one to Dominic's dog later to find out.

Riding away, she glanced back over her shoulder one last time. The animal still hadn't moved, but it did howl again. She shook off a shiver and urged Rebel to a fast gallop.

❧ Chapter Twenty-Four ❧

"Is everyone on your household staff going to come in here today?" Priscilla complained when another maid she'd never before seen came into Dominic's suite with fresh water. "Even your cook delivered our dinner. When has she ever done that?"

They were sitting at the chess table Dominic had had brought up from the parlor. Not exactly what Priscilla had thought she would be doing here today, but she was a good sport and didn't want to tax his wound any more than he did. Priscilla and his mother were the only two people he'd played who had a chance of beating him. Gabriel knew how to play, but he didn't have the patience for the game and usually lost deliberately just to end it.

Dominic moved his queen. "They are probably just curious about what you're doing here when it's been nigh a year since your last visit."

Priscilla moved her knight into position to force his queen to retreat. "And let's not forget the more likely reason: that they already favor your bride-to-be and think I'm stirring the pot against her."

"This is only her fifth day here," Dominic scoffed, although he, too, had observed that Brooke had charmed his household. It seemed as if she'd been there for weeks, not days, probably because he'd seen so much of her in so short a time.

"Or perhaps your servants worry that the Prince will soon own your estate?"

He scowled. "I'll marry her if I have to, I just don't want to. It'll be a marriage made in hell, so why wouldn't I do everything in my power to prevent it?"

"But what if it's not? What if she's nothing like her brother? Whatever Robert has done to deserve your wrath, no one else perceives him as any more wicked than your typical egotistical rake-hell, you know. So why would you condemn your bride just because she's sister to a man you—"

"Matchmaker isn't a role that becomes you, Cilla."

She laughed. "You'll do as you will no matter what anyone says. I was merely distracting you. Checkmate."

He laughed and stood up. She was staying the night and had even offered to sleep in his bed, promising she would be careful of his leg. He had declined the offer, but asked her to keep him company until she was ready to retire. He had hoped Brooke would join them for the meal they'd had a few hours ago. Priscilla had been lying beside him in bed and he'd had his arm around her while they talked. He'd timed it just right, too. The food arrived. But Brooke didn't.

He went to the north window overlooking the

park to watch the sunset. The house was sufficiently angled for him to be able to see part of the sunrise and the winding south road from this window, but the sunset had to spread its light widely for him to see any of it. He saw none of it tonight due to a dark bank of clouds.

"It appears to be raining in the north. It's just as well you didn't try to get home before dark."

Priscilla joined him at the window. "That looks nasty."

"It will likely blow over before you depart in the morning."

"I don't mind traveling in the rain, only in the dark. And the wind appears to be blowing north. That might not even reach us." She glanced down. "Should you be putting pressure on that leg?"

"Only when Gabe isn't in the room. Damned mother hen, he is. It doesn't hurt, Cilla. And Dr. Bates doubled up on the stitches after the first set broke."

"It really doesn't hurt?" She smiled intimately, placing her hand suggestively on his upper thigh that wasn't wounded.

He chuckled, guessing the direction of her thoughts. "I only got rid of the fever two days ago. The wound is merely numb, probably from that witchy paste the girl puts on it."

"You should have married me when you had the chance, darling, then you wouldn't be in this pickle."

That wouldn't have prevented the duels. Whitworth still had to pay for what he'd done. Dominic couldn't share that with Priscilla. She loved gossip too much and couldn't be trusted not to spread the reason for Ella's death far and wide.

However, without that knowledge, she seemed to find his predicament funny. But then she'd also said that she liked the girl's spunk. Women. There was no accounting for taste or their vagaries.

The door suddenly burst open and Gabriel said, "Something has happened to Lady Whitworth. She hasn't returned from her ride."

Dominic started to smile. "Hasn't she?" But then he turned and saw Gabriel's worried expression. "How long has she been gone?"

"It's been at least three hours now. She didn't come back for her dinner."

Then she'd actually left of her own accord. Dominic was surprised. He didn't think his flaunting his mistress in front of Brooke would work, but maybe that, coupled with his anger, had finally chased her away. "That's good news."

"No, it's not. Her maid is frantic. She swears her lady wouldn't leave without her, and I agree. She wouldn't leave on horseback either. Something's happened to her. And it will soon be dark."

All relief fled. "Andrew!" Dominic bellowed. "Bring me trousers that haven't been butchered and my greatcoat for the rain."

"*You* can't go out," Gabriel protested.

"Of course I can. If she dies on the moors, the Prince will think I killed her. I assume someone has already checked the village?"

"That was the first place we looked."

"Go have Royal saddled."

"Dom, please, you can't ride again this soon. I just wanted permission to round up all the men to start searching for her."

"You can do that as well, but there's not many of them with mounts who can search far, and we don't have enough saddles to use my horses. And she's my responsibility. I could wish it was otherwise, but that fact stands. So don't argue with me."

As soon as Gabriel rushed out of the room, Priscilla said drily, "I suppose I'll find a bottle of brandy to take to bed with me."

"You aren't worried about her?"

"Why would I be? I'm sure you'll find her. She probably just rode into the rain and has found shelter from it."

"Possibly."

Wolf followed him out of the room. Dominic entered Brooke's room first to grab something of hers for the dog to smell. Her room was nearly Spartan though, as if she hadn't unpacked—or she'd taken what she wanted with her today. It was still possible that she wasn't lost but fleeing. It would be much more difficult to find someone who didn't want to be found.

Downstairs, his cook was waiting for him and thrust a sack of food at him. "She hasn't eaten" was all she said.

Marsha's worry was evident. So was Arnold's. At the stable, the elderly groom thrust another sack of supplies at him and attached two lanterns to Royal's saddle before he handed off the reins to Dominic.

He heard someone yelling and glanced toward the house. Brooke's maid was running toward him, and Gabriel was trying to stop her. But she shook her arm loose from Gabe and ran forward to demand of Dominic, "What did you do to upset her today? She never takes long rides unless she's upset!"

He didn't have time for this and didn't even address Alfreda. "Take her back to the house," he said to Gabriel before leaving them there.

Dominic rode around behind the pastures before he dismounted to let Wolf smell the ribbons he'd taken from Brooke's vanity. "Find her," he told the dog. He'd taken Wolf hunting enough times to know he could depend on him to catch Brook's scent.

Wolf sniffed around only briefly before taking off in the direction in which Arnold had said Brooke rode off.

Although it was still dusk, he lit one of the lanterns before the rain reached him. Not far to the north, he could see the heavy deluge, which looked like a solid gray curtain hiding the land in the distance from him. Wolf charged toward it without a care. Dominic pulled up. Was he really going to ride into that? For her?

He spurred his stallion forward, thinking now he had another reason to dislike Brooke Whitworth.

❧ Chapter Twenty-Five ❧

The wind was howling through the castle ruins, blowing so hard that moonlight appeared occasionally, but the rain was still so heavy Brooke could barely make out in the eerie light the lone tree, bent by the wind. Lightning was in the distance, but the thunder was loud enough to seem much closer.

Brooke might have considered this something of an adventure if she weren't so cold, hungry, and uncomfortable in her soaked clothes as she sat huddled in a closet with just three stone walls still standing around her. Did castles even have closets? she wondered.

Whatever the space had been used for centuries ago, it was about three feet wide and only about five feet long, but at least it had a stone ceiling that hadn't crumbled yet and a stone floor that was dry. There might once have been a door, but that had long since rotted away.

She'd been sitting there for what felt like hours,

and time was moving excruciatingly slowly. She'd never find her way back to Rothdale in the darkness and the heavy rain. She'd have to wait here until the morning unless someone rescued her, but how likely was that? Alfreda would be worried. Dominic probably wouldn't know or care that she'd been gone so long.

Earlier, as she'd watched a thick sheet of rain bearing down on her, she'd felt daunted yet excited. She'd never seen anything like it. She'd tried to outrun it, but nature was too quick.

She'd stopped as the rain poured down on her and Rebel, not knowing what to do when she couldn't see more than a few feet in front of her in any direction. She'd wondered if Rebel would be able to find her way back to Rothdale if she gave her free rein or just get them hopelessly lost. Then she'd heard the big dog's howling. At least, she'd hoped it was the dog and not something else.

It was those darned rumors about Dominic. And his pet that was big enough to be part wolf. The dog she'd run into today was even bigger, but it hadn't threatened her. Both dogs must simply be a breed peculiar to this area that she'd never seen in Leicestershire. But obviously someone *was* breeding them this big up here in the north, and Dominic could have mentioned that instead of letting her think that a few packs of wolves had survived the extinction.

She turned about and headed back to find the

dog. In a fanciful moment, she wondered if the animal was calling to her. It might be trying to lead her to its home, people, a warm fire. She'd settle for anything that got her out of the rain. But she certainly hadn't counted on an animal den. The big mound the dog had been sitting next to had a hole on the other side of it, and Brooke saw the animal disappear inside it when she got there.

She dismounted and tried to peer into the hole, but it was too dark inside for her to see anything. There was no way she was going into the den, even if it might be dry in there. She looked north instead, where she'd seen the castle ruins. She might find shelter there. With the rain so heavy and clouds so low, she couldn't see it now, but if she rode due north, she might find it. Or the dog might lead her there if she explained . . .

That was a silly notion, but she still spoke into the den. "No thank you, friend, I'd prefer to try the ruins. Would you like to come along?"

She remounted. The dog stuck its head out of the hole and watched her ride away. She glanced back to see if it would follow her, but already she couldn't clearly see much of anything behind her.

She was disappointed when she located the ruins. Little of the castle was still standing. The area was littered with broken stone blocks from walls that had fallen. A fairly large tree stood in what had once been the courtyard or perhaps the remains of a great hall. She hobbled Rebel under the tree where the mare would have a little cover from the rain and carefully started picking her way through the slippery moss-covered stones, looking for shelter.

A partial stone stairway must have led to a higher floor, but nothing was up there now except for wind and rain. She hoped to find stairs that led down to a cellar, but the rain was still coming down in torrents, which limited visibility. She saw a flash of white though when the dog suddenly ran past her. She hurried up and followed it a little way beyond the broken stairway, where it sat down and waited for her. That was when she found her cubbyhole at the side of the stairway.

She stepped inside the small enclosure and invited the dog to join her, but it had already run away. Had it intentionally led her to that room, or had it only sat down to see what she was going to do next? Either way, she called out, "Thank you!" Then she moved as far back in the narrow room as she could go. Leaning against the back wall even though it was covered with moss, she closed her eyes, feeling thankful to be off her horse and sitting someplace dry.

She heard the sound of a horse approaching before she saw the dim light. It was still teeming rain. She stood up quickly and moved to the doorway of her cubbyhole and saw the huge hooded figure holding a lantern and leading his horse to the tree where poor Rebel was hobbled.

Rescue! She was so relieved, even if it might only be someone out looking for his dog.

"Hello!" she yelled.

"I had a feeling . . ."

The wolf. She'd recognize his voice anywhere. The one person she did *not* want to be rescued by. And what the devil was he doing out of bed?

❧ Chapter Twenty-Six ❧

Brooke dreaded getting drenched again but imagined that Dominic wouldn't want to stay here any longer than he had to, so she offered, "If you tell me you can find your way back to Rothdale in the dark, I'll come out."

He didn't answer, which prompted her to change her mind about giving him conditions. She was reluctant to step back into that downpour until she had to. But when he came toward her and handed her his lantern before returning to the horses, she realized they might not be going back to the manor house right away. So she set the lantern in the far back corner of the cubbyhole, out of the way.

She returned to the doorway, but it was so dark she couldn't see him or the horses. Was he looking for a bigger room that was still intact? No, he'd need the lantern for that. She supposed he could just be unsaddling the horses, but he should have examined the room first. It simply wasn't big enough for the two of them.

When he loomed in the doorway again, she moved to the back wall to get out of his way. He had to duck down to enter the cubbyhole. Her head almost reached the ceiling, so he definitely couldn't stand straight in here. He tossed her two leather sacks before he set down a second unlit lantern by the entrance and shrugged out of his greatcoat, which he left outside the enclosure since it was dripping wet. She saw that it had kept his clothes and hair, which was pulled back in a queue, from getting soaked like hers.

"Aren't you going to lead us home tonight? You do know the way, don't you?"

"Yes, but it's not safe. The ground is muddy, the river has overflowed its banks, and there are deep pools of water out there. I'm not willing to take that risk."

Brooke recalled what Arnold Biscane had told her about one of Dominic's ancestors dying in a carriage accident during a rainstorm like this. It was sweet that Dominic cared so much for her safety to wait until morning to lead them home.

But then he added, "I'm not willing to risk Royal's safety when he could slip and break a leg. I'm lucky we got this far without that happening."

Of course, he wasn't thinking about her at all! She gritted her teeth, hoping he'd stay at the opposite end of the small space. The room was far too narrow for them to maneuver around in it.

"Spread out the blankets before you take out the food."

There was food! She quickly shook out two blankets, laid them on the stone floor, and sat down in the back quarter of the room before she reached for the other sack. She found a small meat pie and began eating. He could have sat in front of her, but instead he stretched out on the blankets and curled on his side next to her, resting on an elbow, his head nearly touching the back wall, his legs taking up far too much space now!

She quickly scooted around to face him before complaining, "There's not enough room in here for both of us if you're going to lie down."

"There's plenty. You can lie down, too, just curl up next to me. I've even brought you a pillow."

He meant his arm, she guessed, though he was still leaning on it just then. He didn't sound pleased to have made the offer, either. He was cramped, stuck in a small space with his enemy. Of course he wouldn't be pleased. And his leg . . .

She glanced at his left thigh, concerned. "Does your leg pain you? You haven't reopened the stitches, have you?"

"Would you like me to remove my trousers so you can take a look?" She must have looked so surprised by that suggestion, he amended, "The wound is securely bandaged and no longer pains me very much, due to your ministrations."

Was that a thank-you? She was incredulous until he added, "You can consider this rescue payment for healing me. Now that we're even, you can go home."

He meant *her* home, not his. But the food was taking the edge off her hunger, so she tried not to let that comment darken her mood. "How did you find me?"

"Wolf led me this way."

"Where is he?"

He snorted. "Probably still barking at the fox hole just south of here. I rode up here because I took shelter in these ruins myself one summer during a sudden storm. It's the only shelter in these parts, so I figured you might have found the castle's last intact room."

She wouldn't exactly call it intact, but realized Dominic's big body was blocking much of the wind gusts that blew in. Was that why he'd lain down? If so, that was quite—chivalrous of him.

A dog started barking.

"There he is now looking for me."

Was that Wolf suddenly barking out there? Or was the white dog still in the ruins, disturbed by the sound of Dominic's voice and sensing a threat? But Dominic obviously assumed it was Wolf and called to his pet. Repeatedly. If it was Wolf, he'd probably caught the scent of the other dog because he was now howling mournfully, as if calling to it.

Dominic finally shouted, "Get in here!"

Brooke shrieked when Wolf came into the cubbyhole and shook the rain off his coat before lying down at Dominic's feet with a whimper. Dominic grumbled. Brooke rolled her eyes as she wiped the spray off her face.

Watching her, he asked curiously, "How did you find these ruins in the rain?"

"With help."

"From whom?"

"Witch spirits." She grinned. He snorted, so she simply said, "I'd just passed by when the rain started, so it was easy to get back here."

She didn't think he'd believe that a dog had called her back this way.

"Your maid was frantic when you didn't return from your ride after a few hours. Most of the men on my estate are out looking for you. I thought you'd finally come to your senses and left Rothdale for good."

Then why had he bothered to look for her himself? she should ask, but guessed it would lead to an argument, and that's the last thing she wanted in their small space. She couldn't exactly leave or slam any doors here!

"At least you're not on Shaw land."

Thank goodness, a neutral subject! "Are we still on yours?"

"No. Whoever owns this stretch to the northwest of Rothdale has never occupied it or farmed on it as far as I know."

"Are you sure?" she asked, thinking of the dog's owner.

"Actually, no. I haven't been up this way for several years. Hell, Ian Shaw might have purchased it for all I know."

"You say that as if it's a bad thing. Or were you going to court your Shaw neighbor in order to join your land to hers?"

"She's a pretty girl."

Brooke waited, but apparently he wasn't going to say more, so she pointedly asked, "Do you love her?"

"I barely know her. It would merely have been a useful match to expand Rothdale and settle a couple of disputes."

"Over land?"

"Ten years ago Ian Shaw promised to shoot any Wolfe on his land. I promised to have him thrown in prison if he even tried. But the animosity between our families didn't start over land. Our ancestors five generations back dueled. They used swords back then. My ancestor lost a hand in that fight, which should have ended it, but didn't. Then our great-great-aunts had a notorious physical brawl, which caused a scandal that lasted decades. Those are the two main clashes that I know of. There could have been others since the animosity apparently started long before that, around the same time that the infamous Wolfe curse began. As the story goes, the Shaws reviled and then shunned my ancestor Cornelius Wolfe for flaunting his lowborn mistress in front of them. Cornelius was a hedonist who cared only for his own whims and pleasures, the proverbial black sheep of the Wolfe family."

She shook her head at him. "And you actually think Shaw would have let you court his daughter with all that bad history between your families?"

"Why not?" Dominic shrugged. "It's exactly that—ancient bad history. I'm confident Shaw would quit fretting over our border if his daughter were to become mistress of Rothdale. Besides, the man strikes me as simpleminded."

"Are you sure the daughter isn't simpleminded, too?"

"I doubt I would have cared."

What a sad thing for him to say. "Do you really aspire so low?"

"What else is there?"

"Happiness, love, children."

"That sounds like what you might aspire to."

"But not you?"

"Love is fleeting, as is happiness. I would have got around to having some children, though. I just wasn't in a hurry for them."

"Cynical—at the least, not very optimistic, are you? But happiness and love are possible. Whether they last is entirely up to you. Surely you could agree with that?"

He snorted. "That both require work?"

"Not so much work as a little effort. Or maybe nothing a'tall except acceptance. Sometimes you have to believe you can attain something to attain it."

He raised a single brow. "A philosopher, too? Aren't you full of surprises."

She wasn't put off by his derisive tone. "As for you not caring whether your wife is simpleminded or not, I highly doubt you'd want that trait passed down to your children, so that statement is false. You would care."

"I'm not getting a chance to find out, am I?"

She stiffened. The subject had just turned on them, and this was not the place to get into that argument again, when she couldn't move without touching him, when she felt him against her knees, his legs bent enough to touch her entire right flank and hip. She wouldn't even be able to get out of here without crawling over him.

Wisely, she didn't rise to the bait. She opened the sack of blankets, took out two more, and handed him one. He folded his to use as a pillow and put his head on it. He still had to keep his knees bent, or his feet would have been out in the rain.

"Get some sleep," he said. "It will be morning soon enough. And if the ghosts wake you, ignore them."

She stared. "*What* ghosts?"

"Some of these old castle and guard-tower ruins

are reputed to be haunted. I never believed it m'self, but you never know."

"Is this one reputed to be haunted?"

"I don't know. But in any case, ghosts are harmless, so no screaming. I don't wake well to screaming."

She rolled her eyes. If he hadn't added that, she might have thought he was serious. She couldn't guess what he was up to tonight, teasing, telling obvious whoppers, almost as if he'd grown comfortable with her—even as he still tried to push her away.

But she did *not* want to lie down next to him, even though he'd closed his eyes, letting her know he was done talking. And she didn't think she could sleep sitting up, much as she would like to. No longer the least bit cold, a little too warm in fact with the thought of sleeping beside him, she draped the other blanket over her anyway and lay down carefully on her side, facing away from him.

She had to bend her knees, too, because his legs were blocking her from doing anything else. But she didn't have enough room on her side to bend her legs without leaving her backside pressed against him. She was mortified. She hoped he was asleep and didn't notice that she was touching him again and wriggling around as she tried to get comfortable and couldn't!

"If you're not still in the next second, we're not going to be sleeping tonight."

She wasn't exactly sure what he meant by that, but she immediately stopped moving. Her last thought before she drifted off was that it was pleasant to feel his warmth all around her as the wind howled and the rain continued to pour down outside their ancient shelter.

❧ Chapter Twenty-Seven ❧

Brooke awoke to find herself twisted all around Dominic, but he was likewise twisted around her. How the deuce had they slept like this?

Brooke realized she must have turned toward him in her sleep because her head was tucked between his arm and his chest. One of his legs was stretched out with his foot outside their cubby-hole, but it had stopped raining. His other leg was bent between hers. She was sure that her leg on which his was resting was quite numb. But she was hesitant to move and find out because she was going to be utterly mortified if he woke and found her positioned this way—cuddled up to him as if she wanted to be sleeping this close to him.

"You slept through the noise."

She squeezed her eyes shut as if that might stop the color from shooting up her cheeks. "What noise?" she squeaked, thinking of the ghosts he'd mentioned.

"The horses bred during the night."

Her eyes flared. "They did?!"

He leaned up on his elbow, which made her head slide down to his forearm but allowed him to look down at her. "You're not displeased?"

"On the contrary. I intend to own my own horse farm someday. This will be a good start."

"Who says you get to keep the foal? I charge five hundred pounds to stud Royal."

"Since I didn't contract for that, and it's your fault for not hobbling your stud for the night, you can forgo that charge."

"Is that so?" He ran the back of a finger slowly along her cheek. "But husbands and wives find other ways to negotiate."

"We're not—" *Married yet* got lost under his mouth.

She didn't try to turn her face away, not with her future horse farm apparently at stake. Then she stopped thinking about that altogether.

The taste of him was intoxicating. She parted her lips, letting in his tongue. Her hand curled around his neck under his queue, gently caressing him. His moved down her neck to her chest and hovered over one of her breasts. He merely slid his palm over the tip, making her nipple peak and sending tingling sensations all the way down to her toes. Only then did his fingers close around her breast and squeeze gently.

She might have gasped, his hand felt so nice there. She might have asked him not to stop. But, in any case, his kisses deepened and turned more passionate. His knee rose up between her legs until it pressed against the apex of her thighs. She did gasp this time but it was lost under his mouth. The pleasurable sensation he'd just evoked stayed with her though, and she felt the strongest urge to rub her body against his. Thrilled and overwhelmed as his tongue thrust in and out of her mouth and his hand caressed her breasts, she felt urges that made no sense to her clambering through her body. Yet they were so confined in this narrow space with no room to maneuver, no room to get at what she wanted. She was trapped with him leaning over her, but he could actually . . .

Suddenly the kissing stopped.

"No, as much as you might want me to, I'm not going to make love to you. If I do, you'll never leave Rothdale."

It took her a moment to realize that he was boasting about his sexual prowess. He'd even smiled when he said it! She raised a brow. "You think you're that good in bed?"

"In bed, so I've been told. In this decidedly primitive place?" He shrugged, but still said, "Probably."

She felt like laughing or hitting him with something. Was he serious or just teasing her again? The smile suggested the latter, and she thought again that he must be feeling more comfortable with her, might even be starting to like her a little. But it was a brief thought. Considering everything said and done, she had to doubt it. Then she gasped. Had he just accused her of *lusting* after him?

"What makes you think I want—?"

He put his finger to her lips to silence her. "There's no point in protesting when it's in your eyes, in your soft touch. But if you think that will magically make me love you, you're wrong."

He sat up, apparently ready to leave.

Angry that such amazing kissing could end like this, she said, "You're *not* going to blame me for what just happened."

"I don't. I blame your horse. It's been a long time since I listened to horses breeding. It's quite primal."

He gazed into her eyes when he said that in such a way that she was a bit entranced by him. The feral gleam she sometimes saw in his eyes wasn't dangerous now, it was quite passionate. For a moment, she thought he desired her. But then she dismissed that thought, too.

He smiled again, though this time it seemed mocking when he added, "Obviously I'm not going to mind having you in my bed, but I give you fair warning, you'll never be trusted out of it. You're not going to find love or happiness here, Brooke Whitworth. Children, possibly more than you want, but nothing else. You still have time to flee."

Yes, of course she did. At least, he *thought* she did. Maybe she should tell him about her father's threat to consign her to a lunatic asylum. Or maybe she should poison Dominic as her brother wanted. She was definitely in a mood to poison him right now.

She stood up as he went out to saddle the horses. She stuffed the blankets back in the empty sack, then grabbed the other. She paused though and emptied the sack of food for the white dog in case it was still around or came back to the ruins after they left. She wasn't hungry. She hoped Dominic was.

She'd already seen that the sun was shining, but it felt wonderful to step out into it. What a difference the sun made. The landscape had looked so daunting last night. Now it looked fresh and beautiful, although a few big puddles were in the courtyard. She looked around, but she didn't see the white dog anywhere, though Wolf was running around sniffing everywhere.

"I'm glad I found you."

Did she really just hear that? With Dominic's back to her while he tightened cinches on the saddle, she couldn't be sure. It implied something quite different from what he'd said inside the cubbyhole.

"Why?" she said breathlessly.

"Because your demise on the moors would have gotten the Prince exactly what he wants—a

207

reason to strip me of all tangibles and toss me in prison or hang me."

What an unromantic subject to raise! She should have known better than to attribute meanings to his words that couldn't possibly be true.

But as to what he'd actually meant, she said, "I doubt that. The Prince currently stands on the moral high ground and is being supported for trying to save lives. He wouldn't accuse you and imprison you for something you didn't do."

Dominic laughed derisively. "Royals through the ages resort to any means—"

"And by the by, why didn't you give up looking for me last night? You must have ridden for hours in that rain."

"I did—and was tempted to."

That didn't exactly answer her question, but he was holding out his hand to help her up on her horse. She walked toward him but ignored his offer, able to get on Rebel herself. It just wouldn't be very ladylike, but nothing about this situation was!

Putting her foot in the stirrup, she persisted, "So why didn't—you?" She ended in a gasp when he put his hands on her buttocks and shoved her the rest of the way into the saddle.

"Self-preservation, as I've just explained." He walked back to tie the supplies to his saddle.

When they were both mounted and just beyond the ruins, she glanced back, wondering if the beautiful white dog would reveal itself now so it could watch them leave. Wondering again about where the dog lived, she asked Dominic, "Does Ian Shaw breed dogs?"

"No.

"You're sure?"

"I made sure when I found Wolf."

So the dog must indeed be lost. She supposed she could come this way again sometime when rain wasn't imminent, to try to help it find its way home. It was the least she could do after the dog had helped her find shelter from the storm.

❧ Chapter Twenty-Eight ❧

"Don't you *ever* scare me like that again," Alfreda cried as she ran toward Brooke, who was standing at the entrance to the stable.

"I'm fine. I had some unusual help. I'll tell you about it later."

"At least Lord Wolfe found you. I'm inclined to think more kindly of him now."

Brooke snorted. "Don't. The only reason he went to look for me was because he was afraid the Prince would hang him if I died on the moors."

Wolf had followed her out of the stable as if he were still tracking her. But this was the first time he'd gotten close to her since he and Dominic had found her, and she glanced down to see him

209

sniffing her shoes once again and whining. Really?

She tsked. "You need to make up your mind, Wolf, whether we're going to be friends or not. At least stop being so wishy-washy about it." Glancing at Alfreda again, Brooke sighed. "The other wolf is still determined to push me out the door."

"But are you still determined to change his mind about you?"

"I'm running out of ways to do that. Not one thank-you have we gotten for helping with his wound, though he did acknowledge that he's better because of it. Even so, he doesn't trust my motives. It's almost as if he overheard that last conversation I had with my brother."

"What conversation?"

Brooke looked over her shoulder and saw that Dominic had come up behind them. She felt like groaning but realized he probably hadn't heard that much of what she'd been saying. "It was nothing. My brother was being his usual nasty self—sort of like you," she added, and marched ahead, pulling Alfreda with her.

Thinking of a hot bath and carrots, Brooke passed through the kitchen to order hot water and grab a carrot to take upstairs for the next time she saw the household pet. She supposed she should check on Dominic's wound before she got too comfortable in her tub. If he was going to go to his room. He might be going to someone else's room. He seemed quite healthy—thanks to her. If he was favoring his wounded leg at all, she hadn't noticed.

She washed her face, hands, and arms and quickly changed clothes, but one question was on her mind that she needed to ask before she did anything else. "Did *she* leave?"

"The ex-mistress? At dawn," Alfreda replied.

"Ex?"

"According to the staff."

A bit too friendly for exes, Brooke huffed to herself, but when she put on a new pair of shoes, Alfreda protested that Brooke wasn't waiting for the bathwater.

"I'm just going to make sure the wolf didn't make his injury worse by rescuing me."

"Definitely more kindly—"

"Stop." Brooke rolled her eyes. "I could have survived the night and found my own way home this morning."

"Intentions speak for themselves. He made sure you got home safely."

And might have injured himself doing it, so Brooke wasn't going to argue about it. Alfreda didn't need to know what else had happened in that ruined-castle cubbyhole. If she were more optimistic, she might think Dominic's kisses were a promising sign, a step toward breaking down his defenses—and animosity. But not after the excuse he'd used! Yet one thing she'd been trying not to think about was seeing him unclothed in his bed again and touching him in an intimate way, even if only to treat his wound, after they'd practically slept in each other's arms last night and he'd given her those ardent kisses this morning. . . .

She flushed, thinking of it anyway, and turned away so Alfreda wouldn't notice. Seeing the carrot on the bed, she put it in her pocket.

Alfreda noticed that. "Your breakfast will arrive with the bathwater. Are you too hungry to wait?"

"This is for his dog."

The maid snorted. "That mutt will laugh at you. Dogs only like meat."

Brooke made a face as she left the room. Likely an accurate statement, but she hoped not. She'd feel bad if she'd left the white dog a carrot it didn't want. The sack she'd emptied for it hadn't held much meat. Maybe she could take some meat to the dog the next time she rode out. She owed it something for helping her last night.

A different footman opened Dominic's door when she knocked, but he was on his way out and closed it behind her. As usual, Dominic's eyes were on her before she glanced his way. He was sitting on the edge of his bed unbuttoning his shirt. He'd already put on those altered trousers again, though it didn't look as if he'd unwrapped the wound yet to check it.

"Don't worry"—she moved toward his bed—"I

know you've already seen quite enough of me for one day." And night. "I just want to check—"

"You prattle too much, *Doctor*," he said sarcastically. "Do what you will, then go."

She gritted her teeth until she realized he was probably in pain again. Pain and testiness seemed to go hand in hand for him.

"If you wouldn't mind?" she said neutrally, indicating his bandage.

"You may."

He'd always unwrapped the bandage himself—until now. Contrariness just got added to the mix. And he was pretty much sitting on the bandage. How was she supposed to unwrap it?

That question was answered when he stood up on his right foot, putting no weight on his injured leg. She quickly bent down and unwrapped the cloth before he changed his mind and made the task more difficult for her. The bandage only stuck a tiny bit to the wound before the last strip fell away.

After examining the wound and the stitches, she was pleased. "Good. There's no redness or swelling. It appears that last night's adventure didn't hurt you."

"That's debatable. My shoulder is extremely sore from sleeping on the stone floor."

Brooke ignored that. "Unless you're going to dress again, you can leave the bandage off. The air will allow the scab to harden."

She stood and picked up the red pouch of herbs she'd left on his night table and put it in her pocket. He no longer needed it. Then she picked up the blue pouch.

"I advise you to still rest your wounded leg a few hours each day." She handed him the blue pouch. "And you can sprinkle these ground herbs over the scab when you do. They will help you mend more quickly. If you're going to dress in your normal trousers, though, you should bandage the area first. And don't submerge your wound in bathwater just yet. Partial baths will do."

"You're implying I stink again?"

He didn't. She knew because she'd spent the night beside him. To avoid an argument she decided not to say another word. She turned, about to leave.

"You can do it."

She glanced back to see him sitting on the edge of the bed again and shrugging out of his shirt. "Do what?"

"Bathe me."

She turned around slowly. Color was already brightening her cheeks, but she managed to say, "No, I—I'm afraid my benevolence doesn't extend that far—unless, of course, you are prepared to marry me today?"

She thought that would settle the matter nicely until he replied, "You have wormed your way into my bedroom repeatedly with the excuse that it's already your duty to assist me. So you can't quibble over what sort of assistance your duty entails."

She could, but she had a feeling it wouldn't matter. He was making another of his points, showing her how much she would dislike living with him, reminding her that he'd always make some sort of unpleasant demand designed to embarrass her.

He took it for granted that she would comply, telling Carl, "Bring me a basin of water and a washing cloth."

Brooke's mind raced as she tried to think of a way to put off an uncomfortable situation. "You don't want the water heated?"

"Not necessary. Carl always keeps a small pail of water warming in the fireplace in the bathing room so I don't have to wait for hot water."

Well then. How difficult would it be to rub a wet cloth over him? *Very difficult.* She groaned inwardly. But she needed to show him that his tactics were not going to work. *So be pleasant, as a wife would be,* she told herself.

When Carl walked away after setting the bowl of water on the night table, she wrung out the cloth. At least Dominic was still sitting on the side of the bed so she had easy access to him. But when she stood in front of him, cloth in hand, she was arrested by his eyes. He had such a piercing gaze, as if he were trying to see into her mind, or trying to gauge her reaction to this forced intimacy. He'd tried so many different ways to make her go. Did he really think she would find this chore so odious if she were his wife? She had a feeling that she wouldn't mind it, and that made her blush. She wasn't his wife yet.

She ran the cloth over his face first, slowly, carefully. She tried to ignore how incredibly handsome he was, but couldn't. He had such strong features, chin, nose, the wide brow. Two locks of hair fell on either side of it, too short for his queue. It was like touching strands of silk when she lifted them out of the way.

When she felt the thick morning stubble on his cheeks, she realized the cloth might be too thin. Trying to clean his ears wasn't a good idea, though, because she saw the gooseflesh on his neck. She quickly switched to his shoulder.

"That's the one that aches from sleeping on that hard floor last night." He added softly, "Massage it for me."

She stopped moving her hand, she stopped breathing. Her heart was pounding. If she looked into his eyes, she was sure she would melt on the spot. Yet she had to massage him before he brought up her duty again. The only way she managed it was to imagine it wasn't his shoulder she was kneading with her fingers, so she looked over his shoulder at the bedroom wall. Then she heard his groan of pleasure.

Utterly undone, she quickly grabbed the cloth

again and moved it down his arm. If he asked her to massage him again, she'd throw the cloth at him. Holding his hand in hers, she wiped each finger. She was concentrating so hard on the task she didn't notice right away that his hands weren't dirty. He'd already washed them?

Her eyes went back to his. He could wash the rest of his body himself, too. He could do this so much more easily and quickly than she could.

As she started to say so, his hand twisted around hers and pulled her forward, nearly to his chest. "Remember your duty, soon-to-be-wife. This isn't a matter of necessity, it's a matter of choice. Mine. Continue."

He'd read her thoughts! Hot cheeked, she stepped back to wring out the cloth again, then applied it to his chest. Not softly, but angrily, and for longer than necessary, though that might have been because she got so distracted by how big and broad his chest was and how hard and well muscled his abdomen was. But when she saw how red she was leaving his skin, she stopped abruptly. He hadn't said a word of protest.

Contrite, she decided to finish as quickly as she could and get out of there. But when she leaned around him to reach his back, her breast brushed against his upper arm, and she felt the same wonderful sensations she'd experienced that morning when he'd brushed his palm against her nipple. *Oh, God.*

She quickly backed away to rinse the cloth out again, then climbed onto the bed and moved behind him to wash his back. More gooseflesh appeared on his skin as she washed the back of his neck. His neck and ears were sensitive. Something a wife might want to remember for future reference. Brooke tried to forget it. His dog helped her to do that by jumping up on the bed and watching her. Considering the animal's odd behavior recently, he made her a little nervous now.

Running the cloth over Dominic's back much more gently because his eyes weren't on her now, she decided to get into the spirit of being a dutiful fiancée and massaged his shoulder a little more. She might as well try anything and everything to get him to love her.

But Wolf had distracted him and he leaned over to pet the dog's flank, prompting her to remark casually, "You say he's not a wolf, but one of his ancestors might have been."

"Possibly. But it doesn't matter. He's quite tame."

Dominic wasn't, but she persisted, "I know wolves are supposed to be extinct on the isle, but how do we know they were all killed off?"

"Because it was inevitable once kings started placing bounties on them instead of just demanding their pelts as tribute. They've been gone for centuries, but the lands in the north are extensive and wide stretches are uninhabited. I suppose it's possible a few packs might have survived, but I'm doubtful."

She had expected him to scoff at her as he had done the last time this subject came up, not support her contention that his dog's wolf ancestors might have roamed the Yorkshire moors more recently than centuries ago.

But then he said, "If you'd stop looking at Wolf like he's more wolf than dog, you might not fear him or believe that rumor about a wolflike creature howling on the moors."

The color returned to her cheeks. "Nonsense," she insisted. "Wolf and I are great friends already, though he does get upset when he smells Raston on my hands."

"Raston?"

"Alfreda's cat that's been catching mice for your head groom in the stable."

"Cats have their uses. Did you think I would object to your bringing one with you?"

"You object to everything about my presence here, M'lord Wolfe."

If she thought that would be a good time for him to deny it, she was mistaken. As long as he couldn't see what she was doing behind him, she reached in her pocket for the carrot and handed it to the dog. He took it and jumped off the other side of the bed and immediately started making crunching noises.

She grinned and was still grinning when

Dominic said, "What's he chewing on? If he's got hold of another one of my boots—"

"It's just a carrot. You didn't know he likes them?"

"So that's how you made friends with him?"

"No, I only found that out just now."

"And why did you have a carrot to give him? For your horse? You are *not* riding off on your own again. You'll take a groom with you henceforth."

"Certainly. And I wasn't—"

She paused when she heard the door to his room open and two servants came in carrying buckets of water. She threw the cloth in her hand at Dominic's back before she shot off the bed and straight for the door.

"Do *not* get your wound wet when you take the bath you *ordered,*" she hissed on the way out the door.

She heard a laugh behind her. He actually laughed!

Beyond despicable. He was positively wicked.

❧ Chapter Twenty-Nine ❧

Brooke made sure not to run into Dominic for the rest of that day by simply staying in her room, even taking her meals there. From the sound of so much traffic coming and going from his room, she guessed he wasn't going to follow her advice to stay off his wounded leg for a few hours a day. She would have thought he'd at least pamper his leg today after so much activity last night and this morning, but obviously not. She even heard him in the corridor later telling Gabriel he was going out to the stable to check on some of his prized horses.

Her run of the house had been brief. And as much as she might be tempted to avoid Dominic and his nasty tactics, she knew she couldn't or they'd never resolve their issues. Well, she had no issues other than his campaign to drive her away. Would that end once they married? Or was his meanness ingrained? Still, she wasn't about to follow him around Rothdale like a lovesick puppy. She needed viable reasons to seek him out and spend time with him now that she no longer had an excuse to enter his room. Why the deuce did he have to heal so quickly?

Alfreda joined her in her room for an early lunch, bringing enough food for them both. "Does he love you yet after you spent the night with him?" the maid asked even before she set the tray down on the little table.

Brooke sat down on the love seat, admitting, "He did kiss me several times, but he had an incredible excuse for doing so."

"Oh?"

Brooke snorted. "He heard our horses breeding

during the night. It apparently stirred his own lust."

"And you didn't take advantage of that?"

"I tried to," Brooke mumbled, then growled, "He stopped, claiming I'd never leave Rothdale if he made love to me."

Alfreda laughed, earning a glare from Brooke across the table. Having coughed her humor away, the maid pointed out, "That was a whopper and you should have recognized it as one."

"Then what was his real reason? I was willing, he even guessed I was."

"Perhaps your wolf is more chivalrous than he lets on and simply didn't want your initiation into the delights of the marital bed to be lacking a bed. And since he's still hoping you'll go home, he wouldn't admit to that, now would he?"

"Maybe." Brooke remembered her own thought last night that it had been chivalrous of him to try to block the wind from her.

"So now that he's healed enough to ride through a storm and back for you, which was a magnificently heroic—"

"Do *not* ascribe to him motives he didn't have. It was self-interest and nothing else that impelled him to find me."

Alfreda tsked as if she didn't agree. "In either case, you need to figure out new ways to spend time with him. Your plan could be working and he just won't own up to it yet. I saw him go out to the stable. Perhaps join him there after you eat? Does he even know how much you love horses?"

"He knows I want to breed them. But that's a good idea and—" Brooke paused when she heard Dominic in the hall calling to Wolf, heralding his return to the house. "Just as well. I would probably have ended up scolding him today for not resting his leg. I'll join him at the stable tomorrow if he goes there again."

"Or ride with him if he starts to exercise that brute he rides. He might even suggest that, not trusting you not to get lost again."

Brooke snorted. "He already said I must take a footman with me from now on."

"So tell him it's more appropriate for him to escort you since he's your fiancé. Be assertive, him or no one."

Brooke chuckled. "Do you know what it's like to be insistent with him? It's like barking at the wind. Both are pointless."

"You're starting to make *me* lose hope, poppet. I know this mountain between the two of you seems insurmountable, especially now that we know he blames your brother not just for his sister's death, but also for the death of her child. I wish you didn't find that out when you read the girl's diary."

"Me, too," Brooke said a bit dismally.

When Alfreda had caught her reading the diary, Brooke had mentioned the part she'd seen at the end of it. Alfreda had offered again that day to make Brooke a love potion to at least get past the animosity and straight to the nicer parts of a marriage. Brooke had declined again. She wanted Dominic to really love her, not just to think he did.

"You should have listened to me the other day," Alfreda said, bringing that up. "This situation is more extreme than we first thought, and that calls for extreme measures. I'm making you that potion."

"But it's not his lust that I want."

"Love, lust, they go hand in hand." The maid stood up and headed for the door. "At least you'll have it on hand in case a situation arises when you think it will be useful."

Because of her harrowing ordeal the previous day, Brooke gave in to her tiredness and went to bed while it was still dusk outside. It was dark when the loud howl woke her. She lit her bedside lamp and looked at her pocket watch. It was half past ten. She grabbed her robe and went quickly to Dominic's room to make sure he was in it, but she was hesitant to knock on his door. What excuse would she have if he *was* in there? But if he wasn't and was out howling on the moors instead? Of course he wasn't. She shook off that ridiculous middle-of-the-night thought. It was just a silly rumor, but she wanted to disprove it once and for all, and not just for her own satisfaction, but so she could support him in debunking it.

She knocked softly and waited. The door opened only a crack. It was Andrew and he said immediately, "He's gone for a walk, m'lady."

Wonderful, just what she didn't want to hear, support for that silly rumor. "Did you hear that mournful howl?"

"Dogs from the village out wandering this way."

Was it? Or were the servants used to making excuses for their lord's eccentric habits? "Where does his lordship usually walk?"

"To the village. He frequents a pub when he can't sleep."

She thanked Andrew and went back to her room, but not right back to bed. A pub, eh? Maybe he had a favorite serving girl there? She was miffed that he was turning to other women instead of her, first his former mistress, now a tavern girl? Wide-awake now, she dressed and left the house, deciding to see for herself.

On this beautiful summer night the wide path to the village was bathed in moonlight. It didn't take her long to get there and spot the one building that was lit up and noisy. She headed straight for it, but stopped at one of the windows to peer inside. She spotted Dominic immediately, taller than anyone else in the room. Gabriel and a half dozen other men surrounded him.

He was dressed casually and didn't even look like a lord tonight. Nor was he acting like one. She was seeing a new side to the wolf and was fascinated, watching him laugh and drink with the commoners, and good grief, was he the one singing? She was impressed that the local men seemed to like him and feel comfortable with him. When Dominic suddenly let out a howl, the other men did as well, and soon they were all laughing about it.

Brooke grinned. No, indeed, that rumor about his being part wolf obviously didn't bother him at all anymore—if it ever did. That thought made her wonder how many of the other things he'd told her about himself were true and how many he'd made up to chase her away.

At least he wasn't there cavorting with women. She turned away from the window to walk back to Rothdale, but gasped when she bumped into someone.

"Steady, lass," the man said. "If you've got a chap in there who's stayed longer than he ought to, come tell him."

Before she could protest, she was pulled into the tavern. She would have bolted right back out if Dominic hadn't seen her immediately. Her eyes locked to his across the room, she didn't move. Then a perky red-cheeked serving girl thrust a drink in her hand and smiled. Brooke felt bad about having had such angry thoughts about the women who worked at the tavern.

"So who is he?" asked the man who had led her inside.

When she glanced at the grinning villager who looked as if he was hoping to see one of the men get yelled at, she probably disappointed him by saying, "I'm Dominic's fiancée."

The last thing she expected was for him to laugh and shout that information to the room. Hoots and hollers filled the room, and men started patting Dominic on the back.

"We heard that gossip," one of the men admitted. "Now we know it's true!"

Another man, who was having trouble taking his eyes off Brooke, told Dominic, "You're a lucky man, m'lord."

Dominic actually smiled, though he replied, "That remains to be seen."

That got quite a few laughs, probably because everyone in the tavern had guessed that she was checking up on him. And how was she going to explain this to him? She took a big sip of the local beer when he started toward her. Then the toasts started, and hearing so many people wishing her and Dominic health and happiness, she couldn't stop smiling.

That might have been why he didn't rush her out of the tavern. After a few more sips of beer, which she'd never tasted before, she stopped worrying that he might be annoyed that she'd come to the tavern.

But he did finally take the half-empty glass from her hand. "Time to go."

She nodded and preceded him out the door and stumbled on the step.

Suddenly, his arm was about her waist. "Do I need to carry you home?"

She looked up at him. "D'you want to? No, of course you don't. Which way is the path to Rothdale?"

He laughed. "Not accustomed to drink, are you?"

"No, well, wine, but rarely. But I'm fine. I just wasn't looking down and forgot there was a step."

"Sure."

His tone sounded teasing rather than skeptical. She should stop hearing what she wanted to hear and remember that he had no reason to be nice to her—yet.

When they reached the path, he let go of her waist. She was disappointed. She liked the way she felt when his arm was around her—so secure, as if she belonged to someone. She wondered if he'd made the protective gesture because his tenants might have been watching them leave the village. Glancing at him, she realized that the man she'd seen in the tavern wasn't the one she knew. No jacket, no cravat of any sort, dressed no differently from the other village men. And they didn't treat him like their landlord; they appeared to like him! She wanted to learn more about the real Dominic Wolfe.

"What was it like growing up at Rothdale?"

He glanced down at her, seeming surprised by

her question. "Wonderful, idyllic, peaceful—at least while my family was here with me."

She shouldn't say another word. Did *everything* have to lead back to his sister's death? But that little bit of beer she'd drunk had made her bold. "When did you know you wanted to breed horses?"

"The day I set loose my father's herd."

She grinned. "You didn't."

"Indeed I did. It was a dare, but I still wanted to see what would happen other than my getting punished for it. Gabe helped me pull down a long strip of fence at the back of the pasture, so there would be a mass exodus, and there was. We couldn't stop laughing as we watched Arnold's father, who'd been head groom at the time, trying to chase down the horses on foot. Well worth the week I had to spend confined to my room. I was only nine at the time."

"So your father raised horses, too?"

"And my grandfather before him. I wasn't sure I wanted to follow in their footsteps until I pulled that prank. It might have been funny when I did it, but I soon regretted it and worried they wouldn't all be caught, in particular my father's prize stallion, who I wanted a get from for my own mount."

"And did you get one?"

"Of course. Royal's sire."

"I'm glad." She smiled, enjoying the genial conversation with Dominic as they walked through the starry night. "Those people in the tavern weren't nervous around you. They remind me of the servants at our house in Leicestershire. They're the people I had the most fun with while I was growing up."

"Your parents allowed you to consort with them?"

"They didn't know." She giggled. "Those servants were my real family."

They'd reached the house. He opened the front door for her, but didn't follow her in. She turned. "You're not coming to bed?"

"You might want to rephrase that."

She didn't know what he meant. Then she did and started blushing. "I wasn't suggesting—"

"No, heaven forbid you do that. But I'm not nearly drunk enough yet to find my bed. D'you think it's easy, sleeping in the room next to yours?"

She drew in her breath sharply, but he didn't hear it; he'd already closed the door to head back to the tavern.

❧ Chapter Thirty ❧

Dominic might not be drunk enough to sleep yet, but neither was Brooke after his last remark. She would have loved to think that he wanted her so much that it bothered him that she slept so nearby, but she didn't believe that. He might have kissed her on two occasions, but neither time had been because he actually wanted to kiss her.

Maybe she should have told Dominic she had been referring to her bed, not his. She giggled, imagining his surprise. Would he have taken her up on the offer? Not before the wedding, he wouldn't.

She sighed and stood at the window overlooking the park, which was bathed in moonlight. She should go down to the kitchen for a glass of warm milk to help her get back to sleep—She saw a white animal loping toward the house. Good grief, the white dog had followed her home and had got inside the hedges?

She hurried downstairs and to the back of the house out through the music room, which had tall French doors that opened onto the wide terrace above the park. She stood at the top of the steps that led down to the gardens and waited to see if the dog would come to her. It did, slowly mounting the steps. Brooke was grinning by then.

"I've always wanted my own pet," she told the dog, feeling brave enough to rub it behind its ears as soon as it was within reach. "Well, one that I don't ride. Would you like to live here? Come along if you do. We'll figure out how to get you settled in, in the morning."

As if it understood her, the dog followed her into the house. She stopped by the kitchen first and grabbed a large bowl of the thick stew she'd had for dinner and took it with her to her room. At least no servants were about to notice her unusual friend.

After setting the bowl on the floor, she closed the door and watched how quickly the dog ate the food. She probably wouldn't be able to keep it here . . . well, not without permission. But after what Dominic had said about Raston, he might allow it. He liked dogs, so why wouldn't he? Of course she knew exactly why: to deny her simply because he could.

She would worry about that in the morning. And she'd have to find out from the kitchen staff what they fed Wolf. Her friend had devoured that large bowl of stew in mere seconds.

She filled the empty bowl with water before she sat next to the dog on the floor to get better acquainted. After it had let her rub it behind the ears, she didn't think it would object to a more thorough petting. It didn't, and when it lay on the floor next to her so she could rub its belly, she was able to see it was indeed a female. Brooke was completely won over. She *would* find a way to keep it.

In the morning when Alfreda woke her, bringing in a fresh pitcher of water, Brooke smiled at the dream she'd had about the white dog coming to Rothdale. It had been so vivid and yet so unlikely, which was why she gasped when she saw the dog sleeping at the foot of the bed.

Her first impulse was to cover it with the blanket until she could explain what it was doing there, but she said to Alfreda, "Don't be alarmed. I've found myself a new pet. It's friendly."

"And why would I worry—that's a big dog. I've already been to visit Raston this morn, so I think I'll keep my distance."

"It's just a dog, Freda."

"Is it? I'll just go assure the staff of that before you take it outside and half the household runs out screaming."

Brooke grinned. Alfreda was being quite pragmatic about it even if she was backing out of the room. "You'll grow to love her!"

"Why does everyone keep telling me who or what I'm going to love?" Alfreda mumbled on her way out the door.

Brooke dressed quickly, talking to the dog all the while. She hoped Alfreda had just been joking about the screaming, but maybe she should clear the way before she let the animal out of the room. But it jumped down from the bed to follow her when she started toward the door, so she stopped and bent down on one knee.

"I'll be back in a few minutes to take you out for a romp. Can you wait? Stay?"

It was obviously used to people. Never a growl, not once showing its teeth, but Brooke still didn't know for sure if it understood her, let alone any simple commands. But it sat on its haunches in the center of the room, let her pet it again, and stayed there while she hurried to the door. She nearly tripped over Wolf as she left the room. He'd been sniffing at the bottom of her door and tried to get past her into the room, but she quickly closed the door before he could. She would introduce the two animals—she hoped they would get along— but not before she had permission to keep her pet. At least Wolf wasn't barking and drawing attention to the secret visitor in her room.

But the worst kind of attention had already been drawn. "What the deuce?" Dominic had stepped out of his room and seen what his dog was doing. "You charmed my dog with that bloody carrot, didn't you?" With Wolf now scratching at her door to get in, Dominic approached. "Does he think you have more carrots in there?"

"Yes," she lied.

But she made the mistake of being too obvious in blocking her door by standing with her arms spread wide. Which is why he pushed her aside to open it. Wolf rushed in, but stopped abruptly when he saw the other dog. Dominic didn't move any farther into the room either.

"That's a wolf," he said incredulously.

Brooke snorted. "And how would you know when you've never seen one?"

"I have and I'll show you, but you're not getting anywhere near that animal again."

She tried to walk around him to put herself

between him and the white dog, but he thrust out an arm to block her. "Stop it," she protested, "it's a friendly dog."

"Do you even know what a friendly dog is like? It would be wagging its tail at you, not sitting there eyeing you like you're its next meal. We have to kill it."

She gasped. "Don't you *dare!*"

The whimpering drew her eyes to Wolf. He had dropped down to his belly and was inching his way toward the other dog, whimpering all the way. Eyes wide, she guessed in amazement, "That's his mother."

"Don't be absurd," Dominic scoffed.

"Use your eyes. That's a lost pup begging its mother to accept him back in the pack."

"You can't keep it."

"And why not? You kept Wolf. Your pet was just as wild when you found him. He tried to eat you."

"He didn't know any better, now he does. But that"—Dominic stabbed a finger toward her majestic friend—"is a wild thing full grown."

"How can you say that when she is calmly sitting there doing absolutely nothing threatening?"

"You can't keep a real wolf indoors."

"I disagree that it's a wolf."

He glanced at her sharply. "Oh, *now* you think they are extinct, when you have twice tried to convince me otherwise?"

She stuck her chin out. "She helped me. She

called me back to the ruins during the rainstorm when I couldn't see two feet in front of me. She knows people. She didn't growl at me when I first saw her. She didn't growl at Alfreda this morning. She's not growling at you when you are threatening her. I want to keep her. She's obviously not a wolf."

In answer he took her hand and pulled her out of there and straight downstairs to the parlor. "What are you—?"

The question was answered when he dug a key out of his pocket and moved to the southeast corner of the large room where the tower wall curved into the house. She'd tried to get into the tower room while exploring the house on her own, but she'd found it locked.

She tensed when Dominic unlocked the door, thinking he intended to lock her up in the tower while he killed her pet. She was ready to fight him tooth and nail, but she was arrested by what she saw inside that room.

❧ Chapter Thirty-One ❧

A chill ran down Brooke's back as she stepped into the gloomy room. Its curved walls were made of rough gray stone just like the floor. A few paintings covered with white cloths, probably to protect them from the dust, hung on the walls. An old chest rested on a low table in the middle of the room. Aside from that, Brooke couldn't see much because the room had no windows. The only light came through the open doorway. Dust motes danced in the light, but she didn't see any cobwebs like in the tower room upstairs.

That grim memory made her ask, "Do you know the condition of the upstairs tower room where you tried to put me when I arrived? It's filled with cobwebs."

"Is it? I haven't been up there since I was a child. But you could have cleaned it. D'you think you're going to just sit here and do nothing if you stay?"

He actually smiled when he said that! She clamped her mouth shut. Implying he would turn her into a servant when he had so many of them in the house was just another of his tactics to make her flee.

"One moment." He left the room. She squeezed her eyes shut, expecting to hear the sound of the door closing, but he came back with a lit candle. She wished he hadn't. His eyes glowed in the candlelight—like a wolf's. It was no wonder the rumors about him flourished.

"What's in the chest?" she asked when he set the candle down next to it.

"Trinkets, jewelry, favorite knickknacks, and journals that belonged to my ancestors."

Journals? She wondered if the missing pages

from Ella's diary were locked in that chest. Did she dare to ask to see them?

"Each one left behind at least one item that is worth keeping. Some are too big to fit in the chest, like this painting. It's two hundred years old."

He took the cover off one of the paintings. She drew in her breath sharply. Two wolves, one pure white, the other solid gray. The animals were lean and predatory-looking with a ferocious gleam in their eyes. Apart from that it was uncanny how closely the white one resembled the dog she'd snuck into the house. No wonder Dominic had brought her here to see it.

"And this one is even older."

He unveiled another painting, but she couldn't take her eyes off the first one. One of the wolves sat as if ready to pounce; the other lay in front of it looking satisfied, as if it had just devoured a large meal. "Who painted this?"

"Cornelius Wolfe's daughter, Cornelia."

"She was able to get this close to the wolves?" Brooke asked incredulously.

"No, she recorded in her journal that she used a spyglass to observe them. There are a dozen more of her paintings in the attic, all of wolves. They obviously fascinated her. And while they might have been considered extinct in other parts of the Isle, they still lingered in the north country in her day. Is there now going to be another Wolfe fascinated by real wolves?"

Brooke was taken aback. Had he just acknowledged they were getting married? She was sure he was just teasing her, so she asked, "Why do you keep this one down here locked away?"

"It's the only one that depicts the wolves close up. It's a beautiful painting. I used to keep it in my bedroom, but when I turned eighteen, I considered it a bit childish and took it down."

"And if the servants saw it in your room—no wonder that rumor about your being part wolf started."

He raised a brow at her guess. "It's a silly rumor that more likely started when I was a young boy and used to howl at school for fun, to frighten the younger boys. But Cornelius's daughter nearly died finishing this one. Her other paintings are more distant views. But for this one she was determined to paint them as if they were right in front of her. It took her months to finish it, to find them in the same pose even though this pair were mates and often side by side."

"How do you know all that?"

"She kept a journal. Many of my ancestors did. They wrote about the family curse and their opinions of it. Some were foolish enough to believe it. But they all blame these two for it."

She finally glanced at the other painting he'd unveiled. It depicted a nobleman of the Elizabethan era dressed in full regalia and standing with his hand on the shoulder of a seated woman who was dressed just as grandly. The pose was typical for a married couple.

"Who are they?"

"That's Cornelius Wolfe, the black sheep I told you about. He was newly titled when this was painted, master of Rothdale, and full of himself. She was his mistress. Some think she was the illegitimate daughter of a nobleman in York, but most think she was one of the Rothdale villagers. But Cornelius raised her status, dressed her like a grand lady, treated her like one, even introduced her to his friends as one because it amused him to do so."

"And gained your neighbors' ridicule and enmity because of it?" Brooke guessed, thinking of the Shaws.

"Yes, but Cornelius didn't care," Dominic said disapprovingly. "As I said, he was a hedonist, entirely devoted to his own amusements. That's all she was to him. When he had this portrait made of them, she was certain he would marry her, but when she suggested it, he laughed at her."

"Not very—"

"Black sheep to the core."

"Oh, I see, *she* cursed your family because he crushed her hopes?"

"Something like that. She left, damning him and his line to perdition. She actually died mysteriously that same day."

"He killed her?!"

"No. There are two different versions of what befell her. According to one, she went home and killed herself; according to the other, she was accused of witchcraft by the village priest, a relative of hers, and was burned at the stake. But no other information about her survived, not even her name. The belief in witches was widespread back then, from the lowest born to the highest noble. It didn't take much a'tall for someone to be accused of being one. People weren't inclined to change their opinion of the woman when Cornelius married ten years later and his first-born died at birth. That tragedy was attributed to that woman's curse."

"But death happens, whether by accident or illness."

Dominic gave her an odd look. "Of course. Our family certainly doesn't have a monopoly on death, and we've lost other members prematurely who weren't firstborns. If the Wolfes are cursed with anything, it's bad luck."

"If Cornelius's mistress's curse was as broad as you said it was, and Cornelius's firstborn died as a baby, how did the 'twenty-fifth year' get added to the rumor?"

"Another mystery, considering only three of my ancestors died at the age of twenty-five, my father being one of them. So it's more that we aren't expected to survive *beyond* that year and no first-born ever has."

"Not one?"

"Not one."

"How did your father die?"

"He and my mother were at the orchard. He climbed an apple tree to pick one for her and fell. It wasn't a tall tree, but the fall still broke his neck. She had the orchard burned after the funeral. It wasn't replanted until after her mourning period."

"I'm sorry."

"As you said, accidents happen."

"Have you read all the journals?"

"No. One is written in Latin, a few in French. I was too impatient to learn those languages."

"I know French. I could teach you—or read the French journals to you."

"You think you will be here to do that?"

She made a face. He didn't notice because he was putting the covers back over the paintings. She stepped out of the room ahead of him. She still had to convince him to let her new friend stay, but had to prepare herself for failure. He'd shown her that painting of the two wolves to convince her that keeping a pet like that was foolhardy, and maybe it was, despite how tame that beautiful animal seemed. She was surprised Dominic had even made the effort to convince her the animal was a wolf when he didn't have to.

So she was incredulous when he stepped out of the tower, locked the door, and said, "I will have an abode built for her behind the hedges on the east lawn, away from the horses. But if she spooks the herd, or if a single animal dies, she will have to go. I do this against my better judgment. It will not take much for me to change my mind."

She wanted to thank him effusively, but if he knew just how grateful she was, he might change his mind. So she just nodded and hurried back upstairs to make sure Wolf had survived the meeting with his mother, if indeed she'd guessed correctly about their relationship. It could merely be that Wolf recognized a more formidable opponent and had acted accordingly—which was sort of what she'd been doing with the wolf she was to marry.

❧ Chapter Thirty-Two ❧

Brooke got so involved with the two dogs, wolves, whatever they were, that she lost track of the time that day. She decided to call her friend Storm in honor of how they met. And she supervised the building of Storm's abode herself, insisting not only on a shed where she could get out of the rain, but also a hole dug in the ground, which might be the kind of shelter she was more used to. Dominic tried to enclose the small area with a six-foot-high fence, but he had it torn down before it was finished when Wolf almost hurt himself trying to jump over it.

From the moment the two animals met, they were nearly inseparable. They romped across the moors like puppies. They both accompanied her when she exercised Rebel, and the mare didn't seem to mind them. However, Royal did when Dominic tried to join them. Dominic wasn't all that pleased that his pet preferred to stay outdoors near Storm than in the house with him. But he didn't force the issue. He solved it instead by letting both animals in the house that night. The staff wasn't happy about that. Brooke was. But Storm behaved like a dog, not a wolf. So the staff would get used to her in time. If there was time . . .

The marriage banns were read again the next day, her second Sunday at Rothdale. Only one more week until she and Dominic would be out of time. She realized that if he did figure out a way for them to avoid getting married and she went home without bedlam hanging over her head, her parents would never let her keep Storm—she knew them too well—and she would be heart-broken. So there was one more reason why she wanted to marry Dominic—one more reason for her to make him love her. Eventually.

His tactics to get her to flee seemed to have been put on hold after their night in the ruins. It might have been because of the dogs. She'd spent most of her time with them yesterday and again today, but so did he, so she hadn't needed to find an excuse to seek him out. Yesterday he'd even said he expected her to join him for dinner. He might have thought that would annoy her so she didn't let him know that she looked forward to those meals with him.

And she kept it to herself that, in letting her keep an animal he thought was a wolf, he'd completely won her over. Of course, he might be hoping that the wolf would take care of his problem for him, but she honestly didn't think so. What happened that night, though, made her think that he might be getting desperate with only one week left before the nuptials. But it was only a small kernel of doubt. She didn't think he could really fake the panic, and it did seem to be panic, that came over him when a letter from London was delivered to him at dinner.

He stood up immediately. "My mother has taken ill. Pack a valise tonight and go to bed early. We will be on the road by dawn. The coach takes too long to reach the coast. We can get to Scarborough before noon tomorrow if we ride."

"I could follow you in the coach."

"No, you come with me."

"But—"

"You come with me. Rise before dawn so you have time to eat before we depart. I apologize for such haste, but she's the only family I have left."

He gave her further instructions before he left the dining room. She hurried upstairs to tell Alfreda. The maid wasn't happy with Dominic's plan for getting to London in the fastest way possible, especially since it didn't include her.

"It's not safe to ride that fast to the coast," Alfreda warned. "You'll be tired if you're getting up that early. You could bloody well fall asleep in the saddle."

Brooke grinned. "I don't think that's even possible. And he has a small sailboat that he keeps in Scarborough. It will get us to his mother's side much, much faster than a coach. Besides, I've never been on a boat before. This could be fun."

"Or you could get becalmed. Sailboats require one specific thing to move them, and it might not be blowing."

There was that, but Dominic obviously didn't think that would stop them or he would have said they would ride to London instead. "Considering how fast those boats can be, an hour or two becalmed won't make that much difference."

"Or you may never reach London. Have you even considered that? That the desperation you saw in him is about *you,* because he's running out of time to get out of the marriage?"

"Stop it." Brooke hurriedly changed out of her clothes into a nightgown. But she thought of the one thing that might ease Freda's mind. "Do you like it here?"

"Yes."

Did Freda just blush with that reply? Brooke rolled her eyes. Gabriel, of course. Maybe he'd been right in predicting Freda would love him.

"So do I, more than I thought I would. I want to stay. I want him to love me so I can. Going off with him alone could be a good thing."

"Then take this with you." Alfreda put a small vial in Brooke's hand. "The right moment might arise in your journey, and now that you are certain that you want Lord Wolfe, you should use it."

Brooke didn't give the love potion back to the maid, but pointed out, "We're going to be on a sailboat, but I'll keep it in mind after we get to London. You're to pack up the rest of my things and take them to London, since we won't return here before the wedding. Gabriel is to ride with you."

"Is he?"

"I hope you won't kill him before you get there," Brooke teased.

The maid huffed, "As worried as I'll be about you on a tiny sailboat, I make no promises."

⟨⟨⟨ Chapter Thirty-Three ⟩⟩⟩

The wind coming off the water threatened to blow Brooke's bonnet off her head. She was glad she'd tied the ribbons tightly beneath her chin. "You have no cabin?" she said to Dominic as he helped her onto his boat.

"It's a sailboat."

"But—"

"It's designed for short trips along the coast, though I've taken her to London more'n a few times, sailing by the stars."

She had hoped the boat would have a cabin where she could get out of the wind for a while or maybe take another nap, since she didn't get much sleep last night, as excited as she'd been. She'd dozed off on a sofa at Dominic's house in Scarborough for about an hour, just long enough for him to get the boat cleaned, arrange for the horses to be taken back to Rothdale, and have bedding and food prepared for their trip. She supposed she could sleep on a sailboat if she'd slept on the floor of a castle's ruins.

He had a full staff in the Scarborough house, which was lovely. The sitting room had large windows that overlooked the North Sea. It had been her first sight of a huge body of water. She'd be thrilled by this impromptu journey to London if she weren't so concerned about Dominic's pre-occupied mood. He was worried about his mother. But Brooke didn't know what exactly was wrong with his mother aside from her running a high fever, so she couldn't reassure him.

The sailboat was at least twenty feet long, so Alfreda had been wrong in assuming it would be tiny. It had only one mainsail and one smaller sail at the front, both attached to a tall single pole. The floor space was ample, and benches were built into the sides of the boat. She sat down as they left the harbor. It was quite windy. She marveled at the speed they got up to as the boat cut through the blue-green water that sparkled with sunlight. The coast was receding behind them and she began to feel uneasy. She'd never been in a boat before and had never been so far away from land. She wished she knew how to swim. But then she laughed when a gust caught her bonnet and tossed it into the sea behind the boat.

She didn't mention it to Dominic, who was adjusting the mainsail. She braided her hair instead, though it was quite a challenge in that strong wind. With the boat sailing south, she saw the thin green line of the coast to her right and the empty blue sea to her left, though she imagined ships were out there just beyond the horizon.

"D'you think we'll see the English armada?" she wondered aloud.

"It controls these waters. We've already passed several English patrol ships."

He tossed her his spyglass, but when she looked through it, she still saw nothing but sea and sky. "Are they fighting battles out there?"

"No, just guarding against blockade runners. They will fire on boats that try to break through the blockade. That strategy has worked. Since the war began, our fleet has doubled while the French fleet has shrunk in half. The blockade prevents Napoléon from getting the materials he needs to build more ships. He wouldn't dare risk the ships he has left by waging a battle in these waters. Besides, his strength is on land, not on the sea."

"Then who exactly is our armada firing on?"

He shrugged. "Ships trying to sneak in French spies, smugglers. The English are simply too fond of French brandy, even at exorbitant prices, for bold sailors, both French and English, not to be tempted to make a great deal of money by smuggling it in. But smugglers work at night, not in broad daylight. However, we're hugging the coast to steer clear of any altercations between our navy and any blockade runners."

A while later, she took a sandwich out of the picnic basket and devoured it. All this fresh air was making her hungry! Then she made her way unsteadily toward Dominic and put the basket by his feet so he could eat. He didn't even look down at it, which made her wonder if it wouldn't be safe for him to take his hands off the wheel.

She'd offer to help him, but she had a feeling he'd decline if not outright laugh at the suggestion. Yet she knew from Ella's diary that he'd taught his sister to sail. Maybe it wasn't that hard. Maybe he wouldn't laugh.

"I could relieve you for a bit. Would it take long to give me a few lessons?"

"Have you ever been in a boat this size before?"

"Well, no, no boat of any size actually."

"Sailing is rather complicated. You'd have to spend weeks out on the water to learn—"

"But you taught your sister—"

He glanced at her sharply. "How do you know that?"

She wasn't about to get Gabriel in trouble for letting her into Ella's locked room, so she said defensively, "You wouldn't tell me anything about her, not even how she died, so I asked the servants. They didn't want to talk about her either, but someone mentioned that she loved to sail by herself after you taught her how."

He was no longer looking at Brooke. His gaze was directed straight ahead. She didn't think he was going to reply, but then she heard, "She was only eighteen when she died nearly two years ago. She'd had a thrilling first Season in London but hadn't accepted a proposal. She had so many suitors my mother couldn't keep track of them all. I was with them in London for the first few weeks, enjoyed seeing my sister so exhilarated by the social whirl, but my work for the military intervened. The army sent me an urgent request for more horses than I could supply, and a long list of horse farms where I could obtain them, most of them in Ireland. The number they needed for a high-priority mission was staggering. I suspected it would take me months to round up the herd, and it did, so I missed the rest of Ella's Season. I even missed her funeral!"

251

Brooke drew in her breath. His anger was back. She heard it, saw it, and guessed he wouldn't say any more now. Yet he hadn't told her what she wanted to know.

She tried to encourage him to continue by asking, "Couldn't anyone else have bought those horses so you wouldn't have had to leave your sister at such an important time in her life?"

"I suppose so, but my contact in the army was used to working with me and trusted me to get them the fastest mounts available. I wasn't told why, but I guessed the animals were for an important new network of spies or scouts on the Continent. In any case, it was stressed that nothing else could take precedence over that mission."

Brooke cringed slightly as she summoned up her courage. "How did your sister die that year?"

"It was early fall. Two of Ella's suitors had followed her to Rothdale after the Season to continue courting her, but Ella didn't favor them and asked Mother to take her to Scarborough for a few weeks before the weather turned nippy, hoping the young lords would leave before she and my mother returned to Rothdale.

"But while they were in Scarborough, she recklessly went sailing by herself on a day that suddenly turned stormy. My mother was frantic with worry when she didn't return after a few hours, the whole town was, nearly every ship and boat in the harbor was sent out to look for her."

"Was she—ever found?"

"Yes. Two days later her body washed up on the shore, miles down the coast. It was so disfigured and battered by the surf by then that my mother couldn't bear to look at it. But there was a locket that was handed to her that confirmed it was Ella. I'd given it to her on her sixteenth birthday and had inscribed on the back, 'Wild one.' It made her laugh and she always wore it with her day dresses. As you can imagine, my mother was grief stricken, and not knowing how to contact me, she had no choice but to hold the funeral a week later.

"When I returned to Yorkshire and learned the devastating news that Ella had died, my mother and I lamented her reckless nature and her bad luck to have been caught in a sudden storm. I blamed myself for not curbing that recklessness. My mother blamed herself for taking Ella to Scarborough. She cried the entire time she told me about the funeral. Some of Ella's girlfriends were there and mentioned they were looking forward to seeing Ella before Christmas at a house party Ella said she planned to attend. A few of her suitors were there and appeared heart-broken. All of the servants from both households were present. Everyone loved Ella. The only odd occurrence on the day Ella died at sea was the hasty departure of her personal maid from the Scarborough house. Later my mother discovered that most of Ella's jewelry was missing. Mother believed the young maid had taken advantage of the worried, distracted atmosphere in the house when Ella didn't return after the storm started to steal a king's ransom of jewelry. The local authorities looked for the girl but she was never found."

Brooke didn't see how any of that series of heartbreaking events related to her brother. In addition to feeling sad, she felt more confused than ever. She didn't dare mention the diary she had secretly read or the damning words she'd found on the last page.

But she could say what she felt in her heart. "I'm sorry your sister didn't make it out of that storm."

"She could have," he said tonelessly. "She didn't want to. But I didn't know that right away. It wasn't until six months after the yearlong mourning period that I thought one night that I could enter her favorite place, her old playroom in the west tower, without dwelling on her death. I picked up her old diary. It was filled with her childhood experiences, some of which included me. But I was stunned to find more recent entries that dated from her Season in London and her return to Yorkshire afterward."

Brooke wondered if the missing pages had still been in the diary when he read it. Or just those last two lines? But those were damning enough. He probably wouldn't have needed any more than that to want to kill her brother. And no wonder he burned that tower. His rage must have started that very night.

Brooke had moved quietly to a bench in front of him. She didn't need to ask what he'd read that night. She didn't want to question him, but he might think it odd if she didn't.

"What was in those more recent entries?"

He didn't glance at her. "She wrote about the wonderful man she fell in love with during her Season. He promised they would marry after he convinced his parents he would have no one but her. She met him secretly so they could be alone together away from our mother's watchful eye. During one of their trysts he seduced her. Ella was stunned and horrified when he told her he wouldn't marry her, that he'd never intended to. It wasn't so much the shame of getting pregnant but the pain of her broken heart and the young man's betrayal that made her 'seek peace and solace in the sea.' She actually wrote that was her intention, that she had no other choice. She even kept his name secret until the final page, when she damned him for ruining her life. No, Ella didn't try to outrun that storm that day, she *let* it take her life."

"I'm so sorry."

He continued as if he hadn't heard Brooke. "I'd never felt rage like that before. I threw the lantern

I'd brought up to that room on the floor and ripped out those damning pages and tossed them into the flames. I almost left the diary there to burn, too, but there were good memories left in it that I thought I might want to read again some-day, or show to my mother eventually, so I put it away in Ella's room. But I didn't try to put out that fire. And I rode straight for London to find the man who seduced my innocent sister and left her with child and laughed at her when she told him—your lying *brother!*"

Brooke flinched. She wished now that she'd never learned the full truth that had been in those missing pages. She could say absolutely nothing in defense of her brother. His cruelty toward Ella was indefensible.

"The wound I gave him wasn't severe," Dominic continued. "I thought it would be enough, but it wasn't. It ate at me that justice hadn't been served. It didn't satisfy the debt he owed, not just for her life but also for the life of her child. Two months later I challenged him again and missed completely, as did he. My rage wouldn't go away. He refused to meet me for this last duel, so I waited a few more months then sent another challenge, which he simply ignored. So I dragged both our seconds with me and tracked him down in London. He couldn't refuse me in front of witnesses." Dominic finally glanced at her and added icily, "*Our* circumstances are an annoyance.

That your brother still lives is an abomination."

"I agree that he's mean, despicable, even vicious," she replied carefully. "No one knows that better'n me. And he doesn't care about anyone except himself, not family, not friends. Someone is going to end up killing him. It's inevitable. But it can't be you. Another attempt will land you in prison if not get you hung."

"Particularly if he becomes *family.*"

The conversation had just turned dangerous, although it had been emotionally charged from his first words about Ella's death. But seeing how furious he looked right now reminded her just how alone she was with him on the sailboat. She'd be panicking soon if she couldn't defuse his rage.

"You know, families don't always get along. Some fight amongst themselves, even brutally. I doubt anyone would raise a brow if you beat my brother senseless from time to time. I know I would if I had the strength for it. And there's not much the Regent could say about it, since it would be a 'family' matter."

Dominic gave her a skeptical look. "You're actually suggesting I beat your brother to a pulp?"

"If he's family, most definitely—as long as it doesn't kill him so you don't get punished for it."

Dominic looked away. At least the rage left his visage, so she began to breathe easier. Giving him an option to look forward to—

"Bloody hell."

She blinked and followed his gaze to the large ship heading their way at top speed. Alarmed, she asked, "Is it going to be able to slow down, or will it ram into us?"

"It doesn't need to get close to kill us."

She didn't know what he meant, but suddenly he was steering madly in the wrong direction, straight for shore. But no dock was there!

❧ Chapter Thirty-Four ❧

Brooke screamed as the shoreline raced toward them or, rather, they raced toward it. They were going to crash!

Dominic yelled, "Hold tight to the rail!"

If Brooke hadn't grabbed it right then and crouched down, she might have tumbled off the boat when it hit the beach. Shaking, she stood up carefully and looked over the side. The rocky shore was less than two feet from the rail. He'd deliberately beached his boat! Dominic's arm was suddenly around her waist as he swung her over the rail to the ground.

"My valise!" she yelled up at him.

A moment later he jumped off the boat with both their bags in one hand and grabbed her hand with the other. "Run!" he yelled without explaining. She was starting to get quite indignant over his bizarre, reckless behavior.

"Won't your boat be stuck now?" she gasped out as she tried to keep up with him.

"I'll worry about that if it survives."

"Survives what?"

He didn't answer, he just kept running inland, dragging her with him. He didn't stop until they reached a huge tree with a wide trunk. She was glaring at him when a thunderous explosion rent the air.

She saw Dominic cringe. That's when she realized what had happened. "Was your boat just blown up? By our own navy!?"

"They must have spotted a blockade runner and chased them, then thought *we* were them. I can't think of any other damned reason for what just happened."

"But you knew they were going to fire at us, didn't you?"

"This is wartime. If the navy had reason to suspect we were French, they wouldn't hesitate. But, no, I didn't think they would actually blow up my damned boat. I just wasn't going to risk it with you on board."

Her brow rose only slightly, but she couldn't resist smiling. He'd beached his boat for her? But he'd lost it, too, and that was a disastrous turn of events for both of them.

"You blowing up the countryside, mate?" a male voice called.

The man walking toward them was young,

short, and wearing a wide grin and a tattered jacket that had once been fine. Brooke wondered if it was a donation from some lord who lived nearby. Dominic appeared glad to see the man. She supposed he could at least tell them where they were if Dominic didn't know. But he probably did because he'd made this trip so many times.

"No, that was an overzealous warship of ours," Dominic was saying.

"Thought you were a Frenchy, did they?" The man chuckled.

"And you are?"

"Just investigating the noise. My village is nearby if you'd like to follow me to it."

"Certainly. I'm interested in acquiring two horses."

"We've got mounts, fast ones, too, but you'll be needing to discuss that with Rory. All decisions are 'is to make." But then four more men and a boy came running through the trees toward them, and the man complained, "I got this under control, Rory, all peaceable-like. I was bringing them to you."

That didn't get the newcomers to lower the weapons they were holding. Even the boy was holding a pistol. Dominic immediately shoved Brooke behind him. She still peeked around his upper arm.

The other villagers didn't look at all friendly.

Rory was the tallest among them, at least that was whom the first man was staring at. He was ferocious-looking, possibly because one of his thick black brows was split right in half by an ugly scar. Another long scar ran across one of his cheeks. He might have been handsome before someone took a blade to his face. Then she noticed another scar, a wide one that circled his neck. It looked like a rope scar from a noose. He must have been nearly hanged. That frightened Brooke the most. Only serious crimes warranted a noose . . .

"What was the noise?" he demanded.

" 'Is lordship's boat got blown out of the water."

Rory's brow rose, the good one, as he looked Dominic over with light gray eyes. They were nearly the same height. Dominic was more muscular, but the man who'd somehow escaped a death sentence was heavier and barrel-chested. But to be the head of the villagers—or whoever they were—he wasn't that old, maybe nearing thirty.

"Are you titled, or just a fancy dresser?" he asked Dominic.

"Titled, not that it's relevant to the situation."

"Oh, but it is."

Brooke felt the muscles in Dominic's arm flex against her cheek; in fact, his whole body tensed. She had a feeling his eyes had just gone feral, too. He was preparing for battle, and that terrified her, considering that five weapons were still pointed right at him.

But she was amazed by his temperate tone when he said, "I would suggest you lower your weapons. We mean you no harm."

Rory shrugged. "Can't say the same. It's too bad about the boat, though. It would've fetched a pretty price. But come along. You'll get to have your say before I decide whether you live or die."

Dominic didn't budge. "I'd like to hear more about your village before I decide whether to accept your invitation."

That caused a few snickers, but Rory had already walked off, assuming they would follow. Someone called after him, " 'E ain't moving, Rory."

Rory glanced back. "Shoot the female in the foot if they aren't walking in front of you in two seconds."

"Do you really want to die today?" Dominic said in a quiet, malevolent tone.

"Oh, ho!" Rory laughed. "And now I have my leverage—the woman. Good of you to volunteer that, mate. But do come along. We'll have a drink and talk before anyone gets hurt, and we'll see if you have something to bargain with."

Dominic put his arm around Brooke and held her tightly to his side before he started walking.

"They're some sort of criminals, aren't they?" she whispered. "This close to shore, maybe smugglers?"

"Without a ship? More likely highwaymen hiding in the woods if they have 'fast' horses— unless that was a lie."

"But it sounded like they'll dicker for our release."

"For promises? Not likely."

"Don't underestimate the power of a titled lord. That Rory fellow probably knows if you give your word, you'll honor it."

She was trying to be optimistic to tamp down her fear, but it didn't work. Dominic wasn't armed. If he tried to fight their way out of this, he was going to get shot, repeatedly, and he was a big target. It was all well and good that he'd threatened to kill their captors, but if *he* died . . .

❧ Chapter Thirty-Five ❧

Brooke looked around the clearing in the woods where the criminals apparently lived. With only four decent-size huts it certainly wasn't a village. A fifth appeared to be under construction; a wagon filled with lumber was parked next to it. She didn't see any gardens or shops, not even a road leading here. A large campfire burned in front of one of the huts. A big pot hung over the fire and benches surrounded it.

A dozen or so people were there, though half of them were women holding young children. Most of them eyed Brooke and Dominic warily, but one young woman smiled shyly at Brooke, as did a few of the children.

They were led to the campfire. Rory picked up a flask on the ground and took a swig from it, then offered it to Dominic, who shook his head. Dominic removed his arm from around Brooke's shoulders when Rory gave her a long look. She realized Dominic was preparing to fight.

Rory took a step back before asking, "D'you need some time to cool off, then? Before we talk? We usually do our robbing on the highways, but we don't turn away donations that come our way."

"You can take what little I have on me, or you can loan me two of your horses and I will return them with a purse containing a hundred pounds."

"Or I can hold you for ransom, gov'nor. A hundred, eh? I'm thinking you're worth a lot more'n that."

"The Prince Regent is already holding me for ransom," Dominic snarled.

The men laughed, obviously not believing him.

"And what's his holiness asking of you?" Rory asked.

"A ring on her finger."

The uproarious laughter when Dominic pointed his thumb at her got Brooke quite indignant.

But Rory stepped closer to her and grinned. "I'd pay that ransom."

It might have been the remark, or because the

264

man was about to touch her cheek, but Dominic suddenly lunged at him. They fell to the ground, and despite there being a half dozen weapons trained on him, Dominic still landed a fist to Rory's cheek before three men dragged him off their leader.

"You might be a lord, but you're not too smart," Rory said angrily as he got back to his feet. "A cooling-off time it is, then. Tie his lordship up and make bleedin' sure the ropes are tight. As for her—"

"I'll be seeing to her," a female voice interrupted.

Brooke turned to see an older woman approaching. Gray haired and gray eyed, she was a little beyond middle years with a weathered face. Her eyes swept over Brooke in a calculating manner before she gave Rory a stern look.

Dominic was struggling so fiercely with the three men holding him that two of them were already on the ground. But four others jumped in to help restrain him. He might still have won that battle, but he stopped trying when he heard the woman add, "D'you not recognize a gently reared lady? She's coming with me, boy."

Brooke held her breath, waiting to hear Rory laugh and tell the old woman to go away. He didn't. Instead he turned to help his men tie up Dominic, and the woman led Brooke to the hut at the far end of the clearing. It was much nicer inside than she had expected. She even found the strong smell of fresh wood pleasant. A double bed had a brightly colored quilt on it. There was a table with four chairs, even a rug on the wooden floorboards. The furniture all looked old and heavily used.

"Make yourself comfy, dearie. I'm Matty."

Brooke swung around when the old woman followed her into the room. "Please, what are they going to do to my fiancé?"

She shook her head. "My boy is mercurial, especially when he sees an opportunity to make us rich. He's sunk his teeth into that idea, now that he knows your man is a lord. So there's no telling what he'll do if it don't happen."

Brooke paled a little more. Had she really hoped to hear a less terrifying outcome? But if this woman was Rory's mother, could she help them? Rory had listened to her and let Brooke go with her. If Brooke could somehow gain her sympathy, maybe . . .

"Rory is your son?"

"Indeed. Rory's a good boy who abides by his own code of honor—usually."

Brooke wondered what that meant but decided not to ask. The woman sat down at the table and indicated Brooke should join her. "You have a nice home. How long have you lived in these woods?"

"Less than a month. We pick a new highway to

work every year. With prices on our men's heads, we can't stay in one area too long, so we build anew each year far from the roads, but not so far that a well-traveled new highway can't be reached in a few hours. How long have you and your man been affianced?"

"I've only known him a week." It seemed so much longer!

The woman looked surprised. "And you're so concerned about him already?"

"He's a good man, a concerned son. His mother has taken ill. We were on our way to London in a tearing hurry because he's so worried about her."

"But you want the marriage?"

"I do, but he doesn't." Brooke sighed.

Matty pointed at her emphatically. "I always tell a girl who believes she's found herself a fine fellow, seduce him if you want him to love you. And you're dealing with a proper lord who wouldn't fail to marry you after he's bedded you."

Brooke had started blushing at the word *seduce*. Alfreda had had the same idea, which is why she'd given Brooke the potion that she had in her valise. But even if she wanted to, how could she now when they might not even be alive come morning?

The woman tsked. "Rory is too unpredictable. It would be a shame if you was to die without knowing what it's like to lie in the arms of such a handsome, virile man as your fiancé. Maybe I can get Rory to agree to let you talk some sense into the lord, convince him to pay Rory his due. Don't worry, dearie. At least, I can arrange for you to spend your last night with him." Matty turned to leave.

"I'll need my valise!" Brooke called out, in case the woman really could do as she'd just said.

But as hours passed, Brooke began to suspect Matty had only given her false hope. Dusk came. She'd been standing at one of the two windows that faced the campfire, and she hadn't caught a glimpse of either Rory or Dominic the entire time. But she could see two guards keeping their eyes on her hut. Was Dominic coming to terms with Rory in one of the other huts? Or was he being beaten now that he was restrained? She was terrified by what might be happening to him and what might happen to her soon. But what if the mother did have enough sway to bring Dominic to her during the night?

Hungry, tired, she still stood vigil at the window, too afraid not to.

❧ Chapter Thirty-Six ❧

"He wants the moon," Dominic said angrily. "I offered him several alternatives, even sanctuary in Rothdale village for him and his friends— against my better judgment."

Brooke had leaped at Dominic the second he walked through the door and was still hugging his waist fiercely. "Did he agree?"

"He still wants the moon. And if he keeps us here too long waiting for it, I won't have anything left to offer him. The Regent will have taken it all."

Embarrassment overtook her when she realized what she was doing, though Dominic was so frustrated he probably didn't even notice. She stepped back. "Did you explain that?"

"*That* is none of his business. Then that old woman called him away. I could hear them arguing behind the hut they had me in, though I couldn't make out what they were saying. But then I was untied and escorted here to you. Do you know why?"

"She's his mother. I think she wants me to convince you to give Rory what he's demanding. She made it sound like this would be our last night if you don't."

"Last?"

"She seems to think the matter will be settled one way or another in the morning."

"Then we need to escape tonight."

"How? The door and the windows face the campfire where there are guards watching this hut."

"I'll break the boards in the back once most of this camp is asleep."

The hut was newly built. She didn't think he could break any freshly cut boards without making a lot of noise that would alert the guards. She didn't see any way out of this if Dominic couldn't come to terms with Rory. But he was here with her now. Rory's mother did come through on that! And Brooke had dug the potion out of her valise as soon as it had been brought to her. But it wasn't going to do her any good if Dominic didn't have a drink she could surreptitiously pour it into.

She could make the suggestion, but she didn't think he would be open to an early wedding night when he was still so determined that there would never be a wedding. But the man excited her in myriad ways, and being alone with him in this small room, with a bed nearby, was affecting her. God, she wished he weren't so handsome. She wished she could be indifferent to him. She wished she could figure out some way to bargain with him so this marriage could be more palatable for *him,* but all she wanted to do was kiss him again. How shameful, but that was certainly his fault for being so adept at it. Yet there wouldn't be a marriage if they couldn't get out of this camp of criminals alive. So this might indeed be her last and only opportunity to find out what it would be like to go beyond the kissing with him.

"Get some sleep," he suggested. "I'll wake you when it's time."

"I'm too hungry to sleep."

The door opened again. A guard stood in the doorway while Matty came in with a tray of food, a lantern—and a bottle of wine! She set the tray on the table and said to Brooke, "Here you are, dearie. This might be your last meal so"—Matty cast a quick glance at Dominic—"enjoy every bite." Then she walked over to Dominic and wheedled him with compliments and pleas to take pity on those less fortunate, great generous lord that he was. Brooke wondered what the woman was up to now, when she hadn't been a bit supplicatory earlier. She supposed Matty might be too afraid of Dominic to threaten him with dire consequences, but then he had taken on a really menacing aura from the moment the weapons had been pointed at them.

Brooke quickly took advantage of the momentary distraction to pour herself and Dominic glasses of wine and slip the love potion into his, and not a moment too soon. Matty came back to collect her tray, setting the dishes on the table. She seemed to be in a hurry to get out of there. The guard who was escorting Rory's mother looked even more wary and quickly closed the door again as soon as she was back outside.

Brooke sat down at the table with Dominic and was delighted to see him drink a good amount of his wine, so she did the same. Not knowing what to expect from him now that he'd imbibed the love potion, and a little nervous because of it, she talked about a dozen different things that were unrelated to their dangerous predicament: the dogs, the horses, his mother's illness, and the advice Alfreda had given her about how to deal with a variety of serious maladies. "It's a good thing I still have all those herbs in my valise. And as soon as we're done eating, I can nap blissfully unconcerned, confident that you'll keep us from any harm tonight. You *are* quite a big man, you know, much bigger than anyone here."

"You sound like a babbling brook."

She gasped. "Don't you dare pun on my name."

"I believe I will dare anything I like." He grinned. "I have a dagger in my boot. I'm amazed they didn't search me for a weapon, but I never leave home without it—just in case I run into your brother when no one else is around."

She rolled her eyes at him as she shrugged out of her pelisse and wondered why he hadn't noticed how warm the room had become. She couldn't seem to get her eyes off his mouth, either, and that led to some vivid thoughts as she remembered how it had felt the last time he kissed her. When she looked at his hands, she imagined how they would feel caressing her breasts. He must be thinking the same thing by now. Why wasn't he carrying her to the bed?

Instead he continued, "And you have reminded

me that I am quite capable of taking on a dozen ruffians. We will be fine. If we get caught escaping, I'll dispose of them quietly."

She giggled, then gasped that she'd done that and jumped up. "I'm so tired!"

"Then get some sleep. I'll wake you when it's time to go."

That had been a hint for him to join her, but obviously not a good one. She couldn't get those sensual thoughts out of her head, was afraid she might scream if he didn't start kissing her soon. She weaved her way to the bed.

"I think you had too much wine."

"Possibly," she mumbled, and started undressing.

She didn't even realize that she'd thoughtlessly taken off her dress along with her shoes and stockings until she heard him groan as she crawled across the soft quilt. But she complained, "It's hot. Aren't you hot?"

She lay down, but then leaned up on her elbows and saw that he looked a little more than surprised, or was he finally reacting to the wine? "I wanted to thank you for Storm, but mostly, for protecting me today."

He raised a curious brow at her. "Thank me how?"

His tone was teasing. She locked her eyes with his and patted the bed next to her. He drew in his breath sharply, but was already walking toward the bed. He lay down next to her and put his hand on her bare arm, moving it up toward her shoulder in a slow caress. "Are you sure?"

She wasn't sure about a single thing in that breathless moment—except that she wanted to feel his mouth on hers again. The leap of her pulse, the rolling inside her that felt so odd, the forgetting to breathe, it was all there to overwhelm her. She answered him by pulling his head down to hers until their lips met.

The touch was exquisite, so soft, pulling her into the kiss with finesse and an unspoken promise. A foray of his tongue, teasing her lips, licking them. She hoped the kiss would escalate to the passion he'd displayed before. She was quite frantic for it, which was why a few moments later, she did the escalating herself, putting a hand on the back of his neck and pulling him closer, much more impatient than she ought to be.

She sensed the passion was there, but he was trying to contain it, and she wasn't sure why, unless—had she drunk from the wrong glass?! It didn't matter, nothing mattered except the urgency racing through her, which was heightened by his every touch. The scrape of his teeth on her neck, followed by the softest kiss to the same spot. One deep, swift kiss, followed by the gentle touch of fingers moving over every part of her face. It was driving her crazy!

She finally gripped his cheeks to keep his mouth on hers, her passion escalating beyond reason.

But he countered that by flipping her over to her stomach, leaning against her back to keep her there, his breath hot on the back of her ear when he said, "Slowly. We have hours."

No, they didn't! They could be interrupted again, the opportunity gone, possibly forever. They weren't exactly behind locked doors just then— well, they were, but they couldn't get out and other people could come in! But she didn't say all that, she was too arrested by what Dominic was doing to her.

Goose bumps spread down her back from the brief kisses he was giving her there. She didn't realize he'd shed his own clothes until she was on her back again and his kisses were no longer soft and slow. Passion unchecked, she was fully caught up in that storm. She thought he was, too, until he leaned back and she saw in his golden eyes that he wasn't going to make love to her there in that little hut. A gentleman after all? Did he think she needed rose petals and soft sheets? She'd been reared by a woman of nature to appreciate nature and enjoy the simple things in life—a swift horse under her, the sun on her face, the wind in her hair, the scent of crushed herbs— and she could add, now, the gentle touch of a man, this man.

She put a hand to his cheek and with the boldness that had overcome her said, "If you think we aren't going to be interrupted, I would like to feel you on top of me—inside me. Please don't stop, not when we're both caught up in this primal storm."

He drew in his breath sharply yet again before a smile slowly curved his lips. Good God, how did that smile make him even more handsome?

She didn't care if she'd just shocked him. She just wanted to feel his weight on her, taste his skin, know the joy of making him hers. She slid her hands over his bare shoulders, dragged her nails gently up his back. He easily removed her camisole, completely baring her breasts to his eyes, then his hands, then his mouth, driving her even wilder for him, if that was possible. She easily pulled off the tie that queued his hair, so she could feel his hair on her skin. She wasn't sure if she got more pleasure from the way he touched her breasts, or the way he admired how plump they were. No, his mouth on them was definitely the best.

Small gasps escaped her as little shocks sparked her pleasure. He seemed to be finding every bit of sensitive skin she possessed, in places she wouldn't have thought could be erogenous—the back of her knees, the tips of her fingers when he sucked on them, behind her neck, places she could touch with no such results. So it was him, only him, or just part of her mounting excitement, possibly that.

He did need to remove her pantaloons, which was not so easily done. She thought he might rip them off when he couldn't find the ties, so she helped, even lifted her hips to make it easier for him. Even that was a caress, the way he did it, his hands on her skin as he pushed the thin stockinette down her legs, over her ankles, then brought a hand slowly back up her bare legs. But the finger he slipped inside her as he reached the junction was electrifying, like nothing she'd ever felt. She let out a sharp gasp as pleasure set her blood racing. She found it incredible that this wasn't even the half of it. If this got even better, she might get addicted.

Like a cat, she wanted to rub her body against him, but settled for wrapping her legs around his hips as his hands and mouth moved back up her body, trapping him right where she wanted him. When his mouth came back to hers, she didn't know he was poised to claim her. It was sharp, swift, her surprised cry caught in his mouth. She definitely didn't like that part, almost pushed him away until she remembered she should have expected that pain and might thank him instead for dealing with it so quickly, especially since it was gone just as swiftly, leaving that glorious feeling of him filling her—and something else. It built, it exploded, ecstasy washing over her. And he hadn't moved yet! The most amazing, delicious sensations flooded her, pulsed around him. He was even looking down at her incredulously. Toes curled, she almost purred.

She couldn't help smiling. He was still looking down at her when a few sweet thrusts brought his own climax. It was amazing to watch. But he collapsed on her then. Her smile broadened. Her hands ran through his hair. She might not mind sleeping like this if they ever got to sleep again.

She pushed away a nasty thought that the danger might not be over and wouldn't be until they were far from this camp. But for the moment she was in a different sort of heaven and wanted to savor every second of it. He seemed to be, too, at least he didn't get off the bed. She was much too languorous to remind him about the vigil he'd intended to keep before she'd distracted him with her invitation. She didn't even blush about that, just drifted blissfully off to sleep.

❧ Chapter Thirty-Seven ❧

She was blushing now! Dominic was swearing at the sunlight coming in through the windows. They'd both slept through the night, their opportunity to escape gone because she'd invited him to make love to her. He got out of bed and retrieved his clothes. She found the tie for his hair, which she'd removed last night, on the mattress and waved it at him.

Taking it from her, all he said was "I keep Storm for Wolf."

She frowned slightly, trying to think why he would say that now, then recalled her thanking him for letting *her* keep Storm. She burst out laughing. He grinned as well. She realized that she must be getting quite used to him if she could laugh spontaneously like that. And he must be getting used to her if he could tease her like that. Her plan to make him love her—eventually—was starting to work, but was she getting caught in the same snare?

Dressed again in all but her pelisse, Brooke had the amusing thought that Regency fashion must have been designed for lovers who grabbed stolen moments. It definitely made it easy to disrobe quickly and re-dress nearly as quickly. She thought about sharing the thought with Dominic, but he was looking quite serious again because they would soon find out if they would be back on their way to London today or never reach it.

Yet she had such confidence that he would handle whatever came their way. She hadn't been joking about that. His size, his quick responses, the way he was preparing ahead for any possibility, it was reassuring even if it didn't remove all of her worry. But that left her mind free to worry over what they'd done instead, or what *she'd* done. If he mentioned it, she would likely go up in flames.

Now that the effects of the love potion had worn off, she was feeling utterly shy about it. She didn't expect Dominic's attitude toward her to change, but she did expect him to stop trying to push her out the door. They weren't suddenly happy young lovers eager to get their hands on each other. Then she had the most horrid thought—that his payback for what Robert had done could be tit for tat, to get her pregnant and *not* marry her. Well, that would be justice served in her mind, but probably not his, so it was a ridiculous thought.

But he *would* marry her now. That doubt was completely gone. As he'd said before, he wouldn't mind her in his bed—which was proven last night. His attitude toward her out of bed was still in question though. Would his animosity miraculously go away, or did she still have to whittle away at it?

She wouldn't have that answer until after their vows were spoken next Sunday. She just didn't have much hope that the marriage would make that much difference, at least not anytime soon. And he did warn her the other night when they'd been kissing in those ruins that making love with her wasn't going to magically make him love her. So it could still take years to develop closeness with this man—if it was even possible. She reminded herself that friends before happy spouses was still a good plan for her to work on.

She still hadn't figured out how she was going to accomplish that other than that she needed to offer him something that would please him, something he wasn't expecting, and not her body, which he could have anytime he wanted. Something else that could form a bond between them. A mystery to unravel? If she could find one. A mutual goal such as horse breeding? No, that was to her benefit, not his. It had to be something *he* would want and she might not like, so he'd know that she was willing to sacrifice for him. She supposed she could offer to poison her brother. . . .

She almost laughed aloud, aware that he would probably jump on that offer, but she'd never make it. She wasn't poisoning anyone, even her despicable brother. And all of which depended on whether they would leave this highwaymen's camp today—alive.

The single rap on the door was startling it was so loud. *Now* they were knocking? But Dominic was in no hurry to open the door. He picked up Brooke's pelisse first to help her put it on.

The door still didn't open. Maybe that was a good sign, courtesy. But Dominic moved to open it now. Rory was out there, and he looked a bit abashed before he waved an arm in a flourish, indicating Dominic and Brooke should leave the hut. Most of the highwaymen and their families were standing nearby to witness this exchange.

"I've decided to accept your last offer," Rory said, though he didn't look all that pleased about it.

Dominic replied, "One hundred pounds?"

"Two hundred, wasn't it?"

"Perhaps I recall one hundred fifty."

"Done!" Rory quickly said, grinning now. "But I'll be taking your coat to seal the bargain." When Dominic just stared at him, Rory added, "It's my only bleedin' incentive, m'lord, so hand it over. Mum might think you'll honor our deal, but I ain't so trusting."

Brooke was incredulous. Dominic shrugged out of his coat and handed it over. It appeared that Matty had had a hand in gaining their release. She'd thought the argument Dominic had overhead yesterday between Rory and his mother had been over Matty's getting Rory to bring Dominic to Brooke's hut, but maybe it had been about this instead.

She saw Matty and went over to her and gave her a brief but heartfelt hug. "Thank you. My fiancé will honor the bargain. You can count on us."

"M'boy thinks I'm an old softy, but I'm just fond of young lovers. Reminds me of my younger years." She gave Brooke a sharp look. "And I'm a good judge of character."

Rory called out, "Do I get one of those hugs?"

"Are we having another row?" Dominic said succinctly, but that just got quite a few laughs.

At the roped horse pen, three mounts were already saddled and waiting. "You'll need to put these on." Rory handed Dominic and Brooke each a blindfold. "Axel will take your reins and lead you out of the woods. We really don't want to build another camp this year, so you understand we don't want you finding your way back to this one. And here's my cousin's address." Rory gave Dominic a slip of paper. "Deliver the horses and the blunt to her. She don't know where to find us, so don't bother asking. Mum didn't want her involved in our business."

Dominic accepted all that with a nod and helped Brooke tie her blindfold and mount one of the horses before mounting the other and tying his own blindfold. "It's actually been a pleasure," Dominic said in parting. "Let's just not do it again."

Only Brooke, who felt a blush warming her cheeks, and maybe Matty, understood that first remark.

At first, it was slow going through the woods, but they moved more swiftly once they reached the road. A ways down it, Axel finally stopped, told them to remove their blindfolds, and handed over the reins, then disappeared through the woods along the road.

Dominic stared after him for a moment. "They'll probably move that camp anyway. That lout was no more trusting than I am and really does think all he's getting out of this is my damned coat."

Brooke kept the grin to herself, inordinately pleased that they were free! "But his mother trusts me—and I told her she could trust you. Was I right?" she asked as he started them down the deserted road at a fast clip.

"I gave him my word," he grumbled. Once their pace picked up to a gallop, she heard him snort quite derisively, "They call these *fast* horses?"

❧ Chapter Thirty-Eight ❧

With every other crisis taken care of, Dominic was back to worrying about his mother as they raced to London. He predicted they would get there by tomorrow night. Apparently they'd sailed that far down the coast before their misadventure with the highwaymen for him to think so. Swapping out the horses for fresh ones at several of the towns they passed allowed them to continue at a gallop. They spent the night at an inn and were on the road again at dawn. Brooke agreed that speed was more important than her comfort; she just didn't bother to say so. And she didn't complain, not once.

But as much as she loved riding, she was quite tired of it by that nightfall. However, she could have walked into the Wolfe town house. Dominic didn't need to pick her up and carry her up the front steps and inside.

The butler let them in, a gray-haired, rotund fellow in his nightclothes. Was it that late? She was tired enough to think it might be.

"Hot bathwater, hot food, and wake whoever you need to, Willis," Dominic ordered. "But point me to a clean room for Lady Whitworth first."

Brooke protested, "Just food will do. I'm afraid I'll fall asleep in a bath."

"Is the lady hurt?" Willis asked as he hurriedly followed Dominic upstairs.

"No, just tired. I may have overdone my haste in getting here. How is my mother?"

"Worse than when I wrote you, m'lord. Thank you for coming so quickly."

Dominic didn't put Brooke down until Willis opened a door for him. She spotted the bed and headed straight toward it, deciding food could wait until morning, too. She glanced back to tell Dominic that, but the door had already closed behind him. She sighed and moved away from the tempting bed. She looked for a mirror to see how badly disheveled she looked, but couldn't find one so she moved to one of the two windows instead. She had a view of the street out front and a single lamppost. Peaceful, with no traffic this late. London! They'd even galloped through the streets, not giving her a chance to see much of it. Tomorrow, maybe . . .

She was looking at the bed again when Dominic

knocked on her door and entered without permission. He held a pitcher of water and a plate of warmed food.

She was too tired to thank him, but she did smile at his thoughtfulness.

"Mother's sleeping," he said. "Even her maid is sleeping. I won't know her actual condition until morning."

"Nonsense, go wake the maid. You didn't nearly kill us today riding here to sleep without some news."

"Her brow is still hot."

Brooke wanted to put her arms around him. He looked so helpless, and in fact he could do nothing to help his mother other than make sure she had the best physician available.

"Summon her doctor in the morning. See what he has to say before you think the worst. And keep in mind, fever does rise at night."

Still looking worried, he nodded and left Brooke. She did no more than wash her face and hands, eat half the food on the plate, and collapse on top of the bedcover. Removing her clothes required too much effort, and she was sore from being on a horse all day. She was half-asleep when it occurred to her that she should have invited Dominic to spend the night with her. She could have offered him more comfort than the little reassurance she'd given.

A maid woke her in the morning with fresh

water, fresh towels, and a chipper attitude, claiming a guest was exciting news for the staff because they rarely had guests that stayed over other than her ladyship's son. Bathwater as well as breakfast were apparently already on the way up.

The room she'd been given was quite utilitarian, with less furniture in it than some of the inn rooms she'd stayed at on the way to Rothdale. The bed was soft, but only one night table with a lamp was beside it. The room had a narrow standing wardrobe, a washstand, a small tin tub without a screen, and a single reading chair. But there was no table, no vanity, not even a bureau, and she looked again and still couldn't find a mirror. It appeared that the lady of the house didn't want overnight guests and made sure if she had one the guest wouldn't stay long.

But among the servants who carried in the buckets of water was a footman with a hard-backed chair in one hand and a small round table in the other, which he set down near one of the windows. Brooke laughed. At least the servants didn't mind having guests.

As Brooke helped herself to a sausage biscuit, one of the maids promised her a more substantial breakfast when she came downstairs—if she could manage those stairs today, Brooke thought. Good God, she was sore from all that galloping. She had only felt it minimally last night. As Brooke stepped into the tub, she hoped the hot water would ease the ache in her legs. It might have helped if she were bathing in a normal tub. But in the little round one she could barely sit down, having to scrunch up her legs. It was more designed to just stand in, get soaped, get rinsed, get out. But she didn't have a maid to help with that, and it would be another couple of days before Alfreda arrived with . . .

Brooke gasped with the belated realization that her valise hadn't been brought to her room yet. She balked at the thought of wearing the dress she'd worn yesterday before it was cleaned.

Then for the second time Dominic entered her room without permission, with just a single rap on the door to announce that he was coming in. Brooke squeaked and tried to sink lower in the little tub, but that was impossible, so she hugged the side facing him, using it as a shield.

"I'm afraid I forgot about this last night, and the footman who saw to the horses merely set it in the foyer." Dominic set her valise on the bed before he approached the tub and put a hand to her cheek. "Good morning."

She was speechless, confused, and definitely hot cheeked. He had to know how inappropriate this was. They weren't married yet—or had he finally accepted that they would be? His attitude had changed since they'd made love, not overtly, but in little ways. He didn't hesitate to touch her now, helping her on and off horses the last two days, carrying her into his house, and just now, a gentle caress. And not one dark feral look since they'd left the highwaymen's camp. She shouldn't read too much into that, she really shouldn't, not when he was still so worried about his mother, and yet she couldn't resist the thought that making love with him might have changed everything between them.

"Do hurry," he continued. "My mother is awake and I'd like to hear what you have to say about her illness."

He left, closing the door behind him. She sighed. Maybe he was just being nice and thoughtful because he wanted her help.

She finished her bath, even managed to wash her hair since the servants had left her two extra buckets of water, though she couldn't be sure that she'd gotten all the soap out.

With his *Do hurry* still in mind, she quickly dried her hair by tossing it about to simulate a breeze, but she almost laughed when she realized she didn't have a hairbrush. Alfreda had been so busy worrying about tiny boats and Brooke's falling asleep on horses and falling off them that the maid had forgotten to pack a brush. Brooke was definitely going shopping sometime today for some amenities, and thankfully she wouldn't have to ask Dominic for money. She had only brought a quarter of her funds with her, leaving the rest with Alfreda, but she had kept the money in her pocket rather than her valise, where the highwaymen might have found it.

With her hair tied back so it wasn't so obvious it hadn't been brushed, and wearing a pale apricot-colored day dress, she stepped into the corridor and didn't even need to ask directions to Lady Anna's room. It was the only room upstairs with the door open.

She approached the bed where Dominic was standing, holding his mother's hand even though she appeared to be sleeping again. A single glance told Brooke the woman might be dying. She didn't need to see Dominic's expression to know that. Anna Wolfe looked so haggard it was hard to tell what she might look like when she wasn't sick. The black hair under her nightcap was matted, she was as pale as white parchment, and even the skin of her lips was cracking. She didn't even have the strength left to open her eyes fully. And it sounded as if she was having trouble breathing.

Brooke immediately filled the glass on the table next to the bed with water and told Dominic to rouse his mother and make her drink it. He tenderly helped his mother to sit up, but she did no more than take a few sips, barely opening her eyes, before she had to lie down again.

Dominic pulled Brooke out into the corridor. "Her doctor just left," he whispered. "Pneumonia, he said. It's usually fatal. And my mother is upset with me for bringing you here. Our talk has debilitated her even more."

"So you explained?"

"She already knew. I sent her a missive from Rothdale right after the Regent's emissary left. Her doctor congratulated her earlier in the week on our forthcoming marriage."

Brooke winced. "So it's become common knowledge?"

"It's definitely making the rounds if even her doctor heard about it. Prinny apparently didn't consider it a secret, but mother is now worried that it will become more than curious gossip and speculation. We don't want anyone to know about Ella."

"No, of course not."

"Can—can you fix her as you did me?"

Brooke had a feeling this was the only reason he'd insisted she come with him to London, especially since she could have arrived before Sunday by coach. A high fever was all he'd said about Anna's illness before they left Rothdale, so Alfreda had given Brooke herbs to treat a normal cold. But pneumonia was a serious illness.

Brow furrowed, Brooke told him, "Alfreda gave me two herbs that might help your mother, but I'm going to need a lot more of both of them, so I need to visit an apothecary today. I also need to talk with your cook to see if your kitchen has

291

the ingredients I need for a broth your mother should drink once a day."

"I have a hack waiting." He took her hand to lead her downstairs and outside.

He'd tried to second-guess her? Or just cover all contingencies? She was impressed.

She was able to find exactly what she needed for the teas, pleurisy root and fenugreek seeds. She would have stopped at another shop to buy a brush, too, if Dominic weren't in such a hurry.

She mentioned it though when they got back to his house before she headed to the kitchen. So she hoped a brush would be waiting in her room before the end of the day—if he was going to maintain this new considerate attitude. She supposed he might just be making amends for their harrowing trip. Or bribing her with kindness to help his mother. She hadn't exactly seen this side of him before their adventure at the highwaymen's camp to know if he was usually like this when he wasn't fighting against a marriage he didn't want. But time would tell. . . .

❦ Chapter Thirty-Nine ❧

"What the deuce did you put in my water?"

Brooke flinched at Anna Wolfe's tone. Dominic came forward in concern to take the glass from his mother's hand, giving Brooke a questioning look. Had she really thought this would be a simple matter? Obviously the mother was going to be a complaining patient just like her son.

With a sigh Brooke said, "A little cayenne and lemon. It's going to help you breathe easier—if you drink it. And the tea I just poured for you will start clearing your lungs of congestion, and, well, frankly, it's going to make you sweat."

"I don't sweat" came the reply ladies tended to make.

"Today you will want to, so be glad when you do. Sweating is a faster means of removing harmful things from your body, which will help you to feel better sooner." Since Dominic hadn't bothered to introduce Brooke, and Anna had already been told she was there to help, she said, "I'm Brooke, in case you were wondering."

"I know exactly who you are," Anna said disparagingly. "*His* sister."

Brooke stiffened and glanced at Dominic. He pulled her aside for a moment. "She's known about what your brother did and what it caused Ella to do for as long as I have. That was something I couldn't keep from her. I apologize in advance. Treating her may not be pleasant."

May not be? Brooke felt a hysterical laugh coming on. Did he think she would refuse to help if she knew his mother despised her as much as he . . . ? But he didn't despise her any longer. He couldn't, not when he trusted her to help his mother.

She nodded and moved back to the bed. Like mother, like son. They even glared the same way! With a sigh she told Anna, "I'm sorry about my brother, but I'm nothing like him."

"You still aren't welcome in my house."

Dominic began, "Mother—"

"She's not and never will be. I told you not to bring this viper in here."

The older woman might be making her feelings quite clear, but her words were slowly uttered, some even wheezed. She'd been helped to sit up halfway in bed. Her eyes were fully open now. Amber eyes like Dominic's.

Brooke thought she ought to leave. Her presence was upsetting the older woman. She started to, but Dominic put a hand on her arm to keep her there before he said to his mother, "She's here to help you at my behest. I already told you this and how quickly she was able to mend me with her knowledge of herbal remedies. Her brother might be despicable, but she can be trusted. However, when you are well, we will both leave if that is still what you want."

"She put *pepper* in my water!" Anna said accusingly. "Or did you not know that's what cayenne is?"

"It does sound odd. But maybe you should see if it does what she claims before you refuse it?" He handed the glass to his mother with a quelling look.

She took it but didn't put it to her lips. Brooke hoped she would when she was done complaining, but she wasn't done yet. Anna told him in a half-beseeching, half-commanding tone, "You can't marry her, Dom. She's a blatant reminder of what we lost."

"You no longer make my decisions, Mother. That burden is on me. And you have gotten worse, not better, according to your doctor. He has given up on you. I will not. So you *will* follow Brooke's instructions and you will cease your complaints about it. Or do you not want to survive this malady?"

"To see you leg-shackled to her? No, I would rather not live for that."

He swore, quite foully, and stalked out of the room, telling Brooke to come with him. But she didn't move right away, having noticed the tears that came to Anna's eyes when he walked to the door. She understood Anna's point of view.

The woman wanted the best for her son. In her eyes, Brooke was the worst.

Dominic was waiting for her at the door. As soon as he closed it, she said, "My presence upsets her too much, when she needs peace and quiet to recover. She won't get that if I go in there again."

"So you're not going to help her?"

"Of course I am. The nice thing about the regimen to combat pneumonia is that I'm not needed to deliver it, merely to do the mixing and steeping. You can make sure she drinks every drop, or her maid can."

"Thank you. I will leave you to it then and return shortly. I need to dispatch that money to those miscreants we spent the night with."

The look he gave her clearly told her that he was remembering what they had done that night. It left her blushing.

✧ Chapter Forty ✧

"And not even a note to say you're back in London?"

Dominic swung around, surprised to see his two closest friends outside the bank, but he had to chuckle at Archer's aggrieved expression. "I rode in late last night. Have you even been home since last night to see if I sent one this morning?"

"Oh," Archer said contritely.

Benton elbowed Archer before saying to Dominic, "Good to see you, old chap. I've got wonderful news, but we hear you do as well. This calls for another celebration."

Dominic raised a brow. "Is that what you two have been doing?"

"I don't know about him," Archer elbowed Benton back, "but *I'm* sober by now."

"Only because we slept with our heads on the table," Benton insisted.

"I would never," Archer said, aghast. "But I did watch you sleep. Quite boring. I surely would have left you there to snore it off if the serving wench hadn't kept me entertained. But this does call for another round. Shall we?"

Each taking one of Dominic's arms, they steered him across the street to one of their favorite taverns. He knew from experience that there was no point in protesting. Besides, he'd missed these two friends, had known them most of his life, having attended school with them.

Archer was the tallest of the three by a few inches. He was often called the golden boy not just because his family had such deep pockets. Blond and green eyed, too handsome by far, he was considered the *ton*'s most eligible bachelor and was at the top of every hostess's invitation list. Benton, while just as handsome with his brown hair and eyes, had developed a bit of a reputation as a gambler, so he didn't receive nearly as many invitations, which might be why he'd been seeking a wife outside London.

It was a shame they didn't see one another more often. Benton had been in the west courting a duke's daughter, had apparently started wooing her before she came of age to get his foot in the door. Now that was dedication, Dominic thought, to court a woman that long, but he hadn't seen Benton often since his friend had decided on that path, to know if he'd succeeded. But he guessed that was what they were celebrating. Archer visited Rothdale occasionally, so Dominic got to see him more often.

Getting a table, Archer ordered drinks. Dominic felt compelled to note, "You look tired."

"I am tired. Did I not mention I've been up all night making sure Benton didn't get robbed while he slept?"

"You could have taken us home," Benton pointed out. "I would have appreciated a bed instead of a table."

"But where's the fun in that, eh?" Then Archer turned to Dominic. "So tell us, is she at least pretty, this chit Prinny wants you to marry?"

"Wants? What exactly have you heard?"

"It's swirling around town that you're going to marry Whitworth's sister," Archer said. "He's been crowing about it, you know, claiming the Regent himself got you off his back so he won't have to fight any more ridiculous duels with you. Is he really that chummy with Prinny?"

"I doubt he even knows George. But our Prince found out the last duel wasn't the first. And now he's going to strip me of everything if I don't ally with the Whitworths in marriage to end my vendetta."

"What the deuce did Whitworth do to warrant morc'n one duel?" Benton demanded, angry on Dominic's behalf.

"I would as soon not display my rage in this fine establishment," Dominic replied. "Leave it go."

"Really?" Archer complained. "You still won't fess up? We need to get him foxed, Benton."

Dominic rolled his eyes. He probably could tell them what Robert had done, they were his closest friends, after all. But his mother would never forgive him if it somehow got out. He wouldn't forgive himself, for that matter.

So he changed the subject by asking Benton, "If you've been celebrating, does that mean your lady has said yes?"

Benton beamed. "We're to be married next month. You're both invited, of course."

"Then congratulations are indeed in order. But you do give new meaning to the word *perseverance*. Did it really take two years to win her?"

Benton grinned. "No, she was in love with me

within a month. It took two years to win over her father!"

They laughed. Dominic ordered another round. But when Archer started to nod off, Dominic told Benton, "It looks like he really did keep vigil all night. Get him home. I'll see you both later this week."

Leaving his friends, Dominic took a hack to Bond Street to find Brooke a brush and comb set, something beautiful and special, a token of thanks for making this trip with him with few objections. He'd expected more. Any other lady he knew would have been railing at him most of the way. But not Brooke. The woman defied description. She'd faced his animosity with smiles and a stubborn resolve. She was too logical, too pragmatic—too accepting. And too hopeful? Did she really want this marriage? Or was she just more afraid of what would happen if she refused it? Maybe a little of both.

He thought about everything that had happened since she'd arrived at his door and was surprised he had so many memories of her already—and that he recalled every one, even smiled at a few. She was amazing, bold, intelligent, beautiful. And fearless, or mostly so. The woman had met a wolf in the wild and hadn't run from it! Or perhaps she just hid her fears well? She did have a temper, not a harsh one, not one that lasted long. An interesting temper.

She was also sensual and bold for a virgin, yet she'd been just that. And she wanted him. That thought was never far away. She'd wanted him.

He found her the brush set in one of the first shops he passed, then recalled that she was having a birthday around the day they were to marry. He stopped in a few more shops that offered mostly jewelry, but nothing caught his eye until he saw the gold-etched cameo surrounded by tiny light green peridots that nearly matched the color of her eyes. He bought it, only to find out it was actually a locket. Presenting her with an empty locket seemed like only half a gift, so he went in search of an art gallery and found one after he crossed into Old Bond Street.

Shopping done, he headed north again, keeping an eye out for a hack to get him home sooner. So he wasn't looking at the line of shops he passed and didn't see the man who'd just stepped out of one of them. He didn't hear the hail, either. But he definitely couldn't miss Robert Whitworth suddenly stepping in front of him, blocking his way. Or the similarities between the two siblings, which were made more remarkable with the man standing this close to him—the same light green eyes, the same black hair.

"Well, well, my soon-to-be brother-in-law," Robert said with a sneer.

"Still gadding about London ruining virgins, Whitworth? That is your forte, isn't it? I'm sur-

301

prised someone else hasn't disposed of you for me by now."

"And I'm surprised my dear sister hasn't poisoned you yet. She promised she would— oh, I understand now, she's waiting until after the wedding, I suppose."

It felt like a physical blow to his gut. Dominic didn't breathe for a moment. But it was obvious that Robert was just spewing venom to goad him. "She's nothing like you," he said contemptuously.

Robert laughed derisively. "She charmed you, did she? You actually fell for that? She did turn out prettier and more clever than I expected."

The urge was there, powerful, immediate, to kill the man with his bare hands despite there being several dozen pedestrians to witness it. But sanity prevailed, just barely. Dominic still landed a solid punch to Robert's cheek that made him stumble backward several feet.

The surprised look Dominic saw on his enemy's face wasn't appeasing in the least. But it quickly turned murderous until Dominic took a step toward him. Robert moved back even more. He wasn't a fighter, he was a coward, a seducer of innocents, an immoral blackguard of the worst sort.

"We aren't related yet, Whitworth," Dominic spat out. "When we are, you can expect a lot more of that."

❧ Chapter Forty-One ❧

"You have to understand, miss, that Lady Anna has quite a temper and often says things she doesn't mean," Mr. Hibbitt said as he collected Brooke's empty lunch plate from the kitchen worktable. "Why, just last month our lady got so annoyed at the staff that she fired all of us, then spent two days tracking us down to rehire us and warned us never to take her mass firings seriously again."

Brooke laughed, realizing the cook was trying to cheer her up. The short, corpulent fellow was quite different from the Rothdale cook, whom she hadn't fully won over yet. This one was quite talkative. But the remark also made her guess that the whole staff must already have heard about her unpleasant first visit to Lady Anna's room. She had heard some of them whispering while she was making the broth for Anna. When Mary, Anna's personal maid, had come in to fetch her lady's lunch tray and Brooke had added the bowl of broth to it, Mary had insisted that Brooke taste the broth first.

Brooke had been shocked, but she'd kept her tone neutral when she'd replied, "I've already had a bowl. So has the kitchen staff, since it needs to be made fresh daily and will otherwise go to waste. Made with strained garlic and a few other beneficial vegetables, it's believed to aid in repairing tissue damage in the lungs, but it is still quite tasty if you're partial to garlic. And you must see that your lady drinks every drop of it, or Lord Wolfe will be informed that you are hindering his mother's recovery."

The girl, red cheeked, had left with Anna's tray immediately, but Brooke was still smarting over the insult to her and its being witnessed by the kitchen staff.

The kitchen had gotten quite hot while lunch was prepared. As she wiped her brow, Brooke asked Mr. Hibbitt, "Is there a garden?"

"A small one behind the house. Nothing as fancy as the gardens at Rothdale, but it may still be cool there at this time of day. It's just off the morning room."

Brooke smiled and left the kitchen to find the morning room, but passing through the main hall, she saw a grand-looking lady entering the house and heard Willis say, "Duchess, always a pleasure."

"Is my dear friend any better, Willis? She didn't mention her health in the note I just received from her."

"Not yet, but with Lord Wolfe's arrival, we may soon see improvement."

"Indeed, that should cheer Anna." Then the lady spotted Brooke and ordered imperiously,

"You there, send up a pot of tea for me to your lady's room and do hurry."

Brooke might be disheveled from the hours she'd spent in the kitchen, but to be mistaken for a servant was one too many insults in one day. She replied stiffly, "I'm not a servant, I'm Lady Brooke Whitworth."

"Harriet and Thomas's girl? Hmmph!" The lady marched toward the stairs.

Brooke swung about and headed to the back of the house, trying not to grit her teeth. Stepping out into the garden a few moments later, she took a deep breath to calm herself. The small area was filled with summer blooms that offered quite a few different scents, and several short fruit trees for a bit of shade. Stone statues of different sizes were set throughout the garden, with even an ornate fountain at the center. She could hear horses beyond the back fence and went up on tiptoe to see a long stretch of mews where horses and carriages were kept, likely shared by the block.

Heading to the fountain to sit down, she bent over to pick a rosebud, so she was quite startled when she heard Dominic say behind her, "Looking for poisonous plants?"

She straightened slowly, but her frown was immediate. "Why would you say that to me? You know I only use herbs to heal people."

"Didn't you try to put something quite different

in my wine the other night and ended up drinking it yourself?"

She sucked in her breath. He was guessing, he *had* to be guessing, but her sudden red cheeks were probably why he added with a sensual smile, "The results were quite memorable."

She had been far too embarrassed to say anything about the love potion and hoped he hadn't noticed any difference in her behavior that night so she wouldn't have to. But he didn't appear to be displeased by what he'd guessed, quite the opposite. She still couldn't bear to own up to it, when it smacked of desperation on her part.

So she admitted part of the truth. "Rory's mother suggested I seduce you, since it might well have been our last night—ever."

He laughed. "And here I thought you actually had a potion that would send you running to my bed. Too bad."

Was he really amused? There seemed to be some underlying tension—and he did just mention poison. "In any case, you must know—"

"No, I'd have to be a bloody idiot to believe that you would kill me before or right after the wedding. That would implicate a Whitworth. Or does he not care if you're the one who gets hanged for it?"

She was confused. "What are you—" She paused with a gasp, guessing. "You saw Robert!"

"The devil is whom I saw," he snarled.

"What maggot did he put in your head?"

"That you promised him you would poison me!"

She sucked in her breath before she slammed both of her palms against his chest. "And you believed him? Why would I? I aided you. You might also recall that I told you several times I don't like him any more than you do. He did suggest that I poison you after we are married, but it was too preposterous to even merit an answer from me, much less a promise. And truthfully, I didn't really think he was serious, though he also warned me not to like you, said it would be disloyal to my family if I did." She snorted. "I have no loyalty to them. So don't you dare accuse me again of something I haven't done or would ever do. I help people. I don't kill them. And if you are not willing to be logical about this, then I have nothing more to say to you."

She started to walk past him in high dudgeon, but he grabbed her arm. "I didn't believe him. But he did warn me that you turned out more beautiful and clever than he expected and shouldn't be trusted."

"Because he's a vicious, destructive person who wants to enrage you and remind you that he's still walking around unscathed while Ella is dead because of him! I knew the vicious child, I never tried to know the man, preferred to just avoid him altogether. Maybe he hoped you would challenge him right then to another duel, leaving the Regent no choice but to punish you for it. Or he could have hoped you would bring your anger to me, which you did. Killing me would certainly stop you from trying to kill him again since you'd be in prison for it. I'm just guessing. I simply don't know what his motives are or what he's capable of these days."

"He's capable of driving young women to their death and getting away with it!" Then Dominic added, "I don't want you giving my mother any more of your teas or magical potions."

Good God, it felt as if they were right back where they'd started. "Too late!" she said with a furious glare. "She's already had a full pot of my tea *and* the broth today. But don't worry, her maid already insulted me by wanting me to drink it first!"

"That's not a bad idea. Very well, you can give your recipes to Mr. Hibbitt, who will indeed test them first. But I think it would be better if you just stay away from my mother altogether."

She brushed past him, tossing over her shoulder, "I think it would be better if I just stayed away from you!"

❦ Chapter Forty-Two ❦

On her way from the garden to her room, Brooke stopped in the library to grab a book to occupy her for the rest of the day. She was too upset to even look at the titles first. A history of London, not bad for a blind choice, she thought when she was comfortable in her reading chair. But she couldn't concentrate on reading when she was so upset that her relationship with Dominic was deteriorating thanks to his mother's antipathy and her brother's stirring up trouble between them.

As the hours passed, she got more and more downhearted because the progress she thought she had made in making him love her during those last days at Rothdale when they seemed to bond over Storm was undone. She'd been so sure more doors to his heart had opened during their journey to London, when he'd given her the most wonderful night of her life, introducing her to the most remarkable pleasures, and he'd been so sweet and protective of her. All that was undone, too. Now she was afraid Dominic was back to hating her as much as he hated Robert.

Yet she couldn't give up. The marriage still had to happen. Besides, while the situation with the Wolfes and their servants wasn't great, she would have a better future as Dominic's wife than she would have if she returned to her family.

Maybe it was time to bargain with him for one of those marriages of convenience Alfreda had told her about. Or maybe a real bargain in which she gave him something he might want in exchange for—what? She gave it a lot of thought, but could only come up with one thing that would make it palatable for him and not cost him—much. At least he would believe she was serious when he heard what she would accept in return. So she was quite willing to join him for dinner when a maid showed up with the invitation.

But she was still smarting over what he had said to her today, including his pretty much accusing her of trying to poison his mother! So even though she gave him a tight smile when she entered the dining room, she asked, "Is your cook dead yet?"

He laughed. "No, but my mother is breathing easier."

"I'm glad to hear it. You can thank me by not yelling at me anymore."

"I don't yell."

"You did."

"This is a yell!" he yelled to prove his point.

It sounded the same to her. He stood up and pulled out the chair next to him. She sat down in the chair at the opposite end of the long table. It looked as if he might rectify that, standing there a long moment debating whether to put her where he wanted her. She sighed in relief when he started to sit back down in his chair, but apparently he reconsidered and came down to her end of the table and sat in the chair to her right.

If she weren't still so utterly disgusted with him, she might have laughed. Concessions when he'd been so cold and suspicious earlier? But she was mostly angry at her brother, for putting her back to day one with Dominic.

He was wearing a fresh shirt, minus a coat. He'd also been properly dressed as an elegant lord earlier in the day, so he obviously kept a full wardrobe of clothes at this house. Her gown was fresh, if a bit wrinkled. She could have asked one of the maids to steam it, but would probably have been ignored.

"If you're going to continue my suggested regimen for your mother, you need to make sure she drinks at least four cups of each of the two teas."

"You can do that. She won't fight you any-more."

"*You* can. Whatever you told her to change her mind about me isn't going to really change her attitude any more than it does yours."

"It's not about you, it's about lack of choice and what can be lost."

She snorted at him. "What makes you think my family saw it any differently? I was promised Bedlam for the rest of my life if I balked at this

311

marriage. We could have seen it differently, you and I, but you decided I can't be trusted. So be it. Why don't we put that on the table and agree we will never trust each other?"

"You have no reason not to trust me, while I—"

"Ha! When you listen to my brother's lies about me?"

"I'll concede I listened when he said you turned out more beautiful and clever than he expected."

She stared at him incredulously; he said that so calmly, almost as if he were teasing, but he couldn't be, not about this subject. So she clamped her mouth shut. The food started arriving. She ignored it for the moment. So did he. He seemed to be waiting for a rejoinder. Did he *want* to fight? She decided not to give him the satisfaction.

She took a deep calming breath. "Obviously you are never going to like this marriage. And you're going to make sure that I don't like it either. But I'm not leaving. I would prefer to be here with an ogre than back with my family. But tell me, has it even occurred to you that we actually have common ground?"

"What do you mean?"

"We aren't even married yet and you and I still have many things in common, a remarkable number considering we are enemies."

"Such as?"

She had to grit her teeth for a moment. A perfect opportunity for him to claim they weren't really enemies and he didn't take it.

"Such as, we both hate my brother. We both love horses and we even both want to breed more of them. And we both hate our futures being dictated by others. Oh, and we both love dogs. We have even both befriended servants, quite uncommon for the nobility to do. So we marry to force the Regent to look elsewhere for a way to pay off his debts, but that doesn't mean we need to see it as a real marriage if you don't want to. We could probably become friends instead. So let me propose a bargain. We could—"

"Are you trying to make me laugh?"

Her brows snapped together. "No, not a'tall."

"We'll never be friends."

It did sound preposterous from where they stood now, but she still insisted, "Stranger things have happened, and you haven't heard my bargain yet."

"By all means."

"We can marry in name only, you won't even need to see me. I'm used to avoiding 'family,' and I will encourage you to take mistresses. You can even bring them home." She said it all fast, before she lost her nerve, but she hadn't yet added the seal for this bargain. "If you will buy me a thoroughbred for each one, I will be quite pleased. So do have lots of mistresses. I want my own horse farm when your curse catches up with you."

"So now you believe in curses?"

The curve of his lower lip was telling. She had *not* meant to amuse him, but obviously she had. "No, what I think is, you are entirely too reckless with your life, duels, sailing right through blockades that are shooting at every boat they see, and who knows what other risks you are used to taking. It's no wonder they say your family is cursed if the men in it were so cavalier about danger as you are. Besides, if you somehow manage to survive your twenty-fifth year, I would merely add my horses to your stock, as long as I have a say in their breeding program."

"What about our breeding program for my heirs? D'you think you'll get a say in that, too?"

Her cheeks lit up hotly. "Is that your way of saying you don't want a marriage in name only?"

"I believe I've made it quite clear that the one thing I won't mind about this marriage is you in my bed. And based on past experience, I got the impression you won't mind lying with me in that bed."

Brooke blushed. "You're assuming too much!"

Dominic smiled sensually. "Am I?"

Her blush got deeper. "In any case, it doesn't mean you won't still take mistresses. I'm encouraging you to do so."

"You're making a bargain for me to do so."

"Yes, exactly. I will even make suggestions if you like, help you pick them out, as it were—one reason why I thought we might reach a sort of friendship eventually."

"And what is my incentive to agree?"

"To protect them," she said without inflection.

He raised a brow. "Was that actually a threat?"

She shrugged. "I have sharp nails."

"You've given this a lot of thought?"

No, damnit, she hadn't. The idea had just come to her an hour ago. And spur-of-the-moment proposals rarely went well, at least, not without regrets. Had she just backed herself into an unpleasant corner?

But he didn't wait for an answer. "If I'm going to die young, by your logic, why not just wait until all my horses are yours."

"I don't expect you to leave me anything. I expect your estate to go to your mother."

"Your family would make sure that doesn't happen."

"So stop being so careless with your life and don't die. Because I do *not* want them to benefit from this, when it's my brother's fault that I'm here. In fact, if you don't have a will, you should make one and be specific in excluding Whitworths from benefiting. And if I'm not of age yet, name your mother as my guardian so they have no further control over me."

"Thank you, you've given me back my appetite."

She frowned as he started eating the food that had been set before him. "You don't think I'm serious?"

"We shall see."

❦ Chapter Forty-Three ❧

Despite swearing she wouldn't step foot in Lady Anna's room again, the next morning Brooke took the lady's breakfast upstairs herself. She told herself it was just to see how much her teas had helped yesterday, but she really wanted to witness firsthand the supposed change in the woman's attitude. Dominic might think his mother had seen the light, but Brooke highly doubted it.

But the lady was sleeping and had apparently only just nodded off, according to the maid at her bedside, so Brooke didn't wake her and had the servant return the tray to the kitchen to keep it warm. Sleep was more important than food for Anna's recovery, as long as she was eating when she was awake.

She didn't know where Dominic was in the big house and would just as soon not find out. She decided to go shopping, which she hoped would take her mind off her having only two days left until her wedding. Not that they needed to wait until the banns were read for the third time when they had the order and the marriage license from the Prince; she merely assumed they would be waiting until the last minute of the grace period that Dominic had been given.

She fetched her pelisse, then went to find the butler to request the Wolfe coach. "I've a bit of shopping to do, but mainly I'd like to tour the city to see some of the places I read about yesterday."

"Be sure to visit Vauxhall Gardens, m'lady. It's especially colorful at this time of the year, though it warrants a full-day excursion, with so many different entertainments to view."

She smiled. "Just a peek then for today."

"Certainly. I'm sure his lordship will want to take you for a longer visit to the gardens some other day."

Would he? She'd been in three of his houses now and he hadn't given her a tour of one of them. And he knew this was her first visit to London. He should have made the offer to show her more of the city he was familiar with.

The Wolfes' town driver wasn't happy about the tour she wanted, to go by his sour expression, or maybe that was his usual demeanor. The two accompanying footmen were reserved, and neither looked her in the eye. She didn't know these town servants and might not get a chance to, if they weren't going to stay in London.

She didn't know what Dominic planned to do when, or if, his mother recovered, either. He had mentioned that he usually spent at least half of

317

the year in town with Anna, but would he still want to do that when he had a wife? These were things she ought to be able to discuss with him, but when did they ever talk about mundane matters?

She hadn't seen much of London yesterday on the way to the apothecary, not with Dominic in the hack with her and the seat being so narrow their shoulders touched. She hadn't thought of anything but him during that brief ride.

For her first trip to this old town she ought to be more excited. She would have been—if she had come with her mother for the promised Season. Such an odd thought, considering her feelings for Harriet, or the lack of them. Was Alfreda right? Had Brooke repressed those feelings for so long they had really gone, or were they just buried too deep to affect her anymore? She didn't exactly like crying and had done far too much of it when she was younger.

The driver wouldn't go any farther south, but he took her close enough to the London docks to see the Thames and all the ships sitting out in the river. There were so many of them, which made her think again that maybe she should book passage on one and just disappear somewhere in the world.

But Alfreda wasn't there to advise her or agree to go along, so it was just a brief thought. Her friend would probably attribute her revisiting an option they'd already dismissed to wedding nerves. But Brooke wanted the wedding, had wanted it from the moment she'd clapped eyes on the wolf. However, she was nervous now about their wedding night.

After what Dominic had said last night at dinner, she definitely expected to be in his bed for it. In a nice room this time, with wine and maybe some sweets and . . . would it be as amazing as the first time, or horrible? With his feeling trapped by her, listening to his mother disparage her character, and having just been reminded by her brother that he ought not to trust her, it could be the latter.

She did get to see Vauxhall, but declined to leave the carriage to enter it. Willis was right, there would be too much to see in there and she'd rather not go in alone. She did get to drive through Hyde Park though, down the lane that would be filled on the weekend with the carriages of the upper crust of society, since it was a noted place to meet or just be seen. Adjacent to it was Rotten Row, where she hoped to ride Rebel someday. She also saw St. George's church in Hanover Square, where all the high-society weddings took place, and wondered if that's where she was going to be married.

It occurred to her that her parents might often come to these places, but neither of them would ever take her along. She had a brother in London, but she'd never go anywhere with him. She even had a fiancé, but the only place he'd taken her was to an apothecary shop—for his mother. She felt so alone in this town. She didn't even have Alfreda. And the maid wouldn't arrive for another day or two.

She ended the tour on Bond Street and left the coach to find some shoes and maybe another apothecary so she could make a salve for the blister on her foot. Traveling boots weren't meant to be worn daily. The two footmen followed her at a discreet distance; they just didn't enter the shops with her. She entered many of them, even after she found a new pair of shoes, which she changed into immediately, and a few shops farther down the street she even found some calendula for a salve.

She didn't find spending money in the great London shops as much fun as she'd thought it would be, but she continued shopping, or mostly peering in shop windows, because she was in no hurry to return to the Wolfe house. Maybe Dominic would think she'd fled and worry—or rejoice.

She gritted her teeth and entered another shop before she noticed what it was. Fabrics. London fabrics. She didn't need any, had a brand-new wardrobe, yet she couldn't resist seeing the selections to be had here in the biggest port town in the country.

"What the devil, Brooke. I was beginning to think you'd never slow down."

She closed her eyes with a cringe. Had Robert been following her?

"Put this away quickly."

Whatever he just put in her hand, she closed a fist around it instinctively and dropped it in the pocket of her pelisse. That he glanced back toward the front of the shop to see if one of her footmen was looking inside to notice made her even more nervous.

"What are you up to now, Robert?" she demanded.

"Don't take that tone with me when I'm just helping you out."

"Like you did when you told Dominic that I promised to poison him? That kind of help could have gotten me killed, or was that the plan?"

He shrugged. "It would have solved our problem."

She wasn't hearing anything she didn't expect to hear from him. He wouldn't care.

"Whatever you just gave me is going to be thrown away. I'm not going to poison him for any reason, certainly not for you."

"It's not poison," he insisted. "Just something to make him sick and disoriented enough to send you packing. I'll settle for him losing every-thing when he does that."

She didn't believe him. He was too much of a coward to want Dominic to remain alive, destitute or not, not after what Robert had done to warrant those duels.

"D'you really think he's still going to try to kill you after I marry him? He won't, you know. He has more honor than that, to kill family— unlike you. Beating you senseless though, now that's allowed."

She probably shouldn't have ended that with a half smirk. Robert flushed with livid color, but when he raised a fist to her, she thrust her chin out and snarled, "Go ahead, I dare you. I'd love to see you in jail for it. If you think I won't scream murder to see that happen, think again."

"Bitch," he snarled as he walked away.

"Defiler of innocents," she said just loudly enough that only he would hear it.

He didn't stop. She did see both his hands form fists. And he almost broke the door to the shop he slammed it so hard on his way out. But then she'd never spoken to him like that before. Maybe she should have made clear a long time ago just how much she hated him, instead of going out of her way to avoid him. Did he think she had forgiven or forgotten the pain he'd caused her when she was too young to know how to prevent it?

She didn't need to sniff what was in the vial he'd given her before she threw it in a rubbish bin. She didn't doubt it was poison of one kind or another, despite Robert's denial. He wasn't going to stop trying to get rid of Dominic for one simple reason—because he wouldn't feel safe until he did.

✖ Chapter Forty-Four ✖

When Brooke returned to the town house that afternoon, she soon heard about the extra horse his lordship had come home with. But it didn't occur to her until she was resting in her room that Dominic's coming home with a new horse could mean only one thing. He either already had a mistress, or he'd found one that quickly today, or maybe even last night after dinner. Either way, she guessed the horse was for her to seal their bargain. She ought to go have a look at it. If she could stop crying, maybe she would.

"It's that bad, is it?"

"Freda!" Brooke leaped off the bed with a laugh. "You're early."

"I made sure of that. Gabriel didn't like taking turns driving that big coach, but I was persuasive."

"With a clobbering or . . . ?"

" 'Or' worked." The maid grinned.

They had a lot to catch up on . . . well, Brooke did. Alfreda's trip to London was apparently quite uneventful and summed up in just a few words about the unpleasantness of trying to sleep in a moving coach. Brooke's trip was too eventful, but she glossed over most of it and couldn't manage to mention the early wedding night she'd had before arriving in London. She would, just maybe after the wedding, when it wouldn't be so embarrassing and earn her a scolding.

But she did mention her run-in with Robert and Dominic's exasperating behavior, ending with "He spent last night with some other woman."

"Did he? But he's not married yet and you haven't made him love you yet."

"Are you really trying to tell me what happens before the wedding doesn't count?"

"When the wedding wasn't his idea, when he never proposed? Yes, I am indeed. Now if it happens after the wedding, there's an herb I've never stocked that is reputed to render a man incapable of performing in bed. I'll see if I can find some here in London. I've always wanted to test it on someone to see if it's true. I've just never met a man I dislike enough to try it on."

"Permanently incapable?"

"No, of course not." Alfreda winked. "I wouldn't do that to you."

It took a moment for Brooke to realize that Alfreda was just trying to lighten her mood with nonsense. That statement that Dominic's unfaithfulness shouldn't count before the wedding was reasonable, though, particularly since the bargain was *her* idea.

She helped Alfreda to unpack the trunks when they were brought in. But another soft knock came at her door almost as soon as the footmen filed out. She certainly wasn't expecting to see

Dominic standing in the corridor. He was dressed to go out, or maybe he was just returning? She immediately thought of the woman her suspicions imagined he'd been with last night—and again today? Maybe she should have asked for a horse per copulation, she thought with a mental growl.

He handed her a folded card. "I've accepted one of my mother's invitations that included me. Most of her friends expect me to be in town at this time of year. Be ready by eight tonight. Oh, and dress accordingly. It's a ball we'll be attending."

Brooke immediately stopped thinking about him and other women. "A party when your mother is so sick?"

"She's improving. Go see for yourself. And it was her suggestion."

"Do you even dance?"

"With four legs I might be a bit clumsy, but"—he glanced down at his legs—"ah, just two today."

She grinned at his teasing. "I didn't mean to imply that."

"Just that I'm a Yorkshire clod who was never taught?"

She rolled her eyes and teased back, "Yes, that."

"Well, in any case, we have a purpose in going, to show the Prince how famously we're getting along."

"He's going to be there?"

"He might. He's been known to favor Lady

Hewitt's parties with an appearance. They are old friends. So no fighting tonight, Babble."

He walked away. She barely even noticed, the excitement of her first ball already starting to fill her. She turned to tell Alfreda, "Unpack—"

"I heard. I thought you said his mother was ill enough to warrant your rushing to London with him."

"She was, but your recipes appear to be helping. I haven't been back to see for myself. My presence quite upset her, so I've stayed away. She didn't like me a'tall."

"I hated the woman who might have been my mother-in-law. My mother hated hers. You don't need to follow suit. She'll be the grandmother of your children. Make an effort to like her for their sake."

Brooke hadn't considered that. Harriet would be their grandmother, too, whom they would hope-fully rarely see. So it would be nice if they had at least one grandmother to love and dote on them. She nodded and went straight to Anna's room.

The lady wasn't sleeping this time. As Brooke approached the bed, she saw that Anna was no longer quite as pale, and even her lips were smooth again. Her eyes were fully open and alert now, too. Maybe the doctor had misdiagnosed her. The woman definitely didn't look as if she was dying now.

"I was wondering if you would visit your patient again."

Was that a slight smile? "I didn't think you wanted me to, madam."

"I admit I don't make a good patient. I do apologize for that." That was a nice way to put those horrid circumstances. But Anna wasn't going to just ignore it, either. "I hadn't realized how preposterous the threat was, hanging over our heads, yours included. That the Regent would take everything we own, the title, the houses, the coal mines, Dom's ships. He would leave us paupers, giving us no choice in the matter."

"I believe he saw this as an opportunity for himself. For that to backfire on him, he would need to think he's done us a favor instead."

Anna grinned. "I like the way you think, girl. The same thing occurred to me. Indeed, that would stick in his craw, wouldn't it?"

Brooke blushed only slightly when she admitted, "I can't take credit for it. It's your son's idea for us to put on a good performance tonight at the ball he's taking me to, if the Prince is there, to give the impression we are pleased with the match."

Anna cleared her throat. "I'm not going to pussyfoot around the subject, m'dear. I'm sure you know that Dom did hope you would refuse him. He can unfortunately be excessively blunt. But you haven't run home. So be it. I accept that neither of you really has a choice in this. So we must make the best of it, all of us."

A kernel of doubt was in Brooke's mind that those words were sincere, until Anna added, "And—and thank you for healing his leg *and* me. I realize you didn't have to do either, but you've helped us anyway. You have a good heart, Brooke Whitworth. Amazing, considering the stock you come from."

Brooke laughed, couldn't help it. A compliment and a backhanded slur. But considering her own feelings weren't far off the same mark, she said, "We don't get to choose our stock, more's the pity."

"I just want my boy to be happy. D'you think you can do that?"

"If he'll stop blaming me for the sins of others, yes, I do think that's possible."

"Then as Dominic said, the burden is on him."

❧ Chapter Forty-Five ❧

Brooke hugged Anna's final words to her as she hurriedly prepared for the ball. They gave her hope. Had she found the family she'd always wished for in the Wolfes?

Dominic said they would leave at eight o'clock, and she only had a few hours to bathe, dress, and have her hair styled, but with Alfreda's help she managed it.

After combing the last lock of Brooke's lustrous black hair into place, Alfreda stood back and gazed at her. "You look—" Alfreda didn't finish. It even looked as if she might cry.

Brooke grinned. "That bad?"

That got a snort out of the maid. "You've never looked more beautiful. Your mother has done you proud."

That got a snort out of Brooke. "All she did was pick the color of the gown. I got to choose the design."

"I wish she could see you tonight" was said in a mumble, then louder: "I think I will mention to your husband that he should have you painted in this gown."

"Don't do that. Aside from the fact that he won't want any record of me being part of his family, at least not hanging on his wall, his reply will probably make you angry."

Alfreda's brows narrowed. "What's happened to make you lose your confidence?"

"Other than that he jumped on my bargain? Or that his anger is barely below the surface again after he ran into Robert yesterday?"

"What bargain?"

"Never mind. It was just a business deal that might win his friendship someday. I'm at least still hopeful of that. And don't make me late."

Alfreda finished fastening the emerald choker to Brooke's neck. The emerald-tipped pins had already been added to her coiffure, and the bracelet sparkled on her wrist. All three of her ball gowns were made for these jewels, each in different shades of pale green with trimmings to distinguish them. This one was bordered in lime silk with silver sequins. And not one decent mirror in the room other than her small handheld one. But she trusted Alfreda not to let her out the door with anything out of place.

"You should smile when you first see him."

"So he doesn't notice the lack of a tucker? He really didn't like it when I wore that evening gown without one."

"He liked it, he just didn't like what it did to him," Alfreda stated without inflection.

Brooke giggled. She probably shouldn't have known exactly what Alfreda was implying, so she quickly left the room before the maid wondered about it. And she did smile, since Dominic was waiting for her at the bottom of the stairs. She'd draped a thin, tasseled shawl across her chest, since she'd rather he not yet see just how low her décolletage was.

It was the first time she was seeing him in evening attire, the black tailcoat, the dark gray waistcoat under it, and a pristine white cravat tied perfectly, and his dark hair tied back so tightly not a lock would escape his queue. Had his valet come to London, too? She tried to imagine Dominic tying that fancy cravat and couldn't.

"You look very handsome." She managed not to blush saying it.

"I suppose that pleases you?"

She started to frown until she realized, "Yes, of course, you will have the ladies drooling over you."

"I'd rather they not actually do that, but as long as you're pleased, shall we?"

She preceded him out the door to the waiting coach. The driver helped her into it before Dominic could. She sat in the seat on the opposite side of the one where she had sat in the hack the other day, expecting to be across from him, yet when he got in the coach, he still sat next to her. At least there was enough room this time for them not to be touching, though it didn't seem to matter. He was still too close, still filled her mind too much. Just two more days and she would know if marriage to him would make any sort of difference. . . .

"You will dance with no one but me tonight."

She glanced aside at him. "Is that normal for an affianced couple? Actually, are we even that?"

"A royal edict negates the necessity of asking, so, yes, we are, which is why you didn't need a chaperone for tonight. My mother did offer to arrange one, but I declined. I didn't think you would want a chaperone to overhear you pointing out prospective mistresses to me."

Her cheeks lit up hotly. "Is that what I'm going to be doing?"

"Isn't that what you suggested?"

Yes, it was, when she was tossing out incentives to get her bargain sealed. So be it. Bed made, et cetera. She would manage to do this without snapping his head off.

Then she remembered that he probably already had a mistress and had brought home her payment for it. But just to be sure, she asked, "Did you buy me a horse? I was told you came home with one today."

"I did."

"Who is she?"

"The horse?"

"Your mistress."

"I don't have one yet. The horse is for you to ride while you're here, since your mare is at Rothdale. Consider it a wedding gift."

"That was—thoughtful. Thank you. A thorough-bred?"

"Worthy of breeding, yes."

She grinned to herself and almost asked him to stop the coach so she could go have a look at it, but didn't want him to know just how pleased she was. This bargain might work out after all, if she could just think of the horses she would be getting and not think of what he would be getting in return.

✥ Chapter Forty-Six ✥

It could have been a dream come true, dancing with the most handsome man in the room at her first ball. It was intoxicating, exciting. Brooke was dazzled and wanted it to never end.

They'd caused quite a stir upon their arrival when Dominic had her heralded as his fiancée. She didn't need to be warned that London society was aware of Dominic's duels. With the last one so public, it had definitely made the rounds. But if everyone there didn't already know that he was now allying himself with the very family whose heir he'd tried to kill, they certainly did now. They just didn't know why, which became apparent when the couple were stopped several times on the way to the dance floor and she heard such remarks as "Getting your toes stepped on by Prinny doesn't usually turn out so well" and "Should you be thanking Lord Robert now?" and more bluntly "What did Robert do to warrant . . . ?"

Dominic had simply walked away from that fellow. But the entire room was probably dying to question him about his reasons for dueling in the first place. Which did explain why he seemed reluctant to leave the dance floor and they were now twirling to the fourth dance in a row.

He wasn't a coward. She knew that well. She

guessed he was simply delaying the anger that was bound to get poked by the gossipmongers tonight, and avoiding making a scene because of it. After all, their marriage was not a subject he could be civil about. She could be. If he wanted to keep her close, she could fend off . . . actually . . .

"One simple word will fly through the room and convince them we—"

"Was I supposed to be reading your thoughts?" Dominic cut in.

"You're rather good at it, so I suspect you know exactly what I was trying to say. But if you aren't worried about getting badgered with questions about our marriage tonight, then I won't mention a brilliant way to keep those questions from even being asked."

"I'm listening."

"If you kiss me right here and now, people will think the Regent has done us a favor and we are marrying for love."

"So love solves everything, does it?"

"I have no idea if it does or not. But it does explain what you're doing here with me."

"And would ruin my chance of a dalliance forming tonight, or is that no longer your main concern?"

She hadn't thought of that, only of helping him to avoid an angry scene. She ought to stop putting concerns for him before her own. But she was silent long enough for him to stop dancing and draw her close. He did kiss her right there on the ballroom floor, scattering her thoughts, igniting her passion. She heard a few gasps. One might have been her own. She didn't care. Nothing mattered when his mouth was moving so sensually over hers. She was about to wrap her arms around his neck when they were jostled apart, another couple twirling right into them.

Brooke laughed. Still smiling, she also took advantage of the moment and took Dominic's hand to lead him off the floor to the sidelines. No one approached with any rude questions.

She whispered, "I think it worked, or half worked. Though it might take a few minutes for that word to fly through the room."

"I wasn't serious about ruined chances."

"No?"

He shrugged. "It's been my experience that women tend to want what they think they can't have."

She snorted. "What an absurd statement."

"Then you haven't experienced it yourself yet. It's human nature and besets men as well."

She was quite familiar with human nature, or was he still not being serious?

"Besides," he added, "there are too many innocents here tonight, so it didn't matter."

She hadn't yet looked at the people there, having been so enchanted by the lights, the glitter, and the beautiful clothes—her husband-to-be.

But it was quite nice to know that he viewed innocents as off-limits. "Is this a debutantes ball?"

"No, though this Season's crop would still have been invited."

She perused the crowd and concluded, "Not even half the women here are as young as you just implied."

"Aren't they? But then they come with chaperones, and very few chaperones are old and doddering."

She rolled her eyes. "Make up your mind."

A few more small groups of people did still come over to greet Dominic and get introduced to her, friends of his who wanted to congratulate him on the coming nuptials. One rakish fellow said, "If this is what you get for dueling, Dominic, I need to find someone to challenge."

Dominic chuckled. "I would recommend a less painful approach."

The mention of pain had Brooke whisper as soon as they had a moment alone, "How is your pain after four dances? And don't try to tell me you don't still have some."

"You're aware that I had that wound for a week before you and the fever showed up? It had already started to mend prior to that interruption."

"That doesn't answer my question."

He shrugged. "It's tolerable, though it could still use your gentle touch. Maybe another love potion would help?"

He was teasing. She was quite certain she had convinced him there had been no love potion. So she only blushed a little. But that he was smiling assured her that the well-wishing from his acquaintances hadn't annoyed him yet.

But then one old biddy came forward with a new guess: "So it was all about the gel here? The Whitworths were *that* determined you not have her?"

"I know you love to gossip, Hilary, but do try to restrain yourself from creating fiction. I hadn't clapped eyes on Brooke until the Prince sent her my way. The hows and wherefores are quite simply none of your business."

While he might have said it with a smile, his tone had gotten sharp enough for the lady to huff and march away. He wasn't smiling now. That feral gleam had entered his golden eyes, which might be why no one else approached.

Brooke had time to glance about the room again and note that a quarter of the people present were middle-aged, mothers or fathers escorting their daughters. Nearly half were the young people having their first or second Season, there to find love or at least a good match. It was a marriage mart, as Alfreda had sneeringly called it, but where else in the country could so many young people be gathered in one place to meet? Arranged opportunity was what it was, that had become tradition, and Brooke would have been included in their number if not for . . . She thrust that thought aside.

At least she was certain she'd be the only Whitworth here tonight. Robert had been forbidden to bring his debauchery to parties that included debutantes, the only decent thing their father had ever done, in Brooke's opinion. She hadn't overheard that confrontation, but some of the servants had, and she'd caught a few of their whispers about it: "Cost a bleedin' fortune to keep that scandal under wraps." "He dipped into the wrong virgin, he did." "Can't even attend those parties now. How's he supposed to find himself a bride, eh?"

But that was last year before the duels. Did Harriet know about the tragic incident involving Eloise Wolfe or the others? Probably not. After all, she still doted on that worthless son of hers. So did Thomas. He never stayed angry at his son for long, though when he did put his foot down, it stayed down.

Still perusing the crowd, she mentioned, "Now there's a group of ladies your age, and not an innocent in the gaggle. And what about her?"

He followed her gaze and looked as if he was about to laugh. "You'll have to do better than that if you want to convince me that you're serious."

He'd never exactly said that he agreed to the bargain. *We shall see* was all he'd said. So he could just be amusing himself at her expense—or

338

he didn't think she was serious. Suggesting a young woman who was quite plain-looking would definitely make him think she wasn't. So she stomped down all regrets and nodded to a pretty woman who might be a few years older than him, but she didn't think that would matter. "Her?"

"Maybe."

She gritted her teeth and closed her fists on her nails. "You should ask her to dance."

"I will need to find you a guard dog first."

"We left the dogs at home."

She was jesting, so she was a little surprised when he asked curiously, "You consider Rothdale your home?"

She was even more surprised that she did. "Yes, actually. Isn't it going to be?"

He didn't answer, said instead, "You might be thrusting mistresses on me, but I'm not thrusting lovers on you. And I've spotted the perfect guard dog for you, who will fend off all comers."

He started to lead her through the crowd. "You're going to dance with her?"

He glanced down at Brooke. That was amusement in his eyes! "Didn't you just tell me to?"

"Yes, but—"

"I can at least see if she's willing."

"You can determine that from one meeting?"

"Certainly."

Her eyes snapped together and then flared wide when he stopped in front of the supposed "guard dog" he'd mentioned. Oh, good God, not her mother!

"We met years ago, Lady Whitworth, so you might not remember. Dominic Wolfe." He gave the slightest bow. "See that your daughter dances with no one else while I am entertained else-where—at her insistence."

Blushing furiously now, Brooke watched him walk across the ballroom in the direction of the very lady she had pointed out to him, the too pretty one.

"Not a wolf after all," Harriet said. "Or at least, quite a splendid beast. I can't believe we have something to be grateful to Robert for."

"Mother, *what* are you doing here?"

❧ Chapter Forty-Seven ❧

As Dominic walked across the ballroom, he realized it might not have been a good idea to leave Brooke with another Whitworth, especially her mother. Brooke's parents had had specific plans for their daughter, a Season in London and probably a handpicked husband. He wouldn't be surprised if Harriet was the one who had pushed Robert into goading him the other day. The whole family would have wanted him to reject Brooke, but when he didn't, mother and son might still be plotting to that end.

Although his own mother was trying to make the best of a bad situation, he knew she still grieved deeply for Ella and would be reminded of her loss whenever she saw Brooke. These misgivings continued to plague him.

"Your bride-to-be doesn't look very happy talking to that woman," Archer remarked casually as he fell into step beside Dominic.

Dominic stopped to glance back at Brooke. "That's her mother. She said she didn't like her family, but then she's said a lot of things and I haven't a clue what's true or not."

"Now that's a nasty statement, old chap. You won't make progress if you're going to doubt everything she says."

What progress? Dominic wondered. "She baldly admitted she's used to hiding her feelings. At least she was on the up-and-up about that."

"Or perhaps that was a lie?" But Archer suddenly laughed. "And here I thought I envied you when I clapped eyes on her tonight. You said she was pretty. That simply doesn't describe your fiancée. Introduce us. I wouldn't give a bloody damn if she's hiding things."

"No."

Still staring transfixed at Brooke, Archer offered, "I'd be happy to whisk her away for you, out of the country. You can say she was kidnapped. It would be true. No blame on you, then, eh?"

"Just the loss of everything I own."

"So I could wait until after the nuptials before I rid you of this thorn."

"She's not a thorn," Dominic mumbled. "But *you're* becoming a nuisance. Do go away."

Dominic walked away first, knowing his friend wouldn't. Since Dominic had met Brooke, she'd filled his mind in every way. He'd even come close a few times to thinking he could do more than tolerate her. That night they'd spent together, she'd ignited his passions and satisfied him so completely. It would be so easy to love her if . . . *If!* There were far too many of those. Yet here he was approaching another woman with Brooke's blessing to be unfaithful to her because of that silly bargain of hers that he didn't understand.

He'd had every intention of embracing her bargain if it was what she wanted, but he was just realizing belatedly that he didn't want to. Just then his path was blocked, and everything he'd felt the day Brooke arrived at his home returned to him.

The Prince Regent with three of his sycophants just behind him stood in Dominic's way. And looking quite the dandy as usual in his chartreuse satin tailcoat with extrawide lapels and fashionable white trousers. The long length of the pants had apparently been invented by the Regent's good friend Beau Brummell, so of course he would wear them. Most of London already copied

Brummell's unique style. Even the Regent's lacy cravat was likely Brummell's doing, fluffed up exceedingly high, probably to conceal the Prince's double chins. But the man was nearing fifty. No fancy clothes could hide the dissipation of his life.

Dominic had known the royal might put in an appearance tonight; he'd just hoped he wouldn't. And Prinny, as his friends called him, had obviously already been in the ballroom before Dominic and Brooke got there; the commotion his arrival always caused would have alerted Dominic otherwise. Which was too bad. Prior warning would have given him time to mask what he was currently feeling.

"I wasn't told she was a beauty," the Prince remarked, looking beyond Dominic at Brooke, before smiling at Dominic. "You must be pleased."

"You would not care to know what I am, Highness."

Dominic said it so coldly, the Regent looked a little nervous.

"Yes, well, at least you are complying. Carry on."

The small group continued on their way along the edges of the dance floor. Dominic didn't move a muscle, fighting off emotions that could get him hung. To think his life could be changed utterly just because that man couldn't live on the fortune Parliament already granted him; he had to spend that *and* mount up debts that would have long since landed any other man in debtors' prison.

Dominic glanced back to make sure the Regent wasn't heading toward Brooke. He wasn't. One look at her helped to rid Dominic of his rage. Ironic. She usually caused it, but not tonight.

He continued on toward Charlotte Ward. He'd heard that she'd remarried not long after their brief one-week affair; he just couldn't remember what her new husband's name was. Blond with light blue eyes, she was exceptionally pretty, yet she hadn't held his interest for long. Too mercurial in her moods, too clinging. Or had that been Melissa? Too many mistresses; he supposed he might be getting a little jaded.

"Charlotte." He took her hand to kiss the back of her fingers politely before he waved a hand at the dance floor. "Shall we?"

She gave him a brilliant smile and accepted his arm. But they'd only twirled twice before she looked at him with her brow raised to say sulkily, "It took you long enough to come back to me after Priscilla. I can't imagine what you saw in her. By the by, she's here."

"I hadn't noticed." He didn't try to spot Priscilla Highley in the crowd when it was all he could do to not glance toward Brooke again to see if she was watching this performance.

Charlotte huffed. "Don't pretend you have eyes

only for me with a fiancée that looks like yours does."

It was true, no one there could hold a candle to Brooke Whitworth. If he was going to plow through old mistresses and find new ones, it was going to be hard to explain why he might prefer anyone to his own wife.

For the moment he evaded with "It's complicated, arranged, you might say."

That made her laugh. "So you're getting your final oats sowed before the wedding?"

Charlotte would apparently be willing to start up their affair again even though she had remarried. But he found himself choosing a different course. "Actually, I need a favor if you wouldn't mind— and remember we parted amicably."

She gave a good semblance of a pout. "I pretended. I was crushed."

He managed not to laugh. "Is that why you married again so quickly?"

She grinned even as she waved a dismissive hand. "He's incredibly rich. How could I not?"

"That you're no longer a widow makes you off-limits, I'm afraid."

"*Must* you have scruples?" She sighed. "Fine, what favor can I do for you, darling?"

"Slap me and look angry when you do it." She laughed instead, forcing him to add, "Please."

"You're serious? But whatever for?"

"As I said, complicated. But consider, if you

really were crushed when we parted, then it's long overdue, isn't it?"

"When you put it *that* way . . ." She cracked her palm across his cheek.

❧ Chapter Forty-Eight ❧

Brooke never did get an answer from her mother. Two of Harriet's London friends had converged on them immediately for introductions and some sly prying questions. Brooke didn't know them, didn't want to know them, and certainly wasn't going to explain how she came to be engaged to a man who'd tried to kill her brother. Harriet evaded explaining as well, though she managed not tobe rude about it.

Then Dominic was back and leading Brooke back to the dance floor to finish the set that his previous partner had just walked off on. Brooke was bristling. She blamed it on her mother's being there, not because Dominic had just propositioned that woman.

"I hope that hurt," Brooke said without looking at him. It would be a fulminating glare if she did, and she didn't want him to know she was bristling.

"Why?"

She groaned to herself, but she had a ready answer for him. "Because you failed, of course."

"I expected you to be deep in conversation with your mother," he replied nonchalantly. "So you weren't supposed to see that."

"Everyone probably saw it, or at least heard it. And my mother has too many friends here, so she barely said a word to me and certainly didn't distract me from watching your progress—or lack thereof. At least she didn't see it. Just what did you say to that woman to make her rebuff you so physically and so quickly?"

He shrugged offhandedly. "The obvious. It either works or it doesn't."

"How often do you get slapped?"

"Not often."

She huffed. "I'm not going to get any new thoroughbreds this way. Maybe you should use a little more finesse, you know, dance with them a few times, get to know them a little if you don't already know them."

"I was merely humoring you, since she was your choice. Charlotte and I actually have history. In fact, a number of my ex-acquaintances are here tonight. But, discounting them, there are still a few women tonight that I haven't met yet—if you want me to continue."

She didn't, but she couldn't say that, so she forced herself to nod. He seemed not to care either way, yet the "bargain" had abruptly turned his nasty new suspicions to amusement the other night. It continued to distract him, too. And she'd rather have the amusement even if it was at her expense, at least until after the wedding. She definitely didn't want him cold and forbidding on that night. She was still holding out hope that the nuptials would change *something* between them. Think of the horses, she advised herself, think just of the horses.

He left her with her mother again before he went off to find another lady to dance with. Brooke stared daggers at his back as he walked away before she started kicking herself mentally. He'd just given her an out from that absurd bargain and she hadn't taken it. What was wrong with her?! But eventually he would be unfaithful to her anyway, wouldn't he? Because she'd failed to make him love her. So she had to stop getting so, so—furious about it.

"We can have a word now," Harriet said. "Shall we step out onto the terrace for some privacy?"

Brooke took her eyes off Dominic to see that Harriet's friends had moved on. Brooke followed her outside before she accused, "I thought you didn't know Dominic Wolfe a'tall."

"I don't recall meeting him years ago, but a stripling is nothing like a man. If I had known him, I wouldn't have been so distraught—"

Brooke interrupted coldly, "Don't pretend to feelings you don't have, Mother. And what are you doing here?"

Harriet winced before she sighed. "Your father had business in town. I expect we'll only be here for a few days. Thomas suggested I come here tonight to find out how the *ton* was reacting to the news of the forced marriage. He wanted me to assure people that we are happy to comply with the Regent's request to give you to Dominic in marriage. Why aren't you married yet?"

"Dominic was badly wounded in that last duel and got a delay because of it."

Harriet glanced toward the ballroom. "He heals quickly, doesn't he? Your handiwork?"

Brooke raised a curious brow. "You know I'm familiar with healing herbs?"

"Of course I do. You may not have confided much to me over the years, but your maid did."

"Then why did you never ask us to ease your husband's pain?"

Harriet snorted. "Because your father doesn't deserve anything from you—or do you love him just because he's your father?"

"Are you joking? He was just a man who was occasionally present in the house I lived in—one I avoided. What reason was I ever given to love him?"

"Exactly."

"But you did despite his callous indifference."

Brooke felt comfortable making that condemnation. The one she couldn't utter was to include Harriet in her previous remark no matter if it was true, that she'd never been given a reason to love Harriet, either.

But Harriet surprised her. "What makes you think I ever loved him? I admit I had hoped to when I was still young, but it never happened. I adapted instead, learned to tiptoe around his rages, and made him think I was just as callous as he is. It's unfortunate that there are people like Thomas in the world, incapable of love, incapable of being loved. I hope Lord Wolfe isn't like that."

No, Dominic was nothing like that. At least he loved his family, had been willing to risk his life to avenge the sister he'd loved, had recklessly raced to London he was so worried about the mother he loved. If he could ever feel even half that for her, she could probably be happy.

But all she said to Harriet was "He's a good man who cares about friends and family."

Harriet smiled. "When is the wedding to be, then?"

"Sunday."

"May I come?"

Brooke shook her head. "That's not a good idea. He and his mother both despise us Whitworths. You can thank your son for that."

Harriet frowned. "So you are hated?"

"How could I not be when my brother got his sister pregnant. Robert laughed, you know, when she told him. Laughed! It's tragic that she killed herself because of it."

"That's . . . horrible."

Harriet did look aggrieved, causing Brooke to ask, "You really didn't know?"

"No, I didn't. I don't think your father knew either. There was another young lady last year we did find out about when her father came to demand Robert marry her. But Thomas didn't want that alliance and managed to buy their silence instead, before it became a scandal. I believe she was convinced to go abroad to have the child. I had hoped they would give it to us, but Thomas didn't want it. It's appalling that it will be given to strangers instead and I will never get to know my grandchild."

Brooke was speechless. It was like listening to someone she'd never before met. Regret for a bastard her precious Robert had obviously refused to take responsibility for? How many more bastards were there that her brother had carelessly created before Thomas had put his foot down? Actually, Thomas had only forbidden Robert from seducing any more innocent debutantes. He'd placed no restrictions on the rest of the women in England.

But then Harriet added angrily, "If your father has to deal with another of Robert's scandals, there will be consequences."

Brooke blinked, wasn't even sure what Harriet meant until she realized she was referring to what Brooke had just said about Dominic's sister. "What consequences?"

"Thomas promised to disown him."

Brooke almost laughed, but still said sarcastically, "Really? The precious heir?"

"You don't know how angry Thomas was. I'm quite sure he meant it."

"And how will that matter once Thomas is dead?" Brooke demanded. "He's old. He doesn't have that many more years before him. And then there will be nothing to curb Robert's nefarious tendencies."

"Nefarious? He's not a villain. Prone to the same rages your father has and a bit of a rake apparently, but—"

Eyes flared wide, Brooke asked incredulously, "Do you even *know* your son?"

Harriet looked back toward the ballroom and blatantly evaded the question. "This was to be our triumph tonight. Have you even noticed that the men here can barely take their eyes off of you?"

Brooke hadn't noticed that, but her eyes had passed over the room when she'd been trying not to watch what Dominic was doing. She noted quite a few handsome men were present. She'd even guessed she might have fallen in love tonight—if she had come here with her mother. One of them even winked at her when her eyes had passed over him. It hadn't made her blush. It probably should have, but it had simply had no effect on her.

Her mother wasn't done. "Yet because you are

affianced to the wolf, they won't approach. But he can't keep his eyes off of you, either, even though he's dancing with someone else. Why is he doing that?"

Brooke was able to spot Dominic through the open terrace doors. He was dancing with a third lady, yet another pretty one, too. "Courtesy," she lied with gritted teeth, still staring at him. "They are friends of his mother's."

With raised brow, Harriet turned back to her to ask pointedly, "A bit young to be Anna Wolfe's friends, aren't they? You don't mind?"

Brooke barely heard the question. Dominic just got slapped again! She rolled her eyes and looked at her mother to quip without the smirk she was feeling, "Not yet."

Harriet sighed. "Robert lied to us. I didn't realize such a horrific tragedy was the reason for the duels. I didn't think Lord Wolfe would hate you."

That was a strong word. It had applied, but Brooke wasn't sure if it still did, and said, "I'm tolerated, or I was, until Robert showed up and tried to get me to poison him—and made sure to mention to Dominic that I would."

Harriet actually blanched. "You wouldn't."

"If that's a question, then you don't know me any more than you—"

"It wasn't."

"But that *is* your son, Mother. Vicious, capable

of murder, lacking any moral fiber or scruples. There's not a good thing that can be said about him except that he is handsome. A pity, that. He should look as wicked as he truly is. And not another word about that toad."

"Then shall we discuss how jealous you are?"

"Of Robert?" Brooke snorted. "Don't be absurd."

"I meant of your husband-to-be." When Brooke looked away, Harriet added, "No? Well, I need a drink. I suspect you do, too. Shall we?"

Why not? Brooke followed Harriet back inside the ballroom to one of the refreshment tables set about the edges of the room and was amazed when her mother drained a glass of champagne down to the last drop. So she didn't hesitate to do the same thing. Jealous? Was that why she couldn't stop bristling?

❦ Chapter Forty-Nine ❧

"That last one is possible."

Brooke swung around to see that Dominic had finally remembered that he had a fiancée in the room. And how businesslike he sounded. Considering what she'd witnessed, again, it took every bit of will she had not to slap him herself.

Instead she had to whisper because her mother was only two feet away. "But she slapped you, too."

"That was so—" He had started to whisper back but shook his head and led her out onto the dance floor instead so he wouldn't have to. "That was so her husband wouldn't get suspicious."

Brooke's eyes flared wide. "D'you like dueling so much? Shame on you."

"Really? When this was your idea?" he shot back.

"Not with married women it wasn't."

"You didn't specify."

"Now I am. No dalliances that come with husbands who will want to kill you."

"Then the pickings are slim here. I see only one widow and I've already burned that bridge."

She saw whom he'd just nodded at, Priscilla Highley, looking exceptionally beautiful tonight in her emerald ball gown. So he hadn't dallied with Priscilla that day she'd come to visit? Brooke wished she'd known that before she let her anger get her lost and drenched that day. Then again, if she'd known, she wouldn't have found Storm. . . .

"I miss our animals," she said suddenly.

"Do you?"

"And I worry that Storm is going to think I abandoned her and return to the wilds."

"Then we'll find her again."

What a nice thing for him to say! It didn't quite end her bristling, but almost.

"Are we going to stay in London after your mother is fully recovered?"

355

"No."

Brooke decided to be a little fanciful. "D'you think we would have met here, this very night, if none of this had happened and I'd come for my promised Season?"

"Probably not."

"But if we did both attend, would you have sought me out?"

"A virginal debutante? My name isn't Robert."

She tsked. "Just imagine it for a moment and tell me you wouldn't have at least asked me for one dance."

"The line would have been too long."

She laughed. "Then I guess destiny has nothing to do with us after all, and if that's so, something will probably prevent us from marrying on Sunday."

"Maybe one dance."

Her eyes flared. That was quite a concession, allowing that it was destiny that had brought them together—one way or another, that they were "meant to be."

But he spoiled the thought by adding, "But destiny isn't always good. In our case, it could be we are destined to hate each other to the grave."

She rolled her eyes. "Such a pessimist you are."

"How can I not be when you are dooming this marriage from the start?"

"How can you say that when I have been nothing but accommodating?"

"Of course you are, even pointing out which bed I should sleep in. Shall I invite my mistress to the ceremony?"

That got a blush out of her and stirred the bristles again. "If you do, I'll invite my mother and we can all glare at each other."

He smiled. "Then perhaps you want to be both?"

She almost asked both what. But she knew. "Wife *and* mistress? I think you're missing the point."

"No. Maybe if you act like a mistress instead of a stiff dutiful wife, I will be able to tolerate you."

"You already tolerate me," she gritted.

"Do I? What makes you think so?"

She formed a tight smile. "You haven't wrung my neck yet."

He chuckled. "Give me time." She was about to kick him for that rejoinder when he added huskily, "You might want to try it out on the way home tonight, being both wife and lover."

Brooke was shocked by what he was suggesting, but the thought of kissing him again and maybe doing more in the coach was incredibly exciting. But she blushed just thinking about it.

A tall man tapped on Dominic's shoulder to stop them. "I'm glad to see your humor is back, so this is a perfect time for me to insist on one dance with your lady. Give over, old boy. I promise not to abduct her tonight."

"Go away, pest," Dominic replied.

"Not this time." The pest grinned. "Or do you really want all the cupids in town rejoicing and spreading the word about the greatest love of the century, et cetera, et cetera. It really will be a scandal tomorrow if you continue to monopolize her the entire night. And I'm not going away, so you might as well be gracious about it and let me save you from scandal this time."

Dominic tsked and led Brooke and the pest to the edge of the dance floor, telling Brooke, "Archer is a friend, though tonight I'm beginning to wonder," and asking Archer, "Why isn't Benton keeping you occupied tonight—elsewhere?"

"Because he's already hied himself back to the duke's daughter. The poor sod must truly be in love!"

"You're lucky this dance is almost over, and don't even think of not returning her to me the moment it is," Dominic warned.

Archer grinned again. "Absolutely!" He twirled Brooke back out onto the dance floor.

"Was any of that true, about a scandal?" she asked her new partner.

"Course not. You are affianced, after all, so not required to dance with anyone but him. Now if he had refused to hand you over just now when I obviously wasn't taking no for an answer, that on-dit might have made the rounds." Then with a nod of his head to simulate a bow, he added,

"Archer Hamilton, third son, not that it matters since I got stuck with a title anyway."

He was grinning again. Quite an unusual fellow. Taller than Dominic, maybe even as handsome. Golden hair in the current flyaway fashion, deep emerald eyes, an outdoorsman to go by the tan that was nearly darker than his hair. She would have had a wonderful crop of young lords to choose from this year—if she'd got her Season.

"I assume you know Dominic well to have pulled the stunt you just did?"

"Too well, I daresay I'm his closest friend . . . well, at least he's my closest. I am delighted to meet you, Lady Brooke. As for the rest of my credentials; boringly rich, wonderful family, delightful mistress. All I lack is—you."

"I beg your pardon? I could have sworn you just said you were his friend."

"But friendship can't stand in the way of fate. Elope with me. I promise to love you for eternity. And Prinny can't very well drop the ax if a third party absconds with you."

"So you know about the Regent's ultimatum?"

"Certainly. Dom is my best friend, after all."

She snorted. "Or you're his worst enemy to even suggest it. But the Prince must love you. Quite a strategy that will let him steal from the coffers of both families instead of just one."

"You don't think it would work?"

"I think the Regent put you up to this." She

noticed the laughing eyes too late and rolled hers. "You're being facetious, aren't you? I'm not amused."

He sighed. "I've been hearing that a lot lately. Very well, what can I do to help you prod the beast? I daresay he only needs a little nudge."

"You're on his side. Don't pretend otherwise."

"Exactly!" Archer exclaimed. "D'you think I don't want him to be happy?"

"There's no such thing in his household."

"But you're going to change that, aren't you?"

It was a good thing the rest of that dance had been short. Music ended, she made her way back to Dominic's side without Lord Hamilton's assistance. She didn't have an answer for Dominic's friend, any more than she did for his mother.

Dominic hadn't rejoined her mother, was waiting alone on the sidelines for her. When she reached him, he asked, "Did Archer behave himself?"

"He was . . . let's say obnoxiously whimsical. Is he always like that?"

"Only when the mood strikes him. Have you had enough dancing for one night?"

"Indeed."

"Then say good-bye to your mother and we'll go."

"She wouldn't give me the same courtesy, so we can skip that. I doubt she would have approached me at all tonight if you didn't force me on her. And Lady Hewitt is near the entrance. We need to at least have a word with her or your mother will surely hear about it."

"Worried about such a minor faux pas?"

"Not me, but your mother might not think it so minor."

He glanced down at her as he led her to Lady Hewitt. "Are you really concerned for her?"

"Don't sound so surprised. Disturbances of any kind might slow her recovery."

"You didn't exactly take that into account when I was recovering."

She laughed. "And where was there a choice in that?"

That somewhat normal conversation didn't continue after they thanked the hostess and walked to their coach a little way up the street. She was still in a much better mood and was fully aware it was because he hadn't found a mistress tonight. But anticipation was building, too. She tried to tamp it down with the thought that he might have been teasing about kissing her on the way home. But she wanted it to happen. Dare she instigate it? No, she only had a couple more days to wait until she could be that bold.

"Did you enjoy your first ball?" Dominic asked as soon as he sat down next to her in the coach.

"Yes." She sighed wistfully. "Except I thought it might be a little more romantic with a few stolen kisses."

He raised a brow at her. "We kissed on the dance floor."

"That was hardly stolen, and besides, that was just to assure the Regent and other people that we were complying with the marriage 'suggestion.' "

"Ah, I understand. You were expecting something more like this . . . ?"

He leaned toward her until their lips met, softly, teasingly. She was still thrilled and would have said yes, except he stopped too soon. She was about to pull him back to her when she was drawn instead onto his lap.

"Or more like this?" he said huskily.

Yes! He was kissing her deeply now, and the passion flared so fast it was already out of control. She slipped her arm around his neck and moaned deeply in her throat when the top of her gown scraped electrifyingly over her sensitive nipples as he lowered the material. And again as his warm hand fondled her exposed breast. She wanted to feel his bare skin, too, but he wasn't accommodating her. Because it wasn't a long ride? That stirred up a bit of desperation in her. She didn't want this to end! But then his hand slipped beneath her gown and slid up her leg until it reached that most sensitive of places and . . .

"I'll buy you as many horses as you want. You don't need to push me to sleep with other women to get them."

It took a moment for her to grasp what he'd just

said, but then she smiled. "So you can tolerate me now?"

"You're going to be my wife."

Such a wonderful statement. Her smile widened. But he was straightening her clothes, making her realize they were home. He helped her out of the coach and walked her to the door, but then he turned to leave!

"Where are you going?" she asked with a frown.

He paused. "Not where you think. Sweet dreams, Babble."

Her dreams were likely to be more than sweet now. They were likely to be a conclusion of what they'd been doing in that coach! She was still smiling to herself as she entered the house. Just two more days . . .

❧ Chapter Fifty ❧

Brooke overslept the next morning. She wasn't even surprised after all that dancing and even drinking champagne for the first time with her mother. But she felt wonderful, as if a weight had been lifted from her. That silly bargain was over, Dominic hadn't slept with other women, and he'd finally assured her that they *would* be married.

Alfreda's bringing in a tray of food had awakened Brooke, and when the maid saw the smile on her lips, she said, "So you enjoyed your-self last night, did you?"

"It was a magical night." At least the ending was! "I think Dominic and I are going to be more'n just friends now."

Alfreda chuckled. "See? You worried over nothing. At least I don't need to look for that herb now."

Brooke laughed at the jest. "No, I definitely don't want him rendered—incapable!"

At the knock at the door Alfreda turned. "That will be your bathwater arriving, so come and eat. I was told to dress you for your wedding today and there's barely two hours to spare now."

Brooke's eyes flared. "You could have said that sooner! Did I sleep through one whole day?"

"No. And, no, I don't know why you're getting married sooner than you thought. You'll have to ask your wolf."

Brooke smiled to herself, remembering what had happened last night on the way home from the ball. That pretty much explained to her why she was getting married today. Dominic must not want to wait any longer for their wedding night either!

The next two hours were hectic, but Brooke couldn't have been more thrilled. She even had a wedding gown to wear, one her mother had insisted on having made for her at the same time as the rest of her new wardrobe. An elaborate white muslin with a slight train and a tucker dotted with seed pearls. The attached long cloak was bordered in puffy silk flowers.

Harriet had expected her to be married soon after her Season, or at least engaged to be, which is why she had the gown for this wedding. Such high hopes her mother had had. She probably should have invited Harriet despite the animosity she would receive in this house. As happy as Brooke was now, she might have, if the wedding were still set for Sunday. Ah, well. Even if the Wolfes had proven gracious about it, Brooke might not have been, so it was as well that it was too late now.

Dominic came to fetch her, looking every inch a lord of the realm despite the feral gleam in his eyes. Anticipation on his part? Imagining their wedding night—or day? The gleam was so bright he might take her straight to bed after the ceremony! But it was time to leave, or so she thought. He led her down the corridor instead to his mother's room. But Brooke knew Anna wasn't well enough yet to go to a church.

Brooke slowed down, causing him to pause. "You're finally getting cold feet? You should have said so before I sent for the priest."

"You sent for one? Then we're not going to be married in a church?"

"My mother wants to bear witness. I saw no reason not to oblige her."

Married at a bedside? After seeing how grand St. George's church was on her brief tour of London, she was a bit disappointed that she wouldn't be married there. But she hid it and merely said lightly, "If I'd known we were wedding at home, I would have worn something less fancy."

"Nonsense. It's still your wedding. And you look exceptionally lovely."

She smiled. She was marrying this man today. Did it really matter where? And maybe he would tell her how much he wanted her if she mentioned the apparent rush?

"Why is this happening today instead of Sunday?"

"Because the Regent was in attendance last night and is aware that I'm no longer suffering from my wound. It's possible he might visit today or send his man to claim we have forfeited by not marrying as soon as I was recovered. But whether he does or not, I see no reason to wait any longer. Do you?"

She certainly didn't, but that certainly wasn't what she'd just hoped to hear. She shook her head, giving him another smile as he led her the rest of the way to Anna's room. But when he opened the door and waited for her to precede him, she didn't move another step.

"What's *she* doing here?" she whispered.

"I sent a note this morning."

"Without asking me?"

"I thought you would be pleased."

"I thought you wouldn't want her in your house."

Sitting at her bedside and even laughing at something Anna had just said was Brooke's mother. It appeared Dominic had done exactly what she'd thought of doing herself this morning, sending off a belated note. And Anna was smiling. So Brooke had been wrong that there would be animosity with more Whitworths present at the wedding. Both Wolfes were going to be more than gracious about it.

Dominic leaned close to whisper, "Last chance, Babble."

Was he *really* going to keep calling her that? And he could say that with her mother there? She glanced at him and saw the amusement on his face. He'd just teased her about the worst possible subject. If he could do that, it must mean he was no longer opposed to their joining. But then an old doubt resurfaced: they were down to the last few minutes, so he had no choice.

Thank God her father wasn't there, too, to bear witness. Robert would have gotten thrashed at the door. Too bad he didn't try to get in. She would have liked to see that. A splendid wedding gift for her . . . even her thoughts were babbling.

Harriet came forward to take her hand. "I'm not going to say you look beautiful because that wouldn't do you justice, precious. You do look magnificent in that gown, though."

Harriet was grinning. Teasing from both camps today? Brooke was feeling outnumbered.

"Father wasn't invited?" she asked as soon as Dominic continued forward to greet his mother.

"Oh, he was," Harriet replied. "I think he actually wanted to come, at least to meet the groom. But this trip to London undid him. He hasn't left his bed since we got here. But speaking of bedridden, Anna told me she's made a remarkable recovery from her illness, thanks to you."

Brooke raised a brow. "You were already acquainted with Anna?"

"How could I not be when we both socialize in this town? I admit, though, that I was expecting the animosity you mentioned. I hadn't seen her since the duels. Does she know why her son wanted to kill mine?"

"Yes."

"Then she's being duplicitous, treating me as if nothing has happened?"

"I don't think so. She's tasked me with making her son happy. I believe that's more important to her now than any grudge."

"A wise choice, making the best of it. But is that what you want?"

For him to be happy? Brooke had thought of it as a goal, that it would bring about peace between them. But she realized now she did want him to be happy. Oh, good grief, she was in love, wasn't she? Caught in her own snare!

As to her mother's question, she said, "Yes, it would be nice if we could both be happy."

"That's not what I meant."

"I'm sorry I'm late," the priest said behind them, and ushered them both farther into the room so they could get the ceremony started.

❧ Chapter Fifty-One ❧

"Tell me I'm not too late!"

The door's bursting open was loud enough, but the crestfallen expression on the intruding lady's face did more to startle Brooke, shut up the priest, and cause a few gasps. At first, Brooke thought she was one of Dominic's former mistresses who'd come to object to the wedding. But then she recognized the exceptionally handsome woman from her encounter with her the other day in the Wolfes' entrance hall.

"No," Anna answered from the bed. "You're just in time, Eleanor—if you bring good news?"

Eleanor laughed in relief. "The best, m'dear."

"Duchess," Dominic said with a formal bow. "Always good to see you, but Mother didn't mention you wanted to attend my wedding."

"Because I don't, dear boy. I have instead made sure you don't have one. You can thank me in the usual fashion, a dozen roses, a bauble, and, oh, I love candy."

The woman seemed absolutely delighted to have said all that, either unaware of the shock she'd just delivered or pleased because of it. Theatrics? Maybe the duchess was an actress?

But Dominic's frown said he wasn't pleased by her cryptic statements. "Explain, if you would?"

"Let me," Anna said. "I might have misled you, Dom, to think I was acquiescent to this match—"

"Might have?" he cut in.

Anna winced a little. "It was good of Lady Brooke to aid in my recovery, but I'm sorry, I still can't bear the thought of my grandchildren having Whitworth blood. So I asked my dearest friend to intervene and offer the Prince a different alternative."

Eleanor rolled her eyes with a chuckle before saying to Dominic, "George owes me money, so he wouldn't dare not receive me this morning or give careful thought to our suggestion. And I sweetened the incentive by mentioning that you and the Whitworth girl like each other and will indeed marry, so he will get nothing, no money, no property. But if he releases you from this forced marriage prior to its happening, then you'll donate your coal mines to his coffers and sign a pledge not to engage in any more duels with Robert Whitworth. He agreed on the spot, of course. I knew he would."

Brooke was too stunned to speak, too stunned to think!

But Dominic wasn't and turned his eyes back to his mother. "I thought you understood you were no longer to make decisions for me. Why didn't you tell me about this plan before you set it in motion?"

"I didn't want to get your hopes up if it didn't work, but it did, and you can't deny you aren't relieved to be done with that despicable family."

"Regardless—"

"That's quite enough insults," Harriet cut in sharply. "Thank you, Anna, for giving me back my daughter. She deserves much better than you lot."

In high dudgeon, Harriet pulled Brooke out of there. No one stopped her, certainly not Dominic. He was free. He might be annoyed with his mother for not consulting him, but he had to be rejoicing nonetheless. Or he would have stopped her, would have told the duchess no thank you, would have married Brooke today despite his mother's interference . . .

Brooke was in shock or she would have said something to him—congratulations, good-bye, something. She didn't hate him, and they were well acquainted after spending two weeks together. But tears were just under the surface. A single word would have spilled them and she didn't want to leave his house that way.

"I will send the coach back for your things. We're not staying here another moment," Harriet said on the way downstairs.

Gabriel was in the lower hall and smiled at Brooke, "Ah, the beautiful bride. But Lady Wolfe, why are you leaving?"

Before Brooke could reply, Harriet said angrily, "Don't insult us by calling her that! She's still a Whitworth." Then Harriet snapped at the butler as he opened the front door for them, "Tell my daughter's maid to pack everything of hers and be ready to depart within the hour. Make that fifteen minutes, so send some servants up to help her."

Brooke still didn't say a word. She ought to mention the mare Dominic had bought for her. Alfreda didn't know about it, but another time would do. She needed to cry, to wash away what she was feeling, but not in front of Harriet. Her mother wouldn't be the least bit sympathetic and was making a lot of scathing remarks about Anna Wolfe and Wolfes in general. She did seem angry about what had just happened.

Brooke was taken to another town house not far away, and Harriet did dispatch the coach right back to the Wolfe house before taking Brooke inside and upstairs. Her parents' London house, she assumed. She wasn't interested.

But passing an open doorway she heard, "Eh, what are *you* doing here, gel?"

Brooke paused to see her father propped up in his bed frowning at her, but her mother shooed her on. "Two doors down on the left is yours. I will join you in a moment." Then Harriet said cheer-fully as she entered Thomas's room, "Our Brooke is going to have her Season after all!"

Brooke continued on to the room Harriet had pointed out and closed the door behind her. The tears came so fast she could only take a few steps before her vision blurred from them. She didn't know how long she stood there, but the outpouring wasn't washing away this grief.

When she felt loving arms around her, she turned toward them gratefully, sobbing, "Freda, he didn't want   "

"Oh, my precious. He was supposed to fall deeply in love, not you."

Brooke stepped back abruptly, shocked yet again. Comfort from her mother? She quickly wiped her eyes and turned aside. "I'll be fine. I just wasn't expecting to not be married today, and to listen to so much crowing . . . was one too many surprises."

"You don't have to explain. You thought he would be your husband, so you let yourself love him. Your jealousy last night suggested you did. But I was hopeful that you two could get past that and be happy."

"I don't understand. You *want* me to be happy?"

"Of course I do," Harriet said softly.

Brooke didn't believe it and got angry at herself that she wished she could. "Don't pretend you loved me at this late date, Mother. Don't you dare!"

"I warned you she felt neglected and unloved," Alfreda said angrily as she entered the room.

Servants began following Alfreda in with Brooke's trunks and were directed where to set them. Harriet's expression had turned impatient over the interruption. Brooke turned away, trying to think of anything other than what had happened today.

But Alfreda wasn't done scolding. "She went too many years without love, Harry. The times you paid attention to her when she was growing up and Robert and Thomas were away were too few and far between. She doesn't remember how much love you gave her when she was a baby. She remembers none of it!"

Hearing her mother called Harry turned Brooke back around in surprise. She'd never heard Alfreda talk to her mother like this, as if the two of them had been best friends or confidantes for years. Alfreda looked as angry as she sounded as she pushed the last servant out and closed the door on them.

But Harriet was now livid at the condemnation she was getting from a servant. "Go!" Harriet pointed stiffly at the door.

Alfreda crossed her arms instead and blocked that door. "I'm not going. I'm making sure she gets told this time." Then suddenly in a softer tone: "Our poppet is full grown, Harry. She doesn't need protecting anymore." Then more sternly: "And I'm releasing myself from my promise, so you tell her or I will."

"This is the worst possible timing, Freda," Harriet said in exasperation. "She's got a broken heart."

"She's had one of those for nigh fifteen—"

"Enough!" Brooke snapped. "Either tell me what you're arguing about or don't, but stop acting like I'm not standing here listening to every word."

The two older women only glared at each other for another moment before Harriet put an arm around Brooke's shoulders and led her to a long sofa. She hadn't noticed it or anything else about the room. But she sat down with her mother and waited, almost with bated breath. She had to fight again to keep the tears back, deeper ones, more familiar ones. . . .

Harriet took Brooke's hand and turned to face her. "I love you. I've always loved you. I honestly thought you knew it, at least sensed it—"

"I—"

Harriet put a finger to Brooke's lips. "Please don't refute it again until I've finished. Robert was jealous of you when you were born, too jealous. I don't know why he didn't grow out of it. I gave him just as much attention as I gave you, but he didn't like me giving you any. I didn't know what he was doing, sneaking into your room late at night. When Alfreda discovered your bruises, she told me. I tried to have Robert sent away, but your father wouldn't allow it, so I had to distance myself from you just to protect you. And he was always lurking around corners, that boy, watching, listening, almost as if he were trying to catch me in the lie. I hated that situation. You can't imagine how much it hurt for me to pretend I didn't care when I loved you so much."

"You could have explained that to me."

"When? While you were still a child? You were too impulsive and naturally demonstrative. I was afraid that if you hugged or kissed me when Robert was around, he would get even more vicious or cause some serious accident. I couldn't take that risk. But I was with you when they weren't around. Surely you remember that?"

"It was too late. All I remember is being rebuffed."

"Is it still too late?" Harriet had some tears in her own eyes.

Brooke was incredulous that she ended up comforting her mother that day. But all she'd ever needed to hear were those three simple words. It was amazing how quickly they could ease all that old pain.

She smiled and hugged her mother close. "It's never too late."

Much more was said, but none of it mattered now that Brooke understood her mother's past actions and behavior. Harriet's keeping her from dining with the family was to shield her from Thomas's harshness and his notice. Robert took the brunt of that harshness. Harriet's fighting so bitterly with Thomas that he even struck her occasionally, but when he slapped Brooke the one time she let her temper loose on him was when Harriet knew she had to convince him she was on his side in everything and come up with ways to keep Brooke away from him. Alfreda had reported to her every single day, every single thing that Brooke had done or learned. They had become good friends.

"I was so looking forward to this Season of yours and getting you away from Thomas for good, before he realized what a prize you are and started plotting for a marriage you would have liked even less. When we got the Regent's edict instead, I did hope you would be happy with Lord Wolfe. I thought surely he would be getting on his knees and thanking Prinny for giving you to him. I even laughed, imagining it. But it turns out he's a fool instead, preferring vengeance to his own happiness. So be it. We will find you someone wonderful so you won't need to give him another thought."

If only that were possible. Maybe in the next century. But Brooke could try.

"Oh, so *now* she deserts us," Harriet said as she got up and saw that Alfreda had quietly left. "Come, I'll help you unpack. I hope you like the room. I had it redecorated for you to use during your Season."

Harriet started opening the trunks and carrying piles of clothes to a prettily carved bureau. Brooke wondered if her mother had ever before unpacked a trunk in her life. But Brooke got up to help, even if it was absently. Too much had happened that day, finding out about her mother's ulterior motives, finding out how much Anna Wolfe hated her, finding out how relieved Dominic was to be rid of her, even if it did cost him some coal mines. He'd probably thanked Anna as soon as Brooke was out of the room for doing what he hadn't thought to do, bribing the Regent to go away. Why hadn't he thought of that himself? Or did he?

"What are you doing with this old thing?" Harriet said as she opened a fan with a flip of her wrist, then grinned when a paper fell out of one of the panels. "Hiding love letters?"

Brooke was surprised. "No, that's not even mine. It belonged to Eloise Wolfe. I should return it to Dominic."

"That poor girl." Harriet picked up the folded paper and set it with the fan on Brooke's new vanity. "I need to tell Thomas what you said about Robert last night. I might love my son because

378

he is my son, but I don't like what he's become and if he's now plotting murder—"

"Don't say anything about that." Brooke admitted, "I was angry when I said what I did, and angry when Robert handed me that vial. I only assumed it was poison, while he said it wasn't and I didn't even check it to be sure, so it might not have been. I do hate him. If he got disowned, I wouldn't shed a tear about it. But he can't be accused of worse than what you already knew about, his seduction of innocents, and he apparently hasn't done any more of that since Thomas warned him not to. Besides, Dominic is signing a pledge to leave him alone now. That should be the end of it."

"I think I'll have him watched, anyway, just to be sure. It won't be the first time I've had to."

❧ Chapter Fifty-Two ❧

Lunch and then dinner; Brooke was beginning to think Harriet was never going to leave her side that day. Brooke didn't mind at all. She was also used to Harriet's nonstop chatter, but today it didn't seem at all nervous the way Brooke remembered it from her childhood. Today Harriet was just keeping Brooke's mind off *him*. And it mostly worked.

"Your father would like a word, some bit of

formal speech now that you're having your Season."

"I'd rather not."

"Not today, of course. I've explained that you're upset. He doesn't deal well with 'upset.' But sometime this week? It will keep him from coming downstairs to see for himself whom you're receiving."

"I'm not receiving anyone."

"You will. I'm accepting every invitation I have, and there will be a lot more after it's announced that you're a true debutante now."

"Don't overdo it," Alfreda had cautioned during this discussion. "She needs some time to get over the fact that the wolf let her walk out his door."

"Nonsense," Harriet disagreed. "She needs distractions, lots and lots of distractions so she doesn't have time to think about that—"

Alfreda had interrupted to tell Brooke, "Give him a week and he'll be knocking on your door."

She gave him two weeks, two hectic weeks, but she didn't see Dominic at even one of the events Harriet had taken her to, and then she finally found out why from his friend Archer. Dominic had returned to Rothdale almost immediately after their—broken wedding. His leaving London and apparently giving up on her made her even sadder. She wished she were back at Rothdale, too. So many memories she had from her time in that wild, beautiful north country, the fun she had getting to know Dominic, riding Rebel across the moors, finding Storm. How many times could one heart break?

But her mother did her best to fill her days with distractions. She was surrounded by suitors at each event, and *they* were certainly knocking on her door. She did become as popular as Harriet had predicted.

Brooke was able to avoid that talk with her father for at least a week by tiptoeing past his door—*why* was it always left open? or running past it when she heard him talking with a servant. But he did finally bark her name, forcing her to enter that room. He still hadn't recovered from this trip to London. She still wasn't willing to help with the aching joints keeping him abed, especially now that she knew her mother didn't even like him, and Harriet had balked when Brooke had suggested it a few days ago, claiming, "You don't want him downstairs scaring away your suitors."

But maybe she did. She wasn't exactly interested in any of those suitors yet.

"You have some names for me?" Thomas had demanded when she reached his bedside.

"Names?"

"Your mother has assured me that if we leave you to it, you'll make a better match than we can arrange for you. So tell me who you're considering? And speak up, gel. I'm bloody well hard of hearing."

This was last week and she couldn't remember a single name that day because she wasn't ready for this debut now, she couldn't stop thinking about Dominic, and she still just wanted to cry. So she gave him the only name she could think of, even though she'd only seen the man one other time since that ball she'd attended with Dominic.

"Archer Hamilton."

"Really?" Thomas had seemed surprised. "I know the Hamiltons, the marquis and I belong to the same club. Good stock, influential, rich. His son will do, even if the boy's not in line for the title. Who else?"

She'd actually invented some other names, which he promptly refused with a "No, don't know him" and "No, don't know him either," and then said sternly, "Stick with the Hamilton pup."

She'd assured him she would when she certainly wouldn't, but it let her get out of there. She had other things on her mind after she'd read Ella's hidden letter. Then the tears stopped after she got that gift from Dominic a few days later.

The note with it simply said, *For your birthday.* No salutation, no well-wishing, and no signature. But only Dominic would commission the picture in that locket for her, and he must have done it before the cancellation of their wedding and arranged, before he left town, for it to be delivered to her when it was finished. Inside the locket was the tiniest painting of the head of a white dog—or wolf. Storm. She was incredulous that he'd still sent it on to her instead of just throwing it away. But that's when she decided to win him back by finding proof that Ella didn't intend to die—at least not before she had her baby first. If her mother would just stop accepting invitations long enough so she could . . .

"You're not having fun, are you?" Harriet asked that night at Brooke's second ball.

Brooke sighed. "Not really. I know this is the logical thing to do, continue as we would have, but too much has happened and . . ."

"Good grief, don't cry again." Harriet quickly led Brooke out onto a terrace where there were only a few people. "What you're feeling will pass, I promise you. I had so hoped these entertainments would have cheered you up by now. Another man could make you forget about that man if you'd just give one of them a chance."

"And if I don't want to?"

Harriet put an arm around Brooke's shoulder and squeezed. "I should have known a broken heart wouldn't mend in just a few weeks. Go ahead and cry, precious. We'll say it was just dust in your eyes."

Brooke almost laughed, but did admit, "I wasn't going to cry again. I have been distracted, though, by that letter of Eloise Wolfe's that had been hidden in her fan. It was from an abbess, telling Ella she already had a wonderful family from the quaint town of Sevenoaks in Kent who would take her baby and love it as their own. The abbess expected Ella to arrive soon at her foundling house, where she could deliver the baby peacefully."

"No one has a baby peacefully," Harriet insisted. "It's an utter impossibility."

"I'm sure a peaceful environment was what the abbess meant, but in either case, it doesn't sound like Ella was going to kill herself, though Dominic thinks she did and that's a very big part of his rage. I'm not so sure now if that was really her intention."

"You think she went off to have the baby in secret first?"

Brooke blinked. "Maybe, or she intended to but died before she could give birth."

Harriet's eyes widened. "Are you saying there's a possibility that I have a grandchild somewhere in England?!"

"Shh, not so loud, Mother. I don't actually think that a'tall. I think her death was really an accident that day. Her body was found at the time and identified, so it was her. And there wasn't time for her to have her baby first. She fell in love with

Robert during her first Season and died that fall nearly two years ago, before anyone even knew she was pregnant from that indiscretion."

Harriet sighed. "That's two grandchildren I'm never going to get to meet. I do want some, you know. I've truly been looking forward to it."

Since Harriet ended that by giving Brooke a pointed look that clearly said, *Hurry up and give me some,* Brooke quickly continued, "But if I'm right and she didn't die by choice that day, that could change Dominic's perception of the matter entirely. After all, Ella was a willing participant in her seduction, so Robert was only half to blame for that, even if he did mislead the girl. And if I could prove that to him, it might remove the hate he has for our family."

"Oh, precious, don't count on that. Men view these matters differently. Robert damned himself in Lord Wolfe's eyes when he refused to marry his sister."

"I would still like to prove my suspicion. That abbess may still have a letter from Ella, inquiring about delivering her baby to the nuns for adoption. She could well have planned to home after that with some story of lost memory, et cetera."

"Or go off to really kill herself afterward, and if that's in her letter, then it's not something you would want to show to the wolf."

"She wouldn't confess that to a nun," Brooke

insisted. "But the abbess might know in either case."

"Very well, where is that foundling house? We'll pay them a visit tomorrow just to be sure."

Brooke smiled gratefully, even though she knew she was putting too much stock in the outcome. Ella might well have intended to sail to the foundling house that very day and only to pretend to be lost at sea so no one would look for her, but got caught in the storm instead. Brooke wouldn't be able to suggest anything beyond that to Dominic, not when she remembered him repeating Ella's words from those missing diary pages that he'd burned, that she'd intended to "seek peace and solace in the sea." Ella *did* want to die, had felt she had no choice, but she apparently hadn't wanted to kill her baby with her. She'd wanted to have it first and be assured it would have a good home before she ended her life. Dominic needed to at least know this, if it was true, that her death was an accident. That alone might help him to heal from that loss.

And give her a reason to see him again. . . .

❦ Chapter Fifty-Three ❧

The abbess lied to them. Even when she was handed her own letter, she denied writing it, denied ever meeting Eloise Wolfe, even though she admitted Lady Wolfe was such a generous benefactor that her donation allowed their foundling house to expand into an actual orphanage. But the abbess was stern, abrupt, and so obviously not telling the truth, at least not about the letter. She even tore it up into small pieces and tossed it aside! Now Brooke didn't even have that to show Dominic.

It was the last thing Brooke expected to happen when they got there. All she'd wanted was confirmation or at least a letter that Ella had written, but she got neither and had lost what little evidence she'd had. Seeing how disappointed she was, Harriet got furious and lambasted the devout woman before dragging Brooke out of there. But a young nun ran after them as they were getting into their coach.

"There was a lady who came here in the fall that year with her maid."

"You were listening to our conversation with your abbess?" Harriet asked.

"I was in the next room. I—I—"

"Don't blush," Brooke said quickly with a smile. "Eavesdropping is a habit of mine, too."

"What can you tell us about that girl?" Harriet asked. "D'you know if she was Eloise Wolfe?"

"I never saw her. No one did other than the abbess. She stayed with us many months. Crying was heard from her room occasionally, but none of us attended her, only her maid did. She was in complete seclusion to protect her identity, at least until the birthing, when the midwife was summoned. The couple who were to take the child were sent for, but that was before the yelling, or the abbess would probably have waited."

"What yelling?"

"We were all called to chapel to pray for mother and child when the midwife was heard to yell there were complications—too much blood loss. I'm sorry, but the mother rarely survives when that happens."

"You can't tell us for certain?"

"Only that there was a freshly dug grave in the graveyard the next day, and not just a small one. One or both of them had died."

"Surely your abbess at least told you and your sisters the outcome after you prayed for a good one?" Harriet asked. "This might be my grand-child we're talking about."

Brooke started to remind Harriet that was impossible, but the nun answered first. "You don't understand. Only 'ladies' demand complete anonymity when they come to us, and that includes into death, which is why the grave has no marker and why the abbess will never speak of it or reveal their identity. She's bound to silence."

"But you aren't?"

"I am, but I have too much compassion, or so I'm told. You obviously knew the girl and grieve for not knowing what happened to her. I'm so sorry I can't tell you what you hoped for. The common women who come here to give up their babies, they aren't secluded and we aren't kept from them. Too often they die in childbirth, too. And I've said too much. I'll get in trouble if I'm seen talking to you. I must go."

Brook nodded and thanked the nun. She'd expected so much more from this trip. But as she got into the coach, Harriet said behind her, "We're going to Sevenoaks. Ella might have died with those complications, but the child *might* have survived. I have to be sure."

The young nun hadn't even been talking about Ella. Ella had died two years ago. If an orphaned baby was being raised in Sevenoaks, it belonged to some other lady who'd had a similar indiscretion. Harriet was pulling wishes out of a hat, hoping Ella had somehow faked her death even when they'd found her body. But Brooke was too despondent to remind her mother of that.

But Alfreda, who'd been waiting for them in the

coach, wanted to know, "And how will we find this baby in a haystack?"

"I'll speak to the mayor and every priest in Sevenoaks. Someone will know if a couple came home with a baby last year in, when might it have been? April or May? Or if they came home disappointed instead. If they were waiting to adopt one, it would be exciting news for them that they would share with their friends and neighbors. Now let me take a nap, I'm exhausted. I was so excited last night, letting myself hope for the best today, that I got no sleep a'tall."

Brooke was utterly dejected, berating herself for wanting to go to that orphanage in the first place. She should have taken that letter straight to Dominic instead of handing it to a nun to watch it be destroyed. It wasn't conclusive proof of an accidental death but it had been something. And he'd never believe Brooke if she still tried to tell him about it. She wasn't tired herself, but she leaned against Alfreda for comfort.

"Are you really going to let us go all the way to Sevenoaks for nothing?" Alfreda whispered to her a while later when Harriet was softly snoring.

"You could have told her," Brooke whispered back.

"It wasn't my place, but if that baby survived, you need to mention that it can't possibly be any relation to her."

"I will if it comes to that, but we probably won't find any baby there, so she'll conclude on her own that it died with whoever its mother was, which is undoubtedly what happened. But I'm in no hurry to get back to London today; in fact, I'd as soon return to Leicestershire."

"Now don't say that. You won't be finding any husband there."

"Who says I want one now? Maybe come the winter Season I'll feel differently, but now—pretending to enjoy these social events has been extremely difficult when all I can do is think about him. This was a crushing disappointment today, Freda. It was my only chance to end his rage over what he thinks happened to his sister, my only chance to win him back."

"Back?"

"I was very hopeful that our marriage would be a turning point for us, but I didn't get to find out."

Alfreda must have sensed tears were imminent because she abruptly changed the subject with an interesting tidbit. "Gabe seemed out of sorts when he visited me prior to leaving London. He was quite gloomy, actually, and wouldn't fess up to why."

Brooke glanced aside. "I didn't know he left, or that you've seen him since we changed households."

"Of course I have."

Brooke perked up. "How was Dominic? Did he say?"

"Unapproachable. Not pleasant to be around."

"But Dominic got what he wanted. Why isn't he gloatingly happy?"

"Gabe doesn't know. The wolf is apparently keeping it to himself, what's put him in another black mood. Likely his mother is the cause and he can't berate her while she's still recovering."

"I suppose he might be angry that he had to give up his coal mines to obtain his goal," Brooke guessed. "As for Gabe, if he was in the doldrums, it was probably because he was leaving town with Dominic and knew he wouldn't see you anymore."

"No, he said they'd be back, he just didn't know when. But he seemed out of sorts on our trip to London, too. That he didn't want to discuss any of it finally got me so annoyed I showed him the door."

"He came to the house?"

"To my room."

"Oh," Brooke said without blushing.

"Freda, are you getting married?" Harriet asked in surprise, not sleeping after all.

Alfreda snorted. "He's too young for me."

"No, he's not," Brooke put in.

"Well, I'm happy enough just enjoying him when I feel the mood to."

Harriet rolled her eyes before trying again to

nap. Brooke closed her eyes, too, wondering if Dominic hadn't made an effort to see her before he left London because he was angry about something else, specifically his mother's high-handedness. He might want to get over that before . . . Who was she kidding? He had no reason to ever approach her again, and she'd lost hers.

But Alfreda must have been stewing over the previous subject because, an hour later, she said in another whisper, "I thought this trip was just to prove that Lady Eloise's death was an accident. You know if that baby didn't die with its mother and is in Sevenoaks, you're going to have a devil of a time stopping your mother from demanding it be given to her. Why is Harriet drawing the wrong conclusion? You did tell her Eloise's body was found in Scarborough, didn't you?"

"Yes, but she got it into her head that Ella faked her death so no one would look for her."

Alfreda snorted softly. "With her own body?"

"With a piece of Ella's—" Brooke sat up and stared wide-eyed at Alfreda. "Jewelry. The body was only identified by that, and her maid stole her jewelry that day. That could have been the maid who died on that beach, killed and robbed for the rest of the jewelry and tossed in the sea to disappear! Ella might really have sailed to that orphanage that day."

"The woman who went there to have her baby had a maid with her."

Brooke sank back into her seat, having forgotten that. Now she was grasping at straws just like Harriet—unless . . . "She could have gone there with an older servant she'd known all her life, rather than a young maid she might not have trusted yet. And they could have been far enough down that coast to have missed that storm completely."

"She still died, either way."

"Yes, but if her baby is in Sevenoaks—my God, Freda, if I could bring Dominic her child, it would change everything!"

"And put your two families at war for a new reason."

Brooke ignored that to say excitedly, "Tell the driver to drive faster!"

Chapter Fifty-Four

"Don't be alarmed," Dominic told Willis, who was staring agog at the two animals Gabriel was trying to get into the town house. "They're big, but harmless."

The improvised leashes were proving useless. Storm slipped her head out of hers and raced across the hall and up the stairs. Wolf ripped his loose from Gabe's hand to follow, as usual.

"Storm must have caught Lady Brooke's scent," Gabriel suggested with a sigh as he came through the door.

"After two weeks? It's more likely the house, one they're not used to. They'll settle down as soon as they've sniffed out every corner."

Willis finally cleared his throat to say stoically, "Welcome back, m'lord."

But then they heard a screech upstairs and Anna's alarmed cry. "What are two wolves doing in my house?!"

Dominic yelled up, "Actually, Mother, there are three of us here."

Anna appeared around the upstairs corner so delighted to see Dominic back in London that she rushed down the stairs to hug him. She was apparently fully recovered, dressed fashionably, cheeks blooming with health instead of fever. He should be pleased. He would be, if he weren't still so angry at her.

He returned her embrace, but quite stiffly. "The animals are just large dogs from the moors. I brought back the white one because it's Brooke's pet and I need to return it to her."

Anna stepped back to peer at him hopefully. "Dom, have—"

He cut in curtly, "If you'll excuse us, Gabe and I need a whiskey after the long ride today."

He led Gabriel into the parlor and closed the door on his mother. He simply wasn't ready to talk to her yet, but he did need a drink. Pouring them each one, he raised his for a telling toast. "To bad luck: I'm forced by the Prince Regent to marry my enemy's sister. Worse luck: I fall in love with her. Worst luck: My mother interferes, the Regent retracts his decree, and I lose the woman I love."

Gabriel refused to drink to that. "You'll win her back."

"Maybe now that I have Storm on my side. But even if I do, I have less than a year to live to enjoy her."

"You don't really believe in that stupid old curse, Dom!"

"I didn't used to. But now with this recent string of horrendous luck on top of Ella's death and my father's premature demise, I'm beginning to wonder . . ."

"Well, stop wondering. There is no curse. I know because . . . because I'm the one who's supposed to kill you."

Dominic raised a brow. "Kill me? Are you trying to make me laugh? I think you've found a winner of a distraction from my misery, Gabe. Much appreciated."

"As much as I'd like to accommodate, no. You might want to sit down."

"You might want to explain a little faster."

"It's that bloody curse," Gabriel said in disgust. "And it's not even yours. The only curse you have is *my* family, and it's been mostly believed since it was screamed in the 1500s by that damned ancestor of mine, Bathilda Biscane. She was the one who was mistress to the first Viscount Rothdale. The village priest at the time, another relative of mine, had already believed her to be a witch. How else could she have bedazzled her way into a noble's bed if not by casting a spell on him? But the priest couldn't get at her while she was under their lord's protection—until the night she came home to the village in tears. He immediately accused her and sentenced her to burn, but before they could get her to the stake, she cursed her own family, promising that if a Biscane firstborn doesn't kill every titled Wolfe firstborn from that day forward, and before the end of their twenty-fifth year, then *all* of their firstborns will die instead. And she killed herself in front of them, screaming those words and using her own blood to seal the curse."

"And you believe that?"

"That it happened that way, yes. But some of my relatives believed the curse. Soon after Bathilda's baleful theatrics, many Biscanes moved away, some because they didn't want any part of the witch's evil incantations, some because they knew it was superstitious nonsense. Over the next century the curse became a secret that was passed down from the firstborn male of one generation to the firstborn male of the next. Only he could do the deed."

"And you're a firstborn," Dominic said flatly.

"Yes. Arnold didn't relay the secret to me until the night you got that note about your mother's illness and Arnold knew I would be following you to London. He wanted me to act before you married Lady Brooke, so your line would end for good and they can stop committing murder."

"Arnold told you all this? My head groom wants to kill me?"

Gabriel nodded. "He's the eldest living Biscane in Rothdale, my mother's eldest brother. He's terrified that Peter, Janie, and I will die if you don't before the end of this year. He had hoped you wouldn't live this long, which was why he waited so long to tell me I was next in line to kill you. I tried to ram some sense into his head, but he was quite anguished to see you alive when we returned to Rothdale last week."

"You know I'm having trouble believing any of this. Are you sure he wasn't pulling your leg?"

"Do you really think he would have let me leave Rothdale with a story like that if he wasn't serious?"

"I suppose not." Dominic moved to refill his glass, but swung around with the thought. "My father?"

"No! Actually, Arnold assured me that no Biscane still living has killed anyone, not that they weren't prepared to. But all the more recent viscounts, not counting your father, had bad luck with their children, losing their first either at birth or in childhood. But my ancestors have killed some of yours. The gruesome stock I come from, I'm so ashamed!"

Anna tsked as she opened the door and stepped just inside. "As well you should be, Gabriel Biscane."

"Taken to snooping, Mother?" Dominic said drily.

"No, I—well, perhaps briefly, but we need to have a word."

Gabriel tried to get past her. "I'll go."

She blocked him. "No, you won't. Have any members of your family died since Dominic's twenty-fifth birthday?"

Dominic was incredulous. He put the bottle of whiskey back down and tried to keep the harshness from his tone, but wasn't quite successful. "You think to interfere *again?* I will deal with this, it's not your concern."

"Actually, this is, and I meant to tell you on your birthday, but you had that at Archer's house getting your wound treated, the wound you didn't want me to even know about, and then you took yourself to Rothdale to recover so I still wouldn't know about it. And answer my question, Gabriel."

"No, m'lady, not one has died. But if Dom's next birthday comes, my uncle believes that all the Biscane firstborns—me, Peter, and Janie—will die."

"Then I'm happy to disprove that silly curse once and for all." Anna smiled at her son. "You're already twenty-six, darling. There's nothing real about that curse, and your father and I proved it by lying about your age."

Dominic picked up the whiskey again, though maybe he should have pinched himself instead. This sort of bizarre absurdity only occurred in dreams. But twice in one dream?

He took a long swig from the bottle in his hand before he demanded, "How is that possible? The servants would have known when I was born."

"It was your father's idea to disprove that curse once and for all, and now he has, he just didn't live to know it. We were both young when we fell in love during my Season. And I was already pregnant before we married and left on our wedding trip."

Dominic raised a brow. Anna blushed profusely. Gabriel tried again to leave the room, but she put her hands on the doorframe. "We were actually gone for nearly four years. When we returned to England, we claimed you were a year younger than you actually were. Yes, people marveled that you were big for your age, but no one ever guessed why. And now I know that we probably saved your life with our ruse."

She ended that with a glare at Gabriel, but he

was too relieved to care. "I'm going to go send my uncle a missive *and* blacken his eye next time I see him. Thank you, m'lady. I feel so light of spirit now I could float!"

She let him go this time to ask Dominic what she'd tried to ask earlier, "Have you forgiven me yet?"

Dominic drained more of the whiskey. "The one has nothing to do with the other. You didn't save me from a fate worse than death, Mother. You condemned me to a new hell instead."

🎐 Chapter Fifty-Five 🎐

"Maybe no one is home?" Alfreda said when she knocked for the second time.

"I hear babies crying," Harriet insisted. "They wouldn't be left unattended."

The couple they'd been looking for did indeed get a baby last year, then soon after that, another. They were hoping for a third, since they wanted a big family. But Alfreda just rolled her eyes, refusing to repeat for the second time what she'd already predicted. They were going to be let down because even if Ella's child was one of the Turrils' adopted children, they couldn't prove it, the abbess wouldn't verify it, and the couple would certainly deny it, not wanting to give up either child they'd likely come to love as their own by now.

They'd arrived in Sevenoaks late last night, feeling a bit daunted because the town was bigger than they'd expected, having grown from the time it was established in 1605. They'd gotten rooms at a small hotel, and Harriet had gone off to find a few churches, though she'd allowed a visit to the mayor could wait until morning. But she'd had no luck with the churches in the heart of the town and had been directed to try farther out, which they did in the morning.

The pastor at the first one directed them to the Turrils' rather large house on the edge of town. Mr. Turril was a skilled clockmaker, they'd been told. He and his wife had tried for fifteen years to conceive a child before they decided to adopt instead.

As Brooke and Harriet stood anxiously on the front step as Alfreda knocked again, the door opened. The woman who stood there was too young to be Mrs. Turril. Red haired with curious brown eyes and wearing a long white apron, she looked like a servant, perhaps a nanny, because she had a toddler on her hip that neither Whitworth could take their eyes off.

"May I help you ladies?"

From farther inside the house a female voice inquired, "Is that my package, Bertha?"

The maid turned to answer, giving Brooke

enough room to brush past Bertha to find the woman who had just spoken. And there she was, black hair tied back, amber eyes like Dominic's, fashionably dressed. Brooke had never hoped for this, not when there had been not just one but two graves for Eloise Wolfe.

"I know you," Brooke said almost tearfully as she slowly approached Dominic's sister. "I cried with you when your dog died. I laughed with you when you landed a perfect hit to your brother's face with that snowball when you were only twelve. I smiled when I sat on your 'I win' bench in the center of that maze at Rothdale. My God, I'm so glad you're alive, Ella!"

Those amber eyes had gotten wider with Brooke's every word, until the black brows snapped together for a stiff reply. "You are mistaken. I'm Jane Croft, not whomever you're referring to."

"Changing your name doesn't change who you are." Brooke grinned widely. "Don't deny it. Your eyes give you away, so like his."

Even stiffer: "You obviously have the wrong address. Whoever you are looking for doesn't live here. Now I must ask you to leave."

Brooke still wasn't daunted, but before she could reply, Harriet barged in, demanding, "Where's my grandchild?"

"I beg your pardon," the young woman said curtly. "Who the deuce *are* you people?"

"Mother, wait," Brooke cautioned. "This is Ella Wolfe, the child's mother."

The amber eyes were quite angry now. "No, I am not! Please leave."

Brooke quickly said, "I'm Dominic's—was Dominic's fiancée, but I hope to be that again. I love your brother. He still loves you very much and is deeply pained by the loss of you. Your mother still grieves and misses you terribly. The circumstances of your death are what stand between your brother and me. But once he knows that you're alive—"

"You can't tell him!" Ella actually looked appalled, but then tears began streaming down her face.

Harriet was obviously disappointed that she wouldn't be taking a baby home today as she'd hoped, but her words weren't accusing, merely curious, when she asked, "D'you know you have *two* graves?"

Ella swiped the tears off her cheeks. "I should hope so, I arranged for both."

"May we see the child?" Harriet asked hopefully.

"No," Ella said protectively. "I don't even know who you are or how you found me when I took such extreme measures to make sure no one ever would."

Brooke explained, "We didn't know we would find you, not when you wrote in your diary that the baby left you no choice but to take your own life."

"No, I didn't. It left me no choice but to go away to have her. I never considered killing myself and my baby."

"But Dominic said you wrote that you were going to seek 'peace and solace in the sea.' "

"That I wished I could, not that I would, but that was at my lowest point of heartbreak, just a brief tearful thought. But I had to keep the truth from Dominic to keep him from committing murder and ending up in prison for the rest of his life. And the only way to do that was to disappear. I didn't think to pretend to be lost at sea until I sailed past the body of that poor woman on the beach. It was my maid, Bertha, who pointed it out. We stopped to investigate, and that's when the idea occurred to me, to fake my death. I asked Bertha to put my locket on the corpse. You should have heard her complaints, I'm sure they heard them back in Scarborough. So I did the deed, as distasteful as it was, and sent her back on foot to fetch my jewelry so we'd have money to support us, since I couldn't withdraw money from my bank, not after I was 'dead.'

"I intended to give my baby to the foundling house, but once I had it, well, it was love at first sight. The Turrils were disappointed that I'd changed my mind, but they offered me an alternative, to come live with them and raise my child here. It was a satisfactory arrangement for me, since I hadn't really decided where to go after the birth. And they've been wonderful surrogate grandparents. Now I insist you tell me how you found me. The abbess swore—"

"It wasn't her. She even denied writing that letter I found of hers in your fan. But one of the nuns confided a lady had come to them during the fall of that year. I only hoped it had been you, but the nun was sure you didn't survive the complications of the birth."

"I nearly didn't. It was ghastly." Ella shuddered.

"The nun implied you and the child might have died that night, but since she wasn't certain, my mother was determined to look around every last corner, so we came here with high hopes to at least find your baby if it did somehow survive, so we could bring it home where it belongs."

"It belongs with me."

"Yes, of course it does. There's no question about that now. We mean you no harm, I promise you."

Some of the stiffness went out of Ella's shoulders, enough for her to admit, "I knew what the consequences would be for my foolish actions and reckless heart, but I was in love. I even knew his faults, but I was sure I could help him to overcome them. We met secretly so often, I expected I'd get pregnant, so it was no surprise when I did and I was thrilled. I thought it would

406

get us to the altar sooner. More fool me. But even so, I couldn't bear the thought of him dying at my brother's hands, or what would happen to Dominic because of it. I feel terrible about the pain I've caused my mother and my brother, it troubles me deeply, but the alternative would have been much worse."

"But what you feared would happen did happen. There were three duels fought over your death, though neither opponent died. But the Prince Regent intervened and your brother has signed a pledge to give up his vendetta for good. I'm sorry that my brother refused to marry you. He's such a cad. But truly, there's no longer a reason for you to stay here. Go back to your family, Ella. It will be a dream come true for them."

But Ella was suddenly frowning. "I didn't know Benton had a sister, in fact, I'm sure he doesn't. Who are you really?"

❧ Chapter Fifty-Six ❧

Brooke was more nervous than she let on as she waited in the parlor to see if Dominic would even receive her. But she knew he was back in London. Alfreda had a note from Gabriel waiting on her when they got home last night, telling her he and Dominic had returned from Yorkshire yesterday.

So much depended on this meeting, her future, Ella's future, even Dominic's own happiness. And if she didn't do this just right, if she couldn't give him back his sister, then he might hate her even more.

Why couldn't this be simple? Why did Ella still even want to protect a man who had betrayed not just her trust but also Dominic's—his own *friend?* But the wolf that entered the parlor a few moments later wasn't the one she was expecting to see.

"Storm!" Brooke cried in delight, jumping up and putting her arms around the dog and burying her face in Storm's soft white hair.

"You're kissing the wrong wolf," Dominic said as he walked straight to her. He didn't look angry; in fact, he was smiling. Had Ella changed her mind and was already home?

But Dominic was suddenly kissing her and her thoughts scattered every which way. She wrapped her arms around him. She hadn't forgotten the strength beneath her hands, the earthy smell of him, the tantalizing taste. But the thrill was new; it included such relief she could barely contain it. He wanted her!

He picked her up, moved to the sofa, where he sat down to cradle her on his lap, but not before kissing her again and again. Her bonnet fell back on the seat behind her, her hair came loose and tumbled over his arm. Someone closed the door for them. It still wasn't locked, but she was too happy to care.

But she was so shocked when she heard him say, "Marry me, Babble," that she forced them to stop. She was so obviously incredulous that he grinned. "And here I thought having Storm at my side would greatly improve my chance to persuade you. Did it not work?"

She was still shocked, but peered deeply into those amber eyes. "You actually *want* to marry me now?"

After one last tender kiss, he told her, "I wanted to from the night we made love. You've affected me in so many ways—your tender care of me, your concern, your courage, your determination. You got past my defenses so easily, despite who you're related to. I've never known anyone quite like you, Brooke Whitworth, and I want to share the rest of my life with you."

She started to cry even as she smiled at him.

He rolled his eyes and wiped the tears from her cheeks. "It never ceases to amaze me how women can produce a water fountain for the wrong reasons."

Brooke laughed and helped him get the tears off her cheeks. "I'm deuced if I know." But then she said in surprise, "But you let me leave your house. Why did you do that if you already knew?"

"Because I had the thought that without the

Regent's edict casting a pall over us, I could ask you to marry me and you would know it's what I want, not what I was forced to do. And I would know it's what *you* want, if you accepted. I didn't want us to start our marriage under those forced conditions. So even though I'm still annoyed with my mother for interfering, if you say yes now, I will thank her profusely."

Her smile got brighter. "Of course I want to! I did as soon as you stopped growling at me. But the day I left, I was very much in love with you. So why didn't you come to me and ask me sooner?"

"Because your choice had been denied you with me. I wanted you to have it back and all normal options with it. I wanted you to *choose* me, to be absolutely sure of your feelings before I asked you to marry me. You made me love you. I wasn't sure if you felt the same. And you deserved to have that Season you had been looking forward to."

"The Season I haven't been enjoying without you at my side? That Season?"

He looked abashed. "I've been miserable, too, and taking it out on everyone. But I loved you enough to wait for you to enjoy a bit of the Season. Well, I thought you would. However, I hear you ended up with many suitors. Perhaps I should have stayed in town to bare my teeth and snarl at a few of them."

She grinned. "You're pretty good at teasing. Were you always?"

"Only with my sister. She was easy to tease."

Ella! She'd nearly forgotten and now felt like groaning. His reaction could go either way. He might not want to give his word that he wouldn't kill Benton. He might get angry at his sister for putting him through such grief. She wondered if they could get married first before she told him. . . .

Seeing her worried brow, he asked, "What?" But then he guessed. "You're remembering that silly bargain of yours, aren't you? Not that you had anything to bargain for."

She blushed. "No, you told me that on the ride home from the ball. But why haven't you asked what brought me here today?"

He hugged her closer. "Something other than your unspoken feelings for me?"

"Yes, although I did have high hopes that it would lead to what just happened. I did so want to end your grief and now I can. Your sister isn't dead. She's very much alive."

He shot off the sofa, leaving her on it. For a moment she thought he was going to accuse her of lying, his expression was so anguished. "How can this be? Her body was found!"

"That wasn't her." Brooke quickly added, "And she'll come home if you'll swear you won't kill the father of her child."

"I've already made that pledge."

"He's not the one, and before I can tell you who is, I have to hear you swear you won't kill him. Fear of that is why Ella faked her death, Dominic. She doesn't want him dead or you imprisoned for it. So swear. It's her condition that you do, not mine."

"She's really alive?" he asked incredulously.

Brooke nodded. "Both she and your niece are."

"My God, how?"

She told him what she could about the faked deaths without revealing names or locations and admitted how she was able to find Ella. "At first I hoped to find proof that Ella's death was an accident, not a suicide. Then it became apparent that her baby might still be alive. I hoped the child, at least, would ease your pain. We didn't expect to find them together."

"Where is she?"

"I can't tell you."

"Damnit—"

"I can't! She made me promise to hear you swear first."

"Bloody hell, does it not sound like I'm swearing!?"

She understood his frustration. She would have smiled if it weren't so inappropriate with these particular emotions racking him. "That isn't the sort of swearing she wants me to hear," Brooke was forced to say.

Oh, my, there was that feral gleam again, but

412

she didn't think it was for her. Then he paced and did some more of that other swearing. She waited patiently.

He finally stopped and stared at her. "I swear I won't kill him. There, I've said it quite clearly. Now give me the name of who I'm only going to pummel."

"Benton Seamons."

He growled and marched to the nearest wall to punch his fist through it. She hurried over to see what sort of damage he'd just done to his knuckles, tsking at him, "Keep in mind, she doesn't want him to die for what he did, though she might not care if he gets a sound thrashing. But you and your sister can discuss that later."

"Why did she blame your brother instead? Or was that just a ruse to put me off the scent?"

"No, she didn't know you'd read her diary. And it was Robert's fault indirectly, even though he only thought he was helping when he interfered where he shouldn't have. He had become chummy with your friend that summer and learned that Benton was so in debt from his gambling that his father was threatening to disown him. So he steered Benton to a ducal heiress who would be of age to marry in a couple of years, to get in on the ground floor, as it were, a girl who could solve his current problems nicely—and easily cover any exorbitant gambling debts he incurred in the future. It was the only thing that appeased his father enough to pay off his debts. Benton was drunk when he laughed at Ella's news about the baby, but he already knew he couldn't marry her even if he did love her. He broke with her in that harsh manner because he was going to be disowned if he didn't, which would leave him no longer worthy of her in any case."

"Why didn't your brother tell me that?"

"Well, he *did* tell you it wasn't him, you just didn't believe him. And Ella did blame him for ruining her life because he was the one who told Benton he could do better than her and with who. She found that out from Robert before she left London and how badly in debt Benton really was."

"But three duels—why the devil didn't he give me Benton's name?"

"Because he'd given his word to Benton that he wouldn't reveal anything about that summer. Who would have thought my brother could have even a speck of honor in him, to keep that secret even though his life depended on it? But I just found that out from Robert last night when we returned to town. And that being responsible for giving Benton that ducal option has made him feel rather guilty, especially when you accused him of being responsible for Ella's death. He pretty much admitted that he felt he deserved a bullet for his part in it—but not three duels!" Brooke grinned slightly, remembering her

414

brother's frustrated expression when they'd talked of this last night. "He was quite put out when you wanted that third round. He was ready to find Benton himself and beat him into giving you his confession when you cornered him to force that last duel. And when I got dragged into it, he was actually trying to rescue me by goading you to send me home. I'm glad you realized that before I did."

"And that potion he gave you?"

She rolled her eyes. "It was supposed to make you see something grotesque and frightening in anyone you looked at, long enough for you to chase everyone out of your house, including me. It was otherwise harmless. Now, would you like to see Ella today?"

"She's that close?"

Brooke grinned. "Yes. So you should probably let your mother know. Seeing Ella without prior warning . . ."

He chuckled. "Indeed, ghosts tend to cause all sorts of havoc and fainting."

She laughed. "How would you know?"

"A good guess." He squeezed her tightly. "You can't imagine what this means to me, Babble."

Yes, she could.

❧ Chapter Fifty-Seven ❧

Brooke waited until she heard Anna's shriek of joy from upstairs before she went to the parlor's front window and waved toward her waiting coach, giving Ella the signal they had agreed upon to let Ella know it was safe to enter the house. A few moments later a knock came at the front door. Brooke moved into the hall with Storm following at her heels. Her pet wasn't letting Brooke out of sight this soon after finding her again. Brooke was in time to witness Willis's shock when he opened the door. Maybe they should have warned him, too. But with his proper demeanor still absent, Willis was soon hugging Ella; well, it was a bit awkward with Annabelle sitting on Ella's hip.

Ella was laughing when he ran upstairs to let Dominic and Anna know, but her eyes widened when she spotted Brooke and saw what was sitting beside her. Annabelle was excitingly waving toward the "doggy," wanting to touch it, but Ella was cautious and approached slowly. "That's the white wolf that saved Dom and me when we were children."

"She saved me, too, but she's a dog, not a wolf."

"She's a wolf," Ella insisted. "And in London? How's that possible?"

Brooke grinned. "She's my pet. Really!"

Ella glanced at Brooke and shook her head. "Are you a magician? You managed to find me when I wasn't supposed to be found, and you've tamed a wolf. What other tricks have you got in your bonnet?"

Brooke rolled her eyes, but then laughed. "I'll allow I might have tamed at least one wolf."

The wolf she'd just referred to came running down the stairs with his mother close behind him, and Ella and her child were immediately smothered in hugs. Ella and her mother were crying, not at all surprising. Brooke tried to see if Dominic was, too, but his head was bowed over theirs, at least until he reached out and pulled Brooke into that big family hug.

As soon as Annabelle was in Anna's arms and the older woman was cooing over her new granddaughter, Dominic led them into the parlor. Ella had started explaining why she'd taken such extreme measures after Benton had spurned her. Anna only had a few scathing things to say about Dominic's ex-friend during that long explanation, and a few wonderful things to say about Brooke's role in reuniting her family, along with a heartfelt apology.

After Ella finished her story, she asked her brother, "So am I getting more hugs or a scolding?"

"Don't think there won't be one—later."

Ella just laughed at him through teary eyes so like his, until he pulled her across the sofa onto his lap for a bear hug that made her shriek and push away from him, giggling. "I hope you don't crush *her* like that. And when is the wedding to be?"

He grinned. "You assume?"

"She told me a lot about your time together. I *know* you, Brother."

"Today would be nice," Anna put in.

Dominic laughed. "I quite agree. We can find a priest on the way to Whitworth House."

Surprised, Brooke, sitting on his other side, leaned close to whisper to him, "I don't need to be married in my parents' house."

"Why not? We're joining two families and everyone appears to be in London for it."

"But Robert might be there," Brooke warned.

"Your brother has been forgiven—by me. What about by you?"

"No, some things can't be, but after everything I discovered in the last two days, I might have to allow that the man might not be quite the same as the boy. Of course, I could just be so happy that I'll forgive anyone, even him, maybe even my father with his icy heart."

She wished she hadn't said that. Speaking of the devil, Thomas was just coming down the stairs at the Whitworth town house when they all arrived a while later and were let in the front door. Harriet was beside him, helping to keep him steady on the steps.

Brooke called out to her, "We've brought a priest with us, Mother," and then with a laugh at Harriet's look of surprise said, "You were right. He loves me and doesn't want to wait another day for our wedding. Will the parlor do?"

"Certainly!" Harriet stopped when Anna stepped into the foyer.

But Anna, seeing the glare she was suddenly getting, said, "Don't hold a grudge, Harriet. You know what I thought. If we'd had all the facts sooner—actually, our children might not even have met if we did. You and Brooke both had a part in bringing my girl home to us. I can never thank you enough for that, but know that I will love your girl as my own, I promise you."

Harriet blushed a little at those words. But Thomas demanded, "A wedding today?" And then squinting at Dominic: "Is that the Hamilton boy?"

"It's a love match instead, Thomas, and a good one." Harriet got him down the last few steps and steered him toward the parlor. But in a much-lower tone she mumbled, "About bloody time someone gets one of those."

"Eh? Speak up, you know I can't hear that well."

"The Regent's edict, surely you remember we had no choice in this matter?" Harriet reminded him.

Thomas's memory might be deteriorating, but it

419

wasn't always faulty. "I thought that reprobate was bought off," he stated clearly.

"He changed his mind," Harriet lied. "Or did you want to add to the bribe to try and get him to change it yet again?"

Thomas snorted. "A love match will do, no need to waste more coin if the chit actually loves the wolf. I suppose she wants me to give her away?"

"That isn't necessary," Harriet assured him.

Brooke realized what her mother was doing and could feel Dominic tensing up when it occurred to him, too, that Thomas Whitworth could withhold his permission for this wedding, and the priest wouldn't perform it without parental consent. Not that they couldn't find a way to marry some other way, but she'd rather return to Rothdale without the worry that her father might come pounding on the door to demand her back. So she took Dominic's hand in hers and gave him a reassuring smile before she said quite loudly so Thomas couldn't help but hear her, "Actually, yes, let's make this official with you giving me away, Father."

But as soon as Thomas passed into the parlor, Dominic looked down at her and asked without inflection, "Has Archer been courting you without my notice?"

His eyes had just turned feral, making her roll hers. "Your wolf is showing," she teased. "As it happens, it's rather funny how his name came up in this house. Remind me to tell you later."

Ella started to follow her mother into the parlor, but paused to ask, "Is Archer still available? Now that I'm going to be a widow with a recovered memory . . ."

Dominic gave his sister an indomitable look. "Leave my friends alone, minx. I don't want to have to kill Archer after I'm done with Benton."

"You swore—"

"I'm not going to kill him. But he won't walk away from this unscathed, either. He's not going to get what he broke your heart for. The wedding to the heiress won't happen once I speak to her parents and his."

"Oh, well, that's different. By all means . . ."

Having heard the commotion in the hall and Brooke's shout about Thomas giving her away, Alfreda came down the stairs smiling. She didn't need to be told that everything had worked out as Brooke had hoped. But her smile broadened when Gabriel came through the front door. He wasn't about to miss Dominic's wedding and had been dispatched in the Wolfe coach to fetch the priest, who followed him in.

But Gabriel's eyes had gone straight to the maid, and he yelled at her with a cheeky grin, "A double wedding, Freda?"

Alfreda actually blushed, but mumbled, "In your dreams, puppy."

He sighed. "I suppose that's better than your last resounding no."

"Today is for my poppet. Mind your manners."

He must have found that a promising reply because he was grinning from ear to ear when he gave Alfreda his arm to escort her into the parlor. But then Dominic drew Brooke's attention, saying, "Do hurry if you're going to change into that lovely wedding dress."

"I'm not. It would be bad luck to wear it again, and you and I are done with bad luck. I'm ready to make you my husband right now."

Brooke's mother walked her down the improvised aisle that day. But her father did state quite clearly when asked by the priest that, yes, he *was* giving her away, which was the only nice thing Thomas Whitworth had ever done for her. . . .

And then she was Lady Brooke Wolfe, a dream come true. The man who drew her into his arms to seal the union was a better dream come true. The joy in her heart was overwhelming. She cried. Dominic laughed at her when he saw it.

Her brother did make an appearance at the end of the ceremony. He stood in the doorway, wary about getting anywhere near Dominic even though the cause of their discord was in the room. Ella even approached him to say, "I suppose in the end you did me a favor, steering Benton to the proverbial golden goose. I've had enough time to realize he wouldn't have made me a good husband. So why did you?"

"He needed help. You would have got him disowned."

"Yes, but why did *you* elect to fix that for him? Was he an old friend, a best friend? What you did changed not just my family, but yours, not to mention you might have died for it."

"I'd never had many friends, just tagalongs who don't really care about me nor I them. I'd only met Benton that summer, but he showed me there was more to friendship listening, sharing, wanting to help if needed. He was probably the only real friend I ever had—and your brother's a bad shot. The risk wasn't all that great."

Dominic and Brooke joined them in time to hear that. "Shall we try again with what I'm good at?" Dominic asked Robert.

"Bloody hell." Robert backed quickly out of the room.

"I thought you were done with him?" Brooke said.

"I thought that as well," Ella said.

"I am," Dominic replied. "He even knows I am. I'm not sure what he's afraid of now."

Brooke rolled her eyes and went after Robert, stopping him at the front door. She didn't want him plotting to retaliate if he really thought Dominic still wanted revenge. She thought she'd made it clear last night to Robert that Dominic didn't, but maybe it bore repeating.

"He was joking, you know. There won't be any more challenges of any sort."

"Except against Benton now?"

Her eyes flared. "You're going to warn him, aren't you?"

"Shouldn't I? Isn't that what a friend would do?"

He sounded almost anguished, asking that, so she was careful in replying, "Yes, indeed, if he's really a friend, but have you even seen him again since you gave him that boon and he scampered off to secure it two years ago? You got left to deal with the aftermath of that. Did he even know you were accepting duels on his behalf?"

"Yes and yes."

She wasn't expecting confirmation on her guesses. "And he didn't step forward even then to fix that for you?"

"It was too late and he's getting married this week. You got your happy marriage, Brooke, he should get his. You are happy with the wolf, aren't you?"

"For the first time in my life, truly, truly happy. But your friend, if he really is your friend, doesn't deserve that after everything he's done. And he's not marrying that poor girl for the right reasons, is he? Just for more blunt to support his gambling habits."

424

"No, to keep from being disowned. I could imagine the terror of that. And I actually experienced it m'self last year."

"Then warn him if you must, but Dominic has sworn he won't try to kill him. Ella doesn't want that. But I'm pretty sure he's going to get disowned anyway, once Dominic visits Benton's father as well as the girl's parents, and that he *will* do before the wedding. So Benton Seamons won't get the heiress in either case. It's time to bow out, Robert, before you get caught up in a duke's wrath instead."

"It feels like a betrayal to do nothing."

She was surprised enough to remark, "I never thought I would say this, but you're proving yourself a worthy friend, Robert." She would have added *in a callous way,* since people did get hurt by his definition of friendship, but this was her wedding day, so she didn't need to be that blunt. "You'll find some new friends worthy to be yours. You know, we could have been friends like they are." She nodded behind her at Dominic and his sister. "I'm sorry it never happened for us."

She should probably have left that unsaid as well, she realized, when she saw him wince. But then he said, "Jealousy is a monstrous thing when you're too young to know what it is."

She caught sight of her mother joining Dominic and Ella. Everyone was so happy today—except

Robert, and probably Thomas. While Brooke finally had the relationship she'd always wanted with her mother, and she finally had the family she'd always wanted with the Wolfes, she was still reminded by Robert's words that for too many years she didn't have either. Because of his childhood jealousy, his selfishness, his arrogance . . . she forced herself to stop there.

She knew he was about to apologize for that, but she just wasn't ready to hear it. So she nodded and walked away before he said the words that would make her cry or snarl or— she didn't know what would happen. Maybe someday she'd let them find out. . . .

❧ Epilogue ❧

Brooke was laughing when they fell on the bed together. The dogs only looked up briefly to see why, then lay back down in their favorite spot in front of the fireplace. Kissing, and making love, were nothing new to the two wolflike animals that were usually around to witness it. Wolf whined about it once, probably thinking Brooke was hurting his master when Dominic was heard to groan. But Storm nipped at Wolf for the noise and he never made it again.

The rest of the house was quiet, though they could hear Annabelle giggling with her mother in the distance. Dominic had started calling his niece, named in part for her grandmother, Bella instead, and the nickname stuck. Every time Brooke looked at or held the child, she was nearly moved to tears. Bella was so happy and so loved by everyone, the way a child should be raised.

Eloise and Anna both came home with them to Rothdale after their wedding two months ago. Harriet had already visited three times, too. Brooke hadn't wanted a wedding trip, though she did go with Dominic to visit those parents that he'd intended to visit. She'd even thought ahead and brought salve with her just in case he got his knuckles a little bloody, which he did. Only Ella looked a little sad when Benton's name got mentioned. Disowned, disgraced, and apparently without friends to turn to, he'd left the country, no one knew where. He never got to meet his daughter and probably never would now. "Just as well" was the general consensus. The man didn't deserve the precious child he'd turned his back on.

But tonight Brooke had news for Dominic that she'd only just found out today. But when those feral eyes were so filled with passion and were looking down at her the way they were just then, she couldn't think of anything else. Making love with this man was the highlight of every day for her. Sleeping curled against him each night was a close second. She loved him so much it could still make her cry in happiness some-times.

Just now she wrapped her arms around his neck and pulled him down to her lips. They were already naked. They slept like that every night. She hoped they still would when the weather turned cold, though she couldn't imagine being cold pressed to him . . .

He took his time. He didn't always. Sometimes the passion just overcame them both. But when he took his time, he treated her like a sculpture he was creating, molding her with the gentlest of touches. It tended to drive her crazy. Maybe that's why he did it, to hear her moans and cries and demands. She was pretty good at demanding these days, to have him inside her, to feel him so deep. Or maybe it was because she would retaliate the next time and drive him crazy with her hands. They both expected it. Neither was ever disappointed. But laughing tonight, she pushed him over and climbed on top of him to control the pace. Maybe she didn't always do what he expected . . .

Utterly out of breath a while later, utterly replete and in her favorite place curled against him, she remembered. "By the by, we're having a baby."

"Of course we will." He hugged her a little closer. "Lots of them if you want. Didn't I once promise you that?"

"No, I mean, we're already having one. That night in the highwaymen's camp . . ."

He laughed. "You virgins have the worst luck—or the best in this case."

"I quite agree, though I'm not looking forward to the next few months of sickness that come with it, which will be starting any day now."

"I'm sure your witchy maid will have something to ease that for you."

She leaned up to grin at him. "She teased me with no promises, but I'm hoping so."

"Why didn't you tell me sooner?"

She laughed, remembering Alfreda cornering her today to demand the same thing. Alfreda had wanted to know why Brooke wasn't crowing about it when Freda had known about it a month ago.

So surprised, Brooke had replied, "Then why didn't you tell *me* sooner?"

The maid had huffed, "When do I ever get to see you without him by your side anymore?"

Brooke had laughed. "Well, that's true."

"And I expected you to make an announcement about it last month. Did you really not know?"

Brooke gave him the same answer she'd given Alfreda today. "I've been too happy to notice."

Rebel was with foal, too, which had thrilled Brooke when she'd been told. And Storm was also having babies. They'd only just figured that

429

out yesterday. She'd gone off to find her mate somewhere in the wilds, had been gone for a few weeks. They'd searched extensively for her. Wolf had cried and whined for her every day. Then she'd come home a few days ago, scruffy, a little thin, and a little tender. But just then, with both animals on the floor nearby, a howl was heard out on the moors.

Brooke sat up just as both dogs did. "I really hope she hasn't brought her pack home with her."

Dominic chuckled and pulled Brooke back down to him. "*That* would be a problem. It's probably just her mate saying good-bye—until the next time. It's rumored they mate for life, you know. In that, maybe I do have a little wolf blood in me."

Center Point Large Print
600 Brooks Road / PO Box 1
Thorndike, ME 04986-0001 USA

(207) 568-3717

US & Canada:
1 800 929-9108
www.centerpointlargeprint.com